# BATTLELINE ATLANTA

## CIVIL WAR IN GEORGA

A novel by:

Jimmy C. Waters

*Jamie hadn't realized that Sampson was right behind him, but then he grinned at his slave. "Didn't I tell you to stay in that damn trench? Hell Sampson, you ain't even got a rifle!"*

*"Do too got one, Suh! And a powder belt too!" Sampson replied. I grabbed it from dat young, scrappin' boy, dat lil' boy from Walton's Ford named Billy Bender. He got it in de head, few minutes ago; he don't need it no more! His head damn near tore off by some cannon ball 'r sompin!"*

A word of thanks to these folks who helped make this book possible:
The Freelance Design Group: freelancedesign.com
Thanks to Norma D. Snyder, reading and general assistance

Follow Jimmy C. Waters on Facebook as he writes his next novel!
Logon to facebook and search for Jimmy Cherokee Waters!



Civil War photographic images, courtesy of The US Library Of Congress

This and other works are available from the Publisher:

**Currahee Books**™

171 Laurel Mountain Road, Toccoa, Georgia 30577
**www.curraheebooks.com**

10 9 8 7 6 5 4 3 2 1

Printed in the United States of America
ISBN: 978-0-578-14291-3

# Prologue
## Confederate Gold

Lead flew past their heads, as several shots were fired haphazardly from the windows and front porch of Traveler's Rest, beside the Tugalo River in Franklin County of northern Georgia. It was late afternoon on May 23, 1865, and the firing was hot and constant, just as the two loaded wagons roared past on the dusty road. "Those damn Yankees still can't shoot straight. How in hell can they miss me sitting on this old decrepit mule, and for that matter, miss Duncan and Lamar sittin' high as you please on the wagon seats?" The drivers of the two wagons responded to the shots even more slowly than the mule Jamie was riding, but Jamie could see that his friends were not hit, as they whipped their mule teams into more speed.

By that point in the war, Jamie knew not to test his fate with that many Yankees. His eyes told the story as he looked back at his pursuers. He, like his friends had seen war, had both caused and evaluated death many times on many different battlefields, so his eyes seemed to see much farther, much more deeply. They were the eyes of a warrior, a stone cold killer.

He drew his LaMat revolver and popped off a round or two, just as the two wagons roared past his mule and around the bend in the road. He hoped that would be enough to keep the damn Yankee's heads down for a minute or two more. In his mind he was already seeking a plan for escape–two years of war had hardened him, made him practical–his thinking quick, his judgment sure. After all, the treasure in the two wagons was his responsibility.

President Jeff Davis himself had made it clear that the only hope of the Confederacy at that point, was the yellowed, heavy metal in the wooden crates in the bed of the two wagons–the pitiful remains of the Confederate treasury. Jamie would protect that Confederate gold with his life, as would his three friends, friends from childhood along the Tugalo River who were, even then riding aboard the wagons just in front. Only they knew what they carried, so Jamie hoped that the Yankee pursuit that he knew would be coming would be only half-hearted. The damn Yankees believed they'd already won the war anyhow, so why should they chase these two old wagons, and one badly dressed Confederate major on a damned mule? Hell, those Yankees probably thought they were bandits or deserters, out to steal what they could at the end of this dying war. Several more shots whistled past Jamie's head. He'd attracted all the attention since the wagons were already around the bend and out of sight. "Damn Yankees," Jamie thought; "If they ever do learn to shoot, my ass'll be deader 'n old moldy shoe leather!"

He kicked the old mule in the side to coax just a bit more speed–speed that just might save his life. More shots flew past, missing more widely now, thank God. Jamie was sure he didn't want to die in the last days of the Confederacy. Lee had already surrendered the once invincible Army of Northern Virginia several weeks ago, and while Jamie hadn't gotten the word as yet, General Johnston had likewise surrendered the Confederate Army of Tennessee, a pitiful rag-tag army of boys that managed to end the war somewhere up in North Carolina. That had been the last major Confederate force operating along the east coast. The sole remaining Confederate army still active was a pitifully small force of only 8,000 men, and that army sure couldn't do much good way down in south Texas. That was where President Jeff Davis was headed. No, Jamie surely didn't want to die here, not today, not here within sight of his home. He knew the Confederate Cause was long since dead.

"Get your mind on what matters, boy." Jamie told himself, using the very words his father had said to him a thousand times in his childhood. "You won't never get nowhere less'en you can think straight when it counts!"

Jamie smiled to himself, as he thought, "Those damn Yankees are trying to kill me. Hell, they probably will, and what am I doin' but thinking about Pa's dubious, liquored-up wisdoms?" Still those words caused Jamie to take stock of the situation.

His old mule had shown signs of life when the damn Yankees fired at him so he'd finally rounded the bend and was no longer under fire. He knew those Yankees would soon be coming, and their fresh horses would quickly overtake the two wagons and his old mule.

"We need to do something unexpected–turn and fight them maybe?" Jamie didn't realize that he'd spoken his thoughts aloud amid the dying gunfire. Still he tried to recall how many horses he'd seen tied to the rail at the Traveler's Rest Plantation–eight, maybe ten or twelve. While he had complete faith in himself, and his companions, Duncan, Lamar, and Sampson, he knew the four of them, no matter how good they were at shooting Yankees, would be no match for ten or twelve Yankees. Jamie continued to shout out his thoughts without realizing it; "Sons o' bitches probably had Henry rifles too! Load it on Sunday and fire it all week! Most of 'um do by now!"

Duncan replied. "Sharpes or Henrys; makes no damn difference. They'll keep shootin' till they kill us all."

All of these men, tough, leather-hard veterans as they were, nevertheless realized that they couldn't fight that many Yankees. Duncan Carmichael, even before the war, was the best knife-fighter in the whole of Franklin County. That skill with a blade, seemingly any blade, had kept him alive in several tough spots over the last two years. He was a wiry five foot four, and his sleek frame caused many a Yankee to misjudge him in hand-to-hand fights. Those Yankees had ended up dead in one ditch or another in the various north Georgia battles over the years.

Lamar Davis was about as different as he could be from Duncan. He was nearly six feet when most men stood only five six. He was broad of shoulder and some said he could out-pull an ornery mule. It was rumored among his friends that he was nearly as stubborn as one too. He could shoot his rifled musket about as well as any of the veterans on either side by 1865, and he knew he'd personally killed twenty-two Yankees in the last two years, maybe more.

Sampson, their other companion, was Jamie's personal slave, at least he had been until a few months ago. Like many southern officers in the Civil War, Jamie had taken his man along with him two years ago when he went to join up with the Grand Cause. In every single instance, Sampson had lived up to his name. He was by far the strongest man that Jamie had ever known, broad of shoulder, and powerful in his upper body. Further, he was known to be a great hunter. He could seemingly smell out a buck or a bear along the upper reaches of the Tugalo River in those mountains of north Georgia, and like Lamar, he was deadly with a rifle.

In fact by May of 1865, every one of these four men was a tested veteran, but that statement alone doesn't make the point emphatically enough. By that point in the war, each of these men had killed many times and each knew it. They'd had the blood and brains of their enemies on their faces, their arms, and their chests. They killed with bayonets, well-aimed rifle shots, swords, and knives. Further the death they'd brought to others was all over them, like a bloody cloak of war. It was there in the eyes, in the hardness of the expression on their faces. Killing was in their souls. They were as deadly as any four men the Confederacy could muster in the spring of 1865. They were death itself, and every single one of them was just over twenty years old.

Still Jamie thought, even with Duncan, Lamar, and Sampson all shooting, they couldn't fight twelve men. They would have to hide and hide quickly. Once that thought occurred, Jamie knew just the place! He spurred his old mule to catch the wagons that were roaring on ahead down the old Cherokee trail known as the Unicoi Turnpike. In earlier days Jamie would have caught up to those wagons more quickly. He would have been on a horse and not this old mule. But horses were scarce by then in the dying Confederacy, and good horses even scarcer–this old mule was all the once proud Confederacy could offer the twenty year old, battle hardened major in May of 1865.

"Duncan pull up, and turn them wagons to the nigger yard." Every plantation in the south had a "nigger yard," a term quite politically incorrect by today's standards, but accurate to history. It meant the slave village that provided the backbone for, and most of the population of, every plantation in the south in the early 1860s.

Duncan had heard Jamie's shout. He was busy driving like hell, driving as if his life depended on it! Of course, at that point, it did. Sampson was in the back of Duncan's wagon, with his loaded rifle-musket, ready to shoot the first blue coat he saw. By this point in the war, all military protocol was long since ignored between these friends, particularly for this "volunteer only" mission. Even the master/slave relationship between Jamie and Sampson had softened somewhat during the years of war. Each of these four men trusted the others completely. They trusted each other with their very lives, every single day.

Duncan shouted back. "Are you damn stupid, Jamie? Ain't no way outa' there! They'll be here in less than two minutes. I bet them bastards got pissed when you 'n Sampson loosed-off them shots at 'um, too! Hell, they probably even tried to miss us! Maybe they thought that we'd just toss up our hands, surrender to 'um, and then kiss their damned Yankee asses!" Duncan always seemed to have a way with words, as did most of his extended family. The Carmichaels were never known to curb their tongues, or miss any opportunity to swear, and war had only made that characteristic more pronounced in Duncan. Still, he obeyed his orders, and pulled up on the reins. The old wagon slowed down just a bit for the expected turn.

Jamie shouted back still riding his mule beside the wagon. "I ain't got time to crack your skull now, you son of a whore but dammit, I mean it. Pull into that nigger yard there and get into that old barn we used to use for the sheep. We got to hide and they won't ever believe we stopped in here!"

After a moment, Jamie continued. "If we stop here, that might buy us a few minutes, maybe an hour or two, while they chase on down the turnpike!"

Lamar, who everybody called "Lem" was listening to the exchange from the seat of the trailing wagon piped in. "That ain't a bad idea, Jamie, or Major Sir, or whatever the hell!" He said with a smile. Each man knew their friendship would survive the protocol mistake, that is if they themselves survived. "You still got some smarts left, I recon."

"Guess so," Jamie responded. "Sampson, get the damn doors shut, will ya?"

They pulled the wagons right through the center of the slave village on the plantation. The road lay just to the right of the road between Traveler's Rest and a small Methodist church. They knew they were out of sight of the Yankees and with any luck, those damn fool Yankees would ride right past on the road, if only they could get into the old barn quickly enough. They passed several rows of slave cabins, two deep on each side, and then they passed a few more haphazardly scattered on each side of the spur road. Finally, they turned right and headed into the old barn. The old place was big enough for several wagons and thank God, the big double doors were open when they got there!

"I got de door!" Sampson shouted, and he jumped off as the wagon pulled into the barn, even as the wagon rolled to a stop.

Only one woman, the house cook Meely, peaked out of her cabin at the white men and Sampson as they drove the wagons into the barn. Most of the other slaves, some ninety-six in all, that had once inhabited this slave yard on this once prosperous plantation, were long gone. A few were still around out in the field, but most had long since taken to the hills to wait for the Yankees and the Jubilee. With few white men to track run-away slaves in 1865, they had disappeared into the lower ridges of the Blue Ridge Mountains, waiting for the end that everyone knew was coming. Meely thought she saw Mr. Jamie ride past, but she wasn't sure, since he was sporting a long, dirty beard. He wasn't supposed to be home from the war, but she thought it might be him. She decided to just hide in her cabin. She knew that some Yankees were at the big house, and she'd heard the shots only a moment earlier. She wanted to draw no undue attention to herself, so she did what slaves had done for centuries—she made herself invisible whenever danger was around.

Still, even though she was frightened, her heart rejoiced! With the Yankees finally here, she knew she would be alright, unless she got killed by some damn soldier or another! At that thought, she backed carefully away from the only window in the cabin.

Just as Sampson closed the big door to the barn, they saw the Yankees ride past in a wild charge along the main road only forty or so yards away. They figured the damn bluecoats would ride for at least a mile or two following the presumed route of the wagons. Maybe they'd get as far as the next plantation and search there first. That might give Jamie and his men more time. Jamie allowed himself the thought, "Maybe I can get out of this alive! Maybe we'll even succeed in this mission after all!"

"Don't let the Yankees catch you, Major. Ride like the wind, and be careful. That gold is the only hope for our Grand Cause now, and you have the responsibility for it all." Those were the final instructions he'd received from Jeff Davis himself, the President of the Confederacy. Had that really been only six days ago? Jamie, Duncan, Sampson, and Lamar had been dodging Yankees ever since, sleeping mostly during the day and riding at night and then only on the back roads, roads that each one of them knew well. Each of these men had been raised in this valley of the Tugalo River in the lower Blue Ridge, and that is exactly why they'd been chosen for this most important of missions.

Davis and most of the members of the Confederate Cabinet had chosen to escape Richmond immediately after Lee's evacuation of Petersburg in April of 1865. They planned to travel to Texas and join with the small Confederate army there. After a harrowing rail journey through the Carolinas, they'd elected to cross the Tugalo River into Georgia on the Great Philadelphia Wagon Road, which put them at Traveler's Rest, the largest plantation in Walton's Ford. They brought the remains of the Confederate treasury, and several critical government documents with them. They'd then traveled forty miles south on the back roads, since the Yankees seemed to be everywhere. They'd gone to Washington, Georgia where they stayed with a retired Confederate statesman, General Robert Toombs. In his mansion, the final meeting of the Confederate Cabinet took place in May of 1865. History would recognize that as the final act of the Confederate government. All present were sure that the Grand Cause was lost, but President Davis could not bring himself to admit it openly. He was determined to move the Cause forward, so he would see to the delivery of the Confederate treasury, and then make for Texas, alone if necessary.

Still, with so many damn Yankees in pursuit, it was decided that the Confederate gold had to be hidden and then transported in some other fashion to the Confederate States Army in Texas. President Davis and his cabinet decided to split up, and each was to travel as best he could to Texas, where they would recreate the government of the Confederacy. They then planned to initiate a guerrilla war using the small force still in the field. In their minds, the Grand Cause must never die!

Major Jamie Turnbull, a man from the Tugalo River Valley in north Georgia, was originally the company commander of the Thirty-Fourth Georgia Rifles, and more lately, the commander of the Fourth Georgia Regiment. He'd been assigned to Cleburne's Division of Hood's Corps, in the Army of Tennessee, CSA, but after being severely wounded, he'd been detached to other commands. At any rate, he had observed that final cabinet meeting, inscribing the proceedings, as had been his role for the last few months of the war. Once the decisions were made, the group plainly needed an officer knowledgeable of the local back roads. They surely did not need another secretary at that point! Jamie let it be known that he'd come from the area, and he was immediately entrusted with the only future hope of the Confederacy, just over a ton of Confederate gold.

As he and his friends stood in that barn that morning, the Yankees rode past. Jamie found himself wondering what every soldier in every defeated army throughout history wonders: "How did it all come down to this?"

Then Lem's question brought Jamie back into the moment. "Recon they'll come back?" Lamar asked. All four men peered out of the cracks between the sideboards of the old barn, each watching a now empty road.

"Could be a minute. Could be a couple hours." Jamie said.

Duncan looked at Jamie, with that side-ass grin common to every Carmichael along the Tugalo River for well over a hundred years. "Well now Major, Sir," he said, grinning all the while. "Ain't you just got us in a hell of a pickle barrel? Are we goin' to shoot it out with the whole damn Yankee army in this here barn, or did you have another one o' your brilliant plans?"

Sampson and Lamar both smiled, as Jamie replied to his friend. "Damn you Carmichaels all to hell! Can't you ever think of something to contribute, or do you just criticize everybody else?" By now, even in this rather dire situation, each man was enjoying the joking. Theirs was a friendship deeper than most men ever know, a bond that can only exist among men who have gone to war together. Still, each one of them knew their time was quite limited.

Lamar offered the first suggestion. "Could we hide the gold here, instead of up in the caves?" They had planned to transport the gold into the Tallulah Gorge where five waterfalls cascaded down from the high mountains near Panther Creek. There they had planned to bury it in one of the caves where they'd camped as boys.

Duncan, ever quick with a laugh, if not a criticism said, "Yea, once they kill all o' us in this damn barn, they'd never find it buried right there in that damned haystack!" Sarcasm, like an amazing ability to string together curses, was another of the infamous Carmichael traits.

Lamar knew he was right, so he just told his friend to "Go to hell why don't ya?"

Lamar thought for another minute, and then said, "We could dig a hole here in the hogpen and bury it. Maybe they wouldn't dig under them hogs." Then he noticed Duncan looking at Jamie. The hardness around Jamie's eyes meant he was thinking, planning, and each man knew their friend well enough to just shut up and let him think.

After a minute, Jamie smiled and said, "I know just the place to bury it–a place even damn Yankees would never dig up. Even those Yankees won't dig up a grave!"

Lamar looked at Jamie in complete disbelief. "You're not a thinkin' about puttin' this in a grave?"

Duncan smiled again. "Ya thinkin' of old man Devereaux's ain't ya? Hell Devereaux Jarrett ain't been dead for more 'n a month, and you proposin' to dig 'um up already!"

Sampson was terrified at that thought. "Lordy Jesus! We can't go diggin up no grave Mr. Jamie! Not Mr. Devereaux's grave!"

"We got to Sampson. It's the only choice we got!" Jamie replied.

Duncan merely grinned at his friend for a bit, and then said, "You connivin' son-of-a bitch. It just might work!"

Jamie looked at his friends, and smiled. Still, once again, in his heart he wondered, "How did it all come to this?"

## An Author's Note on A Soldier's Question:

Jamie's question was a good one, one that he shared with his family for many decades after the war. He had held the entire Confederate treasury, the entire future hope of the Confederacy, right there in his barn, as he wondered what the future might bring.

But that famous ride with the Confederate gold was near the end of the story, and least confusion overtake us, we should look further back, toward the beginning. The problem, as always in history, is knowing exactly when any story really begins. Was it the Confederate cannon fire at Fort Sumter—that first shot—that began the fighting, or was it the battle of Chickamauga, the first major battle in Georgia? Perhaps it was further back still, at the famed Lincoln-Douglas debates where a young, relatively unknown politician in Springfield, Ohio articulated his position in the statement that is now famous worldwide? "A house divided against itself, cannot stand." Perhaps further back. Maybe that long ago war really began with a duel in Franklin County, Georgia in 1820s. That was the first shot fired, and the first time South Carolina threatened to secede from the Union.

Maybe the true beginning of the conflict was even further back, when those rugged mountaineers, those Jarretts, Prathers, Turnbulls, the Davis family, the Snyders, and the Carmichaels, first came into the Cherokee land in the lower Blue Ridge. They brought their slaves with them in those earliest days. Was that the beginning of this story? Maybe the beginning lay further back, with my people, the Cherokee people, who first lived in these Blue Mountains of north Georgia. When all is said and done, who among us can really know what sets historical events in motion, or where events like wars start or end? What events can truly be said to create causes for subsequent events? Where is the exact beginning of any story?

Time, like the layers of earth, layers only a half-inch or an inch deep, can be carefully peeled back with the shovel, the scowl, or the soft-brush in the hands of a talented archeologist. Eons of time can be exposed to the skilled and the patient, as the probing of the archeologist reveals the marvels of bygone centuries. Under the right circumstances, time, like the ancient earth itself, will tell its tale of the ascent of man. This bloody land of north Georgia tells that story. This particular river—the Tugalo, and these surrounding hills hide those rich layers of time, those many progressions of life, the great leaps forward, and the backward steps in that uncertain trajectory. Who can know really when anything began?

I know a bit of that story. I have unearthed those layers of time before, for my first book about these families, the Jarretts, and their Turnbull relatives, the Prathers, the Waters family, the Davis family, and the Snyders. In that book,

*Blood Oath,* I too, have mused on the meanings of history, like Jamie Turnbull did in that barn so long ago. It is a rich treasure indeed, to hold in my hands, his very thoughts, as written in his letters and those of his wife, as I seek to tell this story, his story. Those letters, along with this rich earth, tell the story of my people, the Principle People, the Cherokee, and of Devy Jarrett's people, Jamie Turnbull's people, and the other families of these mountains; white, red, and black, the peoples living on this land, along this rather trivial north Georgia stream.

In 1863, men came once again, to fight in these Blue Mountains of north Georgia. Jamie Turnbull, a member of the great, the distinguished Turnbull family, married into the Jarrett family, Lem Davis, the slave Sampson, Duncan Carmichael, Dewey Snyder, Owen Collins, Peter Wood, Mike Wellspeak, Mo Hendon, Chad Wilson, Batty Prather, and all of the other men of the Tugalo River Valley. They came again to struggle, to fight and die, in these hills, and now I am left to seek the further truths of their lives, to unearth the further experiences hidden in this hubris, this dark living-ground of the Blue Ridge Mountains. It is left to me to follow them, as well as my own people the Cherokee, in seeking to understand them all a bit better during that long ago War Between the States in Georgia.

As I found out these people, now long dead, were and are worth knowing. In fact, many are, indeed, noble. If that sounds a bit pompous when stated so boldly, then I will ask your indulgence, perhaps your forgiveness for my poor writing skills, my feeble abilities in telling this tale. For their character, their honor, their nobleness, if you will, is indeed obvious in the story of these marvelous families along the Tugalo River of north Georgia. That is the story I wish to tell. I wish to pay homage to them, and if I fail to communicate their story clearly, then the failure is indeed, my own.

For I have learned that indefinable something that drives the rise of man is not limited to one culture, one race, one gender, or to any single group. Nobleness is not a product of education, of culture, or heritage. Indeed, worth of character is not even specific to any single religion or belief system. From the perspective of the scholar seeking to remonstrate on the growth of civilization as a whole, no singular cultural cause that advances human kind can be identified. No group can lay claim any more so than any other, for man's progression through the ages. Rather it is the character of individual men and women that brings forth that growth, that progression. In fact, any culture can move forward at virtually any point in time, if it is nourished with the ideals and the strength of character of even one single worthy individual. Further, the real strength of American Exceptionalism stems from the singular wisdom of freeing one of the fundamental forces in all history—the depth of character of the individual—the intrinsic worth of every man and woman. In fact, the lone man or woman serving his god and striving to better himself/herself and to create a better life for his family—this is the fundamental American reality. From a much broader perspective, this is the primary, perhaps the only cause of the ascent of man through the ages.

That is the very reason that nobleness, that character in all periods, in all circumstances, should be treasured. It is so very rare, yet stems, unexplained, one human being at a time, in the most unusual times. Its existence, its very essence, is so illusory, yet its effect so profound. Worthy men and women change their world, and that must be celebrated, not because human character seeps from specific regions, or religions, or worldly circumstances, but because it seems to be bred somehow, in some misunderstood way, within the very hearts and souls of men. Ultimately all benefit, all rise, because of the nobleness of even one of our fellowmen, regardless of that fellow's affluence, or poverty, or general station in life.

Many men and women show character, show nobleness in their era, and even amid the lesser men and women in the past, I still found greatness. At times, in this exploration of the past, I found character where it might be least expected. Moreover, if the rich earthy layers of time teach us anything, if history itself has any meaning at all, then it tells us that no man or woman who ever walked this earth, is wholly without worth. All contribute something.

So I will write again of the Jarrett family, the Turnbull family, the Carmichaels and the Davis family. Like my earlier book, I will dig again into the promise and the pain of a singular, earlier time, another rich layer of earth, and yet another war, to seek other lessons from these people of north Georgia. I will sift yet another mound of earth, a rich bloody earth tossed up by the great War Between the States, the Great American Civil War, or if you will, the Second American Revolution.

Major Jamie Turnbull, CSA, like his extended Jarrett and Prather families, was a man of deep character, a man of great worth. His slave Sampson, also showed depth of character, along with his friends, Collins, Duncan Carmichael, Batty Prather, Wellspeak and Wilson. Like warriors throughout history, these men understood the essence of war, as did Jamie Turnbull, as he stood in that barn so long ago guarding the last of the Confederate gold. He knew somehow what was gained and what had been lost.

The War Between the States was indeed a cruel, bloody war. Lasting only four years, it still marks a seminal turn in American history. That war defined, and still defines, all who are Americans. That war saw many critical battles here in the Georgia mountains, as men from New York, Alabama, Tennessee, Pennsylvania, Ohio, and Wisconsin came into these hills and fought for them, ultimately seeking the biggest prize of all, the city of Atlanta. While no major battles took place along the Tugalo River itself, many fights took place in north Georgia, and those who then lived along this beautiful Georgia river played a critical role in them, as we shall see.

Let us explore once again what these people did, and why. Let us seek out who they were, these Snyders, Jarretts, Prathers, and Carmichaels; the Turnbull family, the Davis family, and the descendants of a great Cherokee leader, Runs-to-Water. We seek to know how they lived, what they thought, what they fought for, how they died, and finally, how they showed their worth, their nobleness, in their own time. Ultimately, that nobleness, that profound character of such men, is the only topic worthy of such exploration, such writings. Perhaps they can show us more, as they have before. Perhaps, just perhaps, these men and women, these noble families, can show us a bit more of who we are.

**Thus, to the beginning ...**

# Chapter 1
# Chickamauga

## A Letter Home

*Mrs. Mary Turnbull*
*Traveler's Rest Plantation*
*Tugalo River at Walton's Ford, Georgia*
*September 14, 1863*

*My Dearest Mary:*

*I believe that I have reached the mountain on which I shall claim the honor of my birthright as a southern gentlemen, as I have now, at long last, the chance to fight for our Grand Southern Cause! How I have longed for this day for the last two years as you know, while watching others leave me at the University of Georgia, as they rode out gallantly to fight for the Confederacy, while I, considered too young, stayed behind for two long years. Yet now, my time is come; I shall honor that Grand Cause in my struggle tomorrow. I vow to honor myself, to honor you, my beautiful young wife, to honor my family, and my heritage when I first face our enemies. I shall fight gallantly, or I shall die in the Grand Cause of the Confederacy!*

*We are somewhere above Dalton, Georgia, as we await the damn Yankees. The fight will probably happen sometime in the morning or perhaps the next day. It will be the first big fight in Georgia, and the first fight for the 34th Georgia Rifles. I am a bit nervous, and hope that I shall lead my men well and make a good showing of myself. I confess that, though I have two years of college, I am not well prepared to lead men in battle, as I have never even seen a battle. Forgive me for my uncertainties, but I must share them with my wonderful, new wife, as I dare not share them with anyone else.*

*Still, I can think of nothing more important in this moment by our evening fire, than your beautiful countenance. We have been wed only these few months, but I do miss you terribly, and as I write this there are thousands, nay scores of thousands, of other southern men likewise writing their wives and sweethearts. We who write the letters are the lucky ones; those who have no one to write to, they are the unlucky ones. They merely play cards by the fire, or drink themselves silly, or think up new ways to gamble. We all wait for the battle in the morning. Still, I know that I am, indeed a lucky man; for I am confident that no other man writes to a woman as beautiful as you.*

*In the morning we face a Yankee Army of 120,000 on the field, and our force of 75,000 southerners can surely out-shoot them. Yankees haven't shot and ridden all their lives, as southern men have. Most of the damn Yankees are shop-keepers, and some don't even speak English! Still, even we Confederates know the reality of such terrible numbers, numbers that are clearly to our disadvantage. This fight will, indeed be glorious, as we drive the Yankees from their first battle in Georgia. Rumors say that General Longstreet comes south from Virginia with another Confederate army, part of the Army of Northern Virginia, but of course, no one believes that, and no one believes we shall need them. The numbers will not be with us, but that is not much on my mind now. You are.*

*I think of you looking out on the hills of home. This hill on which I sit is not really much different from those of the Tugalo River Valley. This is just a small hill really, like the smaller one in front of Traveler's Rest, which you no doubt look upon this evening from the front porch as you read these humble reflections from one so dedicated to your lovely countenance. We camp near a stream that bears a Cherokee name, Chickamauga Creek. The mountain beyond stands proudly as the last mountain between the evil Yankee army and the soil of Georgia. We must hold those Yankees here and not let them near our homes, for they cannot be allowed to take Georgia, to take Atlanta; for Atlanta is the beating heart of our Confederacy, and it cannot be lost. Still, at this moment the mountain that is on my mind is the one nearest you.*

*Sometimes these Blue Mountains of Georgia, maybe the very land itself, can be larger than our thoughts, larger than our dreams. Sometimes these environs can expand our horizons, our hopes, or maybe even our destiny. At some isolated points on the globe, the very majesty of the earth yields a richness in human hope that seems completely out of proportion to the resources at hand. Such is the land you and I both look upon, the pine clad hills of the lower Blue Ridge of Georgia. These mountains have always been sacred. My family has known of this richness for decades, as has yours. My ancestors, the Turnbulls, the Walton and*

*Prather families, fought the Cherokee just like your Jarrett ancestors did, over these mountains and our place in them. These gentle rolling hills, and the light morning mist that covers a forest-green landscape, converting it as if by some mysterious transformation into a light purplish blue haze, these hills transform every human heart they touch.*

*These mountains and all of the Blue Ridge, are a rich earth. The very dirt under our feet is enriched by the living humus of the fallen poplar, cedar, hemlock, pine, or rhododendron; the decomposition of dead things. But moreover, this land has nourished itself as well on the blood of human conflict. Conquering armies have killed here, first the Cherokee fought here, and later, the valiant King's Mountain Men, our grandfathers among them, fought again over this land. We know this earth; it is ours by right. Our ancestors fought for it, many died for it.*

*Here today the brave men of our Confederacy fight the Yankees who wish to take our way of life, to take our freedom. While we will be victorious, it is a dead certainty that many of us will die here, and once again the ground will be freshened by the blood of the bravest, the best of our brothers. Your cousin Duncan Carmichael is here with the 34^th^ Georgia Rifles, as is Thomas Ward, Lamar Davis, Dewey Snyder, Billy Jarrett, Batty Prather, and many others whom you know. Sampson is at my side, as ever, and he fights with the vengeance of ten men. These are all good men, these men of the Tugalo River Valley, and I fear some of the Walton's Ford men might perish on this mountain come morning. Still, that spilling of blood on this earth, as it has over the centuries, will yield an even richer land, a land bountiful in so many ways, yet unconquerable, and seemingly always just out of one's reach.*

*It is the mountains beyond my view that call to me now–the mountains along the Tugalo River near Walton's Ford, where you sit tonight. With the viewing of each distant crest, or each rolling hill, the human mind can but wonder what lies beyond, and thus our thoughts, our dreams, and our very existence can be captured by these mountains–mine has been tonight, as I think of you. This rich, bloody frontier, this good earth is fed by ourselves, and the land, these mountains, are always larger than our imaginings.*

*For the first time tomorrow, I and all the rest of the 34^th^ Georgia will face the enemy. For the first time the Yankees promise to try and enter the soil of Georgia, and I would die rather than allow it! Still, I wonder what this might mean. In my darkest times, I've considered the future of our Glorious Cause. When Vicksburg fell only three months ago, the Confederacy was split in half, and when General Lee left Gettysburg, he left many thousands of dead Confederate men on that Yankee field. How long can the Confederacy pay such a dear price for our freedom from Yankee tyranny? The very constitution that our grandfathers fought for has been trampled by that monkey Lincoln, and if we lose, I don't know what type of country we shall have, if such a poor estate may even be called a country. It will not be worth much, since freedom will not long survive if the Grand Cause of the Confederacy is lost. Freedom from government tyranny, freedom to defend our property, and even our very lifestyle will surely die with a Yankee victory.*

*It all boils down to taking Atlanta; if the Yankees take these hills of north Georgia, they can then threaten Atlanta. While Richmond is our capitol, Atlanta is the heart of our land; it is the Yankee's goal.*

*All of the bullets and beans for our massive Confederate armies from Mobile, Alabama all the way up to Richmond come through Atlanta, and God forbid that the Yankees take our railroads. The entire south depends on those railroads, and with them the Yankees would control all of our food supply and our transportation. If the Yankees win here, they will have then defeated our brave Army of Tennessee, which is the only true military force to protect Georgia and the Carolinas from the Yankees, as long as General Lee stays busy in Virginia.*

*When General Bragg found out that I was a military man, with credentials from the Georgia Military Institute and the University of Georgia, he insisted that I join his staff as an assistant–one of many unimportant men, I'm afraid. I'm really a glorified secretary, who copies orders, and summarizes previous military actions. On occasion, I get to ride about among the army acting important, and delivering orders. This staff duty does put me more in touch with the goings-on of the army than most, and that is how I hear so many rumors, and sometimes, I can even tell if they are true. General Bragg complains much, and often dictates horribly unrefined letters to President Jeff Davis in Richmond, which I dutifully transcribe for him. Given the number of Yankees in Chattanooga, I cannot tell you what I fear more; the blue-belly army or another sorry letter from a complaining general, a man whom I fear is not up to the task before him.*

*With that in mind, I wish to entrust you with a task. It is my intention to summarize things as General Bragg's staff sees them–since that is my task here anyway. The summaries that I spend endless hours writing for the General's staff are, I suppose, read by someone in Richmond, though I never hear of it. Still, given our present circumstances, it is my intention, should I survive this battle, to begin on the morrow to supply you with secret copies of those documents. I am sorely fearful that, if our cause is not victorious overall, or even if we must retreat quickly, that these documents will be lost forever.*

*I know what you must be thinking; has he gone mad? However, rest assured that these are not military secrets, as you might imagine. I am not that important. In fact, these are not war plans involving future movements of the army at all, but rather these are just summaries of past actions. These after-action reports for Richmond hold no military secrets, since both sides know the events once they have already taken place. Still, these documents are important because they show what we knew and what we intended. They share the thoughts and judgments of our military leaders, and thus in some sense, these show who they and who we really are, as men and as soldiers. They show why we have taken the actions we undertook. For I fear that our story will not be told accurately, if indeed we are not victorious in our Cause. Winners write the histories, and often they write it wrong. At the very least, the University of Georgia would wish to have copies of these documents at some point, since this is the story of the actual history of this war. As such it should be preserved.*

*Thus, my charge to you, my beautiful young wife who so loves to meddle in the affairs of men; if the need arise and I should not return from this war, see that these papers are given to the University that has educated our families for these many decades. I love that distant campus in Athens, and it, like Walton's Ford, brings back many fond memories. I do so love the image of the old arches, the North Chapel, and the delightful debates of my youth in Demosthenian Hall. They all bring a smile to me.*

*I'll send you a summary of the action here along Chickamauga Creek if I can, in the next post. Please preserve it for me. This will be a large fight, and I truly believe these documents may become important in the future.*

*Enough of such meanderings. Do write and tell me more of yourself; I cannot tell you how much such favors mean to men in my position. Tell me everything; tell me what you do each day, or of your grandfather's work on the plantation. Is the farm ready for the hog killing in October after the first freeze? How was the tobacco this year? Are the darkies in line, or have they heard of the promised freedom when the Yankees come, Jubilee, or some such nonsense? Do tell me more of the stories of your grandfather, Devereaux, as you did in your letter last. I enjoy learning everything I can about the mighty Jarrett family of which I'm now, proudly, a member. The mails come through Athens, and can yet reach us here in Dalton through the Atlanta post.*

*As I re-read this I realize I must apologize again to you, my darling for these ramblings. I do seem to move from topic to topic, and you deserve a more endearing note, with many fabulously written lines about your beauty, your delicate face, and your deeply transforming eyes—eyes that speak directly to my heart even now, at this great distance. I am so fortunate to have married you last June, and I treasure the vision of you as my young wife. I can picture you now, sitting on the long porch with your grandfather and all of your family.*

*I hope you do not share this rather dreary letter with them, but rather, laugh out loud as if I had written something witty. Then, when they inquire, please decline to read it to them! They will then believe that a soldier on a distant field has merely been intimate with his young wife. As I write this, my heart leaps to think that I captured the heart of the beautiful Mary Jarrett of Walton's Ford! I am, indeed, the envy of the county!*

*I can almost see you all there on the porch. Is your Grandfather Devereaux having his evening toddy? Is his home brew whisky as good this year, as he hoped? Is your "horrid brood" of younger brothers talking about the war? Note that I've adopted your description of your brothers here! I guess it is the destiny of brothers and sisters to fight occasionally. I bet Meely is there black as night, as I remember. I'm sure that she is ordering everyone around, even while she dotes on everyone's comfort. Is she quite as bossy as I remember? What a servant she is!*

*These last questions startle me, as I re-read them. Have I been gone so long? Where did these last months go? I can't wait to get into this war, even though I secretly dread this coming battle. It is my first, and I shall endeavor to provide a good account of myself, and do honor to you and to my new family. As an eighteen year old officer, I am surely too young to take a wife, but I so wanted to make you mine during that last leave, and I am honored that you consented to marry such a man as I, few prospects in the immediate future, and a war to fight. It has only been a scattering of weeks, but so much has happened since our marriage. I'll not share that for now; the many miles of marching, the drills, and the training all seem inevitably to lead to this mountain and this small creek in north Georgia.*

*Know that I love you and yearn desperately for you. For your consideration, I affirm that no man has ever loved or yearned for his wife more than I at this moment, and I pray God for the opportunity to hold your delicate hand once more. On this evening, as I hear the Whip-o-wills in the hills above, I do not know if we shall see each other again in this life, but with God's blessing, and our undying love, we shall surely love each other forever in the next.*

*I leave now to join the 34th Georgia Rifles, and I will stand or fall with my comrades from the Tugalo River Valley during this battle. I am thankful for that, and of course, no secretary is needed during the battle itself—only runners of orders, and the general has many such men. I thank God that I will fight with the Tugalo men! These men of the Tugalo River Valley are surely the best riflemen in the world. To a man they are forcefully dedicated to this desperate struggle for our rights as men, for our freedom, and for our families at home.*

*As I prepare for this first battle in Georgia, I know that I have a wonderful, beautiful wife, a fine Springfield rifle, a beautiful LeMat pistol, a Grand Cause to which I am ready to commit my all, and strong fine comrades from the Tugalo River by my side. No man could ever beseech a benevolent God for more!*

*At the sunset tomorrow I will write again, so you will not be left wondering.*

*All my love forever,*
*James J. Turnbull, Captain*
*Company Commander 34th GA Rifles,*
*detached to: Gen. B. Bragg, Army of Tennessee*

As Jamie Turnbull folded his brown, tattered letter, he remembered the days when he would write to Mary from the university. Back then he actually used real paper, but that was unheard of in the Confederate States of America at this point. Certainly none could be found on the battle line near Lafayette –all paper was now used for powder cartridges, and thus, stationary had gone the way of sugar, coffee, salt, bacon, beef and most of the other necessities of life. All had ceased to be available, perished as it were, in the name of the Grand Cause.

Jamie hated that fact, as he hated the fact that his gentlemanly years as a university student had been interrupted by this war. He hated the damn Yankee's and surely wanted to rid his beloved Georgia of them. Still, they did seem to be advancing on every front at this point in 1863 and he hated that too. He like many others, was confident in the Grand Cause and ultimate victory, but he'd had nagging fears about the possibility of southern defeat after the disastrous summer of 1863 when Vicksburg and Gettysburg were both lost in a single week. Like all committed southern gentlemen, he could not and would not be the first to admit the failure of the Glorious Cause; he could barely even mention his doubts to his trusted young wife.

Still as he prepared for his first battle, he knew that much of the Army of Tennessee had been bloodied before, but that his unit, the 34th Georgia Rifles, was green and untested. He wanted to fight well, giving a good accounting of himself and his men. With his education he'd been made an officer immediately, a captain in that unit, but wiser heads in the general's office had placed several veteran sergeants under him to give some experience to an inexperienced outfit.

As Jamie sat by that fire in 1863, he was right to question himself. He was, at that moment, yet a boy playing at soldiering. He'd marched himself and his men to infinity and back seemingly, and he certainly knew the battlefield orders and drills. Still, at only eighteen, he knew that he was untested. He'd received his rank because of two years at the university. Except for that education, he'd be the equal of his friends Lem, Dewey, and Duncan, and all of the other Tugalo River men whose families would have never thought to send their sons off for extensive schooling.

Jamie looked himself over, just as he closed the rough paper on which he wrote, the side of a carton which he pretended was stationary. Like all the others who were new he had boots to wear, whereas most of the Confederate veterans by that point did not. More importantly, he had his pride, and he hoped that would carry him through his first bloody battle. That was his final thought before drifting off to sleep by the fire.

Sampson, his trusted personal slave, then laid down beside him and likewise fell asleep, just as he'd done for nearly every single day of his life.

Jamie Turnbull was wrong in only one particular in his letter of September 14, 1863. The battle that was to become the single most bloody battle in the history of Georgia would not begin until five days later, on September 19. For the next three days, September 15th through the 17th, the two massive armies merely danced together in the hills and valleys of the north Georgia mountains, without coming into serious conflict. On September 18, there were several small, scattered fights along fords or small bridges over Chickamauga Creek, as the great armies positioned themselves. However, on the morning of September 19, 1863, the killing began in earnest. Before it was over, 34,000 men would become casualties in these Georgia mountains, and blood would flow again in the creeks and rivers along those hills just west of Chickamauga Creek. Still, none could have known that as Jamie lay down to sleep that evening.

On the same night Jamie wrote his letter, September 14, 1863, at the Traveler's Rest Plantation in Walton's Ford, Georgia, another letter was being written.

*Captain James Turnbull*
*Commander, Thirty-Fourth GA Rifles,*
*Detached to: Headquarters of Gen. B. Bragg*
*Army of Tennessee, CSA*

*My Dear, Dear, Husband,*

*I miss you this evening, and wanted to send you a few lines, since, according to your letters you seem so happy to receive these communications. I hope not to be a bother, or a worrisome wife, but should you enjoy reading these lines, then it brings me the greatest joy to provide them.*

*Yesterday, at the butchers shop in Walton's Ford,Mrs. Angelina Sharpe–yes the rather rotund one whom you refer to as the "old bitty" from Tugalo Baptist Church—called out a friendly hello to Mrs. Turnbull! Please forgive me but I'd quite forgotten that she was thereby referring to me! I'm afraid that I'd expected her to be hailing your mother, who I later learned, was ill-disposed, and in her bed that particular afternoon. In short, I ignored Mrs. Sharpe completely, and literally walked right out of the place without ever once looking back! Only later did I realize what I'd done, and I'm sure I'll pay dearly for that indiscretion in the next few days and weeks. Certainly, I'll need to remember my own name, since now, as a married woman, I have to maintain respectability for our new family in our community!*

*Yes, I'm definitely Mrs. James Turnbull, and I'll have to get used to that. Still, even saying that name seems strange, and yet I am quite moved to be wedded to the gallant Captain Jamie Turnbull, CSA. I am proud of you, and very joyful in our union before God.*

*I don't know if you ever received my last letter, and the section of notes I'd included about my grandfather's establishment of this wonderful plantation of Jarrett's Manor. As I mentioned, it is my intention to prepare several articles about our plantation, and our southern way of life. I intend to place these in newspapers if I can, to demonstrate that we southerners are not the bloody butchers that the Yankee Abolitionists portray. I can no longer tolerate the idiotic ramblings that I sometimes read in the newspapers of the north. Those papers still seem to be available in Augusta and Savannah from time to time, and we get them as the rivermen come upstream to the plantation. Those Yankees write such rubbish about us, and how they think we treat our servants. In truth, I know of no happier darkies than Aunt Fanny, or Meely, or your Sampson. Even the field hands here at Traveler's Rest eat well and they are never beaten.*

*I know you think it simple insanity that I, as a woman, trouble myself with these discussions; we women understand so very little of men's politics. Still, I love you and as your wife, I implore you to realize that I am a proud southerner too. While I cannot fight for our Grand Cause as you do, I do insist that I have my role to play in defending our life here in the south. If my weapon be a pen and ink rather than a rifle, such is a limitation I'll live with, and I won't hear another word about it! I will tell our story for the world to read, and hope that they see eventually the value in things as we do. I want them to know our southern way of life, as we know it, and perhaps, if they are wise, they will then cherish it too!*

*Therefore I shall write. I can do that, and I've learned to write fairly well, if I do say so myself. I shall put articles in the Pendleton newspaper in South Carolina, and maybe even the papers in Athens, Milledgeville, or Atlanta. In those articles, I shall tell the truth of our life here on a southern plantation. I've written several wonderful tales of the family, as told me by my Grandfather, Devereaux Jarrett. He could spin a story like no one else, and his love for this life, this plantation, the crops, his family, and even his darkies was clear in every single word and deed in his life. We would spend hours on the porch here at Traveler's Rest with him talking about how he built this marvelous home, how he profited from the gold mines in Georgia, and built a set of skilled slaves that were, and are, the envy of the county.*

*I love spending time with him since his illness began last year. He lingers still, and we do hope for the best, but I do not believe he will ever leave his bed again in this life. Still, I can see that his wisdom, his stories, will live on. I will see to it! We talk daily and I write down his memories.*

*I also have his diary and his other papers. Those are rich sources of information on the goings-on here in the valley. He has also left the diary of a much older man, James Wily, who fought the battle of King's Mountain in the Revolution! That diary spoke much of the Cherokee in this river valley, and of the earliest settlers and their slaves. I could write many books on how this land was settled, and how many men in Georgia got rich with Georgia gold.*

*With this wonderful information, I can write about our beautiful southern way of life, and how graceful this southern society truly is. I'll send my scribbling to you, and even if I cannot get these notes in the papers, at the very least you will be able to read something more interesting than the tripe delivered up by most of the papers these days–at least the papers I'm seeing. Thus, in my next post, I'll send you a bit more about my grandfather's life here in the Tugalo River Valley. The language will be rough, just as he told it to me, just as it appears in his and Mr. Wily's diaries. Still this was the rough language of a rough land. I was often assured by my grandfather, that this valley was a gritty, deadly frontier in his earlier days. Imagine that my Grandfather Devereaux Jarrett lived here for twenty years while there were still Cherokee in these mountains!*

*I must go now, and see to making peace in some fashion with the old biddy, sorry; I of course mean Mrs. Sharpe. I hope that thought causes you to smile! With love and admiration for you, my dear husband, a gallant Captain of the 34th Georgia Rifles, the strongest brigade of all...*

*Your devoted wife,*
*Mary Jarrett Turnbull*

*PS – Please know that I miss your touch, your smell, and your face with every single breath. How I blush as I re-read these lines! Can a young wife be so bold so as to say such things to her new husband?*

## Friday Night, Around a Confederate Campfire

It all happened around the campfire. The campfire was everything to a Confederate soldier in 1863. It was how you cooked your beans and cornpone, how you warmed up after setting picket duty up on the line. It was where you talked with your friends, and learned of the day's events, or where you wrote your letters home. The campfire was where you spent most of your time, if you were in the Confederate States Army, and any veteran of that war will tell you that for every hour you spent engaged in battle, you'd probably spend five to ten days in camp, and almost all of that time, either on-duty guarding something, or around the campfire.

"They cain't hit a barn with a wagon, les'en you drive it for 'um! I ain't worried one damn bit about them Yankees shootin at me in the morning!" Lem Davis (only his Mama called him Lamar), spit in the fire after that announcement, while his friends simply ignored him. He was giving voice to the worn-out belief that Yankees couldn't shoot straight, and if that belief had ever been true, it was certainly not true by 1863. While Jamie's command, the eighty-odd men of the 34th Georgia Rifles, may have been a new, untested unit in September of 1863, they were in a regiment that included several battle tested companies from the Army of Tennessee. Of course, the Union army opposing them in the Georgia mountains was certainly battle tested. Still, none of the other Confederates in the 34th Rifles wanted to contradict Lem's assertion. In fact they were trying desperately to believe it!

Finally, Duncan Carmichael, another man from the Tugalo River Valley, decided to give his friend Lem some help. "Hell, Lem. Guess they cain't hit you noways, seein' as how you likely to be hunched up behind some log and cryin' like some damn new-born babe!" The others around the campfire laughed at that, and after only a few seconds, Lem cracked a smile to. The banter of a friend can relieve much of the stress of going into one's first battle, and these two men had been friends for all of their lives; they were both seventeen years old that night.

At the nearby fire, sat the officers for the regiment, including Captain Jamie Turnbull, of the 34th Rifles. Jamie was reading an earlier letter from his wife of several months, and enjoying each carefully structured sentence of it! He was only half-listening to his childhood friends at the nearby fire, the fire for the privates. As an officer, he felt he shouldn't laugh at Duncan's joke on Lem, but he did smile to himself, thinking several things he would never have said aloud; "I sure hope Lem is right. Be damn nice if none of those Yankees could shoot straight. Truth be known, I'm just as untested in battle as my men are!"

The fight that was to become the infamous Battle of Chickamauga began with some scattered fighting on September 18, 1863, but by that night, the 34th Georgia Rifles, had still not fired a shot. They'd marched, of course, first this way for two miles along the creek, then back the same way, as the Confederate commanders tried to position their reserve forces, forces that were yet to be tested in battle. They sent those units where they thought they might need them. On the afternoon of September 18, Jamie's unit had smelled cordite from an earlier fight on a ridgeline that same day. Still, they'd walked over that small portion of the battlefield twice, once going, and once coming, and had yet to see a Yankee. The generals on both sides were consolidating their armies for a major blow to one-another, and that typically resulted in some units on both sides recrossing the same terrain. To make matters worse, their unit had ended up camping in exactly the same spot as they had the night before, literally using the same fire pits. They'd been in the area for four days at that point, and all of the useless marching had occasioned many comments among the ranks, as do all such stupidities in every army in history!

One interesting thing had happened as they'd marched along that day, first northwards up a dusty track and only six hours later, southwards back down the same track. The only surprise the whole day had been when they'd been passed by a bunch of damned Indians!

Lem was the first to notice those Cherokee. The 34th was resting beside the creek in their up-and-back march, as the Cherokee strolled past. The men of the 34th Georgia Rifles didn't think much of what they saw. Lem was the first to comment. "What the hell is that? Cain't them fools even march?" he asked, as the Cherokee walked past.

## Author's Note

To understand that question, one must understand something of the Cherokee, my race, and my people. The main clans of my tribe, the Cherokee people, had been forcibly relocated, forced out of the Georgia mountains only twenty-three years before the outbreak of the Civil War. That forced march—the famous Trail of Tears of 1838, would for all time, mark one of the blackest days in American history. Sixteen thousand Indians, mostly Cherokee, had been forced from their homes, driven from farms they owned, and moved half-way across the continent. Only about eight thousand had finally arrived on their new lands in Oklahoma. My own family survived that bloody march. Still, a small group of Cherokee had remained in the North Carolina mountains only a hundred miles or so from the Chickamauga battlefield, and, when the war began, they, as southerners, had chosen to fight for the Confederacy. It was this group that passed the 34th Georgia, while the Georgia men were taking a break in the grass beside the road along Chickamauga Creek.

The Cherokee however, were not of a single mind on this war. Many wondered why they should fight on any side. The United States government, the Union government, had driven them from their homes, but no government in any southern state had shown great love for them either. In fact, courts in all southern states treated the Cherokee as second class citizens, at best. Most wondered why they should fight at all? Why not merely hide, again, deep in their mountains?

The answer is both simple and profound. The Cherokee fought for the south in that war, for the same reason that many slaves and free-blacks fought for the north; they sought to earn the respect that had been denied them! Of course, the Cherokee were relatively free, at that point, and southern states basically left them alone as long as they stayed out of sight, deep in the rugged Carolina mountain country, those Great Smoky Mountains. There they farmed, and made no trouble. Still, the Cherokee were second class citizens, and they proposed to use the War Between the States to do something about it!

In those distant days no self-respecting people would play what is today known as the "victim card," that most pathetic attempt to gain political advantage by presenting oneself as a "victim." No, in those days, neither the blacks fighting for the north nor the Cherokee fighting for the south would debase themselves in that manner. Instead, they wanted the honest respect of their fellow citizens, and they chose the honorable way to achieve that goal. Both groups wanted such respect, and both proposed to earn it!

The Cherokee had initially organized themselves into a rough regiment, some eight hundred strong; Cherokee men from the hills of North Carolina and Tennessee. They served under Major William Holland Thomas, a white man, who had proved over the decades to be a true friend of the Cherokee people. While owning only a few slaves themselves, these men thought of themselves as Cherokee first, and North Carolinians second, and while they were not terribly vested in the idea of southern secession, they were determined to fight for the south. Thus was born, the Thomas Legion. The unit had quickly been recognized by the Confederate authorities, and was merged into the Confederate States Army.

And that is how a bunch of Indians ended up meandering along Chickamauga Creek, ready to fight for the Confederacy in September of 1863.

Strangely enough, it was that meandering that Lem and the others noticed at first, and "meandering" really is the best word to describe the manner in which the Cherokee moved; at least it will have to do. The one thing that all self-respecting Cherokee men absolutely refused to do was march, to walk in step with others in an orderly fashion. While the Thomas Legion had been drilling like all armies in those days, they never mastered the art of coordinated marching. To a man, those Cherokee thought coordinated marching to be undignified! These same Cherokee could perform close order-battlefield drills under fire; they could quickly position themselves into line-of-battle, or wheel right or left, changing directions while under fire, but marching together they absolutely refused to do. No self-respecting Cherokee would debase himself by marching in time, any more than anyone would look directly into the eyes of his elders or his commanders! Each would have been a sign of disrespect, either of one's commanders or of oneself!

For that reason, no Cherokee could ever be said to have "marched" correctly. Rather, when they moved along the road, the Cherokee would meander, or stroll, or simply walk, all in relatively slow, but very dignified fashion that characterized all Cherokee, as if each man was walking along independently, without being in the company of eight hundred or so of his fellow Cherokee. Thus, was their dignity maintained, and their independence, their balance in life, exemplified.

Cherokee soldiers would win many honors in that war. Some would prove brave to the point of near suicide, while others fought like the demon-warriors from which they had descended. One Cherokee, Stand Waite, would become a Confederate General, commanding thousands of men far to the west. He won the honor of being the last Confederate general of the entire war to surrender. Yes, these Cherokee were excellent soldiers. They could do all of the battle drills. They could ride, move, and fight with a cohesion that rivaled any well trained fighting force of that era, and they could shoot as well as any soldiers in history. The one thing they absolutely could never bring themselves to do, was march.

## That Same Friday Afternoon, Beside Chickamauga Creek

That meandering gait was the reason for the comments from the men of the 34th Georgia Rifles.

Duncan responded to Lem's question. "Them's Cherokee. I heard they was commin. Wonder if'n they'll be worth a damn when the fightin' starts?"

Dewey Snyder spoke up next, laying in the grass beside Lem, while chewing his wad of tobacco. He spit out a wad, then said, "Sure don't look like much, do they? Don't recon' they knowd their right foot from their left, 'lest when it comes to marching."

Lem then answered. "Hell, I don't recon' they'll be worth much at all. How could they know which way to turn in battle? How can they drill on the battle commands?"

Duncan spoke up again. "Still, my granddaddy said they sure 'nuf put up a fight in Georgia back during the Cherokee Wars. They was mighty fearsome warriors back then! And they'd steal you blind! My family still tells the stories 'bout runnin' from the Cherokee raidin' parties!"

"Well," Batty said. "Hope we ain't got to fight near 'um. My family says every damn Injun on God's green earth stinks to high heaven, same as niggers!"

They all laughed at that, as the last of the Cherokee meandered by. The men in the Thomas Legion, of course, had heard the comments. They'd heard such ridicule all their lives, so they paid little attention. Those men were clearly, poor white trash, and they looked it, laying there filthy and unshaven, beside the beautiful Chickamauga Creek, a creek that bore, after all, a Cherokee name. Didn't they know that they debased the Great Spirit's creation merely by being so dirty and lying so close to a beautiful creek? The Cherokee of the Thomas Legion did what Indians have always done for their own peace of mind; they ignored those white men completely. They had come to the big fight to fight, and getting sidetracked by these white trash crackers would merely be a waste of their time. They walked on, never once looking at the men beside the creek.

The Battle of Chickamauga, a fight that would begin in earnest in the early morning of September 19, 1863, was the first real battle in Georgia, which is why both the Thomas Legion and the 34th Georgia were there. The Confederacy was calling in all of its units for this fight. Of course, there had already been several smaller fights along the Georgia coast, battles over one fort or another, and it is an ironclad truth that no battle ever seems like a "small fight" to those who are in it.

Still, Chickamauga was to become something quite different. It would be a truly massive battle for those blue-clad Georgia hills, as over 120,000 men tried to kill each other in a battle line only three miles long. It was larger than most battles in the entire war, and more men died on that field than any other fight in the entire Civil War, with only one exception; Gettysburg.

Chickamauga would be studied by students of the art of war for well over one hundred and fifty years, and would ultimately rival any battle in history for sheer savagery. In only two days, Chickamauga would become, by far, the bloodiest battlefield in Georgia, and one of the bloodiest ever fought in the Western Hemisphere.

And all of this death would happen, basically because both of the opposing generals were idiots. To make matters worse, both of those idiots, those commanding generals, were simply wrong in their assumptions about what was happening, and of course, such mistakes often cost the lives of thousands of men. The Union General Rosecrans thought he could sneak a Yankee force into the Georgia mountains piecemeal. He'd divided his men into three different columns as he marched into northwest Georgia, and only one Union force, the Army of the Cumberland, was moving deep into the Georgia mountains. Their task was to approach, and possibly capture a small mountain town named after another general in an earlier war, the town of Lafayette, Georgia. The other two Yankee armies could not really support the Army of the Cumberland, as they were much too far away. Still the Army of the Cumberland was a powerful force, some 66,000 men strong.

Meanwhile, Confederate General Braxton Bragg made the mistake of thinking he was attacking the northern flank of the Yankee force. His goal was to drive that Union army to the south and west, out of Georgia and into the rugged mountains of north Alabama, away from the other Yankee forces that he knew were up in Tennessee. Of course, he was wrong in that assumption; his attack did not strike the northern flank of the Union force. He hit that Union army directly in the middle, and thus he attacked the strongest section of the Union line!

It is a fact, obvious throughout history; when commanders make stupid mistakes, men die. That truth would be proven on the battle line of Chickamauga, as thousands of Union and Confederate men were sacrificed because of two equally stupid generals.

## Friday Night, At the Campfire

After their idiotic up-and-back march, the 34th sat around their campfire, that Friday night. Owen Collins, a new man in the unit and a veteran of an earlier campaign, chose that moment to respond to Lem Davis' earlier comment. He took a sip of some moonshine that he wasn't supposed to have in camp, and said, "What I seed of them damn Yankees up in Virginia, they can shoot for fair! Don't let nobody tell you no different! At least they shot pretty good up by Richmond in 62! By then, them damn Yankees had been fightin' for pert' near a year, and many a man died. I'm jest sayin' I wouldn' go a showin' myself upright if'n I was you. You'll live longer if'n you stay behind your logs and fire your musket from the trenches in the morning, jest like the rest of us!"

One of the younger boys sitting by the fire, Batty Prather, looked up in some confusion. In some fit of ultimate stupidity, his mother had named him Sebastian Thomas Prather. The Thomas name had come from his great-grandfather, old Tom Prather, a man who'd fought in the American Revolution, and been rewarded with a nice farm along the Tugalo River in Georgia. However, the name Sebastian was borrowed from the leader of a traveling theater group who occasionally stopped in Walton's Ford and presented a show to the local citizens. Batty's Mom thought the name quite dignified, but of course, none of the kids in that neighborhood found the name to be distinguished at all! Being somewhat resentful of the pretentiousness of such a name, his friends began to call him by a shorter, and somewhat insulting version of his name—thus, Batty Prather.

Batty looked over at Owen and asked? "When did you see Yankees shootin' at anybody?"

Duncan Carmichael grinned, and then answered for Owen. Facing the younger boy he replied. "Collins here sure don't look like much, but he was wounded in his shoulder up in Virginia, Batty. He's joined up with us now, but he's seen fightin' before, so you'll be showin' him some respect, right? He seed the Yankees fight, and he figured out how to live through it. We'll all be learnin' from him, I recon."

Batty responded quickly. "No disrespect intended, Owen. I just didn't know you'd fought the damn Yankees before. What unit was you with then anyway?"

Owen took another swig of the shine that he'd bought about a mile away at one of the many gristmills along Chickamauga Creek. "I was with the North Carolina 26th 'cus my Maw was from up in Carolina, and we was visiting up there when the war broke out. That unit formed up right before the big fight in '61 at Manassas. We was all piss and vinegar back then, just like you boys. We knew we could ride and shoot, and them damn Yankees was all shop-keepers, teachers, or lawyers from up north. We figured they'd never held a rifle before, so why couldn't we beat 'um? Hell, we couldn't wait until we got into it."

Owen paused, as he reflected on his earlier battles. His thoughts were rigidly honest and absolutely horrifying, and his face grew grim, as all around that campfire were quiet. Then he continued. "I drilled with 'um for only a month or so before that fight, and you talk about scairt! In that first fight, I seed grown men cry, southern men, when them damn cannon fired the first salvo at us. I think the cannon was the worst. All of us had heard rifles shot together before. Hell, at any good turkey-shoot you can hear fifty rifles fire all at once, but them cannon, firing all together, ten, or twenty, or fifty. There ain't no sound ever made by man like the sound of them cannon firin' all at onect! You feel 'um, as much as hear 'um, and they'll take the wind out'a you right quick, if you stand too close. They shake your bones and crush the breath out'a you, if you're close, or if'n them cannon shells land near you. And every one of them damn cannon blasts is there for one reason—to blow you all to hell!"

Batty considered that for a moment, then asked, "But could the Yankees shoot straight or not, Owen?"

Owen looked quietly across the campfire at the young man, realizing he'd not made his point, and not knowing how he could. As the others watched Owen and Batty sitting across from each other, every man there saw the contrast; no more obvious contrast in experience has ever before been seen on this planet. For any man who has ever faced a hot battlefield before, the difference in those two faces—Owen's and Batty's—was as clear as night and day. One man had seen, felt, and tasted battle, and the other was as green as a new-born babe!

Of course Owen knew what Batty wanted to hear, and he certainly didn't want to insult the young lad. After another moment he spoke again. "At Manassas in '61 there was confusion everywhere, and some of the Yankees didn't know which way to point a rifle, that's sure. But by the time they got near to Richmond in '62 Batty, they was soldiers, I mean real soldiers, good soldiers for sure. One more thing, I heard. Some of them damn Yankees 'll be usin' repeating rifles, or at least some did yesterday down at Chickamauga Creek. They can shoot five times by the time you reload onect, and that'll for sure kill ya!" Here Owen paused, for a final moment, then he continued. "You damn-well better stay behind your logs tomorrow, unless we got to charge. That way, you'll stay alive!"

Again, all was quiet around the campfire. Finally, Batty spoke. "Sorry, Owen," he said. "Guess I got a lot to learn. I recon' we'll all be lookin' to you 'bout what to do, when the lead starts flying." Batty's conciliatory statement seemed to satisfy everybody. In fact, most of the men had ignored his earlier questions anyway, and simply continued to stare into the campfire. The exchange however, was heard by Jamie over at the officer's campfire, and it caused him, yet again, to wonder about his own preparedness for war.

## Saturday, The Killing Begins

The contrast between Owen Collins and Batty Prather proves one undoubted point recognized by veterans worldwide, throughout history: After a man faces war, he is never the same again.

No one can say how war, how battle, changes a man, as it had already changed Owen Collins, but all who have been on the battle line understand that reality. It is something in the disposition, the hardness of the face, the look in one's eyes. In a much later war in southeast Asia, it would come to be known as the thousand-yard stare. It is a look that can, seemingly kill; it reaches out from one's face. It is a look that decimates others; that look steals one's very soul.

Duncan Carmichael, Lem Davis, Batty Prather, Dewey Snyder, all would find out early on the morning of Saturday, September 19, what war was like. They would, for the first time, learn of war, and thus, they would learn of themselves, if they survived. They'd been roused at five in the morning, well before there was any hint of sunlight, and they'd moved about half-a-mile to some prepared trenches facing across a field. The 34th Georgia Rifles, and the other units in their regiment were placed beside three other Georgia regiments, toward the northern end of the Confederate line, about two-thirds of a mile forward of Chickamauga Creek.

Strangely enough, the creek that gives this battle its name played no real part in the battle itself. On September 18, there had been a few smaller fights at several bridges or fords along the creek, and several of the Yankee units had, indeed, been using the Spencer repeating rifle, but the real fight over the next two days, was nearly a mile to the west. By nightfall on September 18, two massive armies, 66,000 Union men and 60,000 men in the Confederate Army of Tennessee, were camped only a mile apart. The Union force was camped roughly along a three mile stretch of the Lafayette Road, a north-south dirt track that served as the main road to Chattanooga. The Confederate army was a bit more scattered but was approaching from the east, and camping in various fields, beside whatever road they were using.

At that point, each army still harbored incorrect assumptions about where the enemy was. Bragg still believed he would be attacking the northern flank of the Union force, when he was attacking the middle, and Rosecrans believed he was facing only a small portion of the Confederate force. Many men would die because of those incorrect assumptions.

Jamie and his men had been staring out from behind their logs, standing in a freshly dug ditch about four feet deep, with three logs forming a slightly higher embankment before them. Sampson had run to the back to get all the water and ammunition he could carry, but he carefully made note that Jamie's section of the trench was at least as deep as everyone else's. Strangely enough, the battle began that day, not with a massive cannonade, or dramatic charges, but because some of the Union boys from some nowhere town in northern Indiana got thirsty.

With no water to speak of along the Lafayette Road, several groups of Union men, maybe fifty in all, took their Spencer repeating rifles and moved to a tree-line where they thought there might be a creek. Finding no creek in that tree-line, they began to move through the next field on the Kelly Farm, and that is exactly where the killing began. They found no water, but did run smack into a Confederate picket line, which, in that locale was only twenty yards or so in front of the main Confederate trenches. Thus, when those Confederate pickets began firing at the terrified Yankees, they roused an entire Confederate regiment. At that point, fifty Indiana men were targets for 1,243 other men in the Georgia 34$^{th}$ and the 2$^{nd}$ Georgia Infantry. Within ten minutes, Jamie, Lem, Owen, Batty, and Duncan, had fired several times, and each had dropped a few of the terrified Yankees, who ran hell-bent back to the tree line. There, the Union men took positions behind trees, and began to return fire to cover their comrades who were still fleeing the field.

Owen and Batty, the antagonists from the argument the previous night around the campfire, fought side by side, and Owen seemed to be keeping an eye on Batty, in the way an older brother might watch his younger brother. Both fought like demons, loading and firing, loading and firing; tearing open powder cartridges with their teeth, pouring it down the barrel, sticking in a lead shot, and ramming it all home; firing again.

However, one factor was clear even in that first major fight at Chickamauga, the Spencer repeating rifle would be a dominant force in that battle. The Confederates, of course, were using the tried and true Springfield Rifled Musket, and its clone, the Enfield. Those weapons were accurate out to two hundred or so yards, and fired a soft-lead minie-ball that had a tendency to tear itself apart once it hit the human body. Horrible internal wounds would result from that type of wound, and many a man died when one bullet splintered into five, or six separate pieces inside his chest. That is why this weapon was the principle weapon for both sides earlier in the war, from 1861 through the early months of 1863.

The Springfield rifle did however, have one major drawback; like almost all rifles at that point, it was loaded one bullet at a time, from the end of the long barrel. Men using the Springfield, or its cousin the Enfield, inevitably stood up to load the rifle, and used their teeth to tear open a "cartridge," a finger-sized small container filled with gunpowder, which they poured down the barrel. They then put in the minie-ball, and rammed it all home with a long ramrod. Tearing open dozens of powderbags in that loading process had a tendency to turn their face black around their mouth as their sweat and tears mixed with the powder in their teeth. Ten minutes into a battle, men firing the Springfield looked like black-face demons from hell, and with that complicated loading process, men using the Springfield could only fire about three times per minute, as the eleven individual steps in the loading process took up the rest of the time.

In contrast, the Spencer repeater was loaded with seven rounds at a time, in a magazine slung beneath the barrel. Bullets were then fed into the barrel for firing with the cock of a simple leaver. Thus, in one minute, a Yankee could load his rifle, fire seven times very quickly, at seven different targets, and then load again in less than a minute. In that sense, the Spencer was an important factor—a force multiplier in today's terminology—that made one Yankee the equal of three or four Confederates in terms of firepower. That rifle, at Chickamauga Creek, was a game changer.

As Jamie, Duncan, Lem, Batty, Dewey, and the others loaded and fired across that field, each noticed that fifty or so Yankees were putting up an amazing rate of fire, and each knew he was facing the Spencer repeating rifle. While none of the Georgia men had ever seen one, other Confederates had, and all knew of that destructive power of that single rifle. As men from both sides rushed to see what the noise was about, the fight grew, and by 7:30 AM on September 19, 1863, the Battle of Chickamauga was on!

A Union General, George Thomas, was in charge of that section of the field. He was a graduate of West Point, and had been in the army for many years, where he'd risen up through the ranks. While remaining true to his oath to the Union, he was strangely enough, from southern Virginia. He had chosen to remain in the Union army when the war began, so he served in Yankee blue, and while that was somewhat unusual, a story from his childhood is even stranger.

As a youth, his family had owned slaves in the town of Jerusalem Court House in southern Virginia. At the age of nine, he'd fled his home with his mother in the middle of the night, running from the most famous slave revolt in American history—Nat Turner's Slave Rebellion! Maybe his fear that night, as a nine year old boy, running through the woods with his mother, from armed rebellious slaves, played some role in his decision to fight with the Union. If so, he did not share those musings after the war, so like many questions of history, we are left but to ponder.

Thomas' Union boys were facing an equally famous southern commander, the cavalry Commander Nathan Bedford Forrest. Forrest was, by all accounts, the best cavalry commander in the war, bar none—on either side of the conflict. That is high praise indeed, when compared to immortal warriors such as Phil Sheridan, Billy Sherman, or the famed Confederate Commander Jeb Stewart. Stewart had become infamous for the flamboyant trick of taking his cavalry of

2,000 dedicated southern horsemen, and circling entirely the Union Army of the Potomac, a massive force, some 120,000 men strong. He'd done that twice, earlier in the war.

In contrast to Stewart, Nathan Bedford Forrest was not given to such theatrics. In fact, he considered such antics childish, so he dedicated his not-inconsiderable military talents to one thing and one thing only—killing Yankees. At that singular skill, he was very, very good.

It has often been said that Nathan Bedford Forrest could "smell a battle" and many times predict the outcome before the first rifle was fired. With no formal military training at all, he could read terrain, and he seemed to just "know" how men would flow across a field, or down a hillside when they were under fire. He could predict with uncanny accuracy, where his enemy would emerge from a tree-line, or a mountain pass, and thus, he seemed to just know where to place the bulk of his cavalry, his cannon, or in some cases, his infantry. Forrest always positioned his forces for maximum advantage, and few were the times when he did not come out victorious. More so than any other cause, his decisions were one reason that the Union force would be routed in several smaller fights on September 18 at Chickamauga, though he played no part in the final Confederate victory on that bloody field.

When the firing heated up that morning, both of these very capable commanders heard the noise and asked exactly the same question at virtually the same time; "What the hell's going on up there?" Each commander then began to feed men into that early morning fight over an otherwise unimportant field at the Kelly Farm.

General Forrest, though he typically commanded Confederate cavalry, happened to be the ranking man at the northern end of the Confederate line at that moment, so he took command of both the cavalry and the infantry in the immediate area. Like Thomas, he began to send men toward the sound of the guns, without really realizing what was going on. Thus did the Battle of Chickamauga Creek begin. Because a few Yankees that morning were thirsty, 34,000 men were wounded and 4,000 men would die.

Rifle fire dominated the battle for nearly ten minutes. The Yankees with Spencer rifles were kicking up quite a fuss, but no one had thought the big fight—a fight that everyone knew was coming—would begin at that singular cornfield. At that point, no cannon were set up anywhere near that particular cornfield, so the thunder of cannon was not heard, at least initially. Still the noise from nearly a thousand rifles was horrific, and the smoke from those massed rifles was already clouding the battlefield on both sides. About fifteen minutes after the firing began, a cannon battery was set up behind the Confederate trenches. None of the men in the 34th Georgia Rifles had heard the order to fire the four Napoleon cannon in battery, but they certainly heard the noise! Imagine a clap of thunder so loud it shakes your chest, and nearly sucks the breath from you.It assaults your ears and your eyeballs, and literally rattles the bones in your chest. Then imagine that pounding multiplied by four. Nothing commands one's attention on a battlefield like massed cannon fire, and the unexpected firing had exactly the same effect it always had—it terrified men on both sides of that field. Many peed their pants, at that first sound!

Trees, earth, blood, and the body parts of ten Yankees were all flung in the air when the first salvo hit their tree line sanctuary, but the very sound of those guns had terrified the untested 34th Georgia Rifles too! Some of the men didn't realize that cannon on either side were usually fired over the heads of their own troops, and a few Confederate men actually ducked from fear that the cannon shot from those guns might take their own heads off! Several more peed in their britches when the next rounds blasted from those Napoleons, but none of them realized it at the time. To make matters worse, the Yankees soon managed to set up a battery of their own, and those six massive guns were aimed directly at the position of the 34th Georgia Rifles!

The Napoleon was a short-barreled cannon that was the mainstay of both armies during the early years of the Civil War. It was basically a massive shotgun, in that the barrels were not rifled, so anything that could be placed in the barrel on top of the powder-bag could become a deadly projectile. They weren't particularly accurate, but they killed many a man, simply because so many of those guns were used by both sides in the war. A gun-crew of six to nine men prepared each cannon, and they typically fired in battery, with four or six gun groups firing together. They could shoot up to twice a minute, so the sound of massed cannon was almost constant on Civil War battlefields, and if a man was close enough to those guns, he felt the pressure blast of the firing in his chest, his stomach, his lungs, and his eyeballs. That is a feeling like nothing else in the experience of man.

The Napoleons fired a range of projectiles, explosive shot, or solid shot, up to 1,000 yards, and the fire-blast from each firing tore from the end of the gun and reached thirty or forty feet toward the enemy. That fire could, and sometimes literally did, cook men alive, if they happened to be charging toward the Napoleon when the cannon was fired, or merely standing in the wrong place at the wrong time. These cannon also added most of the blinding smoke to the Civil War battlefield, so much smoke that, once the cannon began on both sides, they effectively provided a smokescreen that prohibited enemy commanders across the battle line from seeing what the opposing units were doing.

Jamie, like every green Confederate in that unit, was filthy by then. He was loading and firing his Springfield, just like his men, and shouting to them by that point. "Keep a steady fire, but don't waste shots! We'll get them blue-bellies outa those trees directly, so shoot when you can hit something!" He was pleased with himself, that he'd managed to control his terror enough to continue commanding his troops. He'd seen Owen Collins, a veteran, give him an appraising look right after the fighting began. Seemingly satisfied, Owen had nodded to Jamie, and then resumed his deadly work.

## The First Rebel Yell

Just then a runner arrived with orders. Jamie lowered his head to hear amid the confusion, as the man literally shouted directly into his ear. Then Jamie nodded his understanding, and shouted to his men above the firing. "Men, prepare to move out. Leave packs here. Take only water and forty rounds of ammunition. Fix your bayonets!"

Bayonets were even then, an archaic, and virtually useless, artifact of history. While they were used as weapons until well into the 20th century, they had not been particularly effective weapons on any battlefield since the American Revolution. As armies became equipped with rifled muskets like the Springfield in the mid-1800s, the real killing took place at a much greater distances than in Washington's time, rendering the bayonet almost meaningless. It is a historic fact that less than 5% of all wounds in the Civil War resulted from any type of blade, and that included both the swords worn by officers, and all of the bayonets on the battlefield. With both the rifled musket and the repeating rifles changing the battlefield during the Civil War, blades were, by then, virtually useless as fighting weapons. Even the famed Confederate General Stonewall Jackson complained of the uselessness of his sword in battle. He was never known to draw his sword, either in battle or in drill, and in fact, it had rusted and fused within its scabbard. Like that sword, the bayonets on the battle lines of the Civil War, were already obsolete.

With that fact calmly noted as a historical footnote, it is also a fact, that nothing terrified the infantry soldier in 1863, either north or south, more than the order to fix bayonets. That order represented the probability of close-order fighting, and not a single man in either army wanted that type of battle. No man in history, even good knife fighters like Duncan Carmichael, ever wished to die by being skewered on his enemy's blade, and when bayonets were ordered, the fighting was sure to get nasty.

Then came the next inevitable order, shouted by a Confederate commander behind the battle line; "Charge!" So they did. Dewey, Batty, Owen, Lem, and Duncan, then Jamie, along with Sampson in the van; they moved simultaneously with nearly a thousand other Confederates, standing, jumping, and moving forward over their logs.

And that was exactly when it happened for the first time in Georgia, at least the first time in the War Between the States. As those Confederates charged the Yankee rifles, they did something that had not been heard in the entire state of Georgia since the American Revolution, they began a scream, a high-pitched yell that had become known by that point as the Rebel Yell. For nearly all of those Confederates, it was their very first time making that noise!

The idea of yelling in battle to give oneself confidence and strength had originated almost exactly a hundred years before among Cherokee warriors in the same north Georgia hills on which those armies fought near Chickamauga Creek. The Cherokee knew that screaming in battle was powerful medicine, and gave one strength. It also terrified one's enemies, so they had screeched and screamed when they went into battle along the frontier in the Cherokee Wars of the 1760s. By the time of the American Revolution, many white frontiersmen were using the same battle tactic, screeching and screaming together during a running advance to give oneself strength. Thus, the sound that became known as the Rebel Yell predated the Civil War by at least one hundred years. It was a Cherokee war tactic from the Cherokee wars of the 1760s, and had probably been used by my people, the Cherokee, for centuries.

The Rebel Yell had not been heard in Georgia during the Civil War, prior to its use on the fields at Chickamauga Creek for one simple reason—no significant fights had taken place in Georgia during the first two years of the Civil War! There had been several small battles near the coastal forts, but Confederates were typically defenders in those fights and not aggressors—thus no Rebel Yells were heard in those smaller fights. The Rebel Yell was an aggressive weapon, used only while charging one's enemy. It meant your force was moving forward; it meant that those facing you were soon to die, that the real killing was soon to begin.

Moreover, the Rebel Yell is a misnomer. The sound itself was not truly a yell. It was more of a barking screech, a cross between a barking dog and a horribly wounded animal. It was a high-pitched yelping! When one man did the Rebel Yell, the yelping merely sounded abrasive, irritating to the ear. However, when an army barked or screeched that yell in unison, the sound was truly terrifying!

Many stories attest to the impact of that fearsome sound. Some fights, by all historical accounts, were actually won by that aggressive yell. Union men were occasionally so terrified that they fled the battle, once they heard an advancing Confederate force screeching that Rebel Yell. It was truly a terrible sound to the Union men in that war.

One can hear it even today, an authentic Rebel Yell. One perceptive journalist in 1928, using what was then, state of the art recording equipment, recorded an actual Rebel Yell from a living Confederate veteran. Thomas Alexander had fought with the 37th North Carolina infantry, and was one of the few living veterans who had actually used the Rebel Yell in battle. By 1928 there was some debate about what the actual Yell sounded like, and in some early movies, Hollywood had gotten it quite wrong. The journalist wisely sought to preserve the actual sound for history, so he took a simple tape recorder to a Confederate Veterans meeting. That 1928 recording, along with several other recorded examples, has survived for all time, and we can even now, hear the sound of a true Rebel Yell from someone who actually screamed that sound in battle.

Moreover, in 2007, using the most modern digital recording and sound manipulation techniques, the Museum of the Confederacy in Richmond, VA, re-mastered that singular Rebel Yell, and then multiplied a thousand fold. Thus, today, anyone can actually hear a true Rebel Yell from a thousand voices **(www.youtube.com/watch?v=dfHylwlq9Ow)**. That sound, even today, is still terrifying.

Of course, that sound, on many battlefields of the Civil War, was multiplied in impact by the other sounds of battle, by the smell, and by the terror; the earth-shaking sound of scores of cannon—a sound that could, and often was, heard twenty miles away. Added to that universe of palpable noise was the abrasive pop, the crackle-firing of uncounted rifles, as well as the shouts of wounded men, screams of officers, and the baying of wounded, dying horses or mules. Smoke, noise, and gory death defined the Civil War battlefield. In a day before smokeless gunpowder was invented, each rifle spewed forth a flame and burst of grey-black smoke nearly ten feet from the barrel. When that is multiplied by hundreds or thousands, the smoke and noise blinds everyone on the battle line. Of course, the cannon of the day were much worse than the rifles. Firing the same powder, they spewed forth flame and smoke, and no cannon ever fired alone. Even today, there is no sound, there is no experience, in the known universe like a Civil War battlefield.

As Jamie and his men moved forward, they could barely see twenty feet in any direction; the smoke and noise together blinded and deafened them. The noise of the fight simply seemed to get louder with each passing minute. During the charge, Jamie was firing his LaMat pistol, rather than his rifle, since, as an officer, his job was to keep the riflemen in his unit firing and restrain them from running when they faced the enemy. His weapon did little good, but he was blindly firing into the smoke directly in his front, and he shouted his orders as he continued to run forward. "Keep up men, and stay in line. We'll find the bastards soon enough!" He fired again, and paused to reload behind a tree-stump, and as he paused, he was bumped from behind.

"Sorry Suh!" Sampson shouted. "But I's glad you did take up behind dis tree! We's way out in front o' everybody!"

Jamie hadn't realized that Sampson was right behind him, but then he grinned at his slave. "Didn't I tell you to stay in that damn trench? Hell, Sampson, you ain't even got a rifle!"

"Do too got one, Suh! And a powder belt too!" Sampson replied. I grabbed it from dat young, scrappin' boy, dat lil' boy from Walton's Ford named Billy Bender. He got it in de head, few minutes ago; he don't need it no more! His head damn near tore off by some cannon ball 'er sompin!"

Jamie tried to picture a face for young Bender, but couldn't. While he knew all the Tugalo men, some others had joined the unit from other areas—mostly because they were relatives of his boys. Jamie didn't know them all. As he finished loading, he grinned at Sampson, and looked around the tree-trunk for any Yankee targets. However, sticking his head out into the open attracted the attention, and the fire, of nearly an entire brigade of Union men from New Jersey, who happened to be opposing the 34$^{th}$ Georgia Rifles that morning. Bullets flew past like stinging bees, as Jamie ducked behind his tree again, and when he did, he realized that he was lucky to be alive.

"Might want to keep ya' head down, Suh!" Sampson shouted, as he peeked around the other side of the tree and fired. As he reloaded, he shouted, "Suh! Recon' we best get on back to our men soon, a-fore them Yankees figure out ain't but two of us?"

Jamie had two thoughts instantly. First, he thought, "That makes a hell of a lot of sense!" His next thought surprised him somewhat. "I'm fightin' my first fight for the Confederacy, and ain't no white man in sight, but here's my man, Sampson, right beside me, just like always!" For a split second, Jamie realized the absurdity of that thought, but just then the Confederate cannon fired a massive salvo, and again sent smoke and flame flying across the battlefield. Let's go Sampson. Let's get the hell out'a here, in that smoke!" Jamie shouted, as he began to run back toward his men, or where he thought his men ought to be!

Of course, he ran only ten yards or so, before he jumped the stump of a massive oak tree that had been taken down by cannon fire only moments before. He landed right on top of Duncan Carmichael, and no sooner had he landed, than Sampson jumped beside him, landing on Batty Prather, who shouted, "Get off me, you damn nigger," as he shoved Sampson away.

"Damn you Batty!" Jamie shouted. "You shut the hell up! That nigger was up there with me killin' Yankees, while you was back here pissin' your pants, 'n hidin' behind this damn log!"

By that point, Batty had concluded that he'd never win an argument with anyone in his entire unit, particularly his captain, so he took the wiser course of action and shut up. Duncan just grinned, and said, "We lost you in the smoke, Jamie, and some damn fool shouted to take cover, so we holed up behind these few logs. Hell! We ain't even seen a Yankee to shoot at yet, since we charged! They's probably holdin' up somewhere in this smoke too!"

That observation was true, so the firing of rifles soon died down. The cannon on both sides kept up the firing for a time—maybe ten minutes more—but then that died out too, and only sporadic rifle shots were heard in that section of the field. However, by then, other units had moved up to the south of the 34th Georgia Rifles, so there was an increase in firing in that section, some two hundred yards below Jamie's position. As he and the Georgia 34th fell back to their original position, they grabbed their wounded, along with a few Yankee wounded. They left the bodies from both sides, until they could collect them under the flag of truce that was seen on virtually every Civil War battlefield towards the evening after a big fight.

"Shouldn't we get our dead off the battlefield?" Batty Prather asked, as he struggled to carry five Springfield rifles back to the Confederate lines.

Owen Collins, carrying a wounded Union man with him, merely said, "We'll have a detail get 'um later. Ain't nothing to do for 'um now, no ways."

They walked on, hearing the sounds of firing many hundreds of yards away. Then, as Batty picked up another weapon from a dead Confederate, Owen asked, "Are ya checkin' them rifles for powder?"

Batty said, "What 'a yuh mean?"

Owen said, "You be careful pickin' up them weapons. Many of 'um are loaded."

Batty bent down to get the rifle, and asked, "Cain't I just fire it, 'n see?"

Owen, much the wiser man in the ways of war, said. "Don't ya dare fire them damn rifles! That damn gun could blow us up to Tennessee! You just take the ramrod and slide 'ur down the barrel. Then you sight that ram and figure how many loads o' powder ya got in there!"

That made no sense to Batty, so he asked. "What 'a you mean, how many loads? What fool would load more 'n once without firing it?"

Owen just took a deep breath, as he carried the unconscious Yankee along across his shoulder. Then Owen spoke up again. "You did alright, Batty. Yer' Mama would be proud o' you! You weren't scairt at all, and you fired your rifle each time you loaded it! I was watchin' ya see? Still, some men are scairt when they get into in their first fight. I've seen men, some older 'n you, get so scairt' they can't even load their rifles." Owen thought for a moment, taking another deep breath, as they continued to walk through the smoke back toward their own lines. "Some men do just the opposite; they jest keep 'a loadin' their rifles, and never fire 'um!" Owen took a deep breath, as they continued to walk along, then he continued. "You just use the ram and check to see how far it goes in the barrel, to see if you got a loaded rifle, or one with two or even three loads o' powder and shot in it!"

In that assertion, Owen has summarized a little known fact. In the heat of war and the terror of the battlefield, many men were so terrified that they literally forgot to fire their weapons. Others simply could not bring themselves to kill another human being. Maybe it is fear, or a deep religious sense of the wrongness of taking a human life. Perhaps it is some genetic factor that makes killing a member of one's own species so repugnant, but it is a fact. A substantial portion of every army in history could not actually fire their weapons at their enemy. In every battlefield in the Civil War, as the weapons were picked up after the conflict, many were found unfired. Many others were loaded with multiple charges of powder and shot! If a Springfield was fired in that condition, with two or three charges of powder in the barrel, it would simply blow up, killing all who were standing near it. In one example noted by historians, a Springfield was picked up on the Gettysburg battlefield, with more than half the barrel taken up with loaded, but unfired minie-balls and gunpowder. Some unknown Confederate had loaded that rifle eight separate times without firing it! Thus did Owen, seasoned veteran that he was, make sure that Batty checked each rifle he picked up as they moved back to their original line.

## Out Gunned

The first day of the Chickamauga battle was a north-to-south affair, with the major battle actions taking place on the north end of the line early, and then moving along the lines to the south. As different units became engaged at different times, fighting would flair up like the re-emergence of flames in a burning home, and then die back down, with the major actions taking place as if they had been in a planned sequence, from north to south along the battle line. This sequenced set of independent battles resulted in a relative peace for the 34th Georgia Rifles from about 9:00 AM on September 19 until early in the afternoon.

Jamie saw that the men replenished their ammunition, gathered what they could from fallen comrades, and hid from their unseen enemy. Confederates ducked behind their logs and in their trenches to keep out of sight and out of danger. Every so often, maybe twenty minutes apart, the Yankee artillery commanders would send over a few shots, just to let the southern boys know they were still there. One lucky cannon shot hit a limber for a Confederate gun. That wagon was loaded with gunpowder, and the explosion blew several horses well into the next century, sending a spray of oak splinters, blood, and horseflesh for twenty yards in every direction. Three of the gun crew were killed, with one of those being blown nearly apart. Still, other than that lucky shot, nothing much else happened to the 34th Georgia for almost four hours. The men had no orders to move, so they stayed in their trenches, content to let others do the fighting for a time.

At about 1:00 PM that afternoon, the 34th did come under fire, from a

Yankee unit that had been ordered to advance and confront the enemy. Because of the relative silence from their field on the Kelly Farm, the Yankees seemed to have forgotten that the 34th Georgia was even there! At around 12:45 PM, a Yankee regiment, newly arrived on the battlefield from Chattanooga and unaware of the fight that morning, had been flung into the field from the north end, thus missing the bodies of the fallen Union men in the tree line on the western side of the field. The explosion craters surely let the Yankees know they were on a battlefield, but they apparently didn't realize that Confederates were still in the opposite tree line only sixty yards away. The inexperienced Union commander of this particular force had not even arranged his men in battle lines. Believing that his enemy was at least a mile to the south where battle sounds suggested another fight was raging, this Union major had his men in a marching column as they entered the field, and while they avoided the explosion craters, a few men began to notice what looked like several dead bodies to their west—thus most of these Union boys were looking away from the Confederates when the entire regiment, including the 34th Georgia opened on them. That first volley from nearly a thousand Springfield muskets was a wall of minie-balls, deadly projectiles that couldn't miss over a sixty yard distance! That first volley was essentially a massacre.

"Give, 'um hell, boys!" Jamie shouted, as he fired his weapon, along with over a thousand other men. "I don't want a single one of 'um leaving that field alive!"

All the Confederates fired at once, and then began the reloading process, and while that first volley decimated the Union force, there were still over seven hundred Yankees in that field, and every single one of them had a Spencer repeating rifle. By then however, not a single Union man was standing. If those Yankees hadn't been wounded by the first volley, it had quickly dawned on them that they made much less of a target if they lay down in the explosion craters from the earlier fight. Most found a hole in the ground fairly quickly, but others merely lay down behind one of their dead comrades. One Yankee tugged on a body to reposition it to hide behind, only to get cussed at by his comrade, a man severely wounded, but very much alive. Thus, within only fifteen seconds of that first Confederate volley, as the Confederates hid behind their logs, quickly completing their eleven steps to reload, the Yankee Spencers opened up, and once those rifles began firing, the roar was continuous. Those Spencers sent back a wall of lead toward the 34th Georgia, and the noise seemed to go on forever, with no break for reloading at all!

Duncan shouted to his friend, as they both ducked low in their trench. "Hey Lem. Recon we pissed 'um off a bit?"

Lem grinned at his friend's sense of humor, even when under deadly fire. The pop of the Spencer repeater rifles was a higher sound than the Springfield musket, as the Spencer used less powder. Still those Union rifles sounded continuously, as Yankees searched for targets between the logs to their front. Most defensive works in those days were built as a trench in the ground with two or three firing logs on the top, facing the enemy, and the works of the 34th Georgia were no exception. The highest log was usually raised a bit, so the Confederates could fire their rifles between the top log and the one below it, without ever sticking their head up above the top log. Of course in this fight the Yankees were so close, they could easily aim between those logs, and the Spencers were accurate, as well as fast. Men all along the Confederate line began to fall, many wounded in the head or face by bullets that had literally found the crack between the logs.

Jamie was one of the few Confederates who could fire back fairly quickly, since he was using his six shot LaMat pistol. That revolver gave him multiple shots but he wanted to make each one count, so he held his fire unless he saw a clear Yankee target. Even amid the noise of the guns of the Union men, Jamie still noticed the relative quiet down his own line. His entire command was busy reloading their old, single shot Springfields. At just that moment, during that first reloading pause, Jamie had a horrid fear. It was the same dread that would occur to Confederate battle line commanders throughout the Chickamauga battle, and without realizing it, Jamie spoke out loud! "If the damn Yankees realized that nearly every one of my boys is reloading, the whole Yankee line could charge us, and we couldn't do nothin' but spit at 'um!"

Sampson, who had never been more than eight feet away, heard him, and responded. "They'll be on us, sure, less'en we can keep 'um off for a few more seconds." Just at that moment, the Confederate artillery, apparently awakened to the fact that there were again some Union men in the open field before them, fired their four Napoleons. They were good gunners, and managed to drop their shot carefully but strategically, just past the Confederate line, and right on the heads of the Union column in the open field.

Jamie fired his LaMat at one Union man, a lower level commander who was dumb enough to stick his head up to see where the enemy cannon fire came from. That Union man, a lawyer from Pittsburg, died that very second in the northern most cornfield of the Kelly Farm in north Georgia.

Jamie said to Sampson, "Them cannon 'll keep 'um down another minute or two, I recon." Then he turned and shouted to Lem, who was firing his weapon about ten feet away, on the other side of Sampson. "Lem! Move down the line and tell the men to work together and coordinate their fire. Every man works with the man beside him, and only one man fires at a time. His partner has to hold his load for at least the count of ten before he fires!"

Jamie didn't know if his men would understand or follow those orders. Hell, he didn't know how many of his men could count to ten, or how many would be likely to do so in the middle of a battle. Still, he sensed what every commander throughout history knows; an unloaded weapon is a useless weapon, and being able to deliver fire at any point in time is the very essence of battle. If it took twenty seconds to complete eleven steps in the reloading process, then half the men holding their fire for ten seconds should assure that some men held loaded rifles most of the time. Jamie concentrated to see if anything else could be done to counter the horrid reality of the Yankee Spencer rifles, but he could think of nothing. Coordinated fire was his only option, and that would only work if his men would actually do it.

While the Yankee commander and his two senior subordinates lay dead in the field, another subordinate had taken command, and he was not nearly as stupid as his predecessor. He'd quickly realized that the Confederate fire was volley fire from Springfield muskets, so he realized he'd have a brief reloading pause, after the massed Confederates fired their weapons a second time. At just that second, they did. This Union man quickly realized what had to be done; for to stay in that cornfield under both rifle and cannon fire was suicide!

Had Lem been able to reach every man in the Confederate trench with Jamie's orders for coordinated fire, maybe the expected reloading pause could have been nullified. However, Lem, while spreading those orders, was nevertheless moving very carefully, and thus very slowly, down the Confederate line for one simple reason; he wanted to live past the next ten minutes!

The Yankee now in command in the cornfield had, only seven months previously, been a teacher at a small college near Columbus, Ohio. He wasn't a particularly good commander, but he was educated, and was cunning in a way that history teachers often are. He'd often read about war, about battles, and he knew enough to seize an advantage when he saw one. He ordered a charge at his command against the Confederate works, and he planned to unleash his forces just when the next reloading pause began.

Some believe that time seems to stand still in a battle; that men move independently of time or that running and firing a weapon, reloading a rifle, or perhaps even dying itself, seems to take place in slow motion. However, this is a falsehood fostered by arm chair analysis long after the fact. It is the result of the rehash of history by historians, and perhaps even the pretentions of Hollywood. Anyone who has experienced battle knows that the opposite is true. Time is distilled to its very essence on a battle line, and if seconds seem like hours, it is only because the adrenaline in one's body has one moving so fast, that everything seems incredibly slow when compared to one's own heartbeat. Terror quickens the pace for all who face death in battle, and that makes time seem slow.

Such was the case in this fight. While many men died in every single second of the fight, the fact is that the Union force had only been in the field for a minute or so at that point, and the Confederates had only fired three volleys, when the Union order to charge came. Jamie saw his worst fears realized. Lem had gotten word to only a few men to coordinate fire; he'd only passed twenty men or so, and only some of them had actually followed those orders. After the third volley was fired, the Union commander, the teacher from Ohio, shouted, "Charge!" Union men rose from their holes all across the field, and Jamie thought, "Oh hell! I didn't realize there were so many of them left!" Then he quickly shouted the one order that could still, save a few of his men. It was the same order he'd shouted earlier that day. Once again he shouted, "Fix bayonets!"

Duncan Carmichael, positioned about twenty feet to Jamie's right, shouted to Batty Prather and Owen Collins, "Load 'um up right quick, boys. We're about to jump into hell!"

Within ten seconds, seven hundred Union men were at the top of the Confederate works, and some actually jumped atop the Confederate logs. Unlike the Confederates who were now below them, the Union men still had loaded rifles. They began to fire from atop those logs with no mercy, shooting directly down into the Confederate trench at men who were only four or five feet away. Some of the Confederates hunkered down in the trench and tried to reload their Springfields, while others retreated out of the trench and into some trees about ten feet behind the ditch.

Again Jamie had the presence of mind to realize the only safety lay in a close approach to his enemy. He thus shouted "Charge" and that was enough to prompt some of the Confederates to stop trying to load their Springfields, and begin to fight for their lives. Some men used their rifles like clubs. A few Confederates had their bayonets fixed by then so they stood to the front of their trenches and rammed several Yankees through.

It was one bloody mess, and the phrase hand-to-hand combat cannot nearly express the immediacy of the danger; flying knives, bayonets, explosions of the Yankee Spencer rifles, the flying blood from a slashed gut, or cut cheekbone, blood on your chest—yours or someone else's—and brains in your face; and of course, the death. Some Confederates grabbed the legs of the nearest Union men and pulled them into the bottom of the ditch, where they fought it out, biting, punching, gouging out their enemies' eyes, and doing anything else to stay alive. Lem was now fighting about fifty feet from Jamie, and he was wounded in the shoulder by a Spencer round just as the Yankees climbed the forward-facing logs. Still, he fixed his bayonet and rammed the Union man who shot him, and that man fell right on top of him. Thus did a Yankee body protect Lem from the next few rounds from the Union rifles. Owen and Batty were fighting for their lives, working together. Batty had partially hidden under and behind a now-fallen log at the front of the trench, and when Union men actually jumped down into the trench, he was able to trip one of them, which sent him flying into the knife of Owen.

About that same instant, the Confederate color guard for the 34th Georgia Rifles was killed, and just as the unit flag began to fall Duncan Carmichael grabbed it and managed to stick it back in the ground. Had that flag fallen, it would have been a signal that the unit was falling to defeat, and Duncan wouldn't even consider letting that happen. Duncan had been nicked in the shoulder when he turned for the flag, but some other Confederate had shot the Union man from the top of the logs near Duncan, and that man fell, like so many others, right into the Confederate trench. Duncan grabbed his unloaded Springfield, and began to use it like a club.

Jamie had now fired all of the rounds from his LaMat pistol, and he'd grabbed a Springfield from a dead Confederate near him and was using it like a club. While Union men still poured over the logs about thirty feet down the Confederate line, there were none atop the logs to Jamie's immediate front. He took a moment to look around, and feeling like he should give some order, or have some idea that would save his unit from this onslaught, he looked away from his friends and down the Confederate trench in the other direction, finding the same carnage there.

Bloody men in Union blue and Confederate butternut were fighting for their lives, and amazingly, many of the Union men still had rounds in those damn Spencer repeaters. One calmly sat atop the Confederate logs, and fired down the trench, with his back to Jamie, and Jamie wished he had one more bullet in his pistol for that cocky son-of-a-bitch! Then he saw one of his men from Clarkesville, Georgia a man whose name he couldn't now remember, finish his loading process with the old Springfield, but that man forgot to remove the ram from the rifle barrel. When he fired, his ram shot out the end of the gun just ahead of the minie-ball, and both struck the damn Yankee sitting on top of the logs and calmly firing away. That Union man looked down, rather stupidly, at the three foot rifle ram that now protruded from his chest, and seemed to wonder, what the hell is that?

Still Springfield rifles, while taking a large load of black powder were never meant to take that much over-pressure in the breech. The ram and the minie-ball were simply too much blockage, so the barrel blew up just as the shot was fired, killing the young Confederate where he stood. Jamie wondered what he could do once again, and again he shouted his worries out loud without realizing it. "Unless I come up with something fast, all of us 'll die in this damn ditch!"

Sampson was busy loading a Springfield just to his left, and answered, "Is it time we got out 'a this damn hole, Suh?" He then fired at another Yankee man who had scampered to the top of the logs just beside Jamie.

And just at that second Jamie looked to the top of the logs and into the face of hell itself. No less than three Union men had mounted the trench just above Jamie's head, and he and Sampson both looked into the deadly bore of three Spencer rifles. The Union men, thinking to capture this ranking Confederate, held their fire for just a second, and that terrified Jamie even more. It is amazing how large the business end of a Spencer rifle can seem, and Jamie, unaware of their desire to capture him, knew he faced his imminent death at that very instant. Once again, time stood still.

It was then, right then, that Jamie saw something even more frightening than the deadly weapons pointed at his head. A terror, a dark death, a demon, some muddy-black creature arose from the rear of the Union men, striking them from the rear and side, and he seemed to devour them in a bloody flash. Blood flew as a knife slashed one Yankee side and gut, and only after they were tackled by the demon did Jamie realize that it was a dirty, deadly Confederate, who had somehow gotten behind the Union force. How in hell had that happened? Jamie wondered, then he looked that creature over, even as the Confederate dispatched the other two Yankees with the longest knife that Jamie had ever seen.

The Confederate wore a long flowing overcoat, and sported no beard at all, when most Confederates along the line hadn't shaven in weeks. His face was nearly black from ripping open powder bags with his teeth, and this man also had the longest hair Jamie had ever before seen on a man, reaching far down his back. The Confederate's dark face, dirty coat, and long hair flew in the wind, as he hit the first Union man, slashing at first, and then sinking a long knife deep into his side, and driving him into the next Union man atop the trench. He then swung the knife—Jamie then saw that his other hand held a hatchet or ax of some sort. He buried that deep into the neck of the second Union man in line. The third Yankee saw the terror-demon attack his friends, and was distracted for a split second, but long enough for Sampson to reach out and grab the end of the Spencer rifle, pointing it away from Jamie and himself. He then gave that rifle a tug, and toppled the Yankee into the ditch at his feet. That man died looking into the blackest face he had ever seen, and wondering, "Why is this nigger fightin' for the south?"

Jamie drew a breath as he realized he wouldn't die, and that is when he realized that part of the deafening noise he heard was the Rebel Yell. As realization dawned, he looked into the face of the Confederate before them, that filthy, long-haired, deadly man who had just saved his life, and he said the first thing that popped into his mind. "You're a damn savage!"

That warrior looked back at Jamie, and without thinking, shouted his reply. "You're the damned savage! I'm Cherokee!"

Thus did the Thomas Legion arrive on that bloody field! That was the source of the Confederates who rushed into the fight from behind the Union men, knives in one hand and a battle ax in the other—they knew enough not to even bother with their Springfields. After a few shots had been fired, those guns were useless in this type of fight. With their dirty, great-grey overcoats, different from any Jamie had ever seen before, and their long hair flying in the wind, these Cherokee warriors now did, once again, what their forefathers had done for generations. They fought like demons, and the Yankees before them never realized they were surrounded until it was too late. Those Yankees never stood a chance!

Rifles fired, knives flashed, bayonets still found a chest, or ribcage, or neck to puncture, but the fight was decided when the Thomas Legion had moved swiftly into the north end of the field at the Kelly Farm. Few of the Yankees saw them coming, and the Yankee commanders who were still in the middle of the field were quickly dispatched by the rifles of the Thomas Legion. Within only fifteen minutes the firing stopped all along that section of the line, and the aftermath of the fight began. Yankees that could still walk were rounded up in a bunch just in front of the Confederate trench, and held under guard, as men began to collect the wounded from the field.

Lem pulled himself out from under a Yankee body, and began to count the holes in that man's back. He stopped counting at twenty, when he realized that most of those rounds had been aimed, not at the dead Yankee, but at him! Then as he stood up, he said aloud what every man in that trench had been thinking. "We'd all been kilt if'n them boys hadn't showed up when they did." As he said it, he looked to the top of the trench and stared directly into the face of five Cherokee warriors, men who were calmly sitting atop the head log at the top of the defensive trench. There they sat without compassion, indeed without any outward emotion at all, and simply stared back at Lem. Of course, within a second, each Cherokee looked away; to stare directly at a man too long would show disrespect.

All along the line for nearly a hundred yards of trenches, the same face-off was taking place; the 34$^{th}$ Georgia Rifles in the ditch, wondering how they'd lived through that fight, and atop the logs, Union bodies, and silent, grim Cherokee warriors.

## Authors Note: A Cherokee Family Legend

That scene of course, played out many times in that afternoon fight at the Kelly Farm. Perhaps fifty or a hundred Cherokee actually tackled Yankees atop those logs, saving the Confederates in the trenches below, Confederates with unloaded Springfields. Jamie Turnbull told the story often of being saved from three Yankees by a Cherokee in the Thomas Legion. No one can now say, with certainty, who the particular warrior was that saved Jamie Turnbull's life in that ditch on that day so long ago. What is known is that the family stories of a Confederate veteran from Oklahoma, a man named Corporal Tall-Beaver Waters of the Cherokee Legion, told a similar tale. Those legends state that he saved the life of a white officer of the Georgia 34th Rifles atop those logs at the Kelly Farm that day, and that officer may have been Jamie Turnbull himself. Corporal Waters, a direct descendent of the famous Cherokee Chief Runs-to-Water, tackled three Yankees in one instant and then dispatched them with his knife and his war-hatchet. He had fired and discarded his Springfield rifle previously. Both the knife and the war hatchet that went to war so long ago are still owned by my great grandmother. Thus, in one small eddy in the broader stream of history, I suspect that my family, the family of my grandfather, Runs-to-Water, a great Cherokee chief, interacted yet again, with the great Turnbull and Jarrett families of the Tugalo River Valley.

Duncan Carmichael was the next to speak that day from their section of the trench. He looked directly into the face of a Cherokee atop the logs before him as he put the matter simply, and directly as any Carmichael would; "Them damned savages saved our ass!" That quote, also, is part of the story told by Corporal Waters to his family so long ago.

## In the Confederate Trench

Jamie merely watched those Cherokee, as the fighting died away. He then assigned a detail to collect as many Spencer rifles as could be found that would still fire. He wanted a few of those remarkable guns in his unit, if he could find the ammunition for them.

Just then Sampson said, "Mr. Jamie Suh? Here comes someone important!" Jamie looked around and for the first time in his life he spoke with a man who was a living legend, even during his own lifetime.

Will Holland Thomas, was fifty nine years old that year, and he was leading the Thomas Legion, a unit that had been named in his honor by the Cherokee. Thomas was a white man who had married a Cherokee woman, and been adopted by the tribe. When the order to expel the Cherokee came down from the Congress in 1836 and 1838, Will Thomas had purchased land in his own name for some members of the Cherokee tribe, and those few had been the ancestors for what became known as the Eastern Band of the Cherokee. By 1860, nearly two thousand Cherokee still lived in their tribal homelands in the rugged mountains of North Carolina and Tennessee, and Thomas was serving as their undisputed leader. That tribe had provided nearly all of the men for the Thomas Legion.

Thus was the story told. A white man had served as a Cherokee chief, and in the 1830s and 1840s, had helped his adopted people retain their homeland in the Blue Mountains, and thus their dignity. Most Americans were, by then, shamed by the infamous Trail of Tears and the sufferings of the Cherokee people, and if a few remained in the rugged mountains of North Carolina, a land that nobody else seemed to want, that was fine by them. The story of Will Holland Thomas was, even then, known nationwide among the Cherokee and the whites alike. Of course, to the Cherokee, this man was nearly a God.

"I believe we have seen a great victory here." Thomas said, as he looked into the Confederate trenches. "Have you counted your losses as yet, or counted the Yankee prisoners, Captain?"

Jamie took a moment to realize he was being addressed by this famous man. He had already been told that both his regimental commander, and the adjunct—the second in command—had been killed. Jamie was not sure who was in command of his regiment, but he figured, he was at least in the running for that post, since there were no others who outranked him, so he'd act like he was in charge. He responded to Thomas. "Uh, no Sir. I think we lost a goodly number of men, at least until your boys showed up," Jamie replied. Then he realized that much more needed to be said. "I do want to thank you and your regiment, too. I think you might have saved a good number of my boys today, and I'm eternally grateful for that!"

"Indeed," Thomas replied, as if such a matter was simply the art, or the luck, of war. In a sense, he was right. "Perhaps, after you gather your forces, you and your men could vacate the trenches in this section for a time, and my men will take care of the wounded on the field."

Jamie was a new commander, and he was correct in that every officer above him in the entire regiment was either dead or wounded. Still, even with only a few months in the army, he'd been taught many of the unspoken rules of the battlefield. One such unspoken rule governed who cleaned up. In general, the first unit in the fight, the unit that usually bore the brunt of the action, was spared the necessity to clean up after a battle. Picking up the wounded, the extra weapons, the dead, various body parts, broken equipment, and dead horses or mules was no picnic, and those most bloodied were usually spared that duty. Thomas was merely offering to take on those onerous duties, because his men had fought only part of the battle.

Jamie however, had other ideas. "No Sir, Major Thomas. It will be our honor to take care of this mess. I believe that I and my men owe you a debt of honor that can never be repaid for your great assistance in this victory." With that,

Jamie began to shout orders, and for once, his men readily complied, once they understood his intent. "Men of the 34th Georgia Rifles! Come to the front of our works and stand at attention! Today, we give our heartfelt thanks; today we honor the Cherokee of the Thomas Legion!"

As the Cherokee moved back, nearly eight hundred of them (a few had been wounded in the quick fight, but only a few), men from the Tugalo River Valley and the rest of the Fourth Georgia came out of their trenches, up from the mud and the blood of their very personal fight, and stood in straight ranks. Those men grabbed whatever Springfield or Spencer rifle they could, including ones that were clearly damaged and unable to fire. It simply would not do to render honors to another unit without a weapon in hand!

Owen helped Lem mount the front of the trench, as other Confederates helped their wounded; all who could stand for even a moment would be required for this brief time. Men shouted at their comrades to get up and stand at attention, as they honored the men who had clearly saved their lives. Duncan rudely kicked Batty in the ribs, as Batty bent over to grab a useless weapon for the honors. Duncan said, "Come on, you low-life cur. Get yur ass up and out'a this trench and stand at attention. The Cherokee are marchin' by! We're honorin' the Thomas Legion!"

Within a minute, most of the remaining men of the Fourth Georgia stood at attention in front of their works. A few were guarding Yankee prisoners and they remained in place, but they did turn to look as the Thomas Legion formed. The sergeants and lower commanders of the Fourth Georgia fought quickly to get the men into lines, and in only a minute they stood to ranks, much like a unit during parade drill.

Thomas himself for just a moment, didn't know what to say. He didn't seem to realize the gravity of the occasion; perhaps he hadn't realized that Jamie felt his unit was lost before the Thomas Legion arrived on the field. Luckily, one of his subordinates, a Cherokee from Cleveland, Tennessee, saw what needed to be done, so he shouted orders for his men. "Thomas Legion. Stand at attention in ranks. Face the Fourth Georgia." As men in both units assembled fifteen feet in front of the bloody logs atop the trench, Jamie took his place before his troops, and Major Will Thomas turned to face him. Nothing was said for those few moments, as the men in both units quickly assembled.

Jamie had decided in that time what he wished to say. He raised his voice to a shout, for all to hear, and with his man, Sampson, standing to his side, he shouted. "Major Thomas. My men and I request the privilege of rendering honors to the Thomas Legion. Together we won this fight, but we would not have prevailed without you. We owe you and your men our deepest gratitude!" With that Jamie raised a sharp salute to Major Thomas, which Thomas returned, as he nodded his head slightly.

Having received permission from Thomas, Jamie again shouted. "Men of the Fourth Georgia Rifles, render honors!" To a man, the Fourth Georgia snapped up a sharp salute which they held, as Jamie continued, in his loud, but formal tone. "Major Thomas and men of the Thomas Legion. I and my men thank you for the privilege of fighting with you. We thank you for arriving when you did, and for showing the courage you showed as you charged the enemy across this field! We now hereby dedicate this field as the Field of the Thomas Legion! It shall remain so named, forever, in honor of your gallantry in battle, and the Fourth Georgia would be honored to share the battlefield with you again, any time, and anywhere, in defense of our Grand Confederacy!" Jamie then shouted, once again as his men joined in enthusiastically! "Fourth Georgia. Join me in three cheers! Hip, Hip, Huzzah, Hip, Hip, Huzzah, Hip, Hip Huzzah!"

As the men of the Fourth Georgia raised their cheer, Thomas returned the salute once more, and then responded. "Sir! We appreciate that honor, and look forward to that opportunity. We shall stand with the Confederacy as she calls us. We shall now retire from the field."

With that Thomas' subordinate again shouted to his men. "Thomas Legion, left face! Forward march!"

Once again, Jamie noticed the meandering gait, that slow stately amble so characteristic of the Cherokee, as the Thomas Legion left the field, not a single man marching in time with another. This time there were no snide comments on that marching gait from the 34th Georgia Rifles. As far as the survivors in the 34th Georgia were concerned these men could march any way they damn well pleased!

Batty Prather, standing to the left of Duncan, and helping hold Lem up on his other side, got a bit tired under that burden as the last of the Thomas Legion filed past, and he made the mistake of dropping his salute, just as the last few Cherokee ambled by.

Duncan Carmichael had never been much for saluting, but this was one time that Duncan believed a salute to another man had been duly earned! He proposed to quickly correct Batty's mistake! "Get your damn salute back up Batty, or I'll kick your ass from here all the way into next week! Them men saved your bacon, and you'll, by God, be showin' them some respect. You'll salute 'um just as long as they walk pass, or I'll know why not!" Then Duncan, himself holding a rigid salute for the first time in the entire war, continued. The tone of his voice could only be described as reverent. "Salute 'um well, by God! That there's the Cherokee. That's the Thomas Legion walking by!"

Batty dutifully saluted again, as did every other man in the Fourth Georgia. They remained so until the last Cherokee had left the field.

Only after the Cherokee were gone from sight did Jamie shout, "At ease, men. Dismissed!" Then the 34$^{th}$ Georgia Rifles and the other two companies in their regiment moved to police up the field of battle. On that field, nearly six hundred Yankees lay wounded, with two hundred and eighty of those dead. Jamie's regiment had lost three hundred and forty eight men, including every officer above Jamie's rank. Many men were wounded multiple times, by those deadly Spencer rifles. Still, Jamie had six hundred men to do the grunt work of cleaning up the battlefield, and gathering the spoils. No other Yankees made an appearance that day, and by nightfall, most of the work was done.

Today on that same field, one can hear shouts of children, and the only "crack" to be heard on that field, is not the sound of a Springfield rifle, but rather the sound of a bat hitting a baseball. Still, the Thomas Legion is honored by the playing field that bears their name in north Georgia. The Thomas Legion Field still stands, and is still recognized as a field of honor, even today. It is located just outside of the preserved section of the Chickamauga Battlefield Park, and there, the kids and families of the local recreation league play baseball. On some summer Sunday afternoons various local folks fly kites. That field now, is a place of joy and recreation, not a bloody field of death. Still a simple historic marker tells the tale.

**THOMAS LEGION**

**On this field on September 19, 1863, the Thomas Legion, a Confederate Unit comprised mostly of Cherokee Indians from North Carolina, defeated the Second Ohio, a Union unit. In the attack, the Thomas Legion showed great courage and they saved several other Confederate regiments from complete annihilation. This field was dedicated during the battle itself, as a field which would forever honor those Cherokee warriors, the men of the Thomas Legion!**

## At the Confederate Campfire, Saturday Night

It was at one of the campfires along Chickamauga Creek that night, a fire of the 34$^{th}$ Georgia, that God showed up.

Now God is known for putting in an appearance in the most unexpected of places. He once dropped into an inn-keepers barn, in a backwater nothing of a town called Bethlehem. He wandered one dark Christmas night into the battle trenches of Verdun where the English and German boys, totally without orders, decided to stop killing each other on a peaceful Christmas evening. They left their guns in the trenches and walked unarmed into no-man's-land, that Christmas night, where they drank a toast to each other, and then played a game of soccer. God was, most certainly there, that evening.

God appears from time to time, amid deadly car crashes, as someone's life ebbs away, or he shows up in disasters on the high seas. He certainly put in several appearances on 9/11; a massive office building in New York City, the Pentagon, and in an airliner over an unnamed Pennsylvania cornfield. God seems to show up when people most need him, and often when he is least expected. He was needed that night at Chickamauga.

On that Saturday night in September of 1863, God showed up when a man known for his cursing, his drinking, his barroom brawling, and his amazing skill in killing with his knife made a simple decision. For it was on that very night that Duncan Carmichael decided that he needed to pray.

Duncan Carmichael, as we have noted, well represented that filthy Carmichael clan. Deeply rooted both in the midlands of Scotland, and the Tugalo River Valley of north Georgia, Carmichaels have never been known as genteel folk. Rather, they typically cursed, clawed, hunted, or stole their way to survival, taking whatever they needed and frequently filling up the barns and smoke houses that often passed for jails around the Tugalo River Valley in north Georgia. They'd done so for generations prior to Duncan's birth, and before the war, he'd been no stranger to the local jail himself. The clan also cooked up some of the best homebrew whisky in the whole Appalachian Mountain Range, and that is saying quite a lot! They were, to a man, known to fight dirty, and fight to the death, with a knife, a pistol, a hatchet, a rifle, or simply fists and teeth, your choice. They usually won.

Thus did it cause a moment of pause, when Duncan stood up by the fire that night on the Chickamauga Battlefield and simply said, "I'm off to find that damn preacher. I want him to say a damn prayer for me."

Every head within forty feet turned to stare, some of the men who knew Duncan best were clearly in shock! Owen looked over at his friend as his mouth dropped open. Batty thought he'd misunderstood, so he popped out with the question, "What' d you say?"

Duncan, now walking away, didn't even bother to look back. "Damn it! Cain't you hear? Said I was goin' to pray!" And that is just what he did. This man, widely recognized for sins both imagined and real, went off to seek reconciliation with God on that battlefield.

It should surprise no one acquainted with battle that God showed up, and instigated this desire on Duncan's part. Hand-to-hand conflict often has that impact on men, and while the 34$^{th}$ Georgia had been a green outfit earlier that day, by nightfall on September 19, 1863, they were, to a man, bloodied veterans. Each man who survived that day was, in battle terms, worth at least three untested recruits. Still, that was not on Duncan's mind as he sought God. He was experiencing that most common of feelings, fear for one's own survival. Duncan had seen death, as had every man in the 34$^{th}$ Georgia that day and, like the rest, he believed he would not survive many more days of fighting such as they had seen in that field. If his announcement of his intention to pray was a bit unusual—one does not typically curse God, even as one seeks him out—we can only attribute that to Duncan's extended family, as well as his relatively conflicted nature. Neither he nor his family were godly, in any way, and he'd survived dozens of bloody barroom brawls along the Tugalo River, where his family interacted regularly with the roughest of river-men, those dirty, mean, and some might say strongest of men, who guided the flat-bottom barges along that river. He'd faced knives and guns before the war, and he was no stranger to blood. Still, what he'd seen that day truly scared him. Thus, in this most unusual way, did he seek his peace with God.

He did find a Confederate prayer meeting, and the minister did indeed help him say a brief prayer. History has taken no notice of that prayer, so the substance of Duncan's business with God that evening remains unknown. The Confederate Chaplin leading a service that night, did report being somewhat surprised by Duncan's late arrival. Still, we don't know what Duncan needed or desired, nor should we; for every man's business with God belongs only to he and God alone. We may only hope that Duncan Carmichael found some measure of peace that evening. It is known that after that first fight at Chickamauga, Duncan was in near-constant attendance at those battle field prayer meetings that happened most every evening. Of course, he still fought with the veracity and tenaciousness of ten men; he cussed, he drank, and he gambled to pass the time in camp. Still, his friends did see a subtle change in Duncan Carmichael; a bit less slow to anger, perhaps, and not as frequent with his cursing. Clearly God had arrived at Chickamauga, and he would be sorely needed again, the very next day.

That same evening Jamie was receiving reports from his sergeants as he sat by the officers' campfire. He made notes, as one subordinate or another gave him a count of who was dead and wounded in the various companies, and he knew that as the ranking officer, he would have to compile a preliminary report soon for his superiors. He was sure that his division commander would send a more seasoned man to command the regiment soon, and he could resume command of his company, the 34th Georgia. Still, he needed to get a count of dead and wounded on both sides written up for whoever showed up, and he'd already sent word to the rear that he had assumed command of the greatly reduced regiment. While that regiment had included just under a thousand men earlier that day, Jamie now had about six hundred effectives in the regiment, and only sixty one men in the 34th Georgia.

Thus did he write up his report. He supposed that someone on the staff of General Nathan Bedford Forrest, or maybe even General Bragg himself read those reports. Still, his mind wasn't much in it. As soon as he found a few moments to do so, he began another letter to his wife, Mary.

*Mrs. Mary Turnbull*
*Traveler's Rest Plantation*
*Tugalo River at Walton's Ford, Georgia*
*September 19, 1863*

*My Dearest Mary:*

*We fought in a great battle today, one that will continue tomorrow. I hesitate to tell you much of what I saw and what I did. It was a very large and gruesome fight. While my heart longs to share everything with my dearest wife, I cannot put into words many of the horrors I witnessed. Before you begin to worry however, know that I am well, as is your cousin Duncan, and both Owen Collins and Batty Prather. I know you were friends with those gents at Tugalo Baptist Church, so I wish to let you know that they are all fine, and we all did our best to do our duty.*

*We lost some men today, in the afternoon fight before the Cherokee showed up. You would not know many of the names, as some came from Clarkesville or Rabun County. I'm sorry to inform you that Dewey Snyder is dead. He was fighting at the far end of the line, and I didn't see anything about what happened, but when we mustered to honor the Thomas Legion at the end of the fight, he didn't stand with us. We found his body in the trench later, with three separate wounds in his chest. When official word reaches Walton's Ford, please let his family know that he died bravely fighting for our country. Before we moved his body four or five of the other Tugalo River Valley men said a brief prayer for him. We were honored to know him and fight with him, and as he watches us now from Heaven, please know that his fight is now over. Please go see his family, and help them to understand that we will miss him, nearly as much as they do.*

*Our friend Lem Davis was wounded in the shoulder, but a surgeon described it as a "good wound." By that he meant that nothing in Lem's shoulder appeared broken, and the bullet that hit him was not a minie-ball that would have broken up and taken away much of his back, but a harder bullet that merely passed through Lem's shoulder. It didn't do much damage other than tearing out a hunk of his back up high behind his left arm. It is even possible that Lem may fight again for the Grand Cause one day, but for now he will come home to recover.*

*All should be well with his wound unless it becomes infected. That is not likely, as I watched the surgeon take a long-rod branding iron (he was doing surgery in a barn near the battlefield) and ram it clear through Lem's shoulder wound. The burned meat stunk to high heaven and I'm sure you heard Lem's shout all the way across the state. Still, that pain will save Lem's life.*

*I thought about destroying these last few paragraphs, and beginning his letter over. Perhaps Dewey's death, or that description of treating Lem's wound is to grotesque for my delicate wife. Then I decided to merely leave this letter as is and continue. That medical treatment described herein was much more genteel than many of the sights I witnessed today in this, my first battle. Those I shall not speak of.*

*It seems that I am now in command, not only of the 34th Georgia Rifles, but of the entire Fourth Georgia Regiment! One group of charging Yankees managed to attain position on our works in the battle today, and from there they killed our regimental commander and his adjunct. While any of the three company commanders in the regiment could have been elected by the officers, all of us are new to the battlefield, and I have a bit more education than the others. In short, after the fight, those men elected me for the command. I'm sure the division commander will send someone soon to replace me, but for now I compile lists of the dead and wounded, which I have sent up the chain of command. I guess, for the moment, that I'm no longer detached to General Bragg's command regiment. Still, I find my home among these men of the Tugalo River Valley most congenial.*

*I've not heard, at this point, how our army faired overall today. In our section of the field, we fought two separate engagements, both of which resulted from Yankees showing up by mistake in front of our guns. In the first fight, we charged the Yankees, and drove them off. The last fight, this afternoon, was touch and go for a time, but we prevailed when a regiment of Cherokee Indians, the Thomas Legion, showed up and joined the fight. They fought like demons, like the Cherokee warriors they are, and together we won the day!*

*I'm told that several Confederate units moved forward and crossed the road about a half mile to our front, the Lafayette Road. It seems General Stewart's Division, along with General Hood's, moved forward and held that ground for a time before being driven back. At least those are the rumors. One rumor said that the famous General James Longstreet and twelve thousand men, the First Corps of the Army of Northern Virginia, had arrived on the field after the day's fighting ended. Twelve thousand, tried and true Confederates can make a big difference in this fight, and I'm sure you've often read about General James Longstreet, a Georgia man, who has made a name for himself up in Virginia! I do hope that this rumor is true! For it is obvious to all that this is a big fight, and it is not nearly over.*

*Tonight as I write this, we are on the field and our fires are just behind our trenches. The Yankee army is before us, and we expect to defend those works again in the morning. Once again, in the evening tomorrow, I shall write to my lovely wife, and let her know that I am well.*

*As to your last post, I am honored that you feel you can let your husband know of your desire and your love. It brings meaning to these dark days, and I treasure each letter you send, as well as the sentiments in them. At the risk of being likewise bold, I love you more than I can say, and would give anything at this very moment, merely to hold your hand in mine and look into your beautiful eyes.*

*Your Devoted and Most Loving Husband,*
*Jamie Turnbull, Captain, Fourth Georgia Regiment*

## Authors Note: One Day of War

That letter was not sent on the evening of September 19, 1863. The next day, a postscript was added to it, as we shall see a bit later. For now, in retrospect it is interesting to see, in these few lines, the burst of maturity, perhaps even wisdom that a single day in war can bring into a man's soul. Jamie knew, as he wrote this letter, that in the crucible, in the holy hell of battle, that he would not be found wanting. Indeed, he would meet the challenge, even while realizing that the next day would bring more of the same.

War, indeed, changes a man; it can turn mere boys into men, as Owen had tried to explain to Batty Prather only one day before. At this moment, as the men of the 34th Georgia Rifles fell into sleep, no man on that field needed that lesson again. They had been bloodied, and more war was surely coming the very next day.

By the evening of September 19, 1863, Captain Jamie Turnbull was in command of his regiment on the northern end of the long Confederate works, a line roughly parallel to Chickamauga Creek. It was an oft-told story of that devastating war; regimental or even corps commanders being killed, and commanders in battle advancing quickly. Organization was often quite fluid to say the least, and many times in various fights, command would shift two or three times in a single battle. Jamie's advance from company to regimental commander was not unusual, when a big fight was on. Of course the organizational charts for command show a firm, perhaps even a rather rigid structure, for the Confederate States Army, but that structure was, in reality, only a general goal, or some might say, wishful thinking, by the Confederate government.

## Command Structure, Confederate States Army

| Unit Designation | Count of men | Commander |
|---|---|---|
| Company: | 100 men | Captain or Major |
| Regiment: (or Battalion) | 1000 men | Major or Colonel |
| Brigade: | Four Regiments (4,000) | Colonel, General or Brigadier General |
| Division: | Two to Four Brigades (8,000 to 12,000) | Brigadier General or General |
| Corps: | Two to four Divisions (16,000 to 24,000) | General or Major General |
| Army: | Two to Four Corps (32,000 to 100,000) | Major General |

While this command structure was the overall goal of the Confederate government, it was wholly inaccurate. Never in the entire war did a single Confederate unit enter a fight with the entire compliment of men on the field, and as the war drew on, many units were considerably under strength. Many companies included only thirty to sixty men at the end of the war, and many regiments held an actual fighting strength of two to six hundred. The Thomas Legion, which was in reality a regiment, never numbered higher than eight hundred and seventy five men, whereas Jamie's first company, the 34$^{th}$ Georgia Rifles, entered the war with eighty-nine men on the roster. Most of that number saw action on both September 19 and September 20, 1863, and by the end of that one battle, the company was reduced to sixty one fighting men.

Jamie's count of wounded, dead, and effectives for the fight the next day is likewise telling. In his regiment only five hundred and fifty two men were available to fight on Sunday, September 20, 1863. On Saturday, one hundred and twenty nine men were killed outright, and another two hundred and thirty seven were wounded seriously enough to take from the battlefield. Some regiments had lost 20% to 30% of their strength, causalities that are unsustainable in any fighting unit. Even the lowest ranked man on the battle line realized that when units lose

30% of their power in a single day's fight, any individual man is likely to live only three days. That reality can take the fighting heart out of any military force in history, with only a few notable exceptions, and those are mostly instances in which men have committed themselves to die for their cause.

Several examples do come to mind, in that regard. At Thermopylae in ancient Greece, three hundred Spartans fought to the death against an invading horde of a hundred thousand Persians. At the Battle of the Alamo, a hundred and eighty three men died in their fight for the freedom of Texas, as they faced an army of three thousand Mexicans. History does provide several examples where a few brave men proudly, knowingly, faced death for their cause, and in each case, they died, to a man. Still, short of those examples, a 30% death rate cripples any fighting force, and many units at Chickamauga, both Union and Confederate, faced that loss rate. Few men on either side, would leave those Chickamauga fields unscathed, as we shall see.

Still the fight was not nearly over. On the evening of September 19, 1863, Bragg had indeed learned that General Longstreet had arrived on the field with the twelve thousand men of the First Corps, Army of Northern Virginia. This, and the fighting on September 19, gave General Bragg great hope. That night, he wrote that "Night found us masters of the ground, after a series of very obstinate contests with largely superior numbers." He was wrong in the "superior numbers" bit, but it never hurts a general's reputation to exaggerate his own successes a bit. In reality, Bragg had launched uncoordinated attacks all along his line, and had failed to drive his enemy from the field. Still, Longstreet's presence gave him hope, and with that in mind, he, of course, did the one thing a commander should always avoid in the middle of a battle. He literally reorganized his entire army.

With a flurry of written, sometimes conflicting orders, Bragg placed a number of regiments and corps under General Polk at the north end of the Confederate line, while placing the remainder of his men in "Longstreet's Wing," at the southern end of the Confederate line. He again planned to attack from the northern end of the line at first light on September 20, and having his various units roll up the Union from north to south. Alas, it was not to be.

## A Fine Sunday Morning in Georgia

The next day was a fine Sunday morning in Georgia, and the killing soon began again. A cold front had arrived on the battlefield during the night, dropping the September temperatures by nearly 25 degrees, but the men merely hunkered down by their fires in the darkness of the early morning and awaited the day, whatever it might bring.

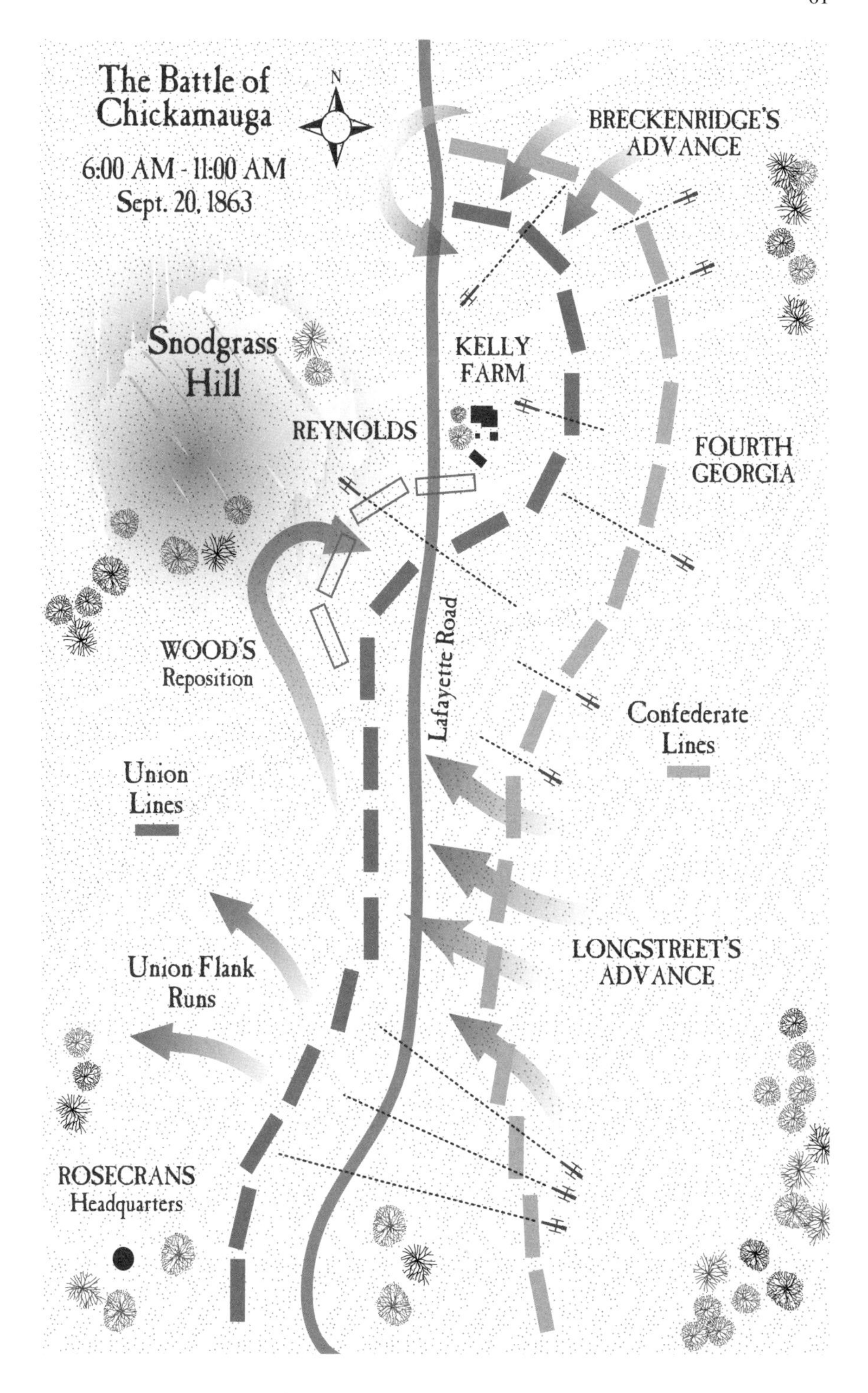

The Battle of Chickamauga
6:00 AM - 11:00 AM
Sept. 20, 1863
N
BRECKENRIDGE'S ADVANCE
Snodgrass Hill
KELLY FARM
REYNOLDS
FOURTH GEORGIA
WOOD'S Reposition
Lafayette Road
Confederate Lines
Union Lines
Union Flank Runs
LONGSTREET'S ADVANCE
ROSECRANS Headquarters

Union forces, ever content to remain behind their hastily constructed works, merely waited. In contrast the Confederate attack was supposed to have begun at dawn, with an attack by Polk's Wing, on the northern end of the Confederate line. The attack was supposed to involve successive Confederate units all down the line, in another attempt to sweep the Union forces away from their base of supplies in Chattanooga, only fifteen miles to the north. Of course, a confusion of orders, many of which had not been delivered to various Confederate commanders, resulted again in a confused, belated attack.

General Longstreet himself, who was to command the southern wing, didn't receive his orders until around 11:00 PM on September 19, which was clearly too late for him to organize his forces. Moreover, the Confederate commander in Polk's wing who was supposed to initiate the Confederate attack at 5:00 AM didn't receive his orders at all! He was casually eating his breakfast at 6:30 AM, when the messenger from Bragg's command found him to ask why he had not attacked earlier, as planned.

The Union forces were no better organized. General Rosecrans himself, rode the length of his line early on the morning of September 20. To his shock, he found large gaps in the line, and several important intersections were unguarded, so he was busily shifting units and making new assignments, even as the Confederate leadership, only a mile or so away, finished their breakfast. While war is, indeed, hell, it is often a totally unorganized hell; so much for the planning and all the good intentions of the generals on either side!

The delay in the Confederate attack was critical. At 6:00 AM on September 20, there were no defensive works on the entire northern end of the Union line at Chickamauga. Because the fight on September 19 had largely been fought along the Confederate works, most Yankee commanders assumed that such would be the case on September 20 also. In short, why cut trees or dig trenches with your exhausted men if you didn't have to? Of course, while sounding reasonable at least initially, that statement is recognized as incredibly stupid by almost anyone who has ever fought in an actual battle. One can get attacked at almost any time, from almost anywhere on almost any battlefield in history. More reasonable Union heads ultimately prevailed, and General Thomas had his men felling trees to build Union defensive works by 6:45 AM. Those works would be tested in slightly less than two hours.

## 6:00 AM until 2:40 PM on September 20, 1863

Around 9:30 that morning, Breckenridge's Confederate Division under Polk, finally got his orders and then initiated the attack on the north end of the Union line. After only fifteen minutes and much to his own surprise, Breckenridge realized that he had, in fact, turned the Union flank at the north end of the entire Union line. Of course, this had been Bragg's intention for the entire previous day, and Breckenridge was ecstatic! Surely his commanders would support him and he could simply roll up the entire Union army! He began to march his division to the south along both sides of the Lafayette Road, sure that victory would soon be in his grasp. However at that exact instant, he was halted by a withering attack from his right. The wily Union General Thomas had seen the danger and thrown in all his forces to stop this attack at the northern end of his line. Further Breckenridge's forces were now separated from the Confederate forces on the left.

Unlike Breckenridge, Cleburne's units further south had run squarely into those newly constructed Union breastworks, and those log breastworks had stopped Cleburne cold in his tracks. Thus Breckenridge was effectively unsupported in his advance, and nothing came of Breckenridge's important breakthrough, other than a few more thousand wounded men on both sides. While Breckenridge's initial advance was to be admired, it could not hide the incompetence of the overall Confederate effort. Missing orders, commanders uninformed they were to lead a dawn attack, and waiting while one's enemy prepares log breastworks, all mark an effort that would embarrass any military leader in the world. The attack on the northern end of the Union line petered out by late morning, as both Breckenridge and Cleburne disengaged.

Because Jamie's regiment, the Fourth Georgia, had been so bloodied the previous day, they were held as Cleburne's reserve force on September 20, and took no part in the morning fighting. They listened to the fight of Breckenridge's forces to their north and west, and heard others in their own division face the Union guns only five hundred yards to their front. Still, after nearly losing everything the day before, even the most hawkish Confederate in the Fourth Georgia was pleased to let someone else carry the fight forward that morning.

However, the Breckenridge attack on Thomas' Union force did have one important result. It led to a confusion of orders, as Union commanders recognized the potential danger and rushed to send forces toward the advancing Confederates. With many different orders being sent forth by several men in Rosecrans' headquarters, it was inevitable that some confusion would result.

Believing that a Union division under Brennan had withdrawn from the Union line to move northward and support Thomas, Rosecrans ordered General Wood's Union Division to the south of Brennan to "close up on Reynolds as fast as possible and support him." That single, simple order is now famous among military historians world wide. It has been studied by military men for a hundred and fifty years, and is now recognized as poorly timed, poorly written, and incorrect in every underlying assumption! That single order resulted in Union defeat for the entire Battle of Chickamauga.

First the term "close up" in the military jargon of the day, meant move in adjacent to a given unit. In contrast, the term "support" meant to move in directly behind that unit. Thus the order itself was contradictory. Rosecrans' order clearly included both terms, and Wood's Division simply could not do both. Moreover, Brennan had requested permission for his unit to leave the Union line and move north, but Brennan had not, at that time, done so. While General Rosecrans believed Brennan had left a gaping hole in the Union line, the fact is there was no hole in the line at all, at that point. However, Wood's unit could not close up on Reynolds, since Brennan's Division was still there, right in the way so to speak, and Wood's men could clearly not occupy the same breastworks as Brennan's. Thus, Wood had to "support" Reynolds rather than "close up" on him. Given Wood's interpretation of a confusing order, rather than shift to the left, Wood, at around 10:45 AM, had chosen to "support" Reynolds, as the only thing he could do. Therefore, in the next fifteen minutes, he began to remove his entire force back away from the Union line, assuming that General Rosecrans would be replacing his men in the line. He intended to follow his orders, as best he could, so he planned to march his force behind Brennan's Division and thereby get behind and "support" Reynolds men on the other side of Brennan's Division.

Only one little thing was wrong with that plan; it left a glaring gap nearly half a mile wide along the Union breastworks where Wood's men had been manning the defensive works! Thus did General Rosecrans stupidity reveal itself once again. On such stupidities, do battles, and history, sometimes turn.

## Longstreet's Good Luck

Just as the Union leadership was making, perhaps, the single biggest mistake in all of military history, General Longstreet and his Virginia boys got lucky. Confederate General Bragg had seen his morning attack slowed down by nearly four hours. That attack ultimately faltered, so he did what many inept military commanders do at that moment. In total ignorance of what was going on before him in the field, he ordered that every single force in his command attack at once. If Bragg had ever had a rationale for that order, it has been either lost to history or ignored altogether, in view of his other, more glaring stupidities.

General Stewart, in Longstreet's wing, received the insane command even before his commander, General Longstreet himself did, so Stewart immediately ordered his men forward. Those poor Confederates rushed directly into a mass of pissed off Yankees, behind strong log defensive works and supported by several cannon batteries. Brennan's Division, Reynolds' Division, and Wood's Division which was now located just behind Reynolds, all poured a withering fire into Stewart's men and the brave Rebel Yell was not a shield against so much flying lead. The result was as predictable as the sun rising in the morning; it was an absolute bloodbath, with Confederate dead and wounded covering the field.

All the while, General Longstreet, who had yet to receive Bragg's order to attack with all forces, was left to wonder what was going on. He asked his staff, "What is happening up there? Has Stewart gone crazy? What the hell is he doing?

Still, as Stewart's men died bravely in those fields before the massed Union guns, Longstreet finally did receive Bragg's order to advance immediately. That is how General Longstreet and the First Corps, Army of Northern Virginia got lucky. As the fates would have it, Wood's Union division was off busily killing Stewart about a half-mile to the north, so Longstreet's Virginia men, twelve thousand strong, faced a half-mile of undefended Union breastworks. When they finally began their belated charge, they didn't even realize no one was shooting back!

At 11:10 AM Longstreet gave the order to advance. Those Confederates raised, yet again, the famous Rebel Yell, and charged forward, as gallantly as any single unit in military history. They charged, as if running into hell itself, across that half-mile front, running directly into what was sure to be a fight to the death, brandishing their swords and bayonets, and screaming like banshees! Still, they were all veterans, so more than a few soon began to wonder why they saw only about twenty or twenty-five Yankee skirmishers before them. As those skirmishers fled, no row of angry Yankees guns was rising above the heavy Union breastworks to their front, no rifles were aimed in their direction! No cannon at all fired on them, and once the few skirmishers were gone, no Spencer repeaters were heard. It became stranger with each running step; where in hell were the damn Yankees?

The Confederates could only run on. When they reached the logs they jumped atop them, and to their shock, they saw nothing but empty breastworks! One cocky Confederate commander atop the logs, was heard to exclaim, "Hell, Boys! Them damn Yankees musta' heard that Longstreet was a 'commin' with the First Virginia!"

They continued past the line, sweeping through the Union rear. As the Confederates ran past the small farm belonging to Amos Brotherton, they charged through the woods and into the next corn field, the Dyer farm, where they saw a row of massed Union cannon, with gun crews ready, but they had no infantry support. After only a moment's hesitation, the Confederates let out another Rebel Yell and charged the guns. The cannon erupted with a horrid, deadly fire, but only once. The gun crews could not reload fast enough, and soon fifteen of the twenty four Union cannon were in Confederate hands, and those Union gun crews joined the other fleeing Union forces. While several Union units on each flank counterattacked the advance Confederates, those men in grey were, by that point, an unstoppable wave, a primal force of nature. Nothing would stop them.

The captured Union guns were quickly turned on the Union forces on either side of the advance, as more and more Confederates poured through the breach in the Union lines. It was at this point that word spread like lightening through both armies; Confederates had broken the defenses and were rolling up the Union line! Knowing of Bragg's desire to push Union forces to the south, Longstreet began to assemble his men to charge through the line and turn the Union army to the south, which is when the real panic began on the southern end of the Union army. Confusion reigned as Union forces seemed to move everywhere at once. Some were trying to counterattack Longstreet's advance, while others were trying desperately to get the hell out of the way of the devastating Confederate advance. One after another, the Union divisions on the southern end of the battle line began preparations to retreat, as their commanders heard of the Confederate breech in their lines. For no commander in history ever wanted to be surrounded and cut off from the rest of his own army.

The Confederates meanwhile did not stop to await orders. On and on they rushed, capturing brigade level headquarters, Union cannon, Union men, and supplies as they moved, and few Union units stood in their way. Within forty-five minutes the Confederates had advanced nearly a mile past the enemy trenches, and Union men still ran before them in nearly every direction. When Polk heard of Longstreet's attack, and received Bragg's order to advance once again with all forces, he issued orders to all his divisions, and the rout of Union forces was on.

## The Fourth Georgia Infantry at Snodgrass Hill

The Fourth Georgia had been held in reserve all morning, that Sunday. Jamie, who had been trying to rest near the remains of the campfire from the night before, had not slept. No one could have possibly slept who was that close to the noise of the battle, but Jamie had rested his eyes for a time. He lifted his head, and he heard a rider arrive on horseback, loudly shouting, "Regiment commander! Regiment commander!"

"Over here, Suh!" Shouted Sampson, who could clearly see that Jamie had been dozing off. By the time the young rider had dismounted with Bragg's order in hand, he was shouting again at Jamie. "Sir, your orders! General Longstreet and the First Virginia have broken through the Union lines and are rolling up the Union southern line as we speak. All Confederate units are to advance on the works before them and attack! It is a glorious day for the Cause!" With

The Battle of Chickamauga
2:30 PM to Dark
Sept. 20, 1863

N

Snodgrass Hill

KELLY FARM

FOURTH GEORGIA

Lafayette Road

LONGSTREET'S CONTINUED ADVANCE

Confederate Lines
Union Lines

that the rider tossed a handwritten order from Cleburne to Jamie, and rode off to find the next regiment commander. Jamie's subordinates had awakened by then and were gathering around him, so he read the orders and then shouted out loud. "Prepare to march! Five minutes! General Longstreet and the First Virginia have broken through!"

With that, a cheer arose from the ranks, as men hastily began to gather their packs, rifles, and ammunition. Of course, Jamie had ordered a resupply that morning, so every soldier already held forty rounds of ammunition and powder for his Springfield or his Enfield. Thus, would the Fourth Georgia join the now famous fight for Snodgrass Hill.

## 2:30 – Dark, September 20, 1863

George Washington Snodgrass, like ninety-five percent of all southern men, owned not a single slave. Rather he did his farming himself, along with his wife and children. He raised corn, some beans, and a few skinny hogs, and managed to scrape a hard living out of hilly, rocky ground about ten miles north of Lafayette, Georgia. At the ripe old age of thirty-one, he was already toothless, and his constant consumption of moonshine rarely helped either his disposition or his health. Still, he lived on his own land, and the view from atop that rocky hill was truly magnificent. He was generally happy, with the companionship of a very skinny woman named Katheryn Sullivan, who hailed from Chattanooga. It was widely debated in those parts, whether or not their union had ever received the benefit of clergy, and the only thing known was that she was, generally, an overworked companion, who had managed to produce seven overworked offspring. They'd built a two room cabin that sat atop a hill that will forever bear his name. As the battle progressed below them, they decided it was probably time to move on down the line, so by 12:00 on September 20, their cabin atop Snodgrass Hill was deserted, and they were hastily leaving the area.

As the Union forces to the south of Longstreet's breakthrough backed up (which is to say, ran like a scattering of frightened rabbits), the overall Union commander, General Rosecrans, took note. His command post happened to be directly behind that section of the Union lines, and when he saw the Union forces rushing past, he quickly realized that the First Virginia was coming to visit. He hastily mounted himself and his entire staff and galloped off to Tennessee. It was said that, once he arrived in Chattanooga later that evening, he finally remembered to ask, "Does anyone know what happened to my army?"

The Union General Thomas, along with many other Union commanders remained on the north end of the field, and by noon they realized they were now fighting for their lives, if not the very existence of the entire Union army. Not knowing if Rosecrans had fled or been captured, Thomas took it upon himself to organize some type or rear-guard defense, and as he considered the matter, he realized that the hill behind him would provide what was needed—a high location for his cannon, and some good defensive terrain for his men.

Thus around 12:00 noon, Thomas began sending orders to any and all Union forces on the northern end of the Union line; "All forces, retreat at once, and rally on top of Snodgrass Hill!" General Thomas himself never said whether he believed himself in command of the entire Union force at that point; like all great commanders, he didn't wait to find out, but merely began to issue orders that made sense. One subordinate, many years later, reported that he'd heard General Thomas say, "The best thing Longstreet could do for the Union is kill that bastard Rosecrans!" If such a statement was made, it was not recorded by anyone else. Thomas merely sent out orders, sending his staff in every direction, telling all to rally at Snodgrass Hill. Thomas placed all of the cannon he could muster atop the hill, benignly ignoring any objections from any subordinate commanders, who seemed worried about losing control of their unit's cannon. He put several Union infantry units in the trenches at the Kelly Farm, which was right at the bottom of the hill and slightly to the east. The rest he placed to the bottom of the southern side of the hill. Since Longstreet had broken the Union line toward the south, Thomas correctly assumed that the main attack on, what was by then his personal hill, would come from there.

So atop the hill Thomas stood; strong and unmoving, just like the granite hill he defended. Nobody today knows where the name came from, or when it was first used, but this highly capable Union commander, this Virginian who chose to fight with the Union, at some point on that day became known as the "Rock of Chickamauga!" That now famous name was duly earned in the crucible of battle by Thomas' decisions, decisions that saved the lives of literally thousands of Union men. Thus would that nickname stand for all time as the greatest honor any soldier could ever earn. It is not an overreach to say that one of the top five most effective Union commanders in the entire War Between the States was, General Thomas, a Virginian who had, himself, owned slaves throughout most of his life, as had his father before him.

The Confederates, once they hit the new defensive line of Union men, took about an hour to regroup. It was by then early afternoon, and that pause in the fight gave precious time for General Thomas to organize his defenses. Longstreet in particular, seemed rather uninspired about any move forward, at least at first. He and his staff may not have yet realized that the entire Union line was crumbling, so he sat down at noon with his subordinates for a comfortable lunch of bacon and beans. When the Confederates finally did regroup they realized that there was a chance to kill the entire Union army, so the tone at

Longstreet's headquarters changed rather smartly, and Confederates began to charge the mountain defenses at the base of the hill. At that point, they again faced their nemesis on those bloody Chickamauga fields—the Spencer repeating rifle.

By 2:30 that afternoon, the Confederate line reached around the Kelly Farm in a large, semi-circle, to the east of Snodgrass Hill, stretched along the base of the hill to the south, and then followed the horseshoe bend, a low rise from the southwest of the hill, reaching out to the southwest and the hills beyond. The new Union line was by then, a strong defensive line, about two miles long, that was made by hasty log-cutting, and even quicker digging.

The Fourth Georgia faced the Union lines at the Kelly Farm, about a quarter of a mile to the east of the hill. Each time Jamie had received the order to advance, he shouted charge to his men; they screamed the Rebel Yell, and charged the Union forces before them. Each time the charge ended the same; the damned Spencers laid waste the Fourth Georgia Infantry.

"Reckon we'll ever get out'a this damn field alive, Owen?" Batty Prather asked as the Fourth Georgia again, fired on the Union lines at the Kelly Farm. They lay behind a dead horse out in the middle of the field, and while Batty still held a load in his Springfield, Owen was quickly biting off the top of a powder bag to reload his weapon. Batty saw that his friend couldn't speak with a mouth full of the raw end of a powder bag, so he continued. "Them damn Yankees sure don't seem to want to do much retreatin' up on this end of the line!" In that assessment Batty was right. While Longstreet's men had eliminated nearly half of the Union forces, the Yankees across from Cleburne's Division still held their original positions at the Kelly Farm, and seemed to give no indication of a willingness to retreat.

Jamie had just received another order from Cleburne to advance his force, and while he considered it suicide to charge those repeating rifles again, he felt it his duty to do so. More frequently than most of the regimental commanders on the field, Jamie had charged himself into the fire of the enemy, that afternoon, not wanting to send his men into any situation he wouldn't go into himself, and he'd earned an insignificant wound in the shoulder to show for it. He momentarily considered ignoring the orders as he was sure it would merely lead to more death for his men. Maybe he could send a response back to his superiors questioning exactly what his orders meant.

At that moment, another runner arrived with countermanding orders. That page simply read, "Commander, Fourth Georgia. You are ordered to stand where you are. General Cleburne, Commanding."

Jamie didn't realize he spoke out loud, as he voiced his thought. "Well I'll be damned! Cleburne finally extracted his head from his own ass long enough to take a look at what's happening up here!"

Both Sampson and Duncan Carmichael smiled and neither said a word. Jamie had been voicing his thoughts out loud all day without realizing it, and neither Sampson nor Duncan had found much among those thoughts to disagree with, nor did they disagree at that point.

While Union General Thomas had organized a strong defense, it was still clear to Union commanders that the fight was lost. Well over half of the Union forces had disappeared into the mountains by 4:30 that afternoon, and everyone on the battlefield knew that the other Union forces would withdraw after dark. For them to remain on that battlefield would be suicide. At that point, historians have estimated that perhaps 30,000 Union men faced something like 65,000 Confederates. Bragg, Polk, and Longstreet realized that the Union forces had indeed been routed. They also realized that many of those units had been able to escape back into Chattanooga overnight. Thus Bragg, while having won a great victory, had nevertheless failed to drive the Union forces away from their base of supply.

Charge after charge that afternoon had failed to break the Union defense at either the Kelly Farm or the southern base of Snodgrass Hill itself. No level of Confederate bravery could overcome the fire from Spencer rifles, that most formidable of weapons, or the astonishing rate of fire that those Yankees could muster. Longstreet himself later said that he'd made twenty-five separate charges against the southern base of Snodgrass Hill. None breached the new Union lines Thomas had established, and all of the Confederates along the line were taking direct fire from Thomas' cannon atop the hill. Those cannon, perhaps as many as eighty of them, were literally axel to axel atop Snodgrass Hill. Some were older Napoleons, but others were the much more accurate Parrott rifled cannon, and most were firing nearly straight down into Confederate positions. It was, quite literally, a ring of fire raining on the Confederates below, and no one at the base of that hill believed they could take that mountain from such a determined Union defense.

Moreover the Confederate leaders, in fact the Confederate rank and file down to the lowest most inexperienced private, knew that Thomas would high-tail it back to Tennessee when dark came. Some of the Confederates, Longstreet among them, wanted to chase the Yankees and not let them escape. However Bragg, being the inept commander that he was, vetoed that idea, and that decision rendered any further Confederate attacks on the Union line at Snodgrass Hill meaningless. If Thomas was going to leave anyway, why not just wait a bit and let him?

And that is exactly what they did. As the day died, Confederate advances stopped and Thomas and the remaining Union forces slipped away that night, much to the consternation of Longstreet, Nathan Bedford Forrest, and several of the other aggressive Confederate commanders. By 6:00 PM on September 20, 1863, the Battle of Chickamauga, the second bloodiest battle in the entire Civil War, was history.

## None Escape, Unscathed

In most cases during the war, the Union press, like the Confederate press, skewed their reporting in order to favor their own cause. However, with a loss as clear as Chickamauga, even the Yankee press had to maintain some semblance of integrity. Thus did the *New York Times,* on September 21, 1863 report, rather reluctantly it seems, on the Union defeat.

**BIG FIGHT IN GEORGIA! BATTLE STILL UNDECIDED ON SUNDAY NIGHT!**

**The fighting near Lafayette, Georgia, south of Chattanooga resumed this morning, and our center was pushed. After much bloodshed, at 2:40 PM the Rebels ran a charge that broke through our lines. Several Union regiments were badly mauled, and had to retreat from the field. Thus, was our center broken and Union forces retreated in disorder. General Rosecrans grew anxious and ordered his staff and the wounded moved back from the fight. The rebels, exulting over their apparent success, made the air resound with cheers! Still both armies occupy the same ground as when the fight began.**

## Author's Note: Never Trust the Papers

That story proves, yet again, that anyone who believes anything from the press, without checking is a blithering idiot. Rosecrans was a bit more than "anxious." He ran like a scared rabbit, with no regard whatsoever for either his army or his wounded. Both armies were not on the same ground as when the fight began, and to put it mildly, reporting that the Battle of Chickamauga was undecided on Sunday night, was rather like reporting that a dead man lying for a full day in his coffin might be considered slightly under the weather!

However the victory was not as one-sided as it appeared, and the debate over what happened during those several September days in 1863 still rages. In the south at the time, Chickamauga was hailed as a great victory, a victory that drove the mighty Union force back out of the state of Georgia, and protected the all-important railhead at Atlanta. However, Bragg and his Confederates didn't follow-up their victory quickly enough to keep the Union army on the run, so the victory was not a strategic Union defeat.

From the Union point of view, the battle merely pushed the army back for thirty miles or so into Chattanooga. Bragg and his forces did lay siege to Chattanooga after some time had passed, but the siege was broken only two months later atop Lookout Mountain and Missionary Ridge, and from a strategic point of view, the Union army still stood poised to invade north Georgia the very next spring.

Of course, Rosecrans' military leadership was over as a result of the battle. It is a fact of history that few losing generals survive to command again, at least at the same level, and Rosecrans was no exception. As news of the Confederate victory was spread by telegraph throughout the north, Lincoln himself despaired of what to do about command of that powerful Union force in eastern Tennessee. While openly expressing confidence in Rosecrans in a telegram to Rosecrans' headquarters, President Abraham Lincoln himself privately told his secretary that Rosecrans seemed, "Stunned, like a duck hit in the head!"

Even those on both sides who lived through the bloody fight at Chickamauga were not unscathed. Jamie had managed, in the closing hour of the fight, to collect a slight wound to his left shoulder, and while the bullet merely grazed him, breaking no bones, it did tear out a not-inconsequential hunk of flesh, and was enough to give Jamie a taste of the reality of war. Even the men who remained unwounded seemed dazed, if not completely confused, as they wondered how they had survived. In point of fact, how many men in all of recorded history have literally looked into the bore of eighty enemy cannon and survived?

## Confederate Hospital Tent

As Jamie's wound was tended that Sunday night, Lem laid beside him in one of the many hospital tents about a half-mile behind the Confederate trench at the Kelly Farm. Duncan had brought Jamie back from the line, and made a point of seeking out the same hospital tent that held Lem.

"Guess both of you'll get a spell of rest at home along the Tugalo!" Duncan said. "I recon you'll miss the big push to catch them damn Yankees now that we got 'um on the run."

Lem looked over at his friend, and merely grunted. Jamie was the one that replied. "I'll be more than happy to stick around here and see to that business with the Yankees, if you'd be willing to take this wound, you old son-of-a-bitch!"

Duncan merely smiled at his friend, and then resorted to military protocol to offer his response. Snapping into a sharp salute, he said, "Right away, Captain Sir! I'll see to it immediately Sir! And Sir, this humble corporal thinks that the Captain is, like-wise, a son-of-a-bitch, Sir!"

The Confederate doctor who was still busy patching up Jamie, looked somewhat taken aback at the easy camaraderie among these three soldiers. Two corporals typically did not joke in this fashion with a Captain, but these men clearly knew each other quite well, and all the Confederates at the Snodgrass Hill fight had been through hell. Besides, the Captain who had just been cursed by one of his own men, didn't seem to mind it one bit. The doctor quite wisely kept his mouth shut on the foul name-calling, but he did order Duncan from the tent, as more wounded were still arriving from the field and he needed the space.

Jamie then asked the doctor for the use of his pen, and moving to the doctor's desk in the corner of the tent, he penned a brief postscript to his letter from the night before.

*"I cannot tell you of the last day of the Battle of Chickamauga, as time won't allow it before the train leaves with the mail from our camp. I have been slightly wounded and will be coming home with the other wounded men, including Lem Davis. We'll speak of it then.*

*Your loving husband,*
*Captain Jamie Turnbull. September 20, 1863."*

He then dropped the letter into the mail bag inside the hospital tent.

## Author's Note: Chickamauga Today

It is a calm, peaceful place today, that formidable hill, Snodgrass Hill, and the beautiful valley and fields below. It is a field that, for all Americans, is well worth the visit. The Kelly Farm is only one of the many views offered atop Snodgrass Hill, and the many fields and forests one can view from that lofty vantage now speak of great peace and tranquility. For in truth, there are few places on this small planet, as lovely as the beautiful Blue Ridge Mountains of north Georgia, and Snodgrass Hill provides only one of the thousands of vantage points for viewing those mountains.

Both the Kelly Farm and Snodgrass Hill are now part of the Chickamauga Battlefield Park. Chickamauga was one of the first battlefield parks organized by the government of the United States, and that organization was unique at the time for several reasons. While Gettysburg had been preserved as a battlefield previously, only Union positions had been marked on that field after the war; Confederate sites were marked later. At Chickamauga, preservation plans from the beginning involved not only the Union positions but Confederate positions also. In fact, so very many men had died on those bloody fields in Georgia, slightly over 34,000 wounded and dead, that the men who had lived through that fight literally demanded that the ground be sanctified.

It is easy to understand why. This was and is one of the bloodiest battlefields on the North American Continent. Some have argued that the final day at Chickamauga may have been the bloodiest single day of the entire war. However, most historians consider the bloodiest day to have been the fight at Antietam Creek near Sharpsburg, Maryland, that had taken place almost exactly a year prior to the fight at Chickamauga. The reason for this debate is rather simple. Sharpsburg was a one day battle, fought on September 17, 1862, in which 23,000 men were killed or wounded. However, a year and one day later at Chickamauga, serious fighting took place over a three day period, so who can say how many were wounded or died on any given day along that small, now famous creek in north Georgia? At the very least, the final day at Chickamauga, Sunday, September 20, 1863, was one of the bloodiest single days in the history of war, and that simple fact demands recognition.

From Snodgrass Hill, Chickamauga Creek itself appears as but a ribbon of a stream far below the mountain, but that name is famous worldwide. Today hundreds of monuments mark the terrain where thousands and thousands of men died. The field is an amalgamation of unit markers, scattered randomly, with Union blue and Confederate grey/red intermixed, more so than on any other battlefield, because units overran each other quite often throughout both days of the main battle. While no battle lines are stagnant for long, the fight at Chickamauga involved so many twists and turns of fortune that it takes a historian to interpret the timelines of the fight, and the markers from one day to the next, mix into near confusion for the casual visitor.

What is clear, to anyone with a heart to see it, is the raw courage of the men who once fought on those fields. Amid the confusion of signs, mixed together, those of us lucky enough to be able to visualize history can yet see the rush of the Confederates as they charged into the abandoned Union lines in Longstreet's assault. We can actually hear the harsh Rebel Yell amid the imagined black-powder smoke and the thunderous roar of massed cannon, the crack of Confederate Springfields at Snodgrass Hill, along with the quicker pop of the Spencer repeating rifles. These fields, forests, and valleys once saw, arguably, the harshest day of fighting ever seen in this hemisphere, and for the lucky few who sense the vividness of history, this place in magical. It is indeed holy.

While all Americans should visit this field, for Georgians, it is an absolute requirement.

The men who died here, the souls that were lost here, await your visit. Indeed, do come to walk along the now peaceful fields. As a writer, as a historian, I can only assure you, such a visit will change who you are.

# The Trip Home

Soldiers throughout history are as diverse as the cultures from which they sprang. Different beliefs, different gods, different commitments, all are reflected among the men who go into battle, and while there are few similarities among all soldiers, there is at least one; for every soldier, regardless of their culture or where they fall in history, all always cherish the opportunity to return home.

Lem was wounded rather badly and was not able to either ride or walk, so the doctor recommended him for a train to the permanent hospitals in Atlanta. Jamie, however, used his rank and pulled off a minor miracle, he got the Confederate army to do something that actually made sense.

Realizing that he, Lem, and about a dozen other wounded Confederates needed to head, not to Atlanta, but across the mountains to northeast Georgia, he organized two hospital wagons to make that mountain crossing. Under his command, two wagons set off up the trail to the small town of Ellijay, and then Dahlonega, Clarkesville, and finally the Tugalo River Valley. The trip took about three weeks, as mountain trails were, at best, rough. In some cases, even the wounded men who were able, had to dismount and push the wagons through mountain streams, or up various escarpments. As the two wagons progressed, men were left with their families, or relatives who agreed to take them in. By the time the wagons reached the old Cherokee town site of Ball Ground, only Lem, Jamie, and several others remained. There they prepared their camp for the night. It was September 29 by then, and the evening promised to be cool but free of rain, so the men decided to bed down under the wagon and not bother setting up their tents.

Jamie was awakened when a man on the end, a man from Elberton named Peter Wood, grabbed a young girl by the arm and twisted it hard, making the black girl scream. Jamie shouted, "What the hell?"

Peter shouted to him, "I caught this nigger getting into the wagon! She's a slave, and she's sure 'nuf gonna' steal us blind, Captain!"

The girl, she couldn't have been older than ten, still wreathed on the ground as Peter twisted her arm to hold her there. She looked into Jamie's eyes, with a defiance and hatred that Jamie had rarely seen. Peter taunted her. "What say, gal. Whose plantation you from anyway? Aint't you supposed to be home now?"

Lem said, "Just shoot her, and be done with it, Jamie. We need some sleep and we ain't in no position to go runnin' around after no runaways! Gal that size can't be worth too much anyway, particularly if'n she's a thief!"

Peter disagreed. "We got to take her somewhere! She's somebody's property, and we ain't got no right just to shoot her." At that point, they all turned to look at Jamie. He was, after all the only officer, and was thus nominally in command of the wagons and the men in them, at least until he delivered them to their homes in north Georgia.

Jamie looked into the eyes of the defiant child, still half asleep himself. She returned his gaze without flinching, and Jamie reflected that only Sampson, alone among all the black slaves he knew had ever looked him directly in the eye before. As ever Sampson was sitting near him watching the entire proceeding, and waiting like the others, for Jamie's decision.

Wood twisted the girl's arm again and said, "What's your name, gal? Where you from?"

"I'm Bessy," she said, and a turn of her head indicated that she would say no more.

Jamie spoke next. "You stealing food, Bessy?"

Bessy turned back to Jamie, paused a moment, and then surprised everyone by answering. "I got to eat sompin!"

Lem spoke up again. "Just let me shoot her."

For a second Jamie actually considered that, but he had no stomach for it. He was pretty sure that Lem didn't either. Maybe thinking of Sampson is what did it, but Jamie did something uncharacteristic for any slave owner. "Let 'er go," He said, without taking his gaze from that young, defiant face.

Peter didn't believe it. "What? I mean, Captain Turnbull! We can't just let 'er go, can we? She belongs to somebody. She's somebody's property!"

As Jamie continued to look into the young girl's face, Lem answered. "We should just let her go. Why kill her? Some local nigger chaser 'll find her in these woods for sure, and get her back to where she belongs. We sure as hell can't take time to find her home."

Jamie then found his voice. "I said we'll let her go. We got seven wounded men here, two wagons, and four near-dead mules. We still got a long way 'til we get home to Walton's Ford and the Tugalo River. We can't go runnin' off to find out who owns her, and someone 'll pick her up soon anyway. Just let her go, and we'll get back to sleep."

Peter then released the girl's arm, and she was up in a flash and into the nearby woods, quickly as a deer leaping into the forest. "Recon' ya'll 'er right. Besides she caint' be worth too much, and somebody'll find her soon anyways." With the girl long gone, the men laid back down to go to sleep.

## Eyes in the Bushes

Throughout this disturbance, Jamie and the others were being closely watched. In the bushes, just past the dim light of the dying campfire, was a face displaying a supreme confidence. The face showed fierce determination and assurance, and the eyelids drooped just a bit, suggesting both a relaxed countenance, and a watchful awareness, if not some degree of deep, abiding wisdom. The face suggested that this one could withstand anything life could bring.

The face belonged to one of the most remarkable, and most famous women, ever to tread through those mountains of north Georgia. Harriet Tubman had been a slave herself, born into that ignoble station in life sometime around the year 1820. After she escaped from slavery in Maryland, she did something few ex-slaves ever did; she returned to the south where she helped her family to escape. Once they were free up north, she returned again and again to help others find their freedom, and she'd been doing so, since before the war began! She often used the Underground Railroad. Some say she actually created it, that incredible network of Quakers and others sympathetic to the plight of slaves in the south, men and women—black and white—who risked their own freedom to help escaping slaves.

One other factor is important in understanding this remarkable woman of history. Tubman's relationship with God was both deeply personal, and some might say unique. She often said that she experienced direct revelations from God, who, in explicit terms, told her specifically what to do, when to move, and when to remain hidden. Her love for God was deep and abiding, and in her deep faith, she found the strength to do remarkable deeds, again, and again, and again, a story not often repeated in history.

Of course, some have offered a different interpretation of her religious zeal. Tubman had experienced a severe blow to the head as a child, and that is when her self-identified "visions" of God began. For those disposed to debunk all things religious, Tubman merely suffered a head trauma that gave her the illusion of visions of the Godhead, and illusions of self-importance.

Regardless of the cause of her visions, all who study history can agree that those visions and her subsequent beliefs led to many brave deeds and saved the lives of many slaves. For the reductionistic in thought, those relatively simple minds that must have a firm, scientific explanation for all things in this world, perhaps the head-trauma theory brings a sense of relief in the interpretation of this unique historical figure. For others, the hand of God was truly working in the very soul of Harriet Tubman, and was once again, working amid the lowest among us; a self-less slave who became a giant of history.

That same history records that Tubman returned at least thirteen times to various areas of the south, and it is documented that she helped at least seventy slaves escape captivity. She probably assisted many more. She also fought for the Union, and served as a Union spy on several different occasions, first in Port Royal along the South Carolina coast, and later with General Rosecrans' Union army in north Georgia.

Just as the battle for Chickamauga began, she left Rosecrans' service, realizing that when battles begin, spies usually become useless. She planned to use her travels into Georgia to help some of the local slaves escape from the area around north Atlanta. Tubman had thus traveled south, passing through the Confederate army as it moved toward Chickamauga. She knew of a group of escaped slaves in hiding with a Quaker family just outside of Marietta, Georgia, a group she quickly found. They left the relative safety of their hiding place, planning to travel to meet Rosecrans' advancing army. She believed that, if she could only get her last group of escaping slaves up to the Union lines, they would be safe. After all, by that time, President Lincoln had already issued the Emancipation Proclamation, and Tubman merely sought to make that promised freedom a reality for a few more slaves.

Of course, with 175,000 fighting men roaming the mountains of north Georgia, the danger for her small group—herself and eight escaped slaves—was great. To make matters worse, she had learned that Rosecrans had lost a big battle and had retreated further away, making her planned escape all the more difficult. In short, after five days of running and hiding in the woods, her band of runaways was now further away from the safety of Rosecrans' army, and by then they were starving. Against her better judgment, she'd let the young slave girl attempt a theft of food from the wagons they'd spotted ahead in the clearing. It was obvious that few of those men could chase the girl if she did get into trouble, as all of them appeared to be wounded.

Tubman moved most of her group away from the wagons, leaving them in hiding in a creek bed about half a mile away. Then she and Bessy, the young girl, who was a self-proclaimed thief, moved back toward the wagons. When Bessy was captured by one of the Confederates, Tubman was sure she was done for, but she watched from the bushes, and, to her surprise, a Confederate officer made the decision to let the girl go!

Tubman was wise enough to take note of that man's name, rank, and hometown, all of which had been mentioned in the conversation; Captain Jamie Turnbull, of Walton's Ford in the Tugalo River Valley of Georgia. Tubman would remember that man, thinking that at least she'd found another sympathizer, if not an outright resource for the Underground Railroad.

Thus did she watch for a few more seconds, as the girl escaped the camp into the woods. "Yes," she thought. "I'll remember that man. He might come in handy some day."

By October 4, 1863, a wounded Jamie Turnbull, and his man Sampson, rode the last wagon into the yard at Traveler's Rest Plantation, the home of the Jarrett Family of Walton's Ford, Georgia. Several house slaves came running to the door, even before he could get off the wagon. Within a few moments, everyone within hearing distance had gathered to greet Captain Turnbull.

It was one of those moments that one remembers for the rest of their lives. Captain Jamie Turnbull, Commander of the Fourth Georgia Infantry, was, for a time, home from the war.

# Chapter 2
# The Mountain Fighting

## An Autumn of Hope

The autumn of 1863 was, for most in the south, an autumn of hope. Of course, all Confederates recognized the seriousness of the losses in the summer of 1863. The loss of Vicksburg on July 2, 1863 had stolen several important states from the Confederacy—Missouri and Texas among them. Perhaps more devastating, the Confederate Army of Northern Virginia under General Robert E. Lee had been stopped cold at Gettysburg, PA, on July 4, and had then retreated back into Virginia. In some ways it defies reason to think that southerners had any hope after July of 1863, but hope seems to spring eternal in the human heart, and Confederates clung to any indication of strength in their cause. The Confederate Army of Tennessee had won at Chickamauga in September after those horrible losses in the summer of 1863, and by November of 1863, the Yankees were surrounded and under siege in Chattanooga, where Confederate forces were slowly starving them out. The victory at Chickamauga loomed ever larger in the Confederate press, as an important indication that the Union was surely on the decline. In late September and October of 1863, many Confederates seemed to hope for ultimate victory. It was, again, an autumn of hope in the south.

Of course they were not totally unrealistic in that hope. In the north, the popularity of the war was waning as the massive casualties of the 1863 battles were listed in the northern papers. Gettysburg, a three day fight, saw more dead and wounded men than any other battle in the war, but Chickamauga—essentially a two day battle fought only two months later, was the second highest death toll of the war. The desire of some Yankees to end the war immediately by negotiating with the south was a significant cause for hope. Even some newspaper editors in the north were saying that the Union would be better served to merely negotiate with the south, and then let those states simply "Go!"

All of this kept President Lincoln in despair for much of that fall after Chickamauga, and such despair was something of a common occurrence for him. He believed, as he told many of his staff and cabinet, that he would not win re-election in 1864. Thus, many in the Confederacy believed, hoped for, the ultimate victory of their Grand Cause.

Neither Captain Jamie Turnbull nor his young wife, Mary Jarrett Turnbull were among them. They believed, passionately, in the Grand Cause of the Confederacy, which they perceived as freedom from a tyrannical Union government, led by that monkey Lincoln. However, their beliefs on slavery were ambiguous at best. Their families had certainly owned slaves for generations, and they believed it morally wrong to mistreat slaves, often wondering how anyone could mistreat someone like Sampson or Meely. Still, they didn't see the War Between the States as a war about slavery. It was, for them, a war for their own freedom. Such are the complexities of history, and of hope.

Jamie's welcome home had been uneventful, which is to say, virtually non-existent. Knowing that his young wife had chosen to stay at her home, the Traveler's Rest Plantation of the Jarrett family, Jamie stopped by there first where he learned that his young wife, and her entire family were off visiting for several days with family in Athens, GA. Once he established that only slaves were present at Traveler's Rest, he headed off to his own home just up the Tugalo River, where his mother, and two younger brothers greeted him warmly. It was three days before his wife came calling, having returned from Athens and learned of her husband's presence. She rushed to his home, and there they shared a passionate night of lovemaking that would defy our simplistic conceptions of what a southern belle in those days might have known of the art of love. They were young, vigorous, and in love, and well, wars tend to have that effect on younger people.

By the time those two got around to a serious conversation they were back at Traveler's Rest, the larger of the two plantation homes, and the spot where they might have several rooms to themselves. They stayed in what had been the higher priced guest room on the top floor of Traveler's Rest toward the northern end of the house. No less a personage than Governor Joe Brown, the wartime governor of Georgia, had stayed in that very room on his honeymoon some years before, so the two were staying in very fine fashion indeed. By the first week in October, they were free to talk, but for reasons of propriety, they maintained a rather formal tone with each other, at least during the day, or when the night lamps were lighted.

Jamie smiled at his wife over their breakfast of grits and eggs one morning, and said, "Do you enjoy being Mrs. Turnbull, as you indicated in your letters?"

Mary smiled at her husband, and in her jokingly formal way responded, "Why Mr. Turnbull! It is certainly not polite to inquire about a lady's honesty, and I'm sure you realize that I, being a devout Christian, am obligated to swear to my fidelity and honesty in all that I say to my dear husband!"

Jamie could only smile in return at first. Then he responded. "Well Mrs. Turnbull, I would certainly never question the integrity of any single word from your mouth, but I did notice that your answer was almost as meaningless as many of the bone-headed orders I received from some of the idiots leading our army! They too can spout senseless diatribes, and with the glossiest of tongue, say almost nothing!"

"Well! I must say, I'm offended! Perhaps the breakfast displeases you, or my dress today is not to your liking then. For I am sure that such a foul mood could never overtake the husband that I love so passionately, least a dastardly cause be the root of the problem!"

Both smiled, having enjoyed the play of formality, and their fluency of thought and word. In their new marriage, they had managed to achieve in only several months, that most treasured basis for a successful relationship—they had become genuine friends, and truly enjoyed each other's company.

It was over breakfast that morning that Jamie asked about plantation life. While his family had eight slaves, and a small "plantation" upriver, they were not nearly so wealthy as the Jarrett family of Traveler's Rest. In 1861, the Jarretts owned nearly one hundred slaves, when most slave owners owned only one or two slaves, and most of the citizens in the south owned no slaves at all. Thus by antebellum standards, the Turnbulls were only moderately well off, while the Jarretts were the most wealthy family in northeast Georgia.

Mary knew that her husband wanted to understand life on a large plantation. She smiled at his question and said, "I'll share with you a scribbling that I based on stories my family has told me over the years. As I told you in my letters, I hope, at some point, to publish this as a booklet on slavery, the real slavery, just to show that we are not the monsters presented in the northern papers." With that, she stepped quickly out of the room, returning some minutes later, with a set of old pages that, thankfully, has been preserved by history. Handing those pages to Jamie, she said, "This tells of how my grandfather, Devereaux Jarrett built this plantation, with help from the Georgia gold fields."

## Building The Jarrett Plantation

*One Fall Evening At Jarrett's Tavern, 1829*
*as told to me by my Grandfather, Mr. Devereaux Jarrett,*
*Master of Traveler's Rest Plantation*
*written by Mrs. Mary Jarrett Turnbull*

The business deal that would help build this plantation and settle the antebellum history of the lower Blue Ridge took place at Jarrett's tavern, on a cold September evening, and the deal transpired because of a simple event that did not take place. On that particular evening Archie Carmichael showed no promise whatsoever of getting drunk enough to fall into the fireplace.

Archie short for Archibaldy leaned precipitously on the stacked rock wall next to the hearth at Jarrett's Tavern in Walton's Ford along the Tugalo River. He was perched on a three legged stool with only the two back legs actually making contact with the rough wooden floor, and as he slept off his drink, he snored loud enough to be heard clear down to the flatboat docks on the river just over a hundred yards away. There were several flatboats in from Augusta, GA, a growing city about ninety miles to the south down the Tugalo River. Between Walton's Ford and Augusta, the Tugalo changed names, such that the same stream, as it grew in its journey toward the coast, became known as the Savannah River.

There always seemed to be a goodly number of rivermen in Walton's Ford, men who plied those waters, carrying the many trade goods to the Savannah port. They were a tough lot, those rivermen, usually filthy, frequently cursing, and generally untoothed. They often drank their cares away in Jarrett's Tavern as they watched old Archie snore, and perhaps fall into the fire. Archie was known to be one of the major entertainments in Walton's Ford.

Several rivermen thought that Archie would fall into the fire sooner this evening since he'd begun drinking earlier than usual. Some had placed wagers on it. Archie himself had had a goodly portion of the "Prather's Honeydew" a locally famous corn whisky distilled right up-river at the Prather Plantation, and he never failed to sleep for several hours each evening after partaking of such fine local whisky as that. Every once in a while he'd entertain the entire tavern by falling into the fireplace, whereby he'd come alive again, and cuss as only a Carmichael could cuss. It was widely known that Carmichael cussing could rival even the most robust efforts of the roughest rivermen working anywhere along the Savannah.

Of course the Carmichaels themselves, settling downriver from Walton's Ford, made their own brand of sour mash whisky. In fact, the liquor that sprang from the branches of that dubious and rather twisted family tree would, by the turn of the century, make "Gum-Log" Georgia known far and wide as one of the most famous of the liquor cooking areas in the entire southern Blue Ridge. Everyone knew Champ Cobb cooked up a mean brew, but while Cobb's whisky was powerful, it was a bit too strong for Archie's taste. When Archie had a little coin in his pocket, or a chicken or pig to trade, he occasionally drank the upscale whisky made by the Prathers, so on this particular night he treated himself to the finer brew, prior to getting drunk enough to fall asleep on his stool by the fireplace.

Archie frequented the tavern for his evening drinks almost every night, and having a reputation for not holding his liquor well, his evenings were always entertaining to the local crowd and the rivermen. At various times even the local folks in these parts were known to take bets on when Archie would tumble over. The rivermen bet on Archie every night, but then again, they'd bet on anything. Side bets were placed on whether he'd fall toward the front door or the other way, thus landing on the hearth or maybe even in the fire itself. James Wyly once won an entire bottle of imported French wine from Devereaux Jarrett himself, the owner/proprietor of this fine establishment, on just such a bet.

On that memorable evening in 1829, Archie had leaned a bit before he woke up and thus he rolled squarely into the fire in the big floor level hearth. He stayed there long enough to catch his deerskin breeches on fire, and then he rolled on the floor until he put the fire out. By then, the entire tavern crowd was laughing at him, and with nothing but his breeches and pride damaged, he joined the laughter while his pants were still smoking.

Now this particular Carmichael was like most of that scattered, "poor white trash" family, in that Archie could barely name his Mammy and his Pappy, but he wasn't real sure about the latter. He had no clue who his Granddaddy was, though he sometimes wondered. He'd been told by his Mammy that their great Granddaddy had fought with the British when the Cherokee still lived in the Tugalo River Valley, but he didn't know whether to believe that or not. He'd noted that his Pappy wasn't called Carmichael at all, but he'd learned over the years, not to ask too many questions about his family lineage. Archie was like many of the Scottish descendants in the Blue Ridge. He was happy to hunt a bit, raise a decent crop of corn, beans, and maybe a bit of tobacco for sale downriver. He was a poor man, owning no slaves and only a few acres of tillable land with a rough cabin on it. He had a cow for milk, several goats and a few skinny pigs that he'd cut up when his misses needed bacon, but by and large he was a poor man. Still, he enjoyed his woman once or twice a week, and he looked forward to having a bit of corn whisky each evening at the local tavern. He really didn't mind the betting on his anticipated evening tumble. He'd even placed a bet or two on himself over the years. Such was the evening's entertainment in the taverns along the Georgia Blue Ridge in the 1820s and 1830s.

The several folks at the bar across from the hearth lost interest in Archie when he snored again, since it was slightly less loud than the former effort. He'd done it from a relatively stable position and showed no promise at all of an interesting tumble on this night, at least not yet. Talk in the tavern soon turned to other things.

Able Ward took another swig from his glass of Prather's Honeydew, and slurped loudly, mostly to announce that he had something to say. "If you ask me, there's still gold in many of those hills, but gettin to it ain't as easy as it were a year ago. What we need now is a water cannon to eat up the hillsides. There's gold in those mountains sure as my pecker's a foot long, and all we got to do is get it out."

His friend, One-eye Benny, was drinking with him in the tavern. "Hush your fuss, you old coot. You ain't found no gold to speak of in six months, and if your pecker's a foot long, I'll be a caged whore with nothing to do on a weekend!" One-eye had heard much the same thing from Able for damn near two months now, and so he just meant to ignore him. Still he couldn't miss an opportunity to poke some fun at his drunken friend.

Distracted from his thoughts of hidden gold, Able simply had to respond to the slight to his manhood. "Damn too, is a foot long!"

At that point, One-eye gave up entirely, not wishing to discuss the private parts of his friend further. Thus, he now tried the tactic of merely agreeing with him. "Yes, I recon' so," he said. One-eye had learned that this approach was the quickest way to get Able to shut up. For anyone who might be interested, the same strategy works with spouses too!

One-eye Benny had been the man that first tripped over the gold in a creek in the north Georgia mountains, leading to the first major gold rush in the United States. Now, just a few years later, over 10,000 miners were plying their trade in almost every creek, draw, gully, or ditch in the Georgia hills. This perturbed some of the older miners, who shared a saying about the problem. "Piss on the side o' any hill out there; then shout that you see 'color' (the yellow "color" of gold), and five idiots from Savanny or Carolina 'll be pannin' your pee, before you get your breeches back up!"

These miners in the Georgia Blue Ridge were a rough lot, as rough as the rivermen along the Tugalo River, and they didn't well abide idiots and fools. Unfortunately a large number of each had joined in the gold rush.

The placer gold, small flakes of gold that had "floated" downstream from the main gold vain, had been panned out for some time on virtually every creek in north Georgia, Alabama, and the lower mountains of North Carolina. Still many pretended that it just wasn't so—the gold couldn't just run out, so they kept on panning. Others were smarter. They knew the "easy gold" was gone but they still talked up the idea of panning in order to sell their worthless claims. Some of the newer miners never realized they were panning the same sand that other's had panned three or four months before. The old hands like Able and One-eye had less tolerance for newcomers to the gold fields than did most of the others.

These rough gents would have never guessed it but their conversation was being listened too quite intensely by several folks at that moment. Devereaux Jarrett, the young proprietor of the establishment, was serving drinks at the far end of the room, and had been talking discretely with James Wyly, the former owner of this particular tavern. Each was well known in these parts, and each was well respected as a shrewd businessman, though Wyly was much older than

Jarrett. When they heard the idea about the water cannon, each looked into the eyes of the other, and each was thinking the same thing; "Maybe it's time to get one." When they realized they'd had the same unvoiced thought at about the same instant, they merely smiled at each other. These two men thus came to the same business conclusion at the same time, and after some private consideration, each realized that they could do this particular business deal together.

Without voicing that shared thought, Wyly spoke first. "Not me, Devy! I'm much too old to go investing in these new water cannon contraptions, and my other taverns along the Unicoi Turnpike are doing damn well, just as yours is here! Don't go asking me to invest in a water cannon with you! Besides, I'd be dead before that damn contraption could even get here from Philadelphia."

"Don't even think that, Mr. James," Devy said. "You'll out live us all, and I know that if it's a good investment, you won't be left out!" Devy smiled at his long term mentor, a man who had earned his respect; for James Wyly had fought with Devy's father at the Battle of King's Mountain during the American Revolution some fifty years previously. On that night, James Wyly was seventy eight years old, while Devereaux was reasonably young, in his early thirties. These two continued to stare at each other. Each was smiling, because they truly enjoyed each other's company, but in such a business discussion, neither one was blinking.

After another minute, Devereaux continued, "Mr. James. You may be gettin on in years, but you're still the smartest man I know in these parts, and I'll seek your guidance even if you're not investing with me."

Devereaux Jarrett was, by the late 1820s, reaching his prime as a businessman. He'd entered the Tugalo Valley many years previously with his father, and over the years, he'd bought Wyly's tavern and country store. Since that auspicious business deal, Jarrett had made Traveler's Rest Tavern a showplace among the taverns in the Blue Ridge Mountains, and was now well into the process of transforming this from a tavern into both a stage stop and a successful plantation.

Physically Devereaux Jarrett was a smallish man, standing only five feet two inches. He was not a handsome man, and if a newcomer saw him in the street of the village of Walton's Ford, few would have thought him to be a pillar of the community. His face was rather square, and his features seemed chiseled harshly into place. His few changes of expression gave away nothing of his thoughts, even his eyes were both fierce and piercing. Of course, these very features became formidable advantages in the world of business, in that almost everyone underestimated this remarkable man. For times had changed in the small community of Walton's Ford, here in the lower Blue Ridge along the Tugalo River since the early days. No longer was this a frontier settlement as it had been in the 1780s. By the 1820s, businessmen and not frontiersmen were the elite of the day, with Devereaux Jarrett and James Wyly, foremost among them, Jarrett because he was one of the smartest of the younger men in the community, and Wyly simply because he had lived so very long.

The previous generation in the Tugalo River Valley–the generation that had included local legends such as Jessie Walton, Daniel Boone, Andy Jackson, and Early Cleveland, not to mention James Wyly himself—had carved a semblance of civilization out of this rugged frontier of the lower Blue Ridge. It was left to the current leaders of the community–leaders like Devereaux Jarrett, James Wyly, and James Prather–to build empires from the resources here, and Jarrett, like the others, was off to a grand beginning. On that day in 1829, Devereaux Jarrett held clear title to over a thousand acres of fine cleared bottomland, and 13,000 acres of mountains covered with prime timber. He also owned a tavern, a tannery, a smithy, and sixty slaves. He was the richest man in the Tugalo Valley, if not the richest in Georgia.

## The Great Man Arrives

It was at exactly this moment that the unexpected visitor arrived. As the door to the tavern flew open, a gusty cold wind blew in, and a darky named Cassius, who was dressed in a fine dark suit—dressed much better than any white man in the tavern—boldly walked into the front door, scanned the room, and then turned sideways to hold it open to the wind. For a slave, Cassius was a true gentleman, having been purchased at auction in London several decades before. Clandestinely he read the classics, and kept records for his master. He even kept a crude personal diary, which would, much later, become the basis of one of the early "slave narratives" of those years. He spoke with an accent which still displayed his British training, and was one of the few blacks who could easily and with relative impunity, look down his nose at the poor white trash that seemed to be the mainstay in the Tugalo River area.

The Carmichael clan, in particular, hated this uppity nigger, but they couldn't touch him as long as he remained loyal to his master. Cassius held the door as that esteemed gentleman walked in, a man that could and would command attention in any room, even any royal palace, anywhere on earth in those years. The Honorable Senator John C. Calhoun, former Vice-President of the United States, and Senior Senator from the state of South Carolina, entered.

This august personage scanned the room quickly appraising each man present. Of course the various darkies he ignored. Then, his senatorial voice, for he truly had one, rose to the occasion and using a commanding tone that had frequently dominated debates in the halls of Congress, Calhoun shouted for all to hear. "Damnation, Jarrett, pour me something hot and strong. It's cold as a witches' teat out there!"

Everyone in the place, save Cassius, laughed at the Senator's statement. Such was the humor and usage of the crude local lingo of America's dominate politician for that age, particularly when he visited the local folks in the rural south.

Everyone, as they finished laughing, greeted the Senator, with most of the tavern crowd tipping their hats. Cassius shut the door carefully, and then practically ran to fetch a chair, and determining well in advance the Senator's choice in company, he immediately placed it at the table where James Wyly sat. It was clear that Mr. Wyly and Mr. Jarrett were the only true gentlemen in the place, so Cassius knew that his master would wish to sit with them. Each man stood as the Senator approached. The Senator, calmly ignoring his manservant's efforts, merely sat down–knowing full well that the chair would be there behind him.

He then spoke to his friend Wyly, looking directly at him, with those forceful, calculating eyes. "James! What might you and young Jarrett here be cookin' up behind my back? I daresay never a conversation takes place here between the two of you that I shouldn't have to watch out for!"

Wyly smiled at the banter of this rich plantation owner turned politician. Wyly, like Calhoun himself, was a man who could, and did, speak the language of those to whom he was speaking, whoever they might be. He could be as coarse as the lowest rivermen or the crude white trash crackers driving a mule team along the Unicoi Turnpike. Still, in an instant, he could become a true gentleman. "Why John," he said, "Whatever do you mean? Do you cast aspersions on my friend Devereaux and I?"

Devereaux returned to the table carrying a drink for the Senator. "Never you mind, our friend Wyly, Senator. He is just beside himself in your esteemed presence! We are always glad to have your company."

"Thank you Devereaux," Calhoun said, as a mug of whisky was placed before him. After he took a long drink, he belched loudly, as was proper in taverns of the day, and said, "Thank you indeed! Never did man nor beast need that drink more that I do this night!" He then took a more gentle sip of his drink, and eased it down, enjoying the simple sensation of a fine whisky on a cold evening. Afterwards, he looked back at Wyly.

"I cast no aspersions, James. I simply state facts. You two are the wisest businessmen in these parts, and when I see you with your heads together, I figure that you're cooking up another scheme to make some cash. I simply want to be a part of it!" These three businessmen, each a landed plantation owner, and each very successful both on his own and in his various partnerships, were about to embark on a discussion that would transform the Georgia mountains. They would, together, industrialize most of the mining in the gold fields of Georgia.

Wyly responded, with a lowered voice; "Well, there are some things we might discuss, perhaps a proposition in mining." After that statement, Wyly cast a careful glance around the tavern to see who, if anyone, was still listening.

The Senator looked around with Wyly, and seeing Archie still propped up by the fire, giggled to himself and his friends. "I see friend Carmichael is still balanced well; I fear there will be no blazing entertainment on this night!"

"Yes," Jarrett agreed. "I sometimes think he does my business a great service with every fall, but one cannot count on the quality of his performance on any given evening. Alas, Archie shows no promise of falling into the fire."

The Senator laughed again. "Ah, Devereaux, on such intangibles does business most often stand or fall; I do hope you'll forgive the unintentional pun!"

By now, Able and One-eye Benny had moved on to discussions of the idiots they'd seen in the gold fields. Wyly scanned the room and lowered his voice, and began to speak, but then he paused and rested his eyes on Cassius. Calhoun, ever the politician, didn't miss the subtlety. Without looking at this manservant standing behind him, he said, "Cassius, why don't you see if that pretty gal, Meely, has something hot to eat out in the kitchen."

"Yes Sir. May I bring you something Sir?"

"No," replied the Senator. "I'm just fine for now."

"Very well, Sir." Thus was Cassius dismissed from the discussion.

As he left the room Wyly spoke again. "As you arrived Senator, we were contemplating a business venture. Devereaux here was just looking for a partner in some harebrained scheme to purchase a water cannon for use in his mine in the Nacoochee Valley. I fear our friend Jarrett has visions of gold."

## Author's Note: The Taverns of the Blue Ridge Mountains

Traveler's Rest in those heady days of the 1820s and 1830s, was not the plantation home it was to become only two decades later. Rather, the same building was, at that point, a stagecoach stop and a frontier tavern. In understanding the business climate on this newly tamed frontier in those days, one must understand the meaning of the frontier tavern. The taverns on the frontier trails were scattered along each road at a distance of roughly every twenty miles or so, the distance a stage or horse could comfortably travel in a day. However, a tavern was more than a local bar and eatery. Taverns in the 1830s served the functions of a hotel, a highway diner, a hospital, a news establishment, a coffee shop, a convention center, a business center, and on occasion, a courthouse and theater all rolled into one. Any businessman traveling in the lower mountains, for no white man save a brave few explorers like Billy Bartram had ever visited the higher reaches of the Blue Ridge, was dependent upon the taverns along his route.

There were taverns in virtually every Georgia town and crossroads—Dalton, Ellijay, Athens, Watkinsville, Clarkesville, Cornelia, Gainesville, Greensboro, Clayton—virtually every town in upstate Georgia held at least one stagecoach tavern, and among these, Jarrett's Tavern at Walton's Ford was perhaps the most strategically placed. The Great Philadelphia Wagon Road—perhaps the busiest road in Colonial America—ran down the eastern spine of the Blue Ridge from the great northern port cities of New York, Baltimore, and Philadelphia, came right by Jarrett's Tavern in the small village of Walton's Ford on the Tugalo River.

A short section of that once-famous road is still visible today, only a hundred yards in front of Traveler's Rest. From the 1790s until the 1850s, that was a well traveled stagecoach route and a minimum of four or five families a week drove up the trail in their own oxcart, asking the same question, "Is there any land for sale around here?"

In contrast to that well traveled road, the Unicoi Turnpike running into the mountains from Jarrett's Tavern, was used more by single men seeking their fortune, or trail drivers with herds of beef or sheep, or even pigs. That rough turnpike began right at the bottom of the hill by Traveler's Rest, and traversed all the way into the higher mountains, through Cherokee country in the Georgia Blue Ridge, and all the way into Carolina and Tennessee. In that direction, lay the Nacoochee Valley and the Georgia gold fields that many saw as the promise of riches for all. Of course, the Cherokee were still in western Georgia at the time, and some would kick up a fuss every now and again, so the Unicoi was seen in the 1830s as the trail to both riches and danger. Many a young man dreamed of shaking himself free of the duties of the family farm in lower South Carolina or Georgia, and coming through Walton's Ford, he would cast himself headlong down that trail to find what riches or danger it offered. For such are the quests of young men in every age.

With the conflux of these two wagon roads and the last navigable portion of the Savannah River system merging here, Traveler's Rest Tavern was located smack dab on one of the busiest highway interchanges of the early 1800s anywhere in North America. It was, in the 1830s, the main rest stop on the way to the frontier. Jarrett's Tavern, which would soon become known as Traveler's Rest Plantation, was on the Interstate 85 of its day, and it remained a busy intersection from the early colonial period through the 1850s.

Still a tavern like Jarrett's was more than a crossroads. Many frontier taverns and stagecoach stops were the centers of many small communities all across the Blue Ridge. This settlement of Walton's Ford, for example, now included over fifty families, with some two hundred and eighty-five white folks living in the valley. There were still a few Cherokee around in small cabins further up in the hills. Of course no one counted the slaves. Only half a mile from the tavern stood the ruins of a Cherokee ceremonial mound but that small hill had been covered over with trees for sixty or seventy years now, and most folks had forgotten it was even there.

In the Tugalo River Valley, on any evening of the week, if you wanted excitement, a quick drink, or just good conversation, Traveler's Rest Tavern was the place to be. Only the courthouse over in Clarkesville on "hangin' days" was more lively, unless you counted the cock fights, or bear baiting that some local farmer typically held in his barn on Saturday evenings. Of course, few of the community leaders would grace such dubious festivities as those. In the 1830s though, all classes of folks came to the tavern; local farmers like Carmichael, plantation owners like James Wallace Prather, or business men like Devereaux Jarrett and James Wyly. All would show up most evenings at the local tavern where they, along with the rivermen working the flatboats on the Savannah river, would take a dram. They would compare notes on the crops and the weather, gossip a bit, and listen to the day's news. Sometimes they would compare notes on world news, if anyone had received a newspaper from any of the down river towns, Augusta or Savannah.

The taverns like the out-houses of those times, were, in some sense, the great equalizers of the day. No matter how few teeth a man had, how bad he smelled, or how sour his breath, whatever his station in life, every white man who could pay his tab was equally welcome at the local tavern. In this humble way, began the great American dream of equality for all. For every man had his place at the local tavern. Of course, most who lived during that period benignly overlooked the fact that this version of the grand American dream of "equality" did not apply to either blacks or women, and certainly not to the Cherokee. Still, great ideas in history, such as equality for all in the American dream, are rarely born as completely perfected ideas, and it often takes history a century or two to improve upon such profound change.

This is not to say that blacks and women played no part in tavern life; in contrast slaves and women were essential to the functioning of frontier taverns. On this particular evening, in Jarrett's Tavern while the wealthy men of the community discussed their dreams of a water cannon to mine gold, other conversations were taking place throughout the myriad rooms of the tavern, conversations by all races and classes of persons. These conversations, in many ways demonstrated the rich tapestry of the complex southern, antebellum society of those decades. Sociologists of later centuries would absolutely drool over the vast and complex relationships of plantation life, and several conversations were taking place at the very instant that the water cannon and the quest for gold was mentioned upstairs. These have been preserved by virtue of two slave narratives—stories of slaves that were either dictated to others, or written down by slaves themselves during the antebellum period, or immediately after. Both Cassius (who was literate) and Fanny Bricebud (who was not) left slave narratives, and that story has been presented herein, as a counterweight to Mary Turnbull's rather defensive view of plantation life.

## Another Conversation at Traveler's Rest
### *(as remembered in the Diary of Cassius, a Slave Narrative)*

Cassius strolled into the kitchen which unlike most taverns, was not in a separate building outside, but rather was in a rude-dug basement under Jarrett's Tavern itself. Here he met the only slave of the Jarrett plantation which he considered his equal, Fanny Bricebud. Fanny ran the kitchen and directed the house slaves for the Jarretts during those decades at Jarrett's Tavern. She even helped raise the Jarrett children. Thus, she was by far the most important, and most influential, of the Jarrett slaves.

No one seemed to know how or where she acquired her unusual second name. Still, she was very proud of that name, since she had two names and most slaves only had one. No one even knew what a "Bricebud" was, nor was there any family anywhere in the Tugalo River Valley by that name. Still, Fanny loved her two names, every bit as much as she loved picking on other slaves who had no last name. Of course, the plain truth was that Fanny Bricebud loved joking with anyone and everyone, about almost anything.

At that moment, Fanny looked up from stirring the cook-pot over the fire in the fireplace. In the pot simmered a beef and vegetable stew that would do any chef in New York, Charleston, London, or Paris proud. She spotted Cassius and grinned, Fanny seemed to grin at everyone. She noted the fine clothes Cassius wore and she immediately knew, by his presence, that the Senior Senator of South Carolina was visiting upstairs. Amid her grin at Cassius, she asked, "Does the gent'men upstairs need anything?"

Cassius merely shook his head no, as he glanced around the downstairs kitchen; Cassius always seemed to look over things with an air of aloofness.

Having attended to the immediate business of the house slaves, the needs of the whites upstairs, Fanny knew just what to say next to this proud, educated negro from London. She raised her voice, still grinning' and said, "Now who let this hea fiel' hand in de kitchen? Don't ya'll realize we fed the field niggas an hour ago? I suppose' you'll want some o' this stew now?"

## An Author's Note: Slave Society

Fanny had, by that question, insulted Cassius in every way possible. It is a fact that all men, no matter what their station in life, develop governing hierarchies, principles of informal governance, and beliefs in one's position relative to others, in which to abide. These may be called societies. They develop in newly formed nations, colonies, frontier outposts, even in prisons. Indeed, if five people found themselves on a deserted island for more than a day, a society of some type would develop—leader and led, influential, and non-influential. So it was that even the destitute, lowest rank of southern society, the enslaved, developed a ranking/cast system—a slave society.

By calling Cassius a "fiel' han," or field hand, Fanny Bricebud had playfully insulted him, suggesting that he, like most slaves, bore the brunt of the cotton economy by working for long hours in the fields each day. Among the ranks of slaves, field hands were at the lowest point in the pecking order, since they had no skill other than picking cotton or other crops. Next in the slave hierarchy came the skilled slaves, artisans who were highly trained in their respective craft. Many plantations–Jarrett's Traveler's Rest was no exception–developed trained slaves, skilled in one or two important plantation jobs such as tanners, coopers for making barrels, blacksmiths, horse-traders, furniture-makers, cattlemen, or weavers. These slaves were more highly valued than field hands since they could–and often did–bring in income from other farms or plantations in the area. Next were the drivers, who were trusted slaves that had the role of overseeing other slaves. It is a common misconception today that most overseers during this period were white men. In fact many whites did oversee slaves on larger plantations, but smaller plantations often used a trusted slave to allocate the work, and oversee plantation chores and the other slaves, with these drivers working alongside the master.

At the top of the slave cast system were the higher-end servants. Fanny, as a well respected cook was one example, as was the nanny that raised the master's children. Cassius, as a trained gentleman's servant, was also among this group. These were considered the most valuable of slaves. These servants were trained throughout their life for their role, and many southern plantations placed much of the family's pride, indeed much of the honor of the plantation, in the austere training and comportment of their house slaves. These house niggers often lived much better than did the other plantation slaves, or even better than most of the local white farmers. These house niggers certainly looked down their nose at the rivermen, or poor-white-trash farmers. These house slaves were often in view of other plantation owners, and often traveled with the master's family. Thus, they had presentable clothes, good food, a bed every night, often in the big house itself. Fanny, for example, even had her own cottage, a small cabin just behind the big house, a cottage that still stands at Traveler's Rest, today.

It is cruel irony that the slaves themselves readily adopted such a demeaning and rigid cast system and thus, they unwillingly participated in the dehumanization of the majority of the slaves in those days. There were always many more field hands needed by the cotton economy than house servants, but truth be known, this rigid cast system demeaned and enslaved both field hands and house slaves alike.

Still the house servants did serve one critical function in slave society. Good cooks such as Fanny Bricebud, were highly prized, and by virtue of being in the mansion almost around the clock, these slaves provided most of the news to the other slaves on the plantation. This is one reason that the slave narratives of Cassius and Fanny Bricebud can be so detailed—they knew virtually everything that happened at the plantation. In fact, the house slaves often pretended not to hear conversations, even as they eavesdropped on them. They often stood rigid just outside of the main rooms as important conversations were held between their white masters, but this selective-hearing masquerade was quickly dropped when they talked among themselves. At that point, any important news was quickly shared with other slaves on the plantation.

The Traveler's Rest Tavern was, even then becoming the plantation of Traveler's Rest. Like the Prather Plantation just upriver, or the Cleveland Plantation over in South Carolina, Traveler's Rest was in reality, a small city. Moreover, larger plantations had fairly large populations—both black and white, when compared to smaller towns in the area. At Traveler's Rest, over a hundred persons lived, whereas the nearby village of Walton's Ford, held only eighty-some persons. In fact, slaves made up 48% of the total population in Georgia in 1860. Only South Carolina and Mississippi had a higher percentage of slaves to whites in their total population, 57% and 55% respectively. As those numbers indicate, plantations were indeed, the backbone of most small towns in rural Georgia, and throughout most of the south.

At Traveler's Rest, the Jarretts were the masters, with Devereaux Jarrett having built this plantation from the humble beginnings of a much smaller, stagecoach tavern in only twenty years. Their white overseer was a man named Walton, who had a distant connection with the Walton who first owned this property back in the 1790s. His family lived in a small cabin about a half mile from the Jarrett's home. The village of Walton's Ford just at the edge of the plantation, had a population of some eighty-five whites, shopkeepers, rivermen, a minister, the Reverend Richard Cleveland, and of course all of their families.

On the back of the plantation itself, about a mile from the mansion stood the nigger yard as shown by early maps of the area, and plantation notes themselves. Here lived most of the slaves then owned by Devereaux Jarrett. In various mixes of friends or extended families, these slaves managed to survive and indeed thrive in a system in which they had no rights and no political voice. They tended, by and large to themselves, and if they were underfed on some plantations, that was not the case at Traveler's Rest. Here slaves were encouraged to keep "kitchen gardens" in order to grow their own vegetables. They were allowed to hunt for small game on the wooded acres of the plantation, and were provided the services of the matron of the plantation when they were ill. Most importantly, as Mary Jarrett reported many years later, they were never beaten. In simple terms they were valuable property, and no savvy businessman in those days, mistreated his valuables.

## A Discussion Among the Slaves

Cassius, always the gentlemen only smiled at his rude greeting from Fanny Bricebud, a friend he'd known for many years. He replied. "Please don't let me disturb your labors. I can get a bowl myself." Cassius was never one to become flustered at Fanny's sense of humor, and he knew from prior visits that no black voice was heeded as often or as judiciously by both the blacks and the whites on this plantation, as that of Fanny Bricebud! In this woman, he'd truly met his equal, or nearly so. Moreover, he loved her ever present smile, and warm, if joking greeting.

As Cassius filled his bowl from the simmering soup pot over the massive fireplace, he paid his respectful greetings. "Ms. Fanny Bricebud! You have out done yourself this evening! I could smell this delicious concoction while descending yon stairs, and with each step I grew more hungry." With that, he took a spoon from the tray near the fireplace, and took a seat on one of the stools by the large table in the center of the room, only then noticing Fanny's daughter Meely, in the corner of the kitchen peeling potatoes.

Fanny smiled, as she sat back down across the table from Cassius, where she had already begun to chop onions for a casserole she planned for the next day. She continued the conversation.

"Well, I spose' you know what they's up to up the stairs! You sure I don't need to run somepin' up for your Master, the high and mighty hisself? "

Cassius stiffened; he didn't like disrespect towards his master, and didn't understand why Fanny seemed to need to always manifest some. "He is fine, but I should like to take up a piece of pie in a few moments. I'm sure he would enjoy that."

"Hump" was all Fanny said. When she was displeased, which was fairly frequent, she merely "humped."

Cassius took another spoonful of the delicious soup and again, complimented Fanny. "I do sincerely believe that this is some of the best soup I've had in all my days!"

Fanny humped again, and then continued the conversation. "What's the gent'mens talkin' bout up in the high stairs?"

Cassius didn't like to share his hearings, as he knew Fanny Bricebud did, but he also realized that he had some responsibility to do so, and he really didn't wish to insult Fanny, so he shared his knowledge. "They are discussing mining gold in these parts, by using a water cannon, in the distant hills I believe." It was true that Cassius had left the room before that discussion started, but, as noted previously, any self-respecting house servant learned to slow up just out of sight, to catch the beginning of the conversation–this tendency to slow down when leaving a room translated into the white's perception that "slaves were slow moving and slow witted." Of course, that perception merely increased the opportunities for house servants to eavesdrop on important conversations.

Fanny continued with a sarcastic question. "Ain't those folks got enough gold by now?" She paused for only a moment, then said. "Course, don't recon' you can have too much gold!" She laughed loudly, as did Meely and Cassius, at her humor.

## Author's Note: The Slaves Defined Themselves

While Mary Turnbull had remarkable insight into the happenings at Traveler's Rest, there were some things even she was not privy too. Again the slave narratives, and other historical notes from the plantation itself or other whites in the community, allow us to piece together a more clear understanding of other aspects of this complex plantation society, and reconstructed conversations such as that above come from the slave narratives noted earlier, as well as these sources, and what is generally known of slave life. For example, we know that Meely was a name that was passed from mother to daughter for several generations on the Traveler's Rest plantation in those times. From the 1830s until the 1860s, there were at least three Meely's in succession and maybe four, and that fact accounts for the much younger slave with that name, living at the plantation during the closing days of the War Between the States.

Next we know of a much darker side of slavery than was shown by Mary Turnbull's notes. For example, while these various conversations were taking place in the big house, a more sinister hallmark of antebellum society was enacted in the barn behind the house. Here one of the youngest but roughest of the rivermen—Willie Palmer was his name, was busy dropping his pants, in an effort to mount a very fat black woman named Lillybell, who earned some money the only way she knew how.

Lillybell was owned by Walton, the overseer for the Jarrett Plantation, and thus, Devereaux Jarrett could not control this slave as she was the property of another. She helped the overseer's wife sometimes, and managed his still, making as fine a whisky as anyone in the valley during the 1830s. But Lillybell, though fat, was still a "comely wench" in the vernacular of those days. Thus, in the evenings, she plied her trade with impunity in the cattle barn, and, as was required, she gave half of her earnings to Walton, her owner.

In the antebellum world of the day, couplings between white plantation owners, or their sons, and the young attractive slaves was not uncommon, though such pairings were much more common among slaves and the rivermen. Of course, this was often a forced and legally condoned rape of the black women of the day, but this immorality that seems so obvious today was ignored in that period. Indeed, if it was known that a master had sired children with his slaves, it was overlooked or spoken of only in whispers. History records that such luminaries as Thomas Jefferson, a man venerated by history, had numerous children with his slaves, and while it is hard to imagine such things in today's world, most of society in those days merely turned a blind eye toward the inevitable mixed-race offspring. Jefferson's plantation in Virginia had many light skinned slaves, and some even sported the red hair for which the third President of the United States was so famous.

What is less well known about slave society is that some slaves did sell themselves in order to earn money, and Lillybell was known to produce a good time for a ha'penny, for anyone who could pay. She even did it for half-a-pound of bacon from time to time. On this night, young Palmer had partaken of the home brew in Jarrett's Tavern for almost an hour, before he decided to poke around the small cabin near the barn where Lillybell was known to ply her trade. As the Senior Senator from South Carolina began to consider the purchase of a water cannon, and just as Cassius was serving himself some soup, the races were about to mix yet again out in the cattle barn. Such were the complexities of southern plantation society, as spoken of earlier.

The conversation in the barn was probably somewhat more limited than the other two, and while we know such things were taking place on that particular evening, history has, thankfully, not recorded the grunts and groans that no doubt characterized that business. Enough said on this matter.

Such was the tapestry of life on most every plantation in the south during those years, and Mary Jarrett Turnbull, and these slave narratives catalogued much of this rich experience. We are certain that she did not hear the dialogue above among the slaves in the kitchen, as she was not yet born. However, white children and black children often played together and ran together as near equals during their early lives, being forcibly separated only at puberty from each other by the white masters of plantation life. In that context, it is not only possible, but quite probable that little Mary could have hidden in the kitchen with her friend Meely, and eavesdropped on later slave discussions similar to the one reported above. At any rate, Mary did write of such dialogues as if she were there, and with the support of the slave narratives, we can get a picture of plantation life. We also know, from their correspondence that her husband, Jamie Turnbull, cherished these stories.

## Jamie's Visit Home in September of 1863.

As Jamie finished reading his wife's "scribblings" as she called them, he was in awe! How could he have found such a gem? How could he have married a beautiful, obviously wealthy girl, only to find out she had such keen insight into so many things? At that moment, as he put the pages down on the breakfast table, he realized that he loved this woman more than he could ever express. Moreover, he knew he would have to work hard all his life, to keep up with her humor, her intelligence, and her wit. As he reflected on that thought, he could imagine nothing worse than his wife becoming bored with him; with the somewhat slower fluency of his thoughts, while hers were obviously, so deep and insightful.

Thus did Jamie Turnbull reach a point early in his marriage that some men reach only after several decades living with the same woman. He knew at that moment that he would never truly fathom the depths of this wonderful creature, his wife. Further, he wanted to accomplish that task much more than he could ever express. As he looked over at Mary, he also realized that such a desire provided an excellent basis for a long and happy marriage. In that sense, Jamie suddenly understood a fundamental truth of the ages. Every happy marriage ultimately rests on a man's appreciation of the unpredictability of the female mind.

"Mary," he said. "These are truly wonderful. I cannot adequately express how much I enjoyed reading these pages! This must be published, as it does present our world in such a different light from that of the northern papers."

"Oh, thank you so much for the compliment, Captain Turnbull! But do rest assured that the important tales of our lifestyle are yet to come. When I next write, I expect to share what my Grandfather Devereaux told me of the fire-eaters!"

Turnbull didn't understand that sentence, and his face showed it, even before he asked, "The what?"

Mary merely laughed, happy that she could entertain her husband so! "Fire-eaters" was a term that my Grandfather used for the men who defended our way of life! Calhoun was certainly a fire-eater, but, alas, he died before things came to a head." Mary paused and looked over at her husband. She then looked back down to finish her needlepoint stitch and said, "You'll just have to wait for more on the fire-eaters. But, my dear Captain Turnbull, it does mean a great deal to me that you have such regard for my scribblings. I do want to show who we really are and how we really live, and that may be my best contribution to this war. My grandfather and my father own slaves and those slaves do provide the labor for the plantation, but it is wrong to argue, as do those damn Yankees, that all slaves are ill-treated, or that slavery caused this horrid war! No slaves were ever treated any finer than Fanny Bricebud, or Senator Calhoun's slave, Cassius! Aunt Fanny is still practically a member of our family, though she is now very old, and rarely leaves her cabin. Still, I do so want to tell our true story!"

"And tell it you shall!" replied Jamie. "There could be no better explanation of who we are as southerners, or who our slaves are, than these pages. You and I will live to see this story told!"

At that Mary paused, not knowing whether she should share her next thoughts with her new husband. However, she quickly decided she should. "James," she said, at once becoming much more intimate, and lowering her voice. "I hesitate to tell you one of the things I have heard, something not in my scribbling."

"My dearest," Jamie responded. "What is it that so concerns you?"

Mary took a deep breath believing that she was about to upset Jamie's world, and not wanting to do so, but thinking it necessary. "There is talk that I've overheard, of some of our slaves here at Traveler's Rest helping runaways. There is even talk of them running themselves, once the damn Yankees come! "

Jamie looked at his wife aghast! "Certainly not!" he said. "Why would anyone here run, or even help runaways? Your slaves are not ill-treated, not at Traveler's Rest. They are given good food, time off from work, and even medical care when they are sick! Why should any want to run away, or help other escaping slaves?"

In that question, taken from Mary's later scribblings, lay the stupidity of most southerners in those times, if not the ultimate demise of the entire Confederate economy! White southerners in those days, did not believe that slaves desired any station in life other than slavery. Of course, all realized that an occasional malcontent might stir up some trouble now and then, and slave rebellions terrified all in the antebellum south. Still, actual slave rebellions were quite rare, and when slaves were treated fairly and provided for, no southerner believed that they might long for freedom!

By our standards today it seems almost unbelievable that an entire population of southern planters—all of whom were highly educated men and women, men and women of seasoned judgment, refinement, and taste—could be so blinded by their own beliefs, so as to not understand that ultimately, all human beings want freedom; that none wish to be the property of others. Still, it is neither fair nor reasonable to judge the conduct or beliefs of those in history by standards forged many decades later.

Beliefs are, in many ways, the hardest things to change and many highly educated populations have chosen to partake in a wide variety of arcane beliefs over the centuries. Roman citizens knew their empire would last through history, expanding all the while, until it finally expanded beyond its own capacity to govern itself. The beliefs of the Roman citizenry, ultimately led to the downfall of Rome. Much later, German citizens believed in a charismatic leader, virtually worshiping him, as the savior of their country. Further, Hitler fed his people a steady diet of false beliefs that ultimately led to the doom of the Third Reich in only ten short years. We cannot judge these men and women in those societies, nor can we judge southerners, based on today's standards. However, we can understand their failures. By believing in a bankrupt system of slavery, they doomed themselves, and Mary's scribblings, capturing so much of her thoughts, as well as Jamie's, can give us insight into that process.

"Tell me what you have heard," Jamie said.

Mary replied. "It wasn't much really. I was going down to the kitchen, and heard Aunt Fanny arguing with Meely. It seems that Meely was asking about rumors that the Yankees would be here soon and would set the slaves free! She wanted to know if she should wait, or merely slip out one night and look for a Yankee camp."

Jamie thought for a moment and then said. "Perhaps I should have a talk with her, or your grandfather should! Perhaps we need to tell her we can still sell her down the river!"

"Oh my dearest husband," Mary said. "Grandfather would never sell a slave away from her family for asking a question, but I am afraid he might discipline her severely, if he knew. I hesitate to tell him."

"Dearest, I think you must tell your grandfather, and let him decide what's best."

"But my dear James, Grandfather has never whipped a slave, and never sold one down the river. Besides, I'm not sure what I heard really, maybe just the musings of a young girl looking for excitement."

Jamie then shared his thoughts in a way that could certainly not be considered characteristic of any southerner in those days. After pausing a few moments he said, "I don't know how our slaves feel about this war. Certainly my Sampson was fighting by my side at Chickamauga; he will be at my side in every fight. The Yankee camp now is way up in Tennessee! How would Meely get there? What do you think these slaves might have heard?"

"I'm not sure," Mary replied. "I'm not sure at all."

According to Mary's notes, the conversation ended there. If anything else was said, she did not record it, but these notes do show that slavery was a topic of conversation among these two well before the Yankee army entered Georgia again, and this also documents that slaves in north Georgia had heard of the coming of the Union army as early as 1863. Further they knew of the promise of freedom that the Union army represented.

## Unexpected Fights in Tennessee

As Jamie remained at Traveler's Rest, recovering from his, relatively minor wound, the weather turned bitterly cold. From the middle of October of 1863, through the middle of November, neither the 35,000 Union men in Chattanooga, nor the 66,000 Confederate men surrounding the town moved much. Unlike camps in the warmer summer months, the winter encampments in the War Between the States, as in all of previous history, tended to be more stable, and much harder to construct. Once such a winter encampment was built, armies were reluctant to leave. While the larger Confederate force did besiege the Union army in Chattanooga, outward signs suggested that neither force seemed to be planning any significant battle during that time. Knowing this, Captain Jamie Turnbull was free to rest a bit longer at his home than he would have otherwise.

Of course much of what is "known" in any war is subsequently proven to be false. The Union commander, General Rosecrans, was planning a retreat, but as soon as his superiors in Washington, DC heard of this, they relieved him and sent an unknown Union general to relieve the siege. Thus did General Sam Grant enter the history books.

U. S. Grant was by some accounts, a drunkard, and also suffered from severe fits of depression. Of course, his president, Abraham Lincoln suffered the same malady of depression, though he drank only sparingly. Grant was, however, that most rare of Union commanders in 1863. He had actually won a few battles, not one or two but several in the west, and that fact alone made him virtually unique among Union leaders. Thus, was he given the command, and ordered to relieve the siege of Chattanooga, and that he did. He sent his friend and his most capable subordinate officer, Crazy Billy Sherman, to root out the Confederates.

Union reinforcements under the command of General William Tecumseh Sherman arrived in Chattanooga on November 21, 1863, and didn't wait a single minute. With an attack on November 23, the Union army began three successive attacks on Confederate forces surrounding the town. On the first day, Sherman's Union forces carried the foremost Confederate position on Orchard Knob. On November 24, Union forces took Lookout Mountain, a formidable hill upon which Confederate cannon could and did command the river approaches to

Chattanooga. The very next day, November 25, 1863, the Union army took Missionary Ridge, the Confederate's final stronghold overlooking the town. With the telegraph service directly from Confederate headquarters to Atlanta, every citizen in Georgia knew of these setbacks by the very next day, and those Confederate defeats led Jamie Turnbull to realize he should have returned to his regiment sooner, wounded though he might be.

In that frame of mind, by late November of 1863, Jamie Turnbull felt he should do something for the Grand Cause, even as he recovered, so he determined to visit the more seriously wounded men who had traveled back to the Tugalo River Valley with him. Thus, it was on a fairly cool Saturday morning that he and Mary set off in the wagon, with a nice side of sweet ham, to visit Lem Davis, and his wife down near Eastanollee Creek. The wagon ride was long and the road seemed full of hard mud holes that were only beginning to thaw. Jamie hoped to get to Lem's home before the mud turned into a real quagmire, but he'd driven on worse roads before, and he knew the visit would take most of the day. Thus, they would return to Traveler's Rest late in the night.

As they rode along for two hours, Mary happily bantered on about this or that in the community, with Jamie practicing that most practical of skills of the married man; studious ignoring! Once every so often, he'd look in her direction and say something like, "Really" and that seemed to be just enough to keep her going for a few more minutes. He could, and sometimes did, tune in to her conversation from time to time particularly when her voice suggested that she'd asked a question of him. Still, most of the time he merely muttered banalities such as, "You don't say!" and she'd go on a while longer leaving him free to consider his own thoughts.

When they reached the Eastanollee Creek turnoff along the Tugalo River Road, Jamie knew they were almost at the Davis farm. Lem's family was not wealthy. They owned no slaves, but they did have clear title to nearly two hundred acres of cleared land, which the extended family farmed together. As Jamie and Mary arrived in the yard, they saw that Lem was laid back and covered in thick blankets on a small bed that had been moved out to the front porch that morning. Jamie spoke first. "I see that nobody wants to keep you in a house for too long, after all the fun camping we did in the army!"

Lem opened his eyes—he'd been sleeping as the wagon arrived—and while Jamie helped Mary from the wagon, Lem's wife, Annabell, came onto the porch. "Why it's Mrs. Turnbull and Captain Turnbull himself! Why I am not dressed to receive such important persons as yourselves! Please, come on up on the porch and have a seat while I get some refreshments! Oh, we are so honored by your visit! Please do come in. I'll have the boys bring in Lem's bed so we can all talk together by the fire. He simply won't stay in the house, you see?" She was clearly somewhat flustered, since in usual circumstances, the Davis family was not likely to receive a visit from members of the richest family in the county!

Lem, smiling by now, looked up from his semi-prone position and joined the conversation by answering Jamie. "Can't stand lookin' at the same damn walls another minute!" As Mary blushed and looked toward the ground smiling, Mrs. Davis cuffed her wounded husband on the back of the head to help him remember his manners." Oh," he said. "Sorry, Captain. Sorry Mrs. Turnbull! Sometimes my mouth says things, cussin' an' such that don't bear repeatin' in front of ladies!"

Jamie was climbing down the far side of the wagon, grinning all the while at his friend's turmoil, so it was left to Mary to rescue the day. "Why Mr. Davis. I'm sure that, married as I am to another of our fine Confederate soldiers, I've heard much worse language than that!" Then she continued. "Now if your boys could fetch the cooked sweet ham from the back of the wagon, I'd like to propose that we eat a bite while we visit. I do hope you and Mr. Davis are free to join us."

That was enough to make everyone comfortable, and Jamie had by then, joined the group. "Perhaps Lem and I could stay here on the porch while you two ladies get the dinner ready inside. I'd like a few minutes to talk with my old comrade, here."

As the two ladies went inside, Jamie took a seat beside the bed of his friend. As is often the way of men who have shared battle, no military rituals were necessary; no preamble required. They each knew what they wished to discuss.

Lem began first. "Nice to see you Captain. You heard about our boys losin' the hills around Chattanooga?"

Jamie sighed. "Surely did, Lem. Don't understand how they could lose them hills, though. I've been to Chattanooga. They are formidable mountains, and a single regiment should have been able to hold them 'til hell froze over."

Lem looked far into the distance of the western field, as if he could nearly see the damn Yankees approaching across the tilled land. "Recon our boys put up a fight, but them hills is sure 'nuf Yankee hills now."

Jamie, by that point, was busy lighting a pipe of tobacco, which he offered to share with Lem. As Lem declined, Jamie spoke to his friend. "Damned Yankees 'll be coming this way soon enough I recon'. Not sure when, mind you, with winter commin' and all. Still, those boys are probably used to the cold, and our Georgia hills ain't as high as some mountains. I don't know if they'll come on into Georgia now, or wait until spring."

They both thought on that matter for a few minutes. Lem was the next to speak. "Recon they'll camp in Chattanooga this winter. Ain't no way they'll want to be in the mountains when the snows come on 'em!"

"Don't know about that Lem. You hear about that Yankee army up in Virginia. The papers said the damn Yankees charged right into General Lee's guns at Cold Harbor! Seven thousand blue-bellies died in seven minutes, the way the papers tell it!" Jamie took a breath at that point, considering his next words. "No army on God's green earth can stand that kind of losses! Don't they understand it? Don't they know we'll kill 'um all, if they charge our cannon like that?"

Lem said, "I did hear of that, but who knows if what the papers say really happened! They say Chickamauga was our great victory, but all I remember is gettin' our ass whipped by those damn Spencer rifles! We damn near lost it, and if'n the Thomas Legion hadn't showed up, we would have."

"Yea, guess you're right. Who knows if the papers are tellin' the truth or not?" As they both reflected on that, each knew the next question to be discussed. Jamie spoke up first. "I guess I'll be goin' back to the regiment soon. I hear Owen Collins has been in command since I left, and my returning don't necessarily mean I'll get my command back when I do get there."

Lem spoke next, "You'll get a command. They can't afford to not use good men who have commanded men in a fight before, and you'll get some command. Still, recon' I won't be joinin' up with you no time soon. This here shoulder got infected for a month, and Annabell says I went crazy for a time." Lem paused, as he reflected on his thoughts. "Doc says I barely made it, but now he says I'll heal up good as new. Yankee bullet didn't get no bone or nothing."

Jamie thought on that a moment. "Couldn't have been a minie-ball then. That damn hunk of lead would 'a killed you sure, hit in the shoulder that low like you was. It must 'a been a smaller ball from one of them damn Spencer repeaters that done for you! They don't break up like a lead minie-ball."

Lem considered that a minute. "Yea, guess that's right. Still, it hurt like hell, what I remember of it. Like getting kicked in the shoulder by the biggest damn mule you ever seed!"

"How'd Annabell take it?"

"Just like you'd figure. She cried for three days, while nursing me before anyone could get her to stop. Prayed every minute, even while she was cryin' too! Prayed like a saved sinner at camp meeting! I never seed the like of it before! Damn near drove me crazy all over again!"

Jamie smiled at his friend, then his face turned serious again, as he gave voice to a thought common to fighting men all over the world. "Ain't no way we could ever tell 'em what it's like, is there? Ain't no way that anyone could ever understand it, without being there. No way in hell!"

Lem knew of no good answer to that question, so he remained silent, as both he and Jamie considered the reality of warriors worldwide. There are few constants in history, but there are some, and among them is the indefinable essence of war. No one who has not been in a battle, a real hand-to-hand fight to the death, can ever understand what such a harsh, horrid, meat-grinder type of fight, really does to a man. In short, only warriors can talk to other warriors.

The rest of the visit was pleasant. Lem's boys moved him inside and propped him on the table as all ate the sweet ham, and some beans and collards that Annabell had cooked for dinner. None of the conversation from that point on dealt with the war, but rather, with the coming winter, the apples yet to be put up, and the amount of corn already stored in the corn bins. The Davis family was about to embark on the fall hog killing a bit later than usual, but still a yearly event to look forward too. After a pleasant meal and a couple hours of conversation, the Turnbulls left on their trek home.

They arrived at Traveler's Rest, very tired, around 10:00 that night in mid-November of 1863. Jamie continued to heal, and within two months, he would again be in the Confederate camp, ready to go, once again, to war.

## Crazy Billy Comes to Georgia

It was a bitter winter in 1863 and early 1864, and that cold spell probably saved Georgia from the Yankee's wrath for a time. Still, by the spring of 1864, a feisty, red-headed firebrand, General Billy Sherman, was firmly in command of the Yankee forces in Chattanooga, and he proposed to accomplish what Rosecrans had failed to do at Chickamauga the previous fall. He was going to beat back the Confederate Army of Tennessee in Georgia and then he was going to take Atlanta. Having rebuilt his Yankee forces, and tripled their strength by importing new men, Sherman had a fighting force of over a hundred thousand Union soldiers, as well as the wagons and mules to move that force and the bullets and beans required to sustain it.

Sherman was a moody man—hence the name "Crazy Billy." He often seemed nearly manic, and was always a firebrand when angry. He shared an illness, what would today be diagnosed as chronic depression, with his friend and mentor, U. S. Grant, and with that mental illness so well documented by history, it is a simple fact that neither of these men would receive a command assignment in any modern army. Sherman once summed up the complicated, though respectful, relationship between these two fighting Union generals, rather directly; "Grant stood by me when I was crazy, and I stood by him when he was drunk. We'll stand or fall together." Still, little was known of either mental illness or alcohol addiction in the 1860s, and both of these men did the one thing that generals absolutely had to do, in order to be well regarded by history. They won battles.

Sherman was a short red-head, with the temperament to match that description. He needed only a few hours sleep each night, and took no care at all for his appearance when in the field. All of his subordinates reported that he was constantly talking, and frequently angry. His memory was vast, and he could, with ease, quote orders he had given weeks before to any member of his staff who was stupid enough to challenge him. In short he was a man that any staffer would be terrified of, but most, nevertheless, enjoyed serving under him for one simple reason; his one saving grace, as noted above, was that he won battles.

Further, he didn't waste men. In most cases, he tended to win battles by not really fighting them! Sherman would rather flank an enemy position than take it by frontal assault, losing thousands of men in the process. He would demonstrate that amazing generalship repeatedly in Georgia in the spring of 1864.

He also shared two other characteristics with his friend and superior General Grant; he hated politicians, particularly if they harassed him by offering their opinions. However, his true wrath was reserved for reporters, whom he considered the "scum" of life. In seeing what passes for journalism today, one can only admire the man's astuteness! He left standing orders with his staff for both; "If a politician shows up in camp, tell him I'm in the field until further notice. If a reporter shows up, shoot him."

However, Sherman had one other characteristic of all great generals; he was an avid planner. He planned everything down to the last, most unimportant detail, and thus, when Sherman came to Georgia, he brought everything he could possibly need! He knew that he would face a determined enemy defending their own soil in Georgia, so he came overly-prepared. Moreover, Sherman believed that, the harsher the war, the quicker the Confederates would request peace terms, so he intended to bring a hard, cruel war into Georgia, and ultimately capture Atlanta—he called the city the "Gateway to the south." He knew that he had the men he would need and all the material of war, fresh from Union factories and shipped by rail, completely unmolested, directly into Chattanooga. He was as prepared for a major offensive as any general in history.

Since the early 1800s, it has been a little recognized certainty of history that industry wins wars. When the materials necessary to make war became mechanical and chemical—guns, cannon, explosives—industrial power became paramount. Any idiot with a simple country forge in either 500 BC or 1350 AD could make a sword, a lance, or a knife, but when wars later employed matchlock smoothbores, flintlock rifles, Sherman Tanks, or F-15 aircraft, the production capacity of industry largely determined who won and who lost.

In World War II, for example, German engineering gave Germany the early victories, since it built airplanes, trucks, and tanks, while the armies opposing them had few, if any. The Polish army, as one extreme example, fielded a large horse cavalry in 1939. That cavalry didn't fare well when they charged, sabers drawn, into machine guns mounted on German tanks and covered by screaming German aircraft overhead. The famed blitzkrieg of the Hun tore up horse-flesh and men alike, as industrial production trumped an insane, if extremely brave Polish cavalry charge in 1939. That was the last documented horse-cavalry charge in history.

Later in the same war, American industry created a war machine such as the world has never seen, with a wartime industrial production still unsurpassed in history. As early as 1942—the first full year of the war for Uncle Sam—American industry could build more Liberty ships than German U-boats could sink! One newspaper headline shouted the fact that one shipyard in South Carolina was turning out a nearly complete Liberty transport ship virtually every four days! While fighting men paid with blood, guts, and for many, their lives for that hard-fought victory in Europe and across over a thousand Pacific islands, it was American industry that made the real difference. GI-Joe certainly did the dirty work on those bloody battle lines, but in many ways it was Rosie the Riveter back at home, that won that war.

Sherman was one of the first commanders in history to realize the importance of industrial production in war, an insight that resulted in two of Sherman's basic strategies; (1) come prepared with everything you might possibly need for war, and (2) utterly destroy any enemy industry or war material you find. Sherman was prepared on both counts.

Thus, when Sherman entered Georgia on May 6, he brought everything. Carefully rebuilding his army since taking the hills around Chattanooga in November of 1863, Sherman had stockpiled supplies—the products of Yankee factories from nearly every Union state—in Chattanooga until the city itself seemed bursting at the seams. His quartermasters had literally run out of warehouse space, and were merely parking cannon, caissons, and extra wagons, all under guard, in fields near the city, while stacking cases of guns, bullets, hardtack, and beans under the cover of tents or merely trees. Thousands of mules, horses, scores of thousands of wagons, hundreds of crates of uniforms, thousands of rifles, and swords were stockpiled. Sherman was taking his Yankee armies to war, and he wanted lots of toys to play with.

As a much younger man, Sherman had been stationed for a time in north Georgia, so he knew the topography. He realized he would fight over, around, and between the rolling hills of the lower Blue Ridge, and he spoke to his staff of the need to prepare for "one big Indian war with many small battles" rather than a single large-formation battle. He knew of the countless small rivers and streams in those mountains, so he had stockpiled thousands of "pontoons," a flat-bottomed boat about twenty feet long that, when anchored side by side and overlaid with planks, made a passable bridge. Sherman's army could cross any river or creek those mountains offered, and they did offer many.

This image from the Library of Congress, shows a Union pontoon bridge across one of the many rivers in Georgia. The pontoons could be stacked on large wagons or train cars for transport, and were so numerous that one Union quartermaster in Chattanooga in February of 1863, facing yet another trainload of pontoons to store, was heard to ask, "Does the esteemed General wish to go only to Atlanta, or would he prefer to have us pontoon our way on over to Europe?"

Later that spring, Sherman's engineers would become experts in "pontooning," crossing both streams and rivers alike. Those engineers

**Union Pontoon Bridge**

constructed pontoon bridges almost as fast as the retreating Confederates could burn the originals. Sherman's cannon and wagons then rolled across the pontoon planks heading for the next fight.

Sherman's supplies of virtually everything impressed even his enemies. When Confederate raiders in north Georgia blew up a railroad tunnel along Sherman's supply line, one Confederate staff officer opined, "It ain't no big thing, blowin' up that damn tunnel. Hell, Sherman's probably brought a spare tunnel with him!" Sherman had, indeed, come prepared to fight, and everyone knew it.

Still there was one other thing that Sherman brought with him into Georgia. He brought a tornado, a dynamo, a self propelled, destructive force of the greatest magnitude, a terror weapon, a walking explosion that could become either the gentlest, most loving kitten, or a horribly vindictive whirlwind to all who stood in the way. She attacked Confederates and Yankees alike and her name was Mary Ann Bickerdyke.

This remarkable woman, like her more famous colleagues Clara Barton and Dorethea Dix, affixed herself to the nearest Union hospital as soon as the war began. Once there, she immediately demanded that conditions for wounded Union soldiers be improved. Standing on that very first day in a rude mixture of mud, blood, vomit, severed limbs, and human excrement that made up the floor of the first field hospital tent she happened to enter, she was appalled at the conditions. That very moment, she began her work, a holy, hell-fire crusade for better treatment of the Union and Confederate wounded.

She commenced on that first day by administering a thorough and complete cursing aimed, in some general way, at the nearest doctor she could find. Her outraged shouts drew the attention of everyone within a hundred yards, and some said, everyone in the next county. Soldiers nearby began to blush as she used a string of vile invective that would have embarrassed any sailor in the world in those days. The wounded hid under their sheets as she ranted on and on, bemoaning the conditions, the filth, in the hospital tent and demanding in the most vulgar and undiplomatic way that the tent be cleaned at once. It was so bad that the poor doctor himself had to be treated for what would later become known as shell shock.

Within minutes that particular hospital tent was moved to dry ground, and Bickerdyke moved on to the next, never even looking back, nor did she ever let go of that righteous fight for better conditions for the wounded. She drafted nurses, she collected bandages, and she demanded cleanliness in her hospitals. She helped bury the mountains of severed limbs that rotted beside every surgeon's tent, sometimes digging the holes herself, and she scavenged for, or simply stole, food for the wounded nearly every day. When various quartermasters complained, Sherman merely turned a blind eye. She was the only woman he allowed into his camp, though that didn't take into account the hundreds of whores who followed along, at a discrete distance behind his ever-advancing forces.

Given her abject disregard of anything that stood in the way of her obtaining better food and care for the wounded, Bickerdyke was roundly hated by the Union medical corps. She did not suffer fools well, and most Union doctors were fools, more ready to cut off a limb than carefully examine or care for the patient. Some doctors called her "the Cyclone;" others used terms such as tornado, damned nuisance, and a few others that are unprintable, even by standards today.

Still this woman did a service for the wounded that all could appreciate. She fought all her fights, angering everyone, all for the sake of "her boys." She remained with the Union forces, and cared for her boys in Sherman's Fifteenth Corps until long after the war ended, resigning only when the last wounded man in the Fifteenth was discharged in 1866. By that point, she was almost worshiped by the thousands of men that her actions had saved. In the fall of 1865, after the war was over, she was asked by Sherman to ride with him at the vanguard of the "Fighting Fifteenth," as they rode in the Union victory parade in New York City. Of all the names, insulting, degrading, or downright vulgar, used about this woman, she preferred the one used by scores of thousands of wounded men, "Mother Bickerdyke."

Sherman had heard many complaints of her iron-fisted tactics in obtaining clean sheets, bandages, and good food for the wounded. Once, he found himself listening to another complaint from yet another doctor whose pride had been wounded by this heavy-handed woman. When the doctor asked if Sherman proposed to do anything, his reply was simple. "Mother Bickerdyke ranks me! Hell! She outranks Lincoln!"

That statement is more important than one might realize initially. When he made that statement, Sherman was in command of over 100,000 men, the second largest army in the world at that moment, second only to Grant's Union Army in Virginia. It could be argued that Sherman was the second most powerful man in the world, but even he could not stop Bickerdyke! She was a force of nature, a tower of strength. Along with Clara Barton and Dorethea Dix, Mother Bickerdyke created what is now known as battlefield medical care. In a day when women generally held little influence and no real political power, it is an ironclad certainty that Dix, Clara Barton, and Mother Bickerdyke changed the world.

Thus, did Sherman and his 100,000 man Union force march forth from Chattanooga on May 6, 1864. Even as they began their trek southward, Sherman's men sang a new marching song; a song that both took a swing at their enemies in Georgia and promised freedom to all men. It was a song that angered any southerner who heard it, because it seemingly invited the very thing southerners feared most, slave rebellion! Moreover, it arrogantly assumed the ultimate Union victory over the Confederate Army of Tennessee, an army that was then encamped in north Georgia. Thus this song did exactly what battle songs are supposed to do; it both inspired the men and it pissed off all the right people.

It was, in essence, a Union song, a song of their beloved flag, the Star Spangled Banner of the USA.

*Hurrah! Hurrah! We bring the Jubilee!*
*Hurrah! Hurrah! It's that flag that makes you free!*
*So we'll sing our chorus from the mountains to the sea!*
*While we're marchin' through Georgia!*

## The Battle of Rocky Face Ridge, Dalton, GA

Rocky Face Ridge is the name of a long, relatively low mountain just northwest of Dalton, Georgia, and in this case, the name accurately describes the mountain. Standing three thousand, two hundred feet above sea level, and just over a thousand feet above the valley below, Rocky Face, with its granite protrusions on both sides, presented a formidable obstacle to Sherman's advance into Georgia. The mountain runs from the northeast to the southwest, sitting exactly across Sherman's planned route. Sherman wanted to follow the route of the Western and Atlanta Railroad all the way to Atlanta, since that railroad would be the supply line for his massive army. As you might have guessed, that railroad cut through Rocky Face Ridge to the northwest of Dalton, just below a granite formation known as Buzzard's Roost.

One other pass cut through the mountain. Dug Gap was three miles further south and, like Buzzard Roost, it was heavily defended by the Confederates. Eighteen miles further south, Rocky Face Ridge ended at Snake Creek Gap, but that was nearly twenty miles away from the anticipated battle, so General Joe Johnston, who then commanded the Confederate forces, was sure it would play no part in the coming fight. He didn't even place guards at Snake Creek Gap. After all, he couldn't guard everything!

Thus in May of 1864, Johnston's Confederate Army of Tennessee was heavily dug in along the top of Rocky Face, with extra strength at Buzzard Roost and Dug Gap. From there, Johnston's Confederate line then cut to the right down the eastern slope of Rocky Face, descending into Crow Valley and stretching some three miles to the east. Just to slow Sherman up a bit, the Confederates had created one more surprise for him astride the gap below Buzzard Roost. By damning the creek that ran through that gap in Rocky Face, the Confederates had constructed an obstacle that Sherman could neither bypass nor ignore, a two hundred acre lake! If Sherman's engineers even tried to use his thousands of pontoons to bridge the lake, the Confederates atop Buzzard Roost could cut them down before they could even hope to construct a decent bridge.

Most folks today, traveling either north or south along Interstate 75, don't even know they're running right through a battlefield, and they would be sorely surprised to know they'd just driven through what was once a lake! Of course, the lake is long gone, but in May of 1864, it was there, right in the gap below

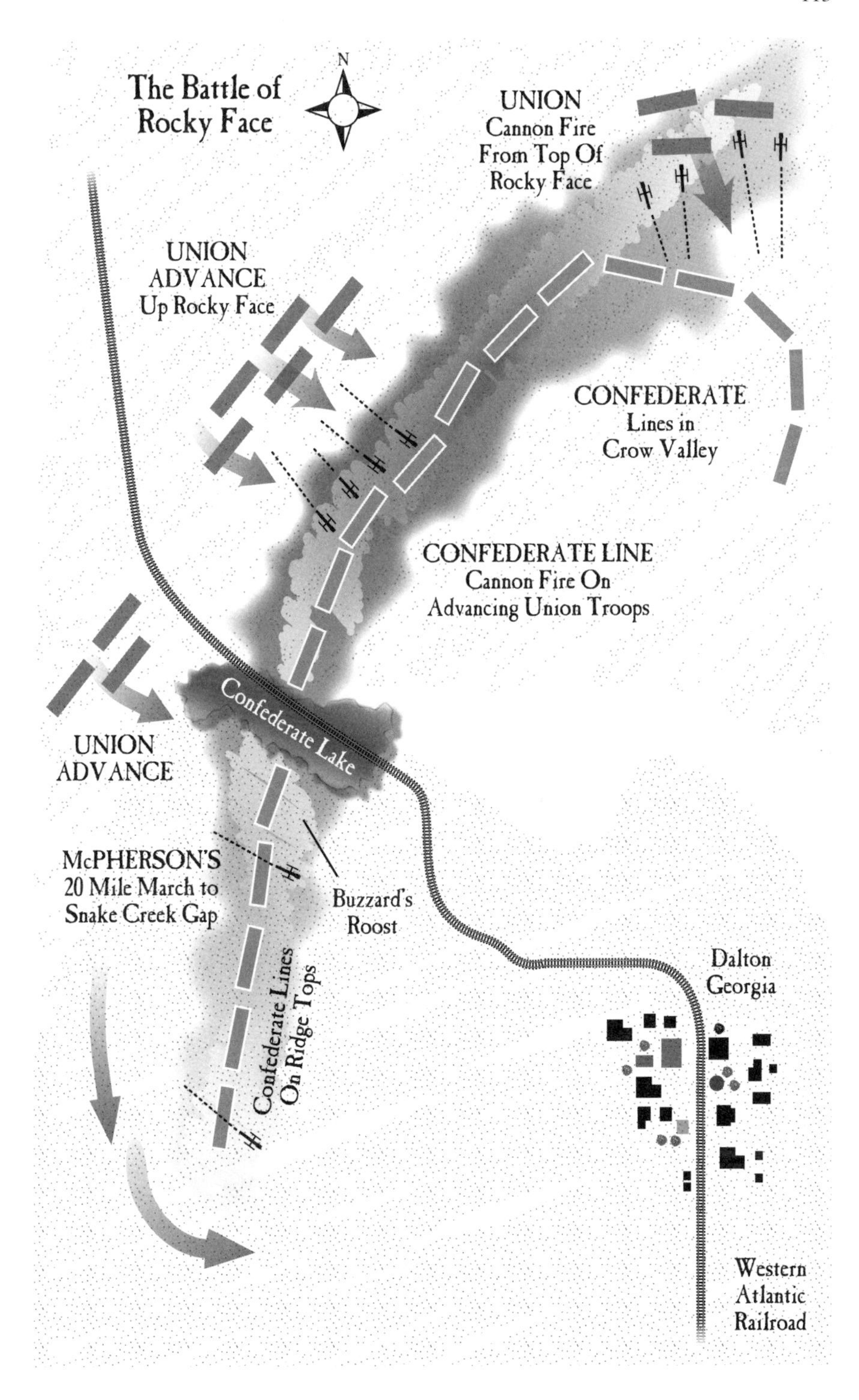
The Battle of
Rocky Face
N
UNION
Cannon Fire
From Top Of
Rocky Face
UNION
ADVANCE
Up Rocky Face
CONFEDERATE
Lines in
Crow Valley
CONFEDERATE LINE
Cannon Fire On
Advancing Union Troops
Confederate Lake
UNION
ADVANCE
McPHERSON'S
20 Mile March to
Snake Creek Gap
Buzzard's
Roost
Confederate Lines
On Ridge Tops
Dalton
Georgia
Western
Atlantic
Railroad

Buzzard Roost, and smack in the middle of Sherman's way. Those near-vertical granite walls of Rocky Face Ridge virtually guaranteed that no Union assault up that mountainside would be successful, and Sherman's men surely couldn't walk on water. Indeed, that fight, like most mountain battles, would have to take place mostly in the passes below.

Jamie Turnbull was back with the regiment by early March. Owen Collins, promoted to Captain, had been in nominal charge of the regiment for those last months, and much to Jamie's surprise, when he returned he was immediately promoted to major, and given command of the Fourth Georgia Infantry once again. Thus, he began a minimal training regime to take in his new recruits, but basically he did what ninety-thousand other Confederates were doing in their camps atop Rocky Face and in Crow Valley—he was waiting for the Yankees.

Almost as soon as Sherman moved out of Chattanooga, he confronted a small Confederate cavalry force at a minor outpost called Tunnel Hill, but he'd swept that force aside on May 7 without slowing his army down in the least. By that evening he was staring at a new lake that wasn't on any of his maps—it wasn't supposed to be there—just below Rocky Face Ridge, a mountain that he could clearly see was bristling with Confederate rifles and cannon. He had to plan something to counter that unexpected lake, not to mention the unassailable Rocky Face defenses, and one can be sure, as that feisty red-head looked over these formidable problems, he was one pissed off Yankee! In that frame of mind, he called together his staff on the evening of May 7, and made his plans.

It was at exactly this point in history that the cleverness of Billy Sherman became apparent. He would rather flank an opponent than fight one, particularly in positions that his enemy had already fortified. That simple, incredibly wise choice on Sherman's part would save scores of thousands of lives over the next two years, and it would take the Confederates a considerable while to realize that this was Sherman's preferred mode of attack. Again and again in the coming months, Sherman would use a "right hook" flanking maneuver to bypass Johnston's Confederate army. He'd send a regiment, a corps, or an entire army many miles to his right, thus flanking the Confederate defensive works.

Moreover Sherman had not one army, but three under his command, and that gave him considerable flexibility in his planning. General Hap Thomas, the "Rock of Chickamauga," commanded a force of 35,000 men, known as the Army of the Cumberland. General Schofield commanded the Army of the Ohio, a 30,000 man Union force, while General McPherson commanded the mighty Army of the Tennessee, 35,000 strong. All three of those Union armies were veteran forces, experienced men bloodied in numerous previous fights. Each would certainly do the duties Sherman assigned. Opposing those Union armies, was Joe Johnston's Confederate Army of Tennessee, and once again, the Confederate Army of Tennessee would fight the Union Army of *THE* Tennessee, just as it had at Chickamauga the previous September.

On May 8, Sherman made his first major move in Georgia. He ordered Schofield's Army of the Ohio to descend into Crow Valley and attack the Confederate forces arrayed before the small mountain town of Dalton. He also ordered General Hap Thomas to make a demonstration attack directly against Rocky Face Ridge, the new, nameless lake be damned!

In the War Between the States, as in many subsequent wars, it has often been advantageous to make demonstration attacks, so Thomas would stage a show against Rocky Face. Historically, such demonstrations were intended to confuse the enemy, and make him think the main attack was coming from a different direction. Thus, General Thomas' attack, it was hoped, would deflect some attention away from General Schofield's move down the Crow Valley. Of course, demonstrations are only useful when they are believable, so only the generals and higher commanders in the Union forces knew which attack was a "demonstration" and which wasn't. Moreover, if you'd been a Union private in Thomas' army looking at the planned attack route straight up Rocky Face Ridge, you'd certainly not give a hoot that your attack was "just a demonstration" even if you'd been privy to that knowledge. You could easily get killed, and many did get killed, in such demonstration attacks. That willingness to sacrifice men in demonstration attacks was, ultimately, the only thing that made demonstration attacks work!

One veteran sergeant in Thomas' Army of the Cumberland looked up at the ridge from the shoreline of the lake almost a thousand feet below. After brief reflection, he said, "Hope you boys can all swim. Way them Rebels shoot, they'll pick us all off'n those rocks right quick, but the lake 'll break our fall!"

Another wasn't that optimistic. He responded. "This'll surely be our grave, boys. Now on your feet and let's get up that damned ridge."

## The Fight On Rocky Face Ridge

Duncan Carmichael, Owen Collins, Batty Prather and the rest of Major Turnbull's Fourth Georgia Regiment looked down from Buzzards Roost, at the advancing Union force in utter disbelief. Duncan spoke first. "They really that stupid? You recon' they'll come all the way up here, right under our guns?"

Batty was hiding behind a rock, just to Duncan's right. "Stupid or not, they's sure as hell commin' up them damn rocks! In a hunert' yards or so, I recon we'll have more to shoot at than we ever figured!" Batty thus summarized the beliefs of most of the men atop Rocky Face Ridge—not a one believed that the Union army would really try to scale those rocks below, particularly under fire.

Jake and Lee Lovorn, two twin brothers who were among the newer recruits to the Georgia Fourth, were hiding behind some cut-oak timbers on Duncan's other side. They were committed to the Grand Cause of the Confederacy, and had done well in their training, but had never before faced a battle. They came from a dirt-poor family near Clarkesville, Georgia, a family that owned no slaves, but they had a good upbringing, and they knew enough to listen to the more experienced men. Normally they kept their mouth shut, at least around the veterans like Duncan, Batty, or Captain Collins. Still Lee was known to run his mouth from time to time, and he couldn't restrain himself, at that moment. "I didn't think there'd be this many of 'um!"

Batty, who was very glad to be the "youngster" in the company no longer, answered. "That ain't too many. Not nearly what we see'd at Chickamauga Creek!"

Duncan, ever the wily veteran, was almost a god to the Lovorn brothers, and most of the other new recruits. "Don't take but one to put a bullet in your ass! Now get your mind on what matters. Check your load, get your next powder packet ready, and clear your rifle sights. We'll be shootin' of'n this mountain in a minute or so, and you'll need to load faster'n you ever done before!"

Lee and Jake responded together. "Yes Sir!" They couldn't have cared less that Duncan held almost the same rank as they did. He'd faced Yankees before, just like Batty Prather and Captain Collins, so he deserved the "Sir!" He definitely outranked them, at least in their eyes.

At just that moment, Major Turnbull and his slave, Sampson rode up. Turnbull dismounted twenty feet or so behind them and, tossing his reins to his man, walked on up to the line. The Lovorn boys didn't know the Major at all, having never been introduced to him before. Still they'd heard he'd been at Chickamauga, and that the other men thought highly of him. However their blood ran cold and their expression froze over, as Major Turnbull began to curse at Duncan Carmichael right in front of their eyes. What's more, they almost fainted when Duncan cursed back at their new officer!

"Damn you, Carmichael! Are you hidin' from them damn Yankees again?"

"Go on straight to hell, Jamie. I ain't got no damn time right now. You go on and piss on somebody else's boots for a change? We 'bout to get real busy up here." Duncan didn't even turn around to face the Major! Thus did two friends relieve a bit of stress just before the Rocky Face fight began. These two men had been friends since forever, and had fought and bled together before at Chickamauga Creek. What's more, they were both about to get into it again with the damned Yankees, so rank be damned. At such moments, friendship, and respect of each other's fighting skills matter most.

The Lovorn boys were terrified for only a moment, since they soon realized that Batty Prather was grinning from ear to ear! By then Captain Collins had walked up to join the talk, but even he knew not to interrupt the Major and Duncan Carmichael.

The Major then looked down the mountain. "Damn Duncan. They really are commin' up that hill, ain't they? I didn't believe it when the messenger brought me the news."

"We're in for something of a fight, for sure, Sir," Batty answered. "But we'll give 'um hell long before they get near us."

"I think so too, Jamie," Duncan said. "It'll be a turkey shoot from here, and if'n them young bucks over there can hit the broad side of a barn with those rifles, we'll be okay, I recon."

Jamie responded. "That's exactly what I wanted to hear, Duncan. You and Batty keep your heads down, and your guns busy. I've ordered cannon-fire when they come fifty yards closer, so you boys open when you can." Jamie then looked over at the new recruits. "You're the Lovorn boys, ain't ya?"

The brothers both responded with a nod, surprised that the Major knew their names. They were much too scared to talk, lest they be cursed too! However, another new recruit spoke up at that moment. Mike Wellspeak had, for some reason, partnered up with Batty, and at just that moment he offered his opinion. "We'll get 'um all, Sir. We can do it!" We've all hunted in these mountains before."

Jamie responded to them all by supporting his subordinate. "Well, listen to the veterans, and all of you follow command of Captain Collins here. We'll all do our duty."

Wellspeak's judgment was sound on the bit about hunting in mountains, even given his relatively limited education. He was mostly illiterate, having never had the opportunity for much schooling. He could read and sign his name, and his counting wasn't so bad. His major saving grace was his shooting. It was rumored that he could hit a gnat on a squirrel's butt with his rifle at a hundred yards, though, in truth, most mountain men would have used a different term for "butt." In his holler in the rugged hills of Rabun County, Georgia, he routinely downed moving deer at two or even three hundred yards, so his assessment of shooting in mountainous terrain was spot on.

When hunting in flat terrain, a rifle shot is relatively easy to aim; simply gage the distance, elevate the shot if necessary, and lead the target a bit. However, in mountainous terrain, the inexperienced hunter will tend to overshoot when firing uphill, or undershoot when firing downhill. In short, unless you've hunted in mountains before, your judgment of the slope is likely to be off somewhat, and Wellspeak knew that lesson well. Moreover, most of the boys in the Fourth Georgia did too; most of those men were from the Georgia Blue Ridge. They were likely to get the aim right on that steep mountain slope, and if they were lucky, the damn Yankees wouldn't.

"I think you're right, Wellspeak. Maybe the Yankees won't understand mountain shooting." Jamie replied. "At any rate, Wellspeak, you and you Lovorn boys; you need to keep your eyes on Duncan and Batty here. Do what they do, or what they tell ya. They been through this before. Do as you're told, and follow Captain Collin's orders. You'll be alright."

"Yes Sir!"

Collins had, by then walked off to inspect another section of the line, so Duncan responded. "We'll keep an eye on 'um Major. Just you and Sampson take care too! You're mighty big targets sittin' high up there, on that damn horse of yours!"

Jamie smiled at the back of his friend's head—Duncan had never once turned around. "I'll do that Duncan. You take care of things here, and take care of these new boys, and I'll see you when it's over." Again he looked over at the faces of Wellspeak and the Lovorn brothers. For a moment, Jamie thought, they're all so young; they can't be soldiers. On that day, Wellspeak was seventeen and the Lovorn brothers were a mere sixteen, only two years younger than Jamie himself.

Without saying another word, Jamie mounted his horse and with Sampson on his mount in the rear, Major Turnbull departed, like Captain Collins, to check on other sections of his line.

The Confederate cannon on the top of Rocky Face Ridge opened up on the Union forces below at 10:00 AM on the morning of May 8, 1863. Thirty four Napoleons were firing in battery, and the sound was all consuming. Duncan and Batty both grinned when they noticed the wet spot on Lee Lovorn's pants, once the cannon roared—the same thing had happened to them at Chickamauga. Still, the Confederate veterans atop that ridge were glad to hear those earth-shaking blasts, and see the heavy fire and smoke pour down the mountain. The new boys, however were terrified!

Today few Americans have ever heard thirty-four fully loaded cannon fire at once. Even most demonstration firings of Civil War cannon today involve only one or two cannon, and those demonstration firings typically fire only about one fourth a load of powder, compared to what was actually used in the War Between the States. No one alive today has ever heard a sound like thirty-four, fully loaded Napoleons.

The fight on Rocky Face Ridge, ultimately turned out to be reversed from the earlier Chickamauga battle. In this fight, the "Rock of Chickamauga" story line was reversed; Confederates were atop the hill at Rocky Face Ridge, and their cannon were slaughtering the men below, firing down the steep mountainside.

This time, it was a Yankee army advancing up the steep slopes. Like that earlier Chickamauga fight, the army advancing up the steep hill-side would take more casualties, and once again, the terrain advantage was difficult to overcome. In simple terms, it is nearly impossible to fire a rifle and climb a mountain at the same time.

Still Thomas' Army of the Cumberland pressed on, and thus did they accomplish what Sherman hoped. Their demonstration did distract attention from the true line of advance. Within fifteen minutes of Jamie's departure, all of the riflemen atop Rocky Face, including Wellspeak and the Lovorn brothers, were firing as quickly as they could reload. The Yankees below were advancing at what seemed to be a relatively slow pace, however, and at times it was difficult to find a target.

Batty wasn't the first to notice, but he was the first to speak about it. In one lull in the fighting, even the Confederate cannon got quiet, and Batty shouted. "It almost seems like them Yankees ain't in the fight, don't it Duncan? I cain't remember a single minute at Snodgrass Hill when I couldn't see a man to shoot at, but here, sometimes, they just ain't nobody movin' down there!"

Duncan once again carried on a conversation without ever taking his eyes from the enemy to his front. "Does seem that way, don't it Batty. I recon' them boys ain't all that much in this fight. Cain't blame 'um though, not when they is down there looking up at this damn hill and these damn cannon!"

Lee Lovorn had heard the comments, and couldn't believe it. Did these two veterans really want more Yankees coming up all at once? He looked over at his brother, silently communicating as brothers often can, his thoughts asking the unspoken question; "What the hell are we in for if those damn Yankees send even more men up that mountain?"

The men all took a few moments to clean their sights, and wash their mouths out with a bit of water. Duncan spoke next. "Next time we got a shot, I want you new men, Wellspeak and you Lovorn boys, to take it. Then, instead of loadin' up again, clean out your rifle. Batty and I'll hold our shot, and clean our guns after we fire next time. Just then, one Yankee poked his head above a rock about one hundred and ten yards down the mountain, and that was enough to get Wellspeak and both of the Lovorn boys to fire. The Lovorns missed, but Wellspeak dropped the man. Of course none of those atop that mountain knew whose aim had been true. One of the Napoleon cannon above them also fired, blowing up the body of the dead Yankee. The new boys then began to clean out their breaches with whatever rags they could grab.

It was at that moment that Lee began to laugh. "Damn, Jake. Your face is blacker 'n grandma's kettle!" And so it was. Neither Wellspeak nor the Lovorns had been in a battle before, and thus, none had rapid-fired their rifles before, at least not for an hour and twenty minutes, as they had on that day. None of those new men had ever been forced to tear open powder-packets, one behind the other with his teeth before, so none had ever established that ring of black powder, spit, and sweat around his mouth prior to the battle that day. By that point all of the men within earshot were grinning, and all, like Wellspeak and the Lovorns, had black rings around their mouths.

Another Yankee down the hill ran from one rock to another, but he never made it, as Wellspeak, along with Batty and Duncan, took a shot. All three hit that man, a poor farmer from upstate Kentucky, who thus died on the slope of Rocky Face Ridge in north Georgia. He left a wife and five small children alone on that farm in those upstate Kentucky hills. The farm was sold out of the family, and strangely enough scores of thousands of Americans pass through that very farm each year. It now comprises part of the land purchased by the state of Ohio to foster the growth of the famous Ohio city that sits just across the river; that very farm is now famous, as a part of the Cincinnati International Airport, an airport for an Ohio City that, nevertheless, sits just across the river in northern Kentucky!

Just after that Yankee died, the Union commanders ordered a further assault up the hill. Again they charged into those deadly Confederate guns. The result was the same—thirty more minutes of one-sided slaughter, but again, the veterans atop Rocky Face Ridge all thought to themselves, "Them boys ain't really coming that hard. I wonder why?"

At that moment both Captain Collins and Major Turnbull were standing close enough to have the same observation, with Sampson, as ever, only five feet away. Turnbull said to no one in particular, "I'm gonna send a runner to tell General Cleburne and General Johnston that very thing; this is only a demonstration at Rocky Face."

Had they had a bird's eye view of the larger battle area, they might have understood more. While the Union advance up Buzzard Roost was seemingly half-hearted, the fight further to the north atop Rocky Face Ridge was much more serious. Sherman had assigned Thomas the demonstration at Buzzard Roost, and up the western side of Rocky Face Ridge, but Schofield's Army of the Ohio, was to fight along the top of Rocky Face, and down in the Crow Valley to the east of the ridgeline, pressing on towards Dalton. Johnston didn't have enough Confederates to turn the twenty mile long Rocky Face into a completely solid fortress, so at the northern end of the mountain, the Union Army of the Ohio simply marched unopposed up to the top of the ridge. From that point, they advanced southward both along the top of Rocky Face and in Crow Valley below.

Once Johnston had received reports from Turnbull and several other line commanders, he began to suspect that Sherman had placed his main advance axis down the Crow Valley, and not at the defenses at Rocky Face. Johnston had created a fortress of about a mile in length northward from the Buzzard

Roost, and then his line turned abruptly eastward. In this area, at the turn of the line and in the valley to the east, the Confederate line was pressed to a much greater degree. As another report of the fighting came in, Johnston finally became convinced that Sherman's main effort would come from the north down Crow Valley.

Still the fighting up there on the north end Rocky Face and in Crow Valley below was close, bloody, and brutal. At one point, the Union force atop the ridge forced the Confederates back several hundred yards, and that allowed the few Union cannon atop the mountain to fire down into the Confederate trenches and earthworks in the Crow Valley below. So occurred an anomaly that was truly unique, a fight that happened only at Rocky Face Ridge during the entire War Between the States. At that point, the mountain was simultaneously occupied by two opposing armies, each of which was firing at the enemy force in the valley below. While Confederates cannon at Buzzard Roost and Rocky Face on the south end fired at the Yankees to the west, the Union cannon atop the north end of the same mountain, fired at the Confederate trenches below and to the east, in Crow Valley. The battle was pressed on all fronts, as well as at Dug Gap, some four miles below Buzzard Roost, where a Confederate blocking force of a thousand men and ten Napoleons was able to stop the Union advance cold. On May 8 and 9, those battles raged, sometimes hot rifle and cannon fire was exchanged, but at other times an unexpected lull would, once again settle over the field.

On both days, the Union Army of the Cumberland had sent a strong force, some three thousand men, to reach the dam that had created the lake in the pass below Buzzard Roost. If they could blow up that dam, the lake would drain and they might be able to force their way through the valley. However, each time, the Confederate fire from Buzzard Roost forced them back. The fight seemed a stalemate, and it remained that way until a bunch of damn Yankees showed up unexpectedly, near Johnston's food supplies.

## Guess Who's Coming to Dinner?

In early May of 1864, the year of Sherman's advance on Atlanta, the question, "Guess who's coming to dinner?" was enough to cause genuine panic in every Confederate heart, from the lowly Confederate private all the way up to General Johnston, the highest Confederate commander. In fact, no housewife hearing that question from her husband today ever feared the unexpected guest more than did General Joe Johnston himself, Commander of the Army of Tennessee, CSA. Of course, he wasn't exactly the first Confederate to ask himself that question on the morning of May 9. That dubious honor goes to a lowly private,

Artemis Stigwell, a sixteen year old recruit who had only recently enlisted in the 23rd Alabama Infantry. It was Stigwell who spotted the unexpected Yankees first.

With a name like Artemis Stigwell, this unfortunate fellow inevitably acquired the nickname "Stiggy" from his Confederate mess-mates. They frequently made "Stiggy Stigwell" a relatively new recruit not to mention a mere boy, get up early to fix breakfast for the several men in his mess. The fare varied from corn meal to fatty bacon, but regardless of the rations, Stiggy Stigwell was always up early, cooking for his group. Around 6:30 AM on May 9, 1864, with the 23rd Alabama Infantry encamped twelve miles south of Dalton, at a small town called Resaca, Stiggy made his discovery. The 23rd Alabama was in route to join the fight up on Rocky Face near Dalton, that morning when Stiggy got up to do his morning chores. Of course, when he awoke he first felt, as do all men, the call of nature. So prior to lighting the morning fire, Stiggy climbed a small hill to the east of Resaca to take his morning piss.

Atop the hill, he relaxed in the early morning sun as men frequently do, and standing there with his britches wide open, he calmly sprayed the few spring flowers growing there on the side of the hill. Then, as nature took her course, he casually glanced across the valley to his side, and his blood nearly froze at the sight!

Standing there with his family jewels still in his hand, he faced five thousand enemy soldiers, most of whom were, by then, carefully taking aim, wanting nothing more than to kill Stiggy as he relieved himself. It seemed, at least to Stiggy, that he was looking at the whole damn Yankee army, and that was the very moment that Stiggy Stigwell made history. As he briefly turned towards the Yankees, he became the only man in the entire history of the Confederacy to have been so proud of his manhood, that he actually pointed it directly into the bore of five thousand Yankee rifles. In retrospect we'll merely note how quickly a gently flowing stream can dry up when a man is facing certain death from that many guns.

Still, Stiggy was lucky that the moment didn't last long. He was young but he was not a fool, so he quickly surmised that his particular weapon, at that moment, was somewhat overmatched. Before he could even get his britches buttoned again, and hopefully a few seconds after his flowing stream ceased, Stiggy was running back down the hill toward his commander doing a respectable impression of Paul Revere, with a slightly different theme. As a few Yankee rifles fired at his backside, he ran downhill in the opposite direction shouting at the top of his lungs "The Yankees are coming! The Yankees are coming!"

While Sherman had used two of his Yankee armies at Rocky Face Ridge, he'd done what he was always inclined to do; he'd sent a sizable force well to his right, to threaten the Confederate supply line, and in retrospect we can consider this as the first "right hook" punch thrown by Sherman's advancing army. It would not be the last on the march to Atlanta. Sherman, who always sought to avoid a major, bloody battle, had sent an entire Union army some twenty miles around the Confederate left flank, and once there, General McPherson and his Union Army of the Tennessee had seized Snake Creek Gap. Again, that gap was so far from the battlefield at Rocky Face that Johnston's Confederates had not even bothered to guard it, and like a frightened rabbit peeking up from his hole in the spring, McPherson sent a small group of only five thousand one mile forward to take a look through the pass. Of course, McPherson realized he'd captured an important gap that could ultimately move Sherman's Union armies much further toward Atlanta, so he dispatched a rider telling Sherman of his good fortune immediately.

Only an hour later, when Sherman heard the news in his tent, he grinned from ear to ear, and shouted to his command staff, "Get the hell in here! We need to plan! I've got Joe Johnston dead!" That assessment, at that moment, wasn't far from the truth. Had McPherson moved his army forward, he would have captured Resaca easily. Besides Stiggy Stigwell, only about eight hundred Confederates were in Resaca that morning. Thus, McPherson's force could have captured the town, moved north, and had his move been quick, he could have virtually encircled Johnston's entire Confederate army!

However one never knows exactly where one stands in battle, and the situation on the front lines always looks a bit more bleak than it might in a command tent many miles away. Back at the head of Snake Creek Gap, McPherson didn't really understand what he might be up against. He'd sent a couple of regiments through the gap and on to the outskirts of Resaca, the small, insignificant railroad town only a mile distant. Of course, that happened to be exactly where Johnston's quartermasters had parked their massive pool of supply wagons, and they were using the rail yard there, to stage the entire battle at Dalton. Thus, train after train of Confederate supplies—food, cannon, ammunition, pigs and cattle on the hoof—all were unloaded in Resaca, and moved by wagon up to Johnston's army in Dalton. Thousands of bullets, cans of beans, kegs of powder, cannon shot, and hundreds of cattle, were literally sitting in railcars on those rail sidings at Resaca, just waiting to be either unloaded by Johnston's men or captured by the Union forces. In fact, the 23rd Alabama was the only sizable Confederate unit on the ground that morning, and they were only there, since that is where the previous evening found them in route to the fight up at Dalton.

Thus the frightening answer to General Johnston's age old question, who's coming to dinner? In that case, a total of thirty-five thousand men; a whole damn Yankee army!

Within fifteen minutes of Stiggy's morning pee, every man in the 23rd Alabama had climbed that hill, and was digging like crazy to toss up some earthwork defenses. They worked atop a small hill to the west of the Resaca railhead, well within sight of the town itself, digging their trenches and quickly felling trees. No defenses had been placed there previously because no one expected a battle there, but even sleepy men can dig amazingly quickly when their lives depend on it. On that particular morning, digging was the thing to do!

Meanwhile the Union General McPherson waited about two miles away with his additional troops. Had he known Resaca was defended only by accident, as it were, with only the one small Alabama brigade in residence, no doubt he would have moved on up that hill and captured the lot! Still he didn't know what might be waiting for him in Resaca, and his orders were merely to capture Snake Creek Gap, and not to move on the Resaca railroad. Thus he decided to await word from General Sherman. On such vagrancies of luck do battles sometimes hinge. Eight-hundred Confederates built defenses that should have been built previously while an army of thirty-five thousand didn't attack, because neither side expected the other to be there. Ultimately neither side knew what the hell was going on!

Thus Stiggy Stigwell's bodily functions had briefly stopped an entire Yankee army, or from another perspective, Stiggy had saved the entire Confederate Army of Tennessee. In retrospect, perhaps his personal "weapon" was a bit stronger than he had thought! Rather funny to note that, when all is said and done, Stiggy's piss was probably one of the most influential bodily functions in history.

About the same time that Sherman got word from McPherson and ordered his Union forces to disengage from their fight at Rocky Face, the Confederate commander, Joe Johnston, likewise received word that his supply line was in danger. His dispatch from Resaca indicated that a Yankee force of indeterminate size was through Snake Creek Gap and was holding before they moved on Resaca, and that only the 23rd Alabama was there to defend the railhead. Within two minutes Johnston had sent his cavalry to the relief of that Alabama unit, and only a bit later, within thirty minutes, he had given orders to his corps commanders; the Confederates would withdraw from their positions on Rocky Face and rush twelve miles to the south to build defenses at Resaca. They had to defend their supply line, the Western and Atlantic Railroad, at all costs!

Thus did both armies move a bit further down the road towards Atlanta.

## Moving On Down The Road

As the situation became more clear in Resaca, both commanders wanted to be the first on the scene, but neither Sherman nor Johnston could move their massive armies quickly. That is exactly how the contingencies and hazards of mountain travel impacted this fight. While Sherman's armies had to travel over twenty miles behind and through the mountains, on small paths and little used wagon roads, Johnston's Confederates had the shorter, more direct route, and a much better set of roads. Johnston won the race, and within a fortnight, both armies had effectively side-stepped nearly twenty miles of mountains, as the fight moved to Resaca, Georgia.

"Wouldn't mind riding that swayback horse o' yours, Major! Could surely rest my feet a bit." Duncan shouted to his friend and commander, Major Jamie Turnbull, as they moved down the road, a road now known as Highway 41 in north Georgia, from Dalton to Resaca. It had taken three days for their turn to come, but as the armies disengaged at Rocky-Face, the time came for the Fourth Georgia Infantry to move out, and take up positions north of the railhead town. The march would take only a day.

At that point, even the newer guys, the Lovorn brothers and Wellspeak, knew that Duncan could joke with their commander in ways none of the others dared. Even Batty who'd been with the unit since Chickamauga wouldn't have asked to ride the Major's horse!

Jamie just smiled to himself, as he rode beside his men, then he replied. "Recon you could use a bit of exercise there, Carmichael. You're getting a bit pudgy around the mid-section, and this little walk'll do you some good. Too much beans and bacon, I recon."

The troops laughed, along with both the Major and Duncan. At that moment, all knew that both beans and bacon were in short supply, and no man could possibly have had too much! Still, this was the commander any fighting man would want; a serious man who minded his troops and knew his way around a battlefield, but who could still, on occasion, joke with his men. Not a man in the entire Fourth Georgia would have wanted a different commander than this brash, young, veteran, Major Jamie Turnbull.

Captain Owen Collins, as second in command, was marching along beside the Fourth Georgia. He then asked, "Major, do you know where we're goin?"

Jamie didn't look back at the man behind him, but he measured his words, certain that they would be repeated down the entire line. "I've been told we'll prepare defenses in a town called Resaca to protect the Western and Atlantic Railroad yard."

"Ain't that the same railroad that was in Dalton?" Batty asked. "If'n it was there too, don't it look like we could 'a road a train car down there instead of marching?"

To Wellspeak, the Lovorn boys, Duncan Carmichael and most everyone else in the marching line, that seemed to be a reasonable question, but most of those veterans were long past expecting the army to make sense. When the Major failed to answer, Owen took it upon himself to respond. "Don't you boys worry the Major, any more now. Besides, most of you is just like Duncan here—getting pudgy around the middle. You could all use a good walk this fine day!" At that most of the men laughed, including Major Turnbull and his man, Sampson, who, as always was riding his mule right behind his master.

When the Fourth Georgia arrived on the outskirts of Resaca only an hour later, they came upon a filthy looking group of exhausted men resting beneath some trees. Major Turnbull shouted down to the first man he saw, a private from the look of it. "Boy! You there! Where is the headquarters tent for Cleburne's Division?"

Stiggy Stigwell, had been digging trenches for three solid days, along with the rest of the 23rd Alabama, and he was in no mood to suffer foolish questions from some officer he didn't even know. Still, the loud Major was an officer, so Stiggy quickly came to his feet, tossed off a poor facsimile of a salute, and then provided the best answer he could. "Sorry, Sir. Not sure about any particular division headquarters, since so many have come to town in the last couple o' days. Most of 'um have set up a bit more towards downtown, just around that turn in the road, but most of the units getting here this mornin' are taking to the line along here." With that, Stiggy pointed to the nearly completed defensive works to his rear.

Jamie made a calculated decision, since he'd been given no orders on where to go. "Captain Collins, you and the men get off the road and rest down here in those woods for a time, while I find out where we are supposed to be. I should be back in an hour or so, but the men could use a rest. Have some of them replenish canteens in the river we crossed back up the road a bit."

With that Jamie and Sampson rode on around the bend, seeking information on where the Fourth Georgia was to camp. When they arrived in downtown Resaca at the depot, Jamie realized just how small the town really was. Only five stores, two churches, a depot, a blacksmith shop, and a livery graced the downtown area. He also noted a tavern on the main street, with five scantly clad females grinning back at him, standing on the second floor porch. He surmised that the tavern also served as the local whore house.

There were five or six merchant's houses, and one hog pen towards the bridge across the river in the distance, not much of a town at all really. Still, he quickly spotted a large tent near the whore house with uniformed men scurrying about, so he headed in that direction. Cleburne was not there, but General Hood was, so Jamie dismounted and tossed the reins of his horse to his man Sampson, before he entered the tent. Hood himself looked up. "Ah, Major Turnbull! The Fourth Georgia is now among us, I see! Good to have you Major. Have you placed your men in the line?"

"My respects to you, General Hood. We've only just arrived, and I was seeking General Cleburne to ascertain where he might want my regiment. My men are resting along the road just inside the new defenses to the north."

Hood looked around his tent. "General Cleburne only arrived earlier this afternoon, and as you can see he is not here at present. He is out positioning his men. Did you say you are camped by the road to the north?"

Jamie replied, "Yes Sir. Until I find where General Cleburne wants me."

"Leave your men where they are for now," Hood responded. "That is the general area in which Cleburne's Division is to man the defenses. You can probably find him out in that direction now, and that is where I'd recommend you seek him. If you have not located him within an hour, do return here, and we'll prepare some orders for the Fourth Georgia at that point."

Jamie snapped a salute, and responded, "Yes Sir," as he turned to leave the tent.

Hood however, interrupted his departure. "Major Turnbull, there is one more thing. Do you have a gentleman named Wellspeak in your unit?"

Jamie couldn't imagine why General Hood, Corps Commander, would even know the name of a new recruit in his unit, and he feared that Wellspeak had already managed to get himself into some type of trouble. Still, honesty was the only option. "Yes Sir. I have the man."

"Good!" said Hood. "Then pick up that negro sitting across the road yonder at the depot. It seems that his family has sent his servant to assist him. That negro has been respectful, but he has become a pest these last few days. Hell, he even insisted that he go to Dalton on foot, until my men stopped him. Please do take him off my hands, Sir."

Jamie managed to cover his shock, and merely replied "Yes Sir," before he saluted Hood and left the tent. He couldn't believe Wellspeak's family owned any negros. While he and other officers, all of whom were gentlemen, frequently had their servants beside them during the war, it was virtually unheard of for a private to bring a man-servant to the fight. Most families didn't own slaves at all in the south, and men who did, usually did not serve as privates in the Confederate States Army. Still, there are exceptions to every rule, and Jamie, upon leaving the headquarters tent, said to Sampson. "Sampson, go over yonder to that slave by the depot, and see if he belongs to Mike Wellspeak! It seems our new recruit now has a man-servant!"

Within a minute, Sampson returned, grinning all the while, with the other man in tow. Sampson was aware of the fact that, until that moment, only the

Major had a man-servant in the entire Fourth Georgia, and for a private to have such a servant when the other officers didn't would only confuse matters. Still he dutifully reported. "Major. This here slave does belong to the Wellspeak family and they sent him along to serve Master Wellspeak in the war."

Jamie looked over the man. "What is your name?" he said.

The slave didn't know any of the men before him, but Sampson had already informed him of who Major Turnbull was, and the fact that he was reasonably kind to his slaves. Thus the new man felt he could at least meet Jamie's eyes briefly as he spoke. "I'm called Ten Cent Bill, Suh! I've come to 'sist Master Wellspeak. I's knowd him since he's just a mite, and the Wellspeak family just got 'nuf money together to buy me for 'um!"

Jamie couldn't help but ask, "What does the Ten Cent mean?"

Ten Cent Bill replied, "Don't know, Suh! I jest been called dat since I was a wee one!" Of course, that was not true. Ten Cent Bill knew exactly where his unusual nickname had come from. He always remembered being an orphan boy, and had been sold twice before he was even nine years old. Once, when he was, yet again, on the auction block in Clarkesville, Georgia, a slave trader had looked him over, and said, "That boy is scrawny and sickly. He won't last a week in the fields in Louisiana. Hell, he aint' worth ten cents!" The name stuck and, while Ten Cent Bill did eventually get sold, he proved that early assessment of his worth to be quite wrong. He worked as hard as any of the slaves, and when he was acquired by a relative of the Wellspeak family in Clarkesville, he'd grown up knowing all of the less wealthy Wellspeak cousins. "Here's my papers, Suh!" He handed a note to Jamie Turnbull.

Jamie noted that it was not addressed directly to Private Wellspeak, but to, "Any Confederate Aurthorety." Thus, after noting the creative spelling, Jamie opened the note and read.

*"This here man is the propertie of Mike Wellspeak, Private, 4 Geiagia Enfranty. We hope he is a saverice to Mike and to the Cause in Dalltan, Geiagia. Please see hem deliveread to our son, Private Mike Wellspeak, and Thank ye.*

*God Bless Ye"*

Spelling aside, it was clear that Mike's parents wanted him to have some help in the war, and they, like Jamie, realized that owning a man-servant might even help Mike get elected officer at some point.

Jamie could only say, "Okay then. Ten Cent Bill it is. You come on along with us. We'll get you to Private Wellspeak."

"Yes Suh! And thank you, Suh," Ten Cent Bill replied, as the three of them moved back down the road, Jamie on his horse, Sampson and Ten Cent Bill, riding together on the mule, following along behind.

## Two Giants Showed Up

At that very moment on May 12 back in Dalton, the final Confederate skirmishers were withdrawing heading hastily down the road to Resaca. Before they were even out of sight, two giants walked into Dalton, and demanded to be taken to the nearest hospital. One was only five feet four, and the other stood just over five feet, so "Giants" might seem to be a strange choice of wording, but history has shown it to be accurate. The tornado that was Mother Bickerdyke was about to explode in that town, and she had Harriet Tubman in tow. As we've noted before, both are giants in history, but neither was so recognized as such on that particular day.

Never a woman to let protocol get in her way, Bickerdyke marched immediately to the building that was obviously the courthouse, and entered. Therein she found the mayor of Dalton busily writing out requests that the Union army spare the town. At that point, Sherman's army had not yet burned any town in Georgia, so the mayor was hopeful that his small hamlet might survive. He intended to give such a written request to every Union officer he could find, but he was clearly not prepared for this female tornado, and the simple authority of her voice, if not its volume, frightened him even more than the Union army which was about to arrive!

"You have some of my boys here from the XV Union Corps. I've come to care for them! We'll also tend any Confederate wounded you may have." Bickerdyke all but shouted. Tubman, obviously just a black nurse in the thinking of this southern politician, was ignored completely as she stood silently in the hallway. As the man looked over these two, Bickerdyke spoke up again. Not wanting to wait even one minute before she got to tend her men, she shouted once again. "Well, man. Where is the hospital? I have men to tend too!"

The mayor finally found his tongue and indicated. "We have four hospitals here. The depot, the Blunt House over on Thurmton Avenue, the Stone Presbyterian Church up the road a piece in Ringold, and the Cook House three blocks to the east. I believe some of the wounded are also in the back yard of this courthouse. Anyone in the square just outside can direct you to any of the other hospitals."

"Thank you. I'm sure we'll find all of them, and we've already been to the Stone Church in Ringgold. While we are here, we intend to care for our boys and the rebels alike, and I will thank you to see that appropriate food is delivered to each hospital, or I shall have to find you again! Should I require anything else, of you, I will let you know." With that Bickerdyke turned and left. The mayor, speechless, sat staring rather stupidly at her departure, and wondering who the hell she was. Tubman merely followed along, having never said a word.

As they walked across the square to the first hospital, Bickerdyke said to Tubman, "You stay with me until our boys show up in town. Then you may go and collect as many slaves, as you can. I'm sure General Sherman can find a use for them digging trenches and such. At the very least he needs the railroad rebuilt from Chattanooga down to here, and I'm sure they can find work that pays a decent wage."

Tubman soon departed on her mission to find slaves, perhaps even a few that did not yet realize they had been freed by the presence of the Yankee army. While she made many trips into the rural south before the War Between the States, as well as behind Confederate lines during the war, she also worked with various Yankee armies during the war, collecting newly freed slaves as the Union advanced.

The very presence of these two, working together in Dalton, Georgia, teaches us something of greatness in history, a fact known by every veteran school teacher and minister, a fact known by all who specialize in bringing out the best in children, as they mature. At that point, in 1864, neither of these women was widely recognized as anything special, and therein lay a lesson for us all. We can never know when and where there might be giants of history among us. We can only watch, and if we are very lucky, we might eventually recognize them. If we are luckier still, as we help them mature, we might also learn from them. These women were truly giants, scores of decades before the feminist movement. Each, in her own way, changed history.

## Fortress Resaca

By May 12, 1864, the small railroad town of Resaca, Georgia had been turned into a formidable fortress. Of course, in many ways, that town had been something of a fortress in the making even prior to the arrival of Stiggy Stigwell and the 23rd Alabama. That was exactly why Joe Johnston chose to make his next stand against the Yankee army in Resaca—it was a natural terrain to defend, and offered many advantages to the defenders.

Resaca was surrounded on the east, south, and the northeast by two rivers, both bearing names from the Cherokee Language, and both were too deep to ford, at least within sight of the railroad bridge at the south end of the town. The Conasuaga River came down from the north, passing the town to the east, and the Western and Atlanta Railroad generally followed this river as it carved its way through the Georgia hills. The Oostanaula River generally flowed east to west, just south of the main town square in Resaca, with the railroad trestle crossing that river south of town. Those two rivers provided a natural foundation for the flanks of Johnston's Confederate defenses.

Also, to the west of the town, ran a string of low hills, including the hill on which Stiggy Stigwell had taken his morning relief only a few days before. Below that hill was a large flat valley of fields that was cut from north to south by a small drainage called Camp Creek. The southern defensive works would ultimately run for four miles along that row of hills from the Conasuaga River north of town to the Oostanaula River in the south. That allowed Johnston to use the natural fortress of the hills and the rivers, and defend not only his railroad but the town of Resaca itself.

As anyone can see, Resaca was effectively a natural fortress even before the Confederates placed their defensive works atop the hills to the west of town. It was a defensive position that Johnston would need. While he still had fifty-four thousand effectives in his Army of Tennessee, Sherman still had three separate armies at his command, a force that now totaled a hundred and ten thousand men. Sherman also had the advantage in firepower, with two hundred and sixty four Napoleons or Parrot rifled cannon at his disposal, while Johnston had to make do with only a hundred and forty four heavy guns.

As those numbers indicate, one hundred and sixty thousand men were thus engaged in a desperate fight in that small, insignificant railroad town, with a population of eight hundred and seventy two souls. Clearly Resaca would soon become a very large battle, and it should not be surprising that the fight at Resaca was to be the bloodiest single fight in the entire state of Georgia, save only the earlier battle of Chickamauga. More men would become casualties at Resaca than in any of the later battles around Atlanta. On those defensive works at Resaca, no less than six thousand men would die.

Today Interstate 75 cuts through much of the battlefield, following north to south, beside Camp Creek, and just to the west of the main Confederate defenses. Like the battlefield at Rocky Face only twelve miles to the north, most travelers on that highway today never realize that they are driving through a bloody battlefield on which thousands of men died.

## The Battle of Resaca

When all is said and done, it is simply amazing to historians how similar the fight at Resaca was, when compared to the earlier fight at Rocky Face Ridge. The Confederates were well dug in along what amounted to a J shaped line, a large fishhook line, running from the north east of town directly to the west, and then turning south. Had one been in a signal balloon slightly to the north of the battlefield, the J shape of the Confederate defensive works would have been obvious. Further, the shape of the Confederate defensive works at Rocky Face Ridge had been almost exactly the same, not to mention the fact that the same defensive and offensive armies opposed each other. It is also interesting to note that this same J shape characterized the Gettysburg Battle almost a year previously. Simply put, when terrain is similar, the battles, throughout history, are likely to be similar as well.

Sherman responded to the Resaca defenses exactly the same way as he'd done at Rocky Face. He ordered an attack all along the Confederate defensive line, and sent his inevitable right hook far to the south of the battlefield, seeking another way to cross the Oostanaula River below the Confederate position. Again, he wanted to get into the rear areas of the Confederate Army. The only difference was that at Resaca, Sherman chose to attack in earnest rather than merely launch demonstration attacks at the Confederates atop those low hills.

One can only guess why he decided to invest so much of his effort in this attack, when he clearly intended to move to the south of the battlefield once again. Historians have debated that point for scores of years, but there are never great odds, when one attempts to out-guess a manic depressive such as Sherman. Let us just say, that Sherman intended to do something at Resaca that he didn't do at Rocky Face. He intended to put his whole army to use, and that decision alone would cost thousands of lives along Camp Creek.

While some skirmishing took place late on the afternoon of May 13, even as both armies were still reaching the future field of battle, the fight began in earnest at dawn on May 14, 1864. With both armies in position, Sherman moved his men forward for the attack all along the line. Thus, did scores of thousands of brave men from New Jersey, Ohio, Wisconsin, Pennsylvania, and New York leave the relative safety of their hills and begin their march towards death in the valley near Camp Creek. The creek parallels Interstate 75 today, with the road only one hundred yards away from the actual creek bed.

The fighting in Camp Creek Valley was particularly gruesome. While Johnston had positioned his main cannon atop the hills to the west of Resaca, he placed an initial defensive line in the valley just behind Camp Creek. At noon on May 14, Sherman advanced Schofield's entire Yankee army into Camp Creek Valley. Nearly thirty thousand men moved into line of battle formation and advanced. Waves upon waves of blue marched beneath their flags into the open to begin their advance. They had to attack across the valley in the open, for almost a mile in the field, all the while under fire from Johnston's cannon, and as soon as they got to within three hundred yards of Camp Creek, Hardee's Confederate Corps sharpshooters opened with their rifles. Those Union forces met devastating cannon and infantry fire, and like most such battles, Resaca promised to be a bloodbath. Sherman also advanced the forces under General Thomas, the Rock of Chickamauga, along the river to the south, and those massive Union forces soon got tangled up with each other, while under

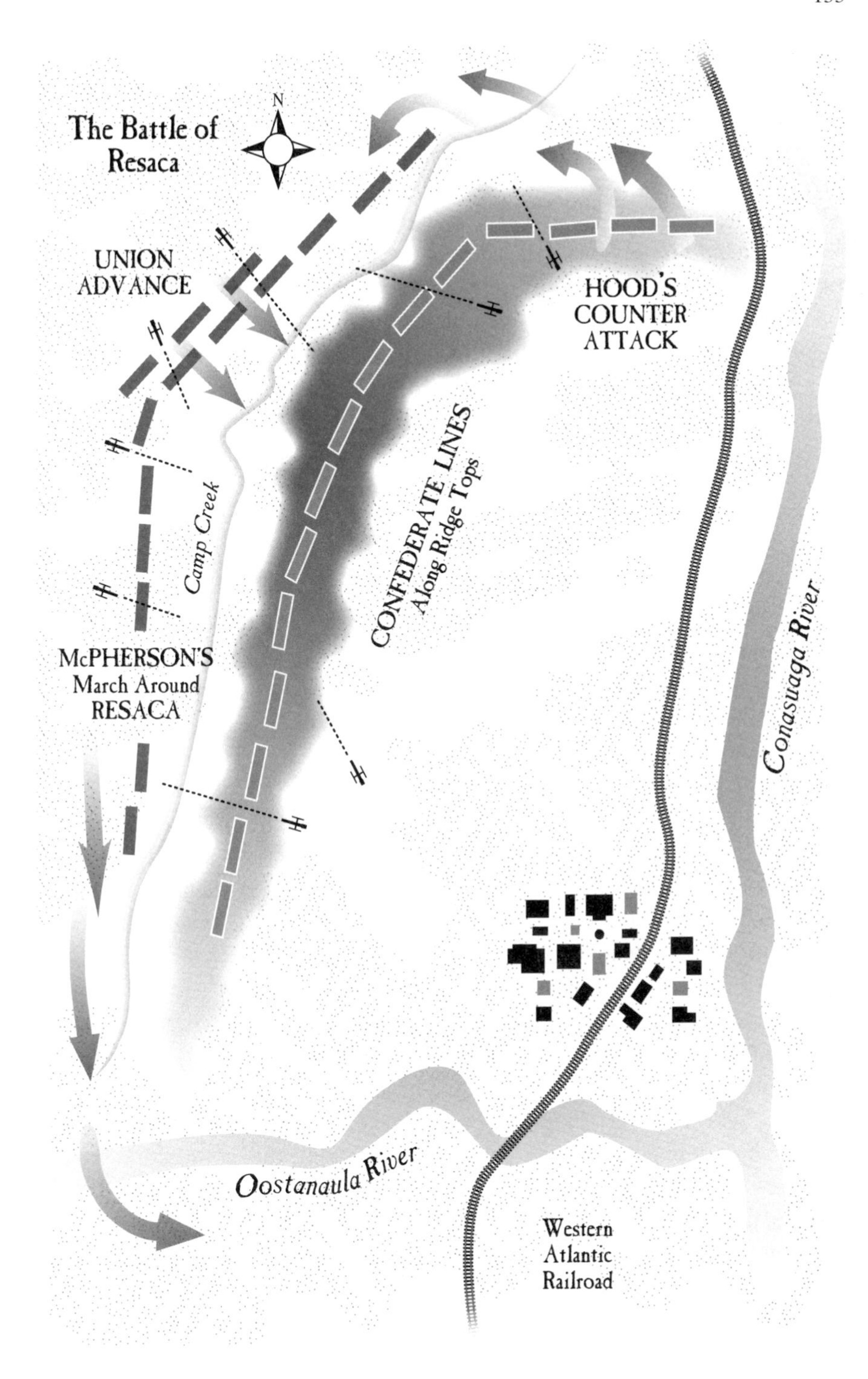
The Battle of Resaca
N
UNION ADVANCE
HOOD'S COUNTER ATTACK
CONFEDERATE LINES
Along Ridge Tops
Camp Creek
McPHERSON'S
March Around
RESACA
Conasuaga River
Oostanaula River
Western
Atlantic
Railroad

devastating fire from the Confederate cannon above. As usual, blue-grey gun smoke covered everything within ten minutes of the opening of the battle, so few of the battlefield leaders in the Yankee force knew what was really going on in the valley before them. The Confederates atop the mountain couldn't see anything.

With no covering hills and little else to hide behind in that valley the Union forces were completely exposed whereas the Confederates had their prepared log and earthwork positions from which to fire. The Yankees advanced and the fighting continued for hours all along the line, with brigades moving up when they could, and finding what cover they could when necessary. The Union men sought refuge in the shell holes from the enemy cannon, or behind dead horses, or even behind dead Union troops. At one point, some of the Union boys actually reached Camp Creek, and splashed through the muddy waters, only to be cut down by the Confederates twenty yards in front of them. Most of the Union forces in the valley never reached that far.

At the bend in the northern end Confederate line, the fighting was even bloodier. Here there was no open valley, no Camp Creek, to deter the Yankee advance. In fact, the terrain was wooded all along that end of the J-curved battle line, so the opposing armies got much closer to each other prior to engaging. With only fifty yards between the forces, and both sides using rifles that were accurate to two hundred yards, anyone foolish enough to show his head was killed almost instantly.

"I can't see any more of 'um," shouted Batty in one lull in the fighting. He was peeking out between the dirt in front of him and his head log. It was around 4:00 PM that afternoon and the Fourth Georgia Infantry was along the bottom of the J shaped line, facing a New Jersey regiment. Jamie was moving behind the line, trying to keep his men in the fight, and making sure that ammunition was available for everyone. He'd heard Batty's shout, and realized that the firing was dying down a bit to his front, so he mounted the parapet just between Captain Collins and Batty Prather, to have a look-see. Sampson was right beside him.

Meanwhile all of the Confederates were quickly reloading, or checking their ammunition pouch. Each man had been ordered to keep forty rounds in his haversack, and given that many could not count that high, those that could were looking into their own bags, and then checking the ammunition supply of others beside them. To a man, they had black powder circles around their mouths, from biting the paper powder bags in the loading process. They'd been eating gunpowder for several hours at that point.

Jamie looked quickly atop the log barrier and gazed into hell. Dead Yankees littered the ground about thirty feet in front of him, and he quickly counted—for no apparent reason—no less than six dead or dying horses. One man's bloody torso hung from a tree limb about seven feet in the air but the rest of his body was nowhere to be seen. Smoke covered the eerie scene, and the screams of the dying were, at that moment, louder than the cannon and rifle fire from the other end of the line. After a few seconds, checking the opposing tree line, Jamie asked Collins, "What's goin' on Owen? Don't see many of 'um up there. Are they retreating?"

Before the officers could have another word, a shout came from just down the line. Duncan, ever willing to offer a wisecrack when he shouldn't, shouted an unwanted answer to Jamie's question. "I don't know Jamie. We been pretty damn busy up here so far!"

Jamie felt like he could have, and probably should have, cut Duncan off at the knees for using his childhood nickname at that point in the battle, but then he realized that nearly every man in the unit was grinning at Duncan's ever-present willingness to joke inappropriately with his Major. Having his men grin at anything in the middle of a fight was probably worth something, so Jamie decided to respond in kind. He shouted, "Thank you Master Carmichael, for your unsolicited wisdom! When you have earned any rank above sergeant, I might give a damn for your opinion. For now, however, if you'd kindly shut the hell up, I'd like to have a word with my officers, here." Noise continued to subside, in that brief lull of the battle.

More men laughed at Jamie's comment; they all knew well that Major Turnbull spoke with Duncan Carmichael before nearly every fight. Still Duncan knew when to hush, so hush he did. Meanwhile, Captain Collins spoke up. "I can't say they're retreating Sir, but they are a bit scarce right now. Looks like they's puttin' out a skirmish line, so maybe we're done for today."

Jamie took a quick look at the sun, gauging the time as mid to late afternoon, since the sun set around 6:30 PM in Georgia in the spring. "Don't bet on that Captain. I've never seen a general that would want to waste this much of the day, particularly when his enemy is right there before him. They'll be coming again, I recon, and if not, then I'll bet General Hood is cooking up something to keep us busy right now."

In this instance, Jamie was both right and wrong. He was wrong in the sense that the Yankees didn't advance any more that afternoon, but instead, tossed out skirmish lines to harass the Confederates. However, Jamie was also right in that General Hood, under orders from General Joe Johnston, was indeed, "cooking up" something for the Confederates to do!

General Hood was widely known to be one of the most aggressive officers in the entire Confederate army, and perhaps the best corps commander in either army. Earlier that afternoon, he had been given just the orders he preferred, and he shared those with his entire officer corps outside of his headquarters tent. "Men at 4:00 PM, we will leave our defensive works, and advance on the enemy directly north of our position. General Stevenson's Division will lead the advance, and General Stewart's will follow him. Our mission is to break their lines, and then wheel to the left, advancing against the open and exposed flank of Howard's Yankee Corps. As we advance, we can assist our forces in Camp Creek Valley, and if we succeed, we can roll up the entire Union force, much as General Jackson did at Chancellorsville up in Virginia. You may retrieve your specific objectives from your division commanders. Godspeed, and do not stop until that whole Yankee army is wiped off the face of the earth!"

Thus when the Yankees were settling into their skirmish lines at 4:15 PM on May 14, the Fourth Georgia, along with the rest of Hood's Corps, prepared for their advance against the blue-bellies to their front. From the Yankee point of view, it was as if the entire bottom of the J shaped battle line began to move forward all at once. Major Turnbull stood beside Captain Owen Collins, as Collins shouted the order; "Advance bayonets!" At that command, the five hundred men in the unit moved forward, adjacent to nearly seven thousand others. The plan was simple; advance in formation until fired upon, then charge like hell toward the enemy.

Jamie Turnbull had his sword held high, as he advanced right in front of the color guard for the Fourth Georgia, with Sampson just behind him. As he looked down the line, he saw all of his men. Most of them were boys, in his mind; those Lovorn boys, for example, and Wellspeak. Others were Jamie's age, like Duncan Carmichael, or even older, like Owen Collins. Jamie noticed that Wellspeak's new slave, Ten Cent Bill, had acquired a firearm and was moving in line right beside his master, and he reflected on that for a moment. In most cases, the Confederates left their man-servants in the camp during the actual battles, and Turnbull himself had tried to do just that with his own slave, Sampson. However, Sampson understood that his job was to protect Jamie Turnbull as best he could, and that meant fighting beside him. Apparently Ten Cent Bill had the same sense of duty toward Wellspeak, his new master.

## Author's Note: Black Confederates

In retrospect, it is interesting to reflect on these servants, these slaves, fighting for the Confederacy. While the black troops fighting for the Union have received much press of late, little attention has been given to the scores of thousands of blacks who fought for the south. Of course, given the modern political bias, it simply makes no sense for black men to have fought for the Confederacy. Why would any man fight for a nation state that enslaved him? Even the question seems to be politically incorrect, but considering that question can provide great insight into those distant times.

First we must recognize that many black Confederates, like Sampson and

Ten Cent Bill, had no initial choice in the matter. They were slaves when the war began, and like Sampson, many were probably the personal servant of one Confederate officer or another. Other black slaves were loaned or rented out to the Confederacy as teamsters, builders, laborers, ditch diggers, or skilled laborers such as blacksmiths. Still it has been shown that many blacks fought for the Confederacy even when they didn't have to do so, and according to news stories in the southern papers of the day, some blacks actually took up arms for the Confederacy of their own volition. Again, it is hard to imagine today; why would any black man fight for a Confederate society in which he was held as a slave? Moreover, few have asked the question, how many black men did so?

As strange as it may seem, the available evidence, old Confederate pension records, news stories of the day, rare photographs, and company rosters for the Confederacy, indicate that perhaps as many as fifty-thousand blacks fought for the south at some point, in some capacity, during the War Between the States. For comparison purposes, approximately six hundred thousand men fought in the entire Confederate States Army, and some four hundred thousand more were in the Home Guard, various southern militias, or other irregular Confederate fighting units. Thus, a total of a million men fought for the Confederacy, fifty thousand of whom were black. These numbers are facts, and cannot easily be disputed; they can, however, be ignored by historians today, and while no one admits it in these modern times, virtually one in every twenty Confederates on the battle line was a black man!

It is intriguing that as recently as 2014, when this book was written, such history is still quite controversial. Clearly such facts do not fit within the politically correct story line today that the war was about slavery. Today's thinkers choose to forget that most Confederates believed they were fighting for their own freedom from the tyranny of a powerful federal government, not for slavery, a theme that rings as true today as it did in the 1860s. Many blacks, free and slave alike, apparently found that rationale to be convincing, at least at the beginning of the war, during a time when even President Lincoln himself insisted that the war was not about freeing slaves, but about preserving the Union.

Of course, the evidence of these black Confederates is there for all to see in the admittedly incomplete records of Confederate veterans, as well as the news stories of the time. There are even several Union sources that date from the war, documenting entire units of black Confederates (**http://blackconfederatesoldiers.com/confederate_states_army_generals_11.html**), and for some detailed information is available. The life of Ten Cent Bill, for example, was well documented. He fought in the CSA throughout the war, and received a pension as a Confederate veteran from the state of Georgia in his old age while spending his last days in an "old Soldier's home" and living right along-side other, white, Confederate veterans in Macon, Georgia. Moreover, his story, and many of his personal effects are preserved in the Cobb County Historical Museum in Marietta, Georgia.

Today, some black men actually celebrate that southern heritage. In fact, *YouTube* presents a couple of interesting videos on black Confederates, that tell of their loyalty to the Confederate Cause in general: **http://www.youtube.com/watch?v=o8hPo6mYnks&NR=1&feature=endscreen** and **http://www.youtube.com/watch?v=_GVIAypsnh8&feature=endscreen&NR=1)**. It is interesting, indeed, to see a black man celebrate his Confederate heritage.

Why would a black man fight for the Confederacy? The answer was simple; loyalty. These men were either loyal to their masters, who in many cases like Sampson and Jamie Turnbull, were also their friends, or they were loyal to the southern states in the same fashion as most southern whites. Sampson had been Jamie's slave all his life, having been partnered with Jamie shortly after Jamie was born. In fact, they'd been together since before either of them could remember, and in situations where the slave was reasonably well treated, such bonds didn't merely disappear because of a war. Thus, did both Sampson and Ten Cent Bill fight, usually right beside their masters, for the Confederate cause.

Today rather than ignore these facts, we would do well to honor those men, even as we honor the black men who fought in Union blue. While history has determined the inherent evil of slavery, the honor these black Confederates showed is worthy of our esteem. In fact, when we honestly look at the lessons of the past, history teaches us quite clearly; honor is colorblind, and loyalty emerges from the heart and soul of a man, not from his skin tone. Moreover, a sense of duty, of bravery, of determined purpose, may be found among all races, and we might also note that these qualities are all too rare. They should be honored and indeed, celebrated whenever we find them, rather than denied when they do not fit our peculiar political perspectives. One can only hope that historians, and perhaps modern society in general, may one day mature into this perspective.

## Hood's Counter-Attack

Thus did this line of men, black and white, move forward in Hood's advance on May 14, 1864. With Major Turnbull and Captain Owen Collins out in front to straighten the line, the men advanced in line of battle, at march step, a pace that would not last long. Within two minutes these Confederates, as well as southern units on both sides reached a point in the foliage where they could be spotted by the Union skirmish line, and the fight was joined.

The advance went as planned for nearly an hour, and General Hood's force was, indeed, living up to his aggressive reputation. Confederate forces, the Georgia Fourth among them, moved forward approximately half a mile, and when they were clearly beyond the Union flank, they wheeled to the left as Hood had ordered, to roll up the Union line. They made good progress, often firing on Yankees from behind the Yankee defensive line, and on three occasions, the Confederates captured one or more cannon that the Union troops had deployed.

However less than ninety minutes after the advance had begun, Hood's nemesis was about to show up, in the form of an unexpected Yankee corps.

In Hood's advance many Union prisoners were taken, and marched to the rear, and it was in one of these rearward marches, led by Owen Collins, that both Mike Wellspeak and Ten Cent Bill first saw the danger. They were guarding prisoners when they spotted a movement of blue in the trees. Union troops were about to attack Hood's advancing Confederate force from the side and rear. Thus it was logical for a small guarding force to see these Yankees first—everyone else in Hood's advancing corps was facing the other way!

As Jamie and the rest of the Hood's Corps moved forward and turned to the west to attack the Yankee positions, an entire Yankee army was just arriving on the battlefield from the north. Hooker's Union Corps, the Union XX, held some fifteen thousand men, and had been the last to leave the battlefield in the Dalton area. Thus they were the last to arrive in Resaca, and their arrival doomed the Confederate advance on the evening of May 14.

As Wellspeak and Ten Cent Bill marched beside a group of Union prisoners back to the east, and then to the south to get back behind the original Confederate lines, Ten Cent Bill looked up and let out a shout. "Look out Mr. Wellspeak! They's Yankees in the tree line there!" He then pointed to the north, where, indeed, the first of Hooker's XX Corps was hiding behind trees and taking aim. Wellspeak, a seasoned veteran, at that point, hit the ground immediately, and shouted to the others, "Yankees in the tree line! Hit the ground! Take cover!" Just as the first shots rang out from the Yankee rifles—thank God they'd not moved their cannon up yet—the fifteen Confederates in the guard force hit the ground seeking whatever cover they could find. Nearly eighty unarmed Union prisoners dropped to the ground also, or scattered in all directions, and the lucky ones ran directly into the Union men hiding in the tree line. A few were, no doubt cut down by the firing from their own army, but such are the vagrancies of warfare. Most made it back into Union hands, just as the Confederates began to fire back.

Captain Collins, one of the most effective small tactics commanders in the entirety of Hood's Corps, was quick to realize what had happened. "Wellspeak!" he shouted. "Get over to Major Turnbull, and tell him a large Yankee force has arrived behind us, and that he needs to get here right quick!" Collins could not have realized that the force he described held over fifteen thousand men, but any Yankees in that particular position were going to prove dangerous, and his quick thinking saved most of Hood's Corps on May 14. Wellspeak and his servant, Ten Cent Bill, had a very impressive footrace, as they ran through the woods behind Hood's advancing Corps, taking only ten minutes to find Major Turnbull and tell him of the danger.

As Collins and the rest of his guard force held the Union skirmish line in place, firing as quickly as they could load, Turnbull brought back an additional hundred men to help in the fight. Batty was one of the first to arrive, along with Duncan Carmichael. "How the hell did Yankees get over there?" he wondered out loud. "We just checked those woods an hour ago!" He seemed almost indignant that a Union force would have the gall to position itself in a location that had previously been secured by the Confederate attacking force.

Duncan took a moment to answer, as he reloaded his rifle. "Just don't seem quite fair do it! Them thar Yankees taking the woods that we checked out!" The sarcasm in his comment was evident.

Batty responded. "Just shut the hell up Duncan! I'm busy over here."

As soon as Turnbull could assess the situation, he shouted virtually the same thing as Captain Collins had only minutes before. "Wellspeak! Run as fast as you can to the front of the advance. I think Stevenson is in charge, since Col. Stewart was hit earlier. Tell Stevenson that a very large Yankee force is in our rear, and that we should turn the entire division to the north to face them. Tell him that otherwise, I fear we might lose our entire division. Now off you go. Move as quickly as you can!" Once again, Wellspeak and Ten Cent Bill began a footrace, and this time, it took them only eight minutes to reach Stevenson, the commander of the Confederate advancing force. He not only stopped the advance cold, but did, indeed turn his forces to face the new threat from Hooker's XX Union Corps to the north. This action saved Hood's entire force.

One hour later, Stevenson's force was back in their original positions. Some men were lost, but Hooker's XX Union Corps had not gotten into position in time to stop the retreat, and the Confederates had captured fourteen cannon, and over three hundred and fifty Union men. Overall the advance of Hood's Corps was something of a victory for the Confederates, but like many battlefield successes, it made little difference in the overall outcome. Both armies were still in position, and it was clear to all that the fight would resume the next day.

## A Grown Man Crying

By early evening on May 14, there was only sporadic fire along the line; the cannon were quiet and each side seemed content to hold position until the next day. Duncan Carmichael, this time accompanied by Wellspeak, Ten Cent Bill, and Batty Prather, all sought out the evening prayer service about a hundred yards behind the Confederate positions, leaving Captain Owen Collins hard pressed to find enough veterans to man his section of the line. Still, he found a few men, enough for the guard duty and the skirmish line some forty yards out front, and this allowed most of the Fourth Georgia some time to themselves.

Camp life between battles was often boring, with much time to oneself around the camp fire, and since most Civil War battles did not involve evening attacks, most of the after dark time during that war was a time for personal pursuits. Drinking or prayer services were two, rather dissimilar ways to spend an evening, and even in brief battles such as Resaca, a sutler's row usually developed that offered many entertainments. Sutler's row, in the War Between the States, was like a small merchant's village that traveled with the army. With over fifty thousand Confederates on the field, it would have been a fairly large number of independent merchants that followed the army, using wagons to transport their goods. When a battle site was selected and the army was likely to stay put for a while, the merchants would set up a street about a mile behind the lines—a row of merchants, as it were, where soldiers could purchase almost anything. Sutler's row typically offered products a man might need, such as razors, plugs of tobacco, pipes, mirrors, soap, etc., or it might offer more rare finds such as real coffee, sugar, eggs—all much too expensive since they were so rare in the south at that point. Women were sometimes an available commodity, along with many varieties of home-grown liquor. Some men bought the women for a thirty minute time slot, while others bought the cheapest liquor they could and simply drank themselves to sleep. One could even pay to have one's own body embalmed and shipped home, should one die on the field. Sutler's row offered everything.

If one was not interested in shopping, and was not on guard duty, one might engage in interesting pastimes around the campfire, that are almost unimaginable today. Lice racing was a favorite sport for both armies. Soldiers simply plucked the lice from their hair, placed one in their personal tin plate, and then wagered over which lice would leave the plate first. One Confederate in Hood's Corps was known to have particularly fast lice, and seemed to win almost all his bets, until it was discovered that he heated his tin plate before every race! The lice managed to move much more quickly when they were being cooked. While no rules governed the sport, it was widely believed that the man had cheated his way to the top! That gent made a considerable amount of cash prior to others discovering his secret! At the very least, we can assume that the men in the Fourth Georgia found ample variety of activities on the evening of May 14, to entertain themselves as they waited for battle the next morning.

That evening, Sampson had gone to find some more ammunition for the Fourth Georgia, at the behest of Major Turnbull, who, himself, was summoned to General Hood's tent for a meeting of officers. Nobody really expected a fight that night, but you could never tell, and you always needed veterans in the line, since new recruits were likely to shoot at night owls, rats, or anything else that moved, thus keeping everyone on both sides awake. Major Turnbull ordered Captain Collins to stay near the line, in case an attack did materialize.

Of course it is a fact of war that, even in indecisive efforts such as Hood's advance on May 14, men die. Near the end of the Confederate advance, Jake Lovorn had taken a Union minie-ball through his throat, and another in his chest. He had been alive for a while, as his brother Lee carried him back to the Confederate lines, but Jake didn't make it all the way back. He bled-out while his body was slung over his brother's shoulder, but Lee only discovered his brother's death, as he lay the corpse down behind the Confederate defensive works. An hour after the fight, he was still sitting there, quietly crying, his mouth open with no sound coming forth, yet tears still streamed down his face. He merely sat seemingly paralyzed over the body of his dead brother, and the other men had, wisely, left him alone with his sorrow.

However, when the others returned from the prayer service, Lee still sat beside his brother's body. None of the men knew what to say, but they knew then that they needed to help Lee in some fashion. His friends and comrades, thus, stood over him, slightly behind. Owen, Batty, Sampson, Wellspeak, and Ten Cent Bill, were all there, watching. All were totally ignorant of what might be said. What, after all, could comfort any man in that position?

It was surprisingly, Duncan Carmichael that came up with the right thing to do. Not only had Duncan been praying a bit since the earlier battles, he'd been studying the Holy Book too. Thus, after letting Lee grieve for a long while, Duncan figured that it was time to help him move on. Duncan moved over and sat on the ground beside Lee and put his arm over Lee's shoulder. He then began to rock Lee back and forth just a bit and began to quote, in a soft voice, that harshest of judgments from the Old Testament; a set of verses known by many a soldier. They are cruel in their certitude, decisive in their judgment of the human condition relative to the whims of fate, but they are also absolute, and perhaps in that harsh decisiveness, they may be said to be somewhat comforting. That evening, it was the only thing that could be said to Lee Lovorn. Sitting beside his friend, with his arm around Lee's shoulder, Duncan quoted those most noble of verses.

*"To everything, there is a season, and a time to every purpose under heaven.*
*A time to be born, and a time to die.*
*A time to plant, and a time to pluck up that which is planted.*
*A time to kill, and a time to heal*

*A time to break down, and a time to build up.*
*A time to weep, and a time to laugh, A time to mourn, and a time to dance.*
*A time to cast away stones, and a time to gather stones together.*
*A time to embrace, and a time to refrain from embracing.*
*A time to get and a time to lose. A time to keep, and a time to cast away.*
*A time to rend and a time to sew. A time to keep silent, and a time to speak.*
*A time to love, and a time to hate. A time of war, and a time of peace."*

Duncan and the others let those noble verses float on the air with a few moments of silence, and, perhaps because of his recent praying, Duncan again found exactly the right thing to say. Lifting his face to the dark of the night, and the canopy of stars he said, "God, we want to ask that, even as you took Jake Lovorn home today, to live with you in Heaven, that you also comfort his brother Lee here, and help him through this trying time. Amen."

The men standing around all joined in with "Amen."

Then Duncan spoke again. "Lee, your brother Jake is with God right now. He's where he needs to be. I promise you, and you need to know this in your heart and your soul! Jake is with the Master now; He is at home, right now. Jake has found his peace."

Another somewhat longer silence, as Lee turned to look at Duncan, then back at Jake's body. At that point, Lee spoke for the first time in hours. "He's home."

Duncan nodded, and then continued, "Yes, he's home."

Another pause.

Then Duncan continued with another memorized, though slightly adjusted, scripture; words that are much more comforting, much more reassuring.

*"For in all these things, Jake is more than a conqueror. I am persuaded that neither death nor life, nor angels, nor principalities, nor powers, nor things present, nor things to come, nor height, nor depth, nor any other thing in all creation shall be able to separate Jake or any of us from the love of God that is in Jesus Christ our Lord."*

Duncan then offered a conclusion. "While we will always remember him, we now know that Jake is home, at last."

At that all of the men of the Fourth Georgia again said, "Amen."

After another moment Captain Collins took charge. Feeling that the impromptu ceremony had concluded, he spoke up. "Lee, you need to come along with me, now. I fancy you could use a drink, so we'll head over to sutler's row for a bit. Duncan, you and Batty take the body on over to the identification tent, and make sure they know who it is. I think they've got a cemetery set up a bit behind the lines here in town. I'm sure there will be a formal ceremony there soon, for all of our brothers in arms."

Collins led Lee back to sutler's row, and the others followed their orders. They then retired behind the southern trenches at Resaca; for the next morning promised continued battle.

## The Resaca Fight On The Second Day

The next morning began crisp and clear, but the heavy air promised a shower at some point later in the day. By that point, all forces had arrived, and everyone expected a truly massive fight. General Johnston had, once again, ordered General Hood to advance to his front along the lower side of the J shaped battle line, and, again, wheel to his left to roll up the Union forces, while protecting himself better against unexpected attacks from the north. The Confederate advance was planned for 9:00 AM, but before they could muster their forces, the battle was joined by advancing Yankees, all along the J shaped line. Thus, on May 15, no concerted Confederate advance ever took place; rather it was all the Confederates could do to stop the successive waves of the Union advance. Sherman had, on that morning sent almost his entire army, some eighty-nine thousand infantry, forward in wave after wave. It was clear at that point; Sherman had brought a massive army to Georgia, and he proposed to use them all!

He sent division after division of Union men directly at the J shaped defensive works, and it was all the Confederates could do to keep their rifles and cannon loaded, with so many targets coming at them at once. When one Union brigade fell on the battlefield, with some of the men retreating, another always seemed to take their place, and no Confederate gun was silent for long. The Union advances continued much of the morning and into the afternoon.

In spite of all of this effort, and the death that accompanies any battle of this magnitude, little was accomplished at Resaca on May 15, other than a massive butcher's bill. After seven hours of nearly constant fighting, the Union advances tapered off around 3:00 PM or so. Men on both sides of Camp Creek and in the woods to the north hunkered down behind their works, and reloaded. Some wondered what the lull was about, having seen nothing that might suggest either a defeat or a victory for either side. Most, however, just counted their blessings—they believed that they may have survived another day of fighting, and that just maybe, they wouldn't have to face enemy guns again that afternoon.

Of course, the men commanding each army knew what was taking place.

Sherman, true to form, had sent another force on yet another right hook, far to the west and south, against Johnston's Confederates, and once again, Johnston saw that his supply lines were in danger. While most of Sherman's troops engaged Johnston's strong positions at Resaca on May 14 and 15, Sherman again gave McPherson the task of moving against the Confederate supply lines to the south about two miles below the Confederate trenches. Once again McPherson had come through, as Sherman's right hook became obvious for leaders on both sides to see.

Crossing some of his forces at Lay's Ferry about two miles south of Resaca, McPherson established a beachhead on the southern side of the river, from which he could threaten Johnston's railroad connection to Atlanta. A few Union men had actually crossed the river on the afternoon of May 14, but they quickly retreated to the relatively safe positions on the northern bank. However, their crossing showed what might be possible, so a much larger Union force crossed on May 15. Johnston once again, became concerned that his entire army might be cut off from Atlanta, and even before the fighting died down on the afternoon of May 15, he was, once more, making plans to retreat with his entire army. He initially hoped to divide Sherman's force, and eliminate the first Union men who crossed the river, but that idea soon changed into a general, though a well-organized retreat. By the end of May 15, it was clear that Johnston would soon withdraw. The bridge over the river was burned by the Confederates as they withdrew.

By the morning of May 17, the Union engineers had used their pontoons to construct a new bridge over the river, and they were hard on the heels of the Confederates. Thus the Battle of Resaca ended, having accomplished little but the death of slightly over six thousand men. Both armies were, once again, moving ever closer to Atlanta.

They left only the dead behind; the dead and the paperwork.

## The After-Battle Summary

*To: The Honorable Jefferson Davis, President*
*From: General Joseph Johnston, Commander*
*Army of Tennessee*
*RE Actions of Late at Dalton and Resaca*

*This is an after-action report, prepared May 16, 1864, concerning the recent fights at Dalton and Resaca. I am pleased to report that we have well defended the mountain passes below Chattanooga against Sherman's Union armies, numbering over one hundred thousand men. Actions at Rocky Face near Dalton, and outside of Resaca have sorely slowed the Union advance into Georgia, and Sherman's forces have been reduced by over ten thousand casualties, while our losses have been significantly smaller. In each case, we were not driven from the field, but abandoned the ground in good order, as a result of Union flanking advances far below our lines. Thus, the spirit of our men is high, and there is no talk of defeat, but of victory!*

*I am repositioning the Army of Tennessee once again, to the south along the railroad that has always been Sherman's main line of advance, and will again hold his forces. However, I regret to inform your Honor that with the current deployment of men, it may be difficult to fight Sherman's forces in an open engagement, as he outnumbers my current strength by almost two to one. I intend to select ground carefully for any future fights, while preserving this army and protecting Atlanta, and I will make Sherman pay dearly for any real estate he captures.*

*However, I do have a request; should the Confederacy make an additional fifteen thousand men available to me, perhaps with General Longstreet at the head of that force, as was the case at Chickamauga, I would be in a position to consider more offensive actions against Sherman.*

*Joe Johnston, Commanding, Army of Tennessee*
*Report Compiled by Major James Turnbull, 4th Georgia*
*Seconded to General Johnston's Staff*

## A Report on the Action After The Action

While Jamie had missed writing the after-action report on Chickamauga because of his rather insignificant wound, when he returned to the army he learned an important lesson; armies have long memories. His name had been written down somewhere as a man of letters, and he soon found, after the fight at Resaca, that he was, once again, seconded to the Commanding General's staff whenever the Fourth Georgia was not in an engagement. Thus, leaving Captain Collins in temporary command, he moved south with General Johnston's staff, during which time, he wrote the after action report above. Of course, he also carefully forwarded a secret copy of that report to his wife, as they had previously agreed. With the burning of Richmond in April of 1865, the official copy of the report above was destroyed. However, it was indeed read, in mid-May of 1864.

Contrary to Jamie's earlier suspicion that no one in Richmond actually read any of the after-action reports, the President of the Confederacy, Jefferson Davis himself, was carefully watching events in Georgia, and studying every detail of all incoming reports, including the one above.

When Jeff Davis read the report, he was seated with his long-time friend, and one-time Secretary of State for the Confederacy, Robert Toombs. Davis' face showed a stern expression as he read and it soon became clear that he was so angry he could explode! "Listen to this mouse, would you Toombs?" Davis shouted, as they sat in Davis' private office in the Confederate Capital Building. "Johnston admits he cannot stop Sherman with his current army! What does he think his job is? What forces does he think I can send him? Would he have us deplete the Army of Northern Virginia? Would he have us sacrifice Richmond for his tiny damn farmer's towns in the Georgia hills? What Georgia mountain top is more important than this capital building? Damn him! I should relieve that sniffling son-of-a-bitch immediately."

Toombs was known as a one-time fire-eater, a Georgia plantation owner, and a passionate defender of the south. However, he was not given to making important decisions based on emotion alone, and he knew to steer clear of Davis' anger. Still, he and Davis had been friends for years, and while Toombs had resigned from Davis' cabinet earlier in the war to serve for a time as a fairly capable general in the CSA, he knew his role was in Richmond, where he served as an unofficial advisor. He still had Davis' ear on important matters, so his opinion was often heeded. He replied, "I agree that this man should be taken out of command, at some point, but it might not be wise at this juncture. His army reveres him, and he is clearly still in the middle of a fight in those hills. Could we not take his command after a victory, even a small one, at some future point?"

Davis considered that. He was known to hate Joe Johnston with a passion, a sentiment that was returned, and both of those men were also known to hold grudges over the long-term. Still, Johnston was the only senior commander Davis had at that moment, since General Lee was busy defending Richmond against Grant in Virginia.

Davis did, in that meeting on May 19, 1864 manage to keep his emotion, his hatred of Johnston, in check. "I suppose you are right, General Toombs. I'll leave the matter with Johnston, at least until he shows us a victory; I do hope he quickly does so."

Major Turnbull never realized, nor would he have ever believed that President Davis was reading reports he had compiled, but that is often the way of things. Written words often take on a life of their own, whether true or not. Johnston's report above was clearly an attempt to put the best light on a couple of defeats, and anyone with an elementary education could make that determination, as easily as had President Davis. Still, it is a historic fact that one of the Tugalo Valley men, Major Jamie Turnbull, was playing a minor role in very significant decisions made in Richmond, even if he didn't realize it.

## The First Confederate Cemetery

The Battle at Resaca did result in one longer-lasting monument, the first Confederate Cemetery anywhere in the country. With no provisions to bury the dead on either side in this cruel war, such burials as did take place were makeshift affairs, and the burial of Jake Lovorn was no exception. His body was quickly put to rest in a shallow grave, with no ceremony, just outside the identification tent, along with hundreds of others.

In this war Union dead were much more likely to be embalmed and shipped home than were Confederate bodies. Thus, the many trains bringing supplies south to Sherman's massive Union army, often returned north loaded with embalmed bodies of Union men, and families across the northern states paid dearly to have their sons, brothers, or husbands returned to them in death, should they die in battle. Thus, many a boxcar that had brought hardtack, ammunition, or cannon to Sherman's army from the north, returned loaded with the Union dead, along with the wounded, and some Confederate prisoners.

It is clear that Confederates were even less prepared to care for thousands upon thousands of bodies than were the Union armies. Confederates throughout the war, were likely to dig makeshift graves near the battle lines and put the dead in together—some of the "graves" were less than a foot deep. In fact, in the several battlefields that saw action twice or more—Bull Run Creek, near Manassas, VA, is one example, graves from one battle were frequently unearthed during the next battle. At the Second Battle of Bull Run, both armies complained of skeletons all across the battlefield, that had been hastily buried in shallow graves over a year before. By the time of Second Bull Run, some of those bodies were completely unearthed even before the fight began!

Jake Lovorn like many other Confederates, was buried in a shallow grave in the front yard of the Green Plantation, early in the morning of May 16, before the Fourth Georgia pulled away. The Greens had the misfortune to have their home just a quarter mile inside of the lower part of the J shaped line at Resaca, so their entire yard was much abused by the digging of shallow graves. When they returned about a week after the fighting ended, they were amazed to find several hundred graves in their yard, and many others in their fields, and some were partially uncovered, presumably by the local wildlife. While their father stood on his porch and cursed, the two Green daughters took up the challenge. They first talked their father into providing some land suitable for a cemetery, then they collected funds. They gathered up several of their slaves from town, and began to re-inter four hundred and fifty Confederates in what was soon to be named the Resaca Confederate Cemetery, the first such permanent Confederate Cemetery anywhere in the Confederacy.

Today this two and a half acres of what was once the Green Plantation, just north of Resaca is quiet and peaceful. It is a stately place shaded by oak and hickory trees, almost all of which date from that time period. Many of those trees were planted over the next two years, as the cemetery took shape. This hallowed ground lies just off Highway 41, about a mile and a half north of Resaca, GA., near the adjacent railroad line and the river. While many burials took place in the cemetery shortly after the battle, this cemetery was officially dedicated after the war ended, on October 25, 1866, the same day as another Confederate cemetery in Winchester Virginia. Groups at both ceremonies believed theirs to be the first Confederate Cemetery to be dedicated to the fallen, but the cemetery at Resaca was being used as a cemetery first, so this small Georgia town has the more accurate claim on that honor.

Like many cemeteries, it is a peaceful place, and one could never tell that within half a mile some one hundred and fifty thousand men fought a deadly, two-day battle. While the Union dead are long-gone, those dead Confederates remain near where they fell, defending a railhead town that was to fall to the enemy in this two day epic struggle. They lie in a large semi-circular pattern, each grave marked by a small fieldstone monument. They rest with their comrades, altogether, the rows of markers descending down the side of a gentle slope with a creek at the bottom, under the canopy of the one hundred and forty year-old oaks. Some of the grave stones mark the spot of unknown Confederate dead. These men, Jake Lovorn among them, have found their peace.

For those one hundred and forty men, there is a fitting tribute carved into a granite monument in the center of the cemetery.

It reads simply:

*We sleep here, in obedience to law;*
*When duty called, we came,*
*When country called, we died.*

Nothing more could be said to honor a man, than this simple epitaph, and like many battlefields throughout history, all that is left today of this massive Battle of Resaca, are the dead.

Of course, as the Confederates moved out, they left behind the rugged mountain passes of northernmost Georgia, and moved into the gentler, rolling hills, hills that are much lower in elevation. As it turns out, however, Dalton and Resaca were not to be the last mountain battles fought in northern Georgia. Even in the lower hills towards the south, there were a few mountains to fight over, and as the Confederates retreated from Resaca from May 16 through May 19, 1864, Sherman's massive Union army moved ever closer to Atlanta.

# Chapter 3
# The Dallas Line

## A Letter Home

*Mrs. Mary Turnbull*
*Traveler's Rest Plantation*
*Tugalo River at Walton's Ford, Georgia*
*May 17, 1864*

*My Dearest Wife,*

*I cannot say how very much I miss you in the last days. I have, yet again, seen much of war, and while I am confident that I lead our southern men wisely, and with some degree of skill, many are still lost in every fight. Sometimes, in weaker moments, I truly despair for our Grand Cause, and I pray daily for the forgiveness of Almighty God for such thoughts. Still, we cannot continue to lose good men as we have of late. There are simply not that many of us, and the Yankees seem to be endlessly ready to die before our guns.*

*I've sent you an after-action report on the recent fights, as I said I would, and while General Johnston puts everything in a grand light, I'm sure that you can read between the lines. While everyone here pretends that all is well, the fact is we lost at Dalton and Resaca because we don't have the men to defend against Sherman's massive Union army. Do hide this report, and know that I plan to send others, when I can.*

*It surely comes as no secret to you that we have removed ourselves from Resaca; I've seen an Atlanta paper that printed the causality lists for that two day fight, so I know it is no secret. I lost many men, but one young man in particular captures my mind, Jake Lovorn, from over in Cleveland. I did not know him particularly well, as he had joined our unit only recently, but watching his brother, Lee, mourn his death was heart rending! Of course, that was only one death, of many. I believe nearly 3000 Confederate men were wounded or died in those trenches at Resaca, and if the Union count is the same, then 6,000 men perished there. That number doesn't approach the fight at Chickamauga last year, but is much larger than the earlier fight at Rocky Face up in Dalton.*

*For now, we move on. I'm writing these lines quickly by a campfire, about twenty five miles south of the last fight at Resaca. We passed through a small town earlier today, but I was literally riding atop my horse nearly asleep, so I didn't catch the name of the place. We'll move, I suppose, until General Johnston finds the place he wishes to defend. Of course, he may know where we are going, but no one else does.*

*You should see this mighty Army of Tennessee on the move! It is a sight to see! Do not make the mistake of the uninformed, thinking that this is merely one large line of men and wagons. No! When an army moves, it is really an entire city that is moving, and rather than move down one road, virtually all roads within a twenty-mile span are used, an intricate network of well-planned movement! First, the generals lay out the main direction and the rally point for the entire army, and then they divide the available roads heading to that spot among the different corps. Usually one corps gets to use one road, by itself, and that is when the move gets complicated indeed!*

*First the corps commanders issue orders as to which divisions will move out at which times and each division moves as a self, contained unit. One division might be scheduled to leave at 7:00 AM and the following division at 10:00 or so. Within each division, each regiment is assigned a specific time to be in line beside the road, and to join in at the rear of the preceding unit. Nothing is easy, but nothing is left to chance in that schedule either. Thus a division moves along with its cannon batteries, its supply wagons, horses, any walking stock—cattle or hogs—its hospital wagons, and in many cases civilian wagons belonging to sutler's row merchants or even their whores.*

*First, the advance cavalry guard moves out on a given road. Then comes the prized, ever protected, cannon batteries and their rolling caissons, usually pulled by nearly dead, very skinny horses, that seem incredibly slow. Next, come the regiments, the thousands and thousands of men in the fighting infantry, followed closely by the hospital and supply wagons for that division or that corps. Finally, in this magnificent line, come the infantry assigned to "rear guard" should a fighting retreat become necessary, and they are followed by trailing cavalry. With infantry in every case following closely behind the horses, I'll leave you to guess how much manure we all step in daily. We don't even bother to clear our boots, as the dust in the next step will merely bring more.*

*Of course, for some lucky units, the railroad toward Atlanta is available, and they get to ride to the destination. For most it is a matter of walking. Still, it is really a sight to see, this moving army, this colossal moving city; thousands upon thousands of men, supplies, cannon, wagons, mules, horses, cattle, and hogs, moving along, and I suppose that twenty or thirty miles behind us, Sherman is moving his massive army in much the same way along the same roads.*

*We play hopscotch along these dirt trails and cart tracks in the beautiful north Georgia hills, trying to kill each other all the while, as we move ever closer to Atlanta. We simply have to stop Sherman soon or Atlanta and its railroads will be lost. Still, we seem, at least thus far, unable to do so; hence my concern.*

*Still all is quiet for this night, at least at this camp. I can go to sleep tonight knowing that I will probably wake up in the morning. It is dark now, and I'm having some difficulty seeing this paper, as I write. Outside my camp tent, Sampson is singing a hymn, and a few others seem to have joined in. Impromptu church services seem to be taking place almost every evening, as we move to some unknown spot for the next battle. Much to the surprise of everyone Duncan Carmichael has found religion; that is really amazing as he was always the meanest, dirtiest drunkard, and the deadliest knife fighter in three counties! Who would have ever thought that such a man would find God in the middle of a war! While he is still the deadliest one among us in a fight, he now leads most of the prayer services each evening, if no reverend can be found.*

*The fire is dying and I am tired, so I will only tell you this; I envision your lovely face, as I sit here. I do not believe I will be able to visit home any time soon, as this endless fighting seems to go, with a battle every week or so. Still, you must know that I love you and long to hold you, my wonderful wife, my bride, in my arms.*

*When I do see you, at some future time, I do not think I will kiss you forthwith; rather I believe that I shall gaze on your face, for a few moments, first, and then I shall know that I am, indeed, in Heaven. Afterwards, a kiss…*

*Yours forever,*
*Major Jamie Turnbull, Commander*
*Fourth Georgia Infantry*
*Hood's Corps, CSA*

As happened so many times in this long War Between the States, two letters from these lovers passed near each other as each passed through the post in Atlanta, heading in separate directions.

*Major Jamie Turnbull, Commander*
*Fourth Georgia Infantry*
*Atlanta Station for Delivery to Hood's Corps, CSA*

*My dearest and most loving husband,*

*Nothing much happens here, as we await news of your victories, so I shan't bother you with boring trivia. I will include this last scribbling of mine, on the history of Traveler's Rest Plantation, since you seem to enjoy these notes so very much. I hope you find them to be a remove from what must indeed, become boring days in camp or on the trail. I shall write more of home a bit later, so for now, these lines on our plantation history will have to do.*

*We hear that General Johnston and the army is near Resaca, wherever that is. At any rate I do hope you are safe. As always, please know that I love you with all my heart and soul. I know that saying this so forwardly is unseemly for a new bride, but it is indeed, the truest expression that Almighty God has placed upon my heart, a heart that is forever, yours.*

*Your Mary*

## More Scribblings on Our Plantation History
### *as told by my Grandfather, Mr. Devereaux Jarrett, Master of Traveler's Rest Plantation written by Mrs. Mary Jarrett Turnbull, May 16, 1864*

My Grandfather Devereaux told me of many past discussions at Traveler's Rest. Many of those discussions changed the very history of north Georgia and, dare I say it, of this nation. I previously sent to you, my dearest husband, an account of the visit by the Honorable John C. Calhoun, when he and several other great men, my Grandfather among them, met here at Traveler's Rest Plantation, and decided to drill for gold using the water-cannon! No one had ever tried that before, at least in north Georgia, but these men did it, and they took thousands of ounces of gold from these Georgia hills by that simple trick. The massive Calhoun Mine near Helen, Georgia, still produces as much gold yearly, as any mine in the world, even today!

However not long after that, the great man John C. Calhoun, became even more frustrated than he had been with the government in Washington City. A bit later he again visited Traveler's Rest and this time, he brought along with him a rather motley crew of fire-eating dragons!

Of course I jest a little here. The men who convened that evening were, not dragons, but were "fire-eaters," so called because of their fiery attitudes towards the outrageous and unfair taxes that were being imposed by the representatives in the Union states! They were so angry at the Union that they "spit flames from their mouths!" at least, according to the northern papers. History has documented that these early fire-eaters, virtually alone, brought the state of South Carolina almost into secession from the Union as early as the 1830s. In fact, according to my grandfather, it is not a stretch to say that these fire-eaters brought this War Between the States—this Second American Revolution—into being, some thirty years before the fighting even started! And the whole thing, just like the first American Revolution of 1776, began over unjust taxes!

The date was July 18, 1832, when the leaders of South Carolina and Georgia discussed, yet again, the pending taxes and ultimately secession from the Union. Men all over the southern states were holding such discussions because of the tariffs proposed in 1828. One of those important, discussions took place at my grandfather's plantation, here at Traveler's Rest. My grandfather remembered that evening well, and told me about it many times.

The great man himself John C. Calhoun, Vice President of the United States of America, spoke first on that night, as he and the other fire-eaters sat on the long front porch of Traveler's Rest. "Gentlemen, thank you for joining me here at Traveler's Rest Plantation, and we appreciate the hospitality of our friend, Jarrett. There is nothing like discussing politics while savoring that nectar, Prather's Honeydew moonshine, such as only Jarrett here can provide!
Now, I come among you today, to announce that I've just resigned from the Vice-Presidency of the United States of America. I can better fend off these, vile, tax-crazed Yankees from a seat in the Senate than from some ceremonial position in the shadow of the great White House! What eternally-be-dammed whelp of a man thought up that meaningless job of Vice President anyway?

"I think of that infernal position as something I call the 'Ain't you dead yet?' office. All the Vice President really has to do on any given day, is look at the President and ask, 'Ain't you dead yet?' If the President either answers verbally or merely breathes, then he clearly ain't dead, and as long as he's still alive, the Vice President has not a damn thing to do until he repeats the same question the very next morning! I tell you esteemed gentlemen, that damned office is totally worthless."

Those fire-eaters always enjoyed a good joke, particularly if it involved the insanity in Washington City, so they all had a good laugh at Calhoun's lines. Then the Great Man spoke again, on a more serious matter.

"No gentlemen. If I'm to fight off these infernal taxes that the Yankees want to force on us, I have to do it from the Senate where I'll have some real power!"

Julien Cobb a fire-eater who served on the faculty of the University of Georgia some seventy miles south of Traveler's Rest, spoke up next. "Indeed, John. I cannot understand it! I simply cannot say why the Yankees believe they should tax our plantations into oblivion. Don't they know that the entirety of southern society will fall, if they do so? Do they not see that we will not, we cannot, stand for it! If you can fight them from the Senate, John, and defeat this ungodly tax on goods from England, then please do so quickly. Otherwise, I fear a fight in the streets of Charleston or Richmond, Savannah, Washington City, or even Atlanta! Personally, I would rather see Georgia withdraw from the Union as continue participating within a government bent on my own destruction."

Edmund Ruffin, the youngest member of the House of Representatives in the South Carolina legislature, had traveled to this meeting with the Great Man himself. His family owned a plantation near Columbia, South Carolina. He had patiently waited his turn, but after several of his seniors spoke, he could hold himself back no longer. "I'm with you Cobb! Damn right, I'm with you! Leaving this unholy Union may be our only option. For I fear, as do you all, that we cannot survive these tariffs. Surely those Yankee gentlemen must see that these taxes would sever our long-standing ties with Great Britain, and force us to buy their more expensive goods from Massachusetts, Connecticut, and New Jersey! That is why the Congress, may Almighty God curse them all, passed the damned tariff to begin with! This tax is at best, a self-serving theft by those northern bastards of our hard earned coin! I'll not stand for it!"

At that point Devereaux Jarrett, the owner of Traveler's Rest and patriarch of the Jarrett family, contributed his thoughts to the discussion. For like most of the men there, he was a wealthy plantation owner, and an international businessman with strong ties to factors in London as well as Paris. "You are right my friends in that we cannot survive these ungodly tariffs, and while the northern states have their own mills and industry, we do not. What we have is cotton, and England wants that cotton and pays for that cotton better than the mills in the Union states do! Thus they wish to tax us on both our exports and imports to and from Europe! Our ties have always been more with London than with Boston or New York, and the men of substance in those northern states wish nothing more than to see the southern states broken. These tariffs are, indeed, intended to ruin us all in the south, and no government has a right to cut the throat of its citizens by ruining their businesses! Don't these Yankees understand that? Are they all mad?"

Calhoun then spoke up again. "I am not sure that we need talk of secession. Rather, we can seek other means to deal with these tariffs, strategies that are within the bounds of the Constitution, or at least, not specifically prohibited by it."

Many of the fire-eaters then spoke up, all at once. "What ideas have you?" "What do you have in mind, John?"

Calhoun let the dust settle from his remarks, with a smile on his face—a face that was usually quite stern and not prone to smiling, except among friends. "I do have a strategy, that is a bit short of secession. We, as a state, should declare this action of the federal congress Null and Void!"

## Author's Note: The First Shots of the Civil War: 1832!

Thus began The Nullification Crisis of 1830s. One might argue that, this crisis was the beginning of the War Between the States, the American Civil War, though these events took place some thirty years prior to firing on Fort Sumter in 1861. The Nullification Crisis was one of the most challenging and difficult periods in early American history. South Carolina did indeed vote to "Nullify" the tariffs—the taxes—in question, and that immediately provoked a constitutional crisis, forcing the question, can a state declare a federal law null within its own borders? There is nothing in the US Constitution that prohibits such a nullification vote, and the Constitution clearly viewed states as the supreme organ of government, superior to the federal authority in most areas, and of course, John C. Calhoun knew his constitutional law. Thus, the fire-eaters of South Carolina decided to try this strategy! By 1832, the South Carolina legislature had passed the Nullification Bill, and both South Carolina and the federal government began preparing their armed forces for what all believed would be a military showdown on that important question. Which authority was supreme; state or federal?

Within a few weeks, that question was on the minds of every educated man and woman in the nation. In fact, two newspaper editors with drastically different viewpoints, ended up dueling each other over this Nullification Crisis in August of 1832. Turner Bynum as a hot-headed opponent of the tariffs passed by the Congress, was soon engaged in rabid debate with another newspaper editor in Greenville, South Carolina, then a small upstate South Carolina town of some four thousand people. In one editorial, Bynum attacked his opponent personally, as well as on his stance on the tariffs, and in the early decades of the 1800s, such personal attacks typically resulted in a challenge for a "duel to the death!"

Bynum's opponent, Benjamin Perry, was a supporter of the tariffs, and thus of the Union. Obviously, he opposed the concept that any state could nullify any federal law, and his paper presented that opinion in a loud, aggressive fashion. When he read Bynum's personal attack, he issued an immediate challenge for a duel, demanding publically the right to defend his honor. Bynum quickly accepted, but that is when both men encountered a big problem.

While dueling was an accepted practice—indeed Andy Jackson, the man then sitting in the White House, had dueled several times in his life—the practice had been declared illegal in the state of South Carolina. Thus, where would two highly visible, public men hold their duel to the death? Where could they go such that the eventual victor of such a duel, would not face murder charges? Someone soon suggested a reasonable option; "Let's all go to Georgia! It's only fifty miles away, and they don't pay much attention to law anyway!"

Thus on August 16, 1832, two men faced each other on a small no-name island in the Tugalo River, in what was then Franklin County, Georgia. Technically the islands in that mountain stream belonged to Georgia, but jurisdiction on an island between two states was always questionable, so an isolated island was selected for the duel. In fact, the island was only seven miles from the Jarrett Plantation, and no doubt, had Devereaux Jarrett known what was to take place that morning he, and most of the other fire-eaters, would have been there! However, neither Bynam, nor Perry, nor their seconds, had shared the information publically, so only four men witnessed the historic occurrence. On August 16 at dawn, two dueling pistols were drawn, and two angry men walked twenty paces from each other, turned, and fired. Both were wounded; however, Bynum's wound was much more severe, and he was dead two days later. Perry on the other hand, recovered, and always opposing secession, he entered politics and served one term as Governor of South Carolina.

It is often strange how events in history seem, at least in retrospect, to be predictably related to other events, and the multiple tensions between states that would lead to the Civil War were complex, and long standing. Still, one can very well argue, as have many historians, that the first two shots of the War Between the States were fired on the Tugalo River on that August morning in 1832, some twenty-nine years before Confederate cannon fired on Fort Sumter in Charleston, SC. Such were the passions over the nullification crisis.

The nation was lucky in the 1830s however, in that cooler heads soon prevailed. A compromise tariff was passed by Congress in 1832, that was somewhat more acceptable to South Carolina, so the state legislature repealed its own Nullification legislation. Thus was the Nullification Crisis and a possible

War Between the States averted in the early 1830s. However, the hostility, the pure hatred, as well as the sectional and economic differences between the several regions of the nation were etched in stone in everyone's mind, and this same fight, and this same question, would smolder for decades yet to come.

Today some historians interpret the War Between the States exclusively as a battle over slavery, and while that may be politically correct in today's world, it is also somewhat moronic, and actually ignores this long complex history. In fact since the ill-fated Articles of Confederation had failed as an early model for a federal government—leading to the adoption of the Constitution—states had varied in their perspectives on a wide range of issues, and on several occasions states had armed themselves for military conflict with each other. Certainly the Nullification Crisis, with both South Carolina and the federal government calling out various militias for the anticipated conflict, represented one tension that led to the Civil War. In "Bleeding Kansas" during the 1850s and 1860s, armed conflict actually erupted, as it had in the Whisky Rebellion in Washington's second term as President. Conflicts between states are nothing new, and while slavery was an important factor, it was only one cause of the War Between the States.

Therefore, more reasoned scholars, more honest men, at least admit there were many reasons for that Great American Civil War, a war that some consider a Second American Revolution. It is a simple fact that the first time the state of South Carolina threatened secession was during the Nullification Crisis of the 1830s, on an issue wholly unrelated to slavery. To ignore that fact is to misinterpret history.

No one knows exactly when the phrase fire-eater was first used, but that term was certainly in use by the 1830s. It did accurately categorize many southern gentlemen of the era, Bynum, Riffin, and Cobb were such men. These were men who did, in fact, "spit fire" in their oratory, arguing forcefully against the growing power of the federal government, a position that is heard loudly today in the growing Tea Party movement, from 2009 through 2014. While secession has not been advanced as a cause by the Tea Party in recent years, a much more limited federal government has certainly been a clarion call of that movement. Further, several states, by 2013, had passed Nullification legislation directed at stopping the federal government small arms, gun control agenda. Thus, those in power today would do well to listen to that message from 1832, rather than denigrate it. It is a fact of history that when any government willingly alienates and demonizes much of its opposition, as the federal government has done to the Tea Party in recent years, societal unrest, often results, sometimes leading to revolutions. Such was the case in both 1776 and 1860, and one can only contemplate the implications of a similar disaffection with large, intrusive government in 2016 or 2020.

Simply put knowing history is not enough. Rather we would all do well to listen to the lessons history teaches us. Clearly, the fire-eaters of the 1830s – 1860s can offer us cautions for today, if we and our federal government, are wise enough to listen.

Further, one can well argue, as have a few historians, that the first shots of the Civil War were fired in 1832, right here in Franklin County, Georgia!

## A War of Shovels

"I'm tired of digging! Ain't Gen'al Johnston got more important work for us?" Thus did Batty Prather sum up his frustrations on May 17, 1864, after hours of digging trenches, as he and the others worked on the fortifications at a small town called Cassville, in north Georgia, only thirty miles south of Resaca. The Western and Atlantic Railroad passed just south of town, and General Johnston had ordered that his Confederate army be carefully entrenched in order to block Sherman's advance along the rail-line. Sherman's army was encamped only twelve miles up the line at a small town called Kingston, GA.

"You're right as hell, Batty! The Gen'al even got the niggers digging on this ditch a bit down the line!" Lee Lovorn chimed in. "Why can't they dig this ditch over here too? Why do we have to do nigger work? Hell, this ain't fit work for no white man! This is a damned war of shovels!"

"Shut your infernal mouths, you idiots, and just keep digging," responded Wellspeak, as he tossed a spade full of red Georgia clay up to the front of the trench. "It don't make no never-mind who digs what ditch, as long as there's a ditch to jump in when ol' Sherman and his Yankees show up! You fools ain't seen much o' his cannon, but I have, so dig'er deep you son-of-a-bitch, and stop complaining!"

At that exchange, Duncan, Batty, Lee, Wellspeak, and all of the others in the Fourth Georgia continued their digging. They were preparing a trench outside of a town with less than two hundred people, most of whom had seen the Army of Tennessee coming and simply left town.

Sampson, the personal servant of Major Turnbull, looked up, as the voices from just down the ditch got louder. He spoke softly, so just the other black men working beside him could hear, and he grinned. "Seems like the white folks can't stan' a bit o' digging! I recon, ain't none of 'um ever really worked before!"

Ten Cent Bill smiled to himself. "Guess not. Wouldn't 'spect much work outa white folk now would ya? I'll bet we end up finishing that ditch too, once we done with this 'um!"

Sampson responded. "Well, dig 'um both deep then. I's been in front o' Yankee minie-balls a'fore, and I can't say as I'd like to face many of 'um without no deep ditch!"

Thus do men of all colors, all stations in life, complain, in the face of hard work. Still if the men are worth a single cent, then the complaining relieves the tension a bit and the work gets done. As those men continued their digging, and their complaining, they were being observed carefully by the eyes of the enemy, from the wooded area only five hundred feet away. Of course, Sherman's army was still encamped in Kingston some miles away to the west, but every army in history has used spies and observers, and the Union forces in north Georgia were no exception. Sherman had his cavalry out in all directions, and he knew that Johnston's men were entrenching in Cassville, but he'd had no solid reports of the locations or dispositions of their exact lines.

Meanwhile in a low clump of bushes, a pair of eyes squinted in a well-worn, well wrinkled, black face. The eyes, like a hawk on the prowl, were watching everything; they missed nothing. No cannon had been observed, but it was clear that work on this section of the entrenchment was moving quickly. The old woman could hear almost every word said by the fifty or so men to her front, but she could barely see their shoulders, which indicated they had been digging for a while. The ditch was about five feet deep along this section of the rise just behind the village. This section of the entrenchment was nearly done, and the diggers only needed to place a firing log or two above the earthworks to protect the men's heads as they fired their weapons below the log. Just as she'd observed at several other sections down the line, the entrenchments were nearly ready, and only the logs and the cannon needed to be positioned.

This would be a strong line, maybe too strong to attack directly, and the wise old woman, Harriet Tubman, had already noticed Sherman's tendency to bypass a strong fortification rather than attack directly. Of course, she would report back to Sherman what she had seen, while gathering in wandering slaves all along her route—taking them to the freedom of the Union lines. Still, by that time, she'd seen it all and could describe the Confederate defenses as well as any army engineer on either side of the line. This Cassville line was a strong defensive line on the top of a sharp rise in elevation, that was almost six miles long. The line included ditches, open fields of fire in front of most of the ditches, and cannon emplacements every three hundred feet or so—a very strong line, indeed.

Thus was Tubman the first to realize, that there would probably never be an all-out assault on the entrenchments in front of her. Sherman, she was sure, would by-pass them. Why waste men in a fight when you can simply go around? She pulled herself, very quietly, back along the ground, never taking her piercing eyes off the men in front of her, and after crawling for twenty or so feet, she was well hidden in the bushes. By then, she's observed construction of virtually the entire line, having watched several different sections since sunrise. She'd also found both ends of the Confederate defensive works.

As she stood, she decided she'd seen enough. Then she looked up at the sun to get her directions—only an hour or so of daylight left. Next, she moved off to the west to find Sherman in Kingston. She walked the entire way, taking her the rest of the day, and most of the night, but when she came to Sherman's camp, thirteen newly freed slaves were in tow. She'd picked them up at a plantation along the Kingston/Cassville road. She asked the first guard in the skirmish line to take her directly to General Sherman's tent, which he did.

Two mornings later Sherman himself, and several members of his staff were sitting astride their mounts and looking through their looking glasses at the same Confederate entrenchments, entrenchments that were, by then, completed. Sherman was shaking his head a bit as he looked at the new fortifications and the Confederates behind them. All head logs were in place, and many cannon barrels were in evidence along the top of the rise, along with rows of men looking back in his direction. It was at that exact moment that Sherman began and ended the Battle of Cassville, with one simple statement; "No way in hell!"

And that's probably why you've never heard of the Battle of Cassville—it never took place. With 65,000 Union men facing Johnston's 50,000 Confederates, who were well dug-in atop the rise behind the town, Sherman decided not to waste his time or his men in that small hamlet of Cassville, Georgia. Just as Tubman had predicted to herself two days before when she looked at those same fortifications, Sherman decided to by-pass them. Of course he had, once again, moved only a part of his massive Union army to Cassville. The day before he rode to Cassville, he'd sent McPherson's Army of The Tennessee, some 35,000 men, on yet another right hook. Sweeping wide to the west of Cassville, McPherson's force missed the Confederate fortifications by over fifteen miles. Within two hours of Sherman's decision, the remainder of the Union armies had begun preparations to withdraw, a fact that many Confederates noted from their ditches.

"Hell, ain't Sherman even gonna give us a bit of target practice today?" Wellspeak said. "I was hopin' to see something to shoot at, after diggin' this nice ditch and all."

Duncan looked over at the younger man, and merely said. "Don't look like they be a comin,' lease ways not right now, do it?"

Batty grinned just a few feet away and responded. "Maybe they heard the Fourth Georgia was over here, and loaded for bear! Hell, that probably scared 'um!"

That brought a grin to all of their faces, as they stood looking at the Union army withdraw their cannon, an army that had never really entrenched. All of the men, Batty, Wellspeak, Ten Cent Bill, Lee Lovorn, even Captain Collins, who was standing a few feet behind the others, could only stare out beyond their breastworks at the attack that never came. Every Confederate in that line at that moment was asking the same question; "Are they leaving? Why don't they attack? What are they waiting for?"

Major Jamie Turnbull, commander of the regiment, was not only dumbstruck; he was righteously angry when the expected attack did not come. "Captain Collins," he shouted to his second in command. "What the hell are they doing over there? Why can't they attack us like those idiots did in Resaca?" He took a moment and spit on the ground from atop his horse, as he sat mounted, only twenty feet or so behind the line.

At just that moment three new men showed up. They came to attention and saluted Turnbull. "Sir, we're reportin' for duty Sir. I'm Mo Hendon, and this here is my cousin Roy Giles."

Then the other recruit spoke. "I'm Chad Wilson Sir, from Clarkesville, GA."

Jamie looked down at the fresh faces, and thought to himself for just a moment, "They look so damn young! Did I look that stupid before my first fight at Chickamauga?" He was gracious enough not to say it. Instead he returned the salute and said, "We can surely use some new men. You men from the Tugalo Valley?"

Wilson had already answered that question, so he remained quiet.

Hendon replied, "Yes Sir. We's from Franklin County down along the Tugalo River, and we knowed Lem Davis. He invited us to join the other Tugalo men in the Fourth Georgia!"

"Well," said Jamie. "We can always use good men, particularly if Lem recommends them." Then Jamie looked back toward the line, and shouted, "Captain Collins! We have new recruits here, Privates Hendon, Giles and Wilson. Put them in the line beside Corporal Carmichael, if you please, and have him show these men around."

"Yes Sir," Collins replied.

Jamie looked back down at the new men. "Men, you learn from Captain Collins and 'specially from Corporal Carmichael. You watch him and ask questions 'bout what he does. He'll get you squared away right quick. Most of all, you be sure and do what he says! He's been at this a while, and if you listen to him real good, he just might be able to keep you alive."

Wilson merely saluted, but Hendon and Giles looked at each other with a worried expression, then looked back up at the Major. "Sir," said Hendon. "Would that be the knife-fighter, Duncan Carmichael, from Walton's Ford? He's been in more scrapes and bar-brawls than most anybody I heard of, including several down in Franklin County!"

Hearing that, Duncan Carmichael stood up a few yards away, and began to climb out of the trench. Once he was atop the earthen mound, he looked at the three new men and slowly grinned. Then he began to walk toward the three recruits. He was filthy from digging the ditch, and he sported a very muddy, seven-inch beard. His long hair was matted against his head from the sweat, and as he advanced, he took his fourteen-inch knife carefully from his breeches, and began to run it across his fingers, never saying a word. While he was still smiling slightly, his eyes were cold—piercing—and he was staring at the new recruits as a rattlesnake might look at an unsuspecting rabbit. He moved to within six inches of Hendon's chest, and stared into Hendon's eyes. Then he stepped to the side, to face Wilson, very much "invading the space" of the new recruits. To a man, the three new recruits could smell his breath, as Duncan, knife in hand, stared in turn, into each man's face from five inches away. Meanwhile, Major Turnbull calmly replied to Hendon's question.

"One and the same boys," said Turnbull. "He's one and the same. Duncan Carmichael is just like his daddy; a knife-fighter, a crack shot, and a thoroughly dangerous man. I truly believe he's the best fighter in either damned army, and if the Yankees don't kill you, he probably will, unless you listen to every word he says and jump when he says jump! You men understand?"

The three privates looked briefly at the Major, and quickly returned their eyes to the dangerous man before them, still standing five inches away, and staring, seemingly, deep into their very soul. Then the new recruits, saluted Turnbull without taking their eyes from Duncan. They feebly said, in unison, "Yes Sir," and Wilson added, "We'll make you proud, Sir."

"I'm sure you will. Now Captain Collins is your company commander, and my second in command, but your boss here is Corporal Carmichael. I believe you can see him standing there before you." Jamie couldn't help himself, so he grinned when he gave the final order. "Corporal Carmichael, please get these new men squared away. Dismissed."

With that Jamie giggled a bit, as he turned away and looked again toward the enemy lines and the attack that still wasn't coming. He waited another few minutes, and grinned to himself, as he heard Batty and Duncan both cursing the new privates in the ditch up ahead. He thought to himself, that Duncan's display had been a bit over the top, but Carmichael would keep those boys alive, if anyone could. With that thought, Jamie looked back across the field.

Finally he could stand the waiting no more, so he shouted. "Captain Collins, I'm riding to headquarters and see if anyone knows what the hell is happening out there. You remain here. If I hear anything other than a skirmish, I'll be back as quickly as possible."

"Sir!" shouted Collins. "I'll keep things in order here, Sir."

Jamie arrived at the headquarters only ten minutes later, just as General Hood was receiving his instructions from General Johnston. Jamie saw maybe fifteen other majors and colonels in attendance, and they were already in discussion. Jamie didn't even have to inquire about the state of the attack; it seems that the same question was on everyone's mind.

General Hood, General Johnston, and the others were standing together just outside of Johnston's command tent, and Hood was speaking as Jamie dismounted only a few feet away. "It seems that Mr. Sherman doesn't want to fight here, at least not today. I've had reports of him moving his cannon out of the line, and hooking up his caissons. He may be withdrawing, Sir."

Johnston spoke next. "I'd like to know the disposition of his forces. Are we seeing all of his men, or is McPherson riding somewhere out there in those woods again? Perhaps if I could ever receive a substantive report from Joe Wheeler's Cavalry I'd have a sense of what is going on!"

Jamie listened a bit more to the comments, but then decided to quietly withdraw—it was clear by then that even the senior leaders of the entire Confederate army were every bit as in-the-dark as he was. Thus, he rode on back to his command having learned absolutely nothing. He reflected a bit, as he rode slowly back to his position. War and life are both like that; in the most dangerous and challenging times, you never know what the hell to expect!

At that moment about twelve miles away in Kingston, GA, Sherman reached his headquarters tent and gave final instructions for his entire command to move west. When the order was given, several staff officers who had not accompanied him to see the enemy entrenchments in Cassville appeared dumbstruck! Was Crazy Billy really moving away from his railroad? It was a completely unexpected move, and one that was very uncharacteristic of Sherman. Ever since he'd left Tennessee in early May, Sherman had planted his army firmly astride the tracks of the Western and Atlantic Railroad. That line was his life-blood, since all his supplies were being shipped by that line right into his southernmost camps. In short, for the entire first half of May, 1864, Sherman had been married to that railroad!

Which is why his orders on May 21, were so unexpected; He chose to leave the railroad and cast off into the wilderness of western Georgia! He decided to leave only a small, rear-guard force behind at Cassville, and move the remainder of his army out to the west, leaving his precious railroad completely. Of course, Sherman knew he was moving into a vast, relatively uncharted wilderness, with only a few roads, and no sizable towns to speak of. In fact, he was moving into what was, at that time, the most unsettled area of Georgia. Unlike the plantation areas along the southern coast, or the areas populated by the gold-rush in the Georgia mountains, that western section of Georgia held virtually nothing, only a few widely scattered farms and one or two rural churches. As his subordinates looked on in his command tent, Sherman studied a map and then placed his finger on the only real settlement, an obscure little crossroads town in that wilderness called Dallas.

He said, "Here, gentlemen, is where we shall rendezvous with McPherson. Alert your commands to move out tomorrow, with an eye toward arriving in Dallas within three days. There are only two roads in that wilderness, so organize yourselves, and your regiments, and make your movements in conjunction with each other. We leave at dawn."

Of course across the lines at Cassville, the frustration continued. No Confederate commander had any clue where the mass of Sherman's army was heading. It was clear within two hours that only a token force was left to their front, and two nights later, even that small force left in the darkness. Johnston knew his army was being flanked but he didn't know if the Union force was to the west or the east of Cassville, so he did the only thing he could do; He moved twenty miles further down the railroad tracks and fortified another strong position right beside the railroad, a place called Allatoona Pass. He was confident that Sherman would never entirely leave the railroad, so he merely needed to build fortifications a bit closer to Atlanta, and wait. Of course, in that instance, Johnston was dead wrong. In fact Johnston had made that most simple of command mistakes. He'd assumed that Sherman would do the same thing after Cassville that he'd done twice before—flank the Confederate line and then follow the railroad. Johnston would learn of his error in only a few days, but by then, Crazy Billy had accomplished a quiet unexpected magic trick. He'd made an entire Union army, a hundred thousand strong, disappear!

## At the Shovels Again

"Damn these shovels, damn this heat, and damn this red Georgia clay! It's like digging into a brick!" Batty had become the leading man in the constant usage of swearwords, since Duncan Carmichael had gotten religion. Of course any of those men, even the three new recruits, could string together a curse that would make a sailor blush, but Batty was probably the best; at the very least, he was the loudest.

"Here we are again, dammit, diggin' another damn ditch that we ain't gonna get to use! Why in hell can't we just hide behind trees, instead o' wastin' all this damn time digging?"

None of the others even responded to Batty's outrage this time around. All of them merely continued to, once again, dig their defensive works. They were preparing a fort on a sixty foot bluff just east of Allatoona Pass, a critical juncture that held the Western and Atlantic Railroad tracks leading south to Atlanta. Major Turnbull had assigned the men to dig one of the forts overlooking the pass, while all the darkies, slaves as well as personal servants, were assigned to dig a similar fort on the other side of the pass. In that way, the rail-line that

Sherman so treasured would pass immediately below the massed cannon that would soon be located in both forts. The cut that held the tracks was no more than a hundred feet wide, so the men working on one fort could literally hear the men on the other, and once cannon were mounted on both bluffs overlooking the railroad, Sherman would find his initial attack, as well as his supply trains, as Batty said, "Blown all to hell!" Once again, the Confederates had constructed a very strong defensive position for Sherman to attack.

This time however, Sherman didn't even bother to look over the position prior to moving around it. History records no dramatic visit by Sherman or anyone on his staff, at the Allatoona Pass defenses for one simple reason; Sherman wasn't headed in that direction. He had already chosen to bypass that section of the railroad, and move toward Dallas, GA, as we have seen, and this was a very wise decision from his perspective. In fact, he controlled the railroad all the way from Chattanooga to Kingston, GA, so he could afford to provision his army from the Kingston depot for a time. Thus, did Sherman leave the railroad and launch his army toward Dallas, and ultimately toward a much larger town twenty miles further south, Marietta, GA. Once again, much to the chagrin of the Confederates, Sherman sidestepped the Confederate defensive line. The southern men were growing very tired of digging ditches that were then merely abandoned, but like the line at Cassville, the forts and other defenses at Allatoona Pass would be abandoned once completed, with no battle having been fought there. Those entrenchments at Allatoona would be the scene of a battle much later in the war, but it is a historic fact that the miles and miles of ditches and forts at both Cassville and Allatoona Pass were unused during Sherman's advance on Atlanta in the spring of 1864.

Thus did the war of the shovels continue, and with all of this movement going on, there was no significant fight between the Union forces and the Confederate Army of Tennessee from May 16 after the fight at Resaca, until the armies again came together ten days later along the battle line in Dallas, GA.

## At the Campfire

All the men were exhausted from their final day of digging, and the Confederates were spending their down-time in various pursuits, as do men in every army. Some were playing poker. Some were betting on lice races. Batty and Wellspeak had gone to sutler's row to purchase a bit of fun, and they soon returned with some fresh whisky that had been cooked up earlier that day. They were well into their cups even before sitting down by the fire, where they promptly passed around the jar. All of the white men by the fire took a drink, except Duncan and Wilson, the new man. Ten Cent Bill, Sampson, and two other black men sat at a nearby tree, playing cards, but of course, they were not offered the white men's jar.

Major Turnbull was off at the general's headquarters doing whatever he did there, leaving Captain Collins in charge once again, but there was little for any commander to do. The positions around Allatoona Pass were virtually completed, so the Confederates did what all soldiers do most of their time—they waited.

The new recruits, Hendon, Giles, and Wilson, all sat by the fire along with the veterans. The new men were still terrified of Duncan Carmichael, as they had been for the last several days, even though he had given them no reason to be, beyond his playful display on the day they arrived. He had taught them a great deal about the fighting, lessons that everyone hoped they learned well. He'd explained what a head-log was for, and how loud the cannon would sound. He'd had them practice quick loading and firing their rifles, while they shot at targets through the smoke of a campfire. He wanted them to understand that smoke blocked one's vision most of the time, and hampered one's aim in a real battle. He'd shown them how to construct a fighting trench. He was in every way possible, trying to get them ready for the hell of a Civil War battlefield.

Still that night all of them sat together, Duncan, the new men, Ten Cent Bill, Sampson, Lee Lovorn, and the others, watching the crazy antics of Batty and Wellspeak—clearly two very drunk men. Batty had the idea first, and shouted too loudly in his excitement, as drunk men often do. "Wellspeak! Want to go watch them boys from Alabame race lice? I bet I can find one in my shorts that'll beat any one they got!"

Wellspeak answered in a drunken slur. "Can't nothing live in your shorts, and if'n it did, I bet you's too drunk to find it!" He then began an uncontrollable giggle, that soon matured into a drunken laugh. Lee Lovorn was sitting on a log, while writing a letter home, but most of the others grinned at Wellspeak's joke. Duncan had noted who sipped from the jar and who hadn't, as it was passed around the fire. After it made a complete circle and was back in Batty's hands, Duncan stood up and terrified one of the new men. "Wilson," he shouted. "You'll be a commin' with me, for a time."

Wilson looked a bit nervous as he stared up at this knife fighter, this filthy demon—for Duncan, like most Carmichaels, not to mention most Confederates, rarely bathed. He merely said, "Sir?"

"On your damn feet, recruit!" Duncan shouted even louder. "You'll be moving out with me in ten seconds, or I'll hide you where you stand, boy!" Then Duncan pretended to reach for the massive knife, a weapon that always remained close at hand, usually stuck in the rope belt holding up his breeches.

Of course, by the time he'd finished shouting, Wilson was on his feet saluting Duncan. Corporals are not saluted in any army in the world, but you may rest assured that Wilson saluted Duncan Carmichael that night. Wilson had no doubt at that moment, who held his life in his hands. By then, everyone else at the campfire was staring at the new man, but a few of the veterans were grinning; Batty, Wellspeak, Ten Cent Bill, and Sampson, all seemed to know what was going on.

"Beside me, recruit," Duncan said, as Wilson fell in beside him. They walked off into the night, heading in the general direction of sutler's row.

Duncan was smiling to himself by then, a smile that Wilson couldn't possibly see in the darkness, but Duncan just couldn't resist a bit more play with this young man. He began, in a stately solemn voice, timing his words to his steps, as he quoted a Bible passage known to soldiers around the world.

*"The Lord is my shepherd: I shall not want.*
*He maketh me to lie down in green pastures;*
*He leadeth me beside still waters.*
*He restoreth my soul. He leadeth me in the paths*
*of righteousness for his name's sake.*
*"Yea, though I walk through the valley of the shadow of death,*
*I will fear no evil. For thou art with me.*
*Thy rod and thy staff, they comfort me."*

By that point in the quotation, the two men had left the comforting light of the campfire, and Wilson was absolutely certain that he was, indeed, walking through the valley of the shadow of death at that very moment. Moreover, he certainly feared the evil that was calmly walking right beside him! For that reason, he was to say the least, surprised at Duncan's next words.

"What do you know of God, recruit?" Duncan said, in a rather calm voice.

Wilson nearly choked at that question, and could only reply, "Sir?"

"What do you know of God?"

At that point, Wilson had the sinking feeling that absolutely nothing in the known universe made any sense, but he was certain of one thing, just as Duncan had suspected, so he spoke up. "God is my only strength, Sir." Wilson said. "He will either keep me safe in this war, no matter what you, 'er, what the Yankees do to me, Sir. God will keep me, just like that Bible passage said."

Duncan then asked, "And what if you die in the fight here?"

Wilson had always been firm in his beliefs, even given his relatively young age. He replied with a bit more courage. "God will either keep me safe in this war, or if I die, he will take me home to Heaven, where I shall live with Jesus for the rest of eternity."

Never before by man, has Christian belief been summarized so succinctly, or so well.

Duncan replied. "I noticed that you didn't partake in Wellspeak's whisky, boy."

Wilson replied. "I ain't got nothing against a sip now and then, Sir. Everybody in camp gets bored to tears. I can see that, and I only been here a day or two." Wilson suddenly realized that he was comfortable now, talking with Carmichael, so he continued. "Hell, Sir. Even my Maw and Paw cook up some mash every few months, like most folks in north Georgia. Maw gives it mostly to the young 'uns, when they get sick, but my folks are known to take a dram or two on Saturday nights."

Duncan then did what every great leader of men does; he opened up a bit, to show this new man who he really was. "It's about the same way at my home. Most Carmichaels drink, and quite a few to excess. Some get trapped in the jar and never get out, and that ain't good for nobody, but if'n you can hold it, a swaller or two never hurt."

Wilson, now confident that neither the conversation nor the nighttime stroll with Carmichael would lead to his imminent death, asked, "But Sir. How is it that you, er… what I mean is, how come…"

Duncan helped the younger man by voicing his thoughts for him. "How come I ain't drinking along with Batty and Wellspeak? How come the meanest knife fighter in three states ain't drunk on his ass all the time?"

Wilson said merely. "I wasn't gonna…"

Duncan shut him up. "Yes you was. You know you was. You wanted to ask exactly that."

Wilson could say nothing. They walked a few steps in silence.

Finally Duncan spoke. "I recon' by now, that I've seen every hell known to man. Even before this war, I'd seen the blood and gore of a true-life, hell-bent-for-death knife fight." Here Duncan paused, but only for a moment. "Now, I've seen war in every ugly way you can. I know what it was like when King David's army slew the Philistines, and I figure this is pretty much the same. I seen wounded horses—they used horses in King David's time too. I've seen good mounts, beautiful horses, scamper across a bloody corn field on three legs, with the other 'un shot away. I've watched men cut in half by a cannon ball. Saw one look down at his own stomach, to find his legs and most of his body gone; I watched the light fade from that man's eyes while he died. I've smelled rotten bodies across the lines, seen men gored by a bayonet, some on my own knife. I've heard the screams of dyin' men; heard many men scream like babies for water or for their Mama, and I've heard more than one curse God with their dyin' breath. I've watched brave men die on both sides. Hell, I've kilt more than my share, 'cause I 'recon I'm good at it. Can't say as I ever liked it much."

Wilson at that point, couldn't help himself. "Then why is it that we still hear the stories, of what you do, 'er, what you…?"

Duncan looked at his companion, grinned and said. "Can't help stories, boy. Most of 'um are true as far as it goes, but that's who I was oncet; who I used to be. It ain't who I am."

Both men paused their conversation at that point. They'd both heard a fundamental truth buried deep in Duncan's words. When all is said and done, men can, and sometimes do, change who they are.

Then after another moment, Duncan continued, "Hell, boy. Those ol' stories even seem to give some strength to the men fighting beside me. The stories sure 'nuf got your attention the other day!"

Wilson said, "Damn sure did, Sir. Damn sure did!"

Then Duncan added one final bit of homespun wisdom that he'd gleaned during the war. "I ain't an educated man, Wilson. I didn't have much schooling before this began, 'cept in knife-fighting I guess. But I do know two things about war. First, every man is scart damn near to death, all the time. Hell, even if he says he ain't, he really is. Second, God is just about the only friend you got in a real fight. Even the guys next to you, guys you know can fight, they'll sometimes get too busy with their own fights to help you much, but God, He's always there, right there, beside you all the time. Hell, any man don't believe that, ain't a man; you got to know the Spirit, you got to know God, to be a real man. Now, don't you ever forget that, you hear!"

They walked a bit in silence after that, each man pondering that statement. Then Wilson realized that they were approaching another camp fire at the very end of sutler's row, and Duncan said. "It's a prayer meeting, boy, and I figured you'd like to come along tonight. Reverend David Ritcey with the 3rd Alabama usually leads one each evening. Sermons ain't none too long, and that man sure can sing!"

"Surely Sir. Thanks for bringing me." Wilson, now near the circle of thirty or so men, merely sat on the ground in the back row, expecting Duncan to do the same. Duncan however, continued on up to the front of the gathering next to the fire, where he was greeted by several of the other men.

Then Duncan walked to the fire in the middle and spoke up. "Guess the reverend is a bit late tonight, but he usually lets me lead the singing, so I guess, we'll start with a hymn."

With that, as Wilson and thirty-two other men turned their thoughts to the divine, Duncan began to sing that richest of hymns—a song popular on both sides of that mighty struggle. It was a hymn of comfort, of certainty in one's faith, and it was all the more popular for that reason during the War Between the States. Once Duncan began, all the other men joined in—for they all knew it by heart.

*"Alas, and did my savior bleed, and did my sovereign die?*
*"Would he devote that sacred head, for such a worm as I?"*
*"At the cross, at the cross, where I first saw the light,*
*And the burden of my heart rolled away.*
*"It was there by grace, I received my sight,*
*And now I am happy all the day."*

Thus, did two men of faith discover each other's comfort in Christian teachings, even as they discovered another fundamental truth; nothing is more powerful or more comforting for men in battle, than a shared faith in God. For that reason, these men would remain best of friends for the rest of their lives, even as they faced hell, again and again, during that bloody war.

## At Traveler's Rest Plantation

That very same night, at Traveler's Rest Plantation, the very same hymn was being sung for a wholly different reason. For a woman who had become an institution at Traveler's Rest was on her deathbed. Fanny Bricebud, long ago the main cook and head nigger for the Jarrett family, was, on that night approaching her eighty first birthday. She had long ago given up most of her duties in the household to younger slaves, her granddaughter Meely among them, and on the same night as Duncan Carmichael and Chad Wilson sang hymns and prayed at Allatoona Pass, a crowd of some fifteen slaves had gathered on the front porch of Fanny's cabin. All suspected that Fanny Bricebud would soon pass, though she had previously been on her deathbed a couple of times. She was very sick, and after all, how long could that old woman live? Still, they knew her favorite hymns, and as they gathered to pay their respects, they began to softly sing the same hymn.

*"At the cross, at the cross, where I first saw the light,*
*And the burden of my heart rolled away.*
*"It was there by grace, I received my sight,*
*And now I am happy all the day."*

At that point, Meely happened to look up from her seat on the porch, and saw several shadows pass by in the distance. Without being obtrusive, she gave her seat to another slave, and said something about using the outhouse. She slowly walked around behind the cabin. From there, she hurried into the trees in the distance, and once in the trees she could circle back behind the old barn without being seen from either the cabin porch or the big house. It took her only two minutes or so before she slipped in the rear door of that barn, but when she didn't see anyone, she softly called out the words "Railroad Jubilee." Those code words, taught to her by Fanny Bricebud only several months previously and known by conductors throughout the southern states, brought exactly the reaction she expected. "Jubilee! Praise God!"

With that counter-code spoken, Harriet Tubman stepped out from a distant horse stall, and said, "Where's Aunt Fanny? This here Conductor don't know who you is."

## Author's Note: The Underground Railroad

With those code words, began a ritual that took place all the way from southernmost Florida to the upper reaches of Wisconsin and Michigan. Escaped slaves along the documented and formalized routes of what became known as the Underground Railroad always sought a friendly place to hide. Some places called "stations," could be used multiple times. As escaped slaves made their way into the Union states or in some cases, all the way up to Canada, they often suffered, went hungry, traveled at night or in rainstorms all to achieve their own freedom. The blessed freedom kept them moving and motivated, and it awaited them as soon as they got to Canada, or during the war, the Union army. Guides on the Underground Railroad were called Conductors, and those Conductors traveled with the slaves, and were responsible for knowing signs and symbols of the Railroad as well as the network of locations in any area where they might hide, or be hidden from the slave hunters. While Tubman was new to Georgia, she knew who to ask about these symbols and stations, and Fanny Bricebud, the house servant, had been using the relatively lax discipline in the nigger yard at Traveler's Rest to help runaway slaves for over two decades. Her daughter, yet another woman named Meely, had helped her for years in that endeavor, but with the daughter's recent death in childbirth, Fanny had initiated her granddaughter, also named Meely, into the movement.

Of course, throughout history slaves in America had chosen to escape whenever possible, and the network of escape routes of the Underground Railroad was formed long before the War Between the States, during the early 1800s. It reached its height in 1850. Over 100,000 slaves used this network of "stations" and "conductors" to help them escape all the way up to the "Drinking Gourd." That code word, all along the Railroad, referred to the fact that two stars in the drinking-bowl end of the Big Dipper constellation point directly in the direction of freedom—they point to the North Star. If escaping slaves followed that star, they ultimately ended up in the northern states, the ungoverned northern territories, or Canada. More than 30,000 slaves escaped between 1840 and 1860 alone, and several hundred of those came right through Traveler's Rest Plantation where they were hidden by the agent, Fanny Bricebud. Aunt Fanny always kept a quilt hung in her one cabin window, and that quilt helped the Conductors identify her cabin among all the other cabins and buildings at Traveler's Rest as the Tugalo Station. Various quilting patterns were utilized throughout the south, as symbols and helpful signs; some meant "conductors and passengers welcome," while others meant "stay away at all costs!" These quilt patterns were understood only by the agents and Conductors along the Railroad.

That night long ago, in the darkened barn at Traveler's Rest Plantation, Meely responded to Tubman's inquiry. "I'm de granddaughter of Fanny Bricebud, and she ain't well. She done told me about de quilts, and that I's to help any who come this way needin' it."

Tubman, with her piercing eyes, evaluated the young girl before her, then spoke up a bit, though still keeping her voice below normal conversation levels. "Y'all come out here, and let's talk a bit with Meely here." She then looked around in various spaces in the barn, and like wraths in some shadowy spirit world, figures began to emerge from several stalls, and around stacks of hay. Meely was amazed only a moment later, when she counted thirteen passengers that Tubman was guiding to freedom.

"We's still got a bit o' bread and some cheese from the last station, but we could use some more," said Tubman. "We be needin' water too. Can you get some here? Just pretend you bringin' some for dem horses."

Meely said,"Ain't no need. Our Massa, Mr. Devereaux had us dig a well right here in de barn, so's we can get water right here. Dat well is right behind you. And I'm thinkin' I can find some biscuits and buttermilk in the big-house kitchen, but it'll have to wait until de slaves leave Fanny's cabin."

Tubman then asked, "Aunt Fanny, dying?"

Meely felt a catch in her throat, but forced herself to answer. "She mighty sick, and she must be damn near eighty year old, if not older. Cain't rightly say she dying, but they sure'uff singing to her and all. Even Mistress Turnbull came out from de big house to da cabin a bit ago, to pay her respects. Dat woman love ol' Aunt Fanny near 'bout as much as all of us! Aunt Fanny Bricebud, she raised up all de Jarretts for near' bout fourty years now!"

Tubman, ever cognizant of her work with the Railroad and always seeking more help for what she believed to be a holy cause, quickly recognized the name she'd heard in a distant forest the previous fall. "Did you say, Turnbull? Turnbull what you said? I though dis was the Jarrett Plantation."

Meely responded. "It do! It belong to Mr. Devereaux Jarrett, but he 'olest daughter done marry a fine man, Cap'n Jamie Turnbull, and Capt'n Turnbull, he stay here for a time last fall, when he got shot in de war."

Thus did Tubman confirm that Captain James Turnbull was associated with this station along the railroad, and she quickly recognized that he was the same man who had released a captured slave girl in the woods of north Georgia, as she was trying to steal food last September. Tubman stood still as she reflected on the matter, and though she didn't realize it, she was speaking her private thoughts softly. "God be praised! This is the second time God done brought dis man to my attention. They is po'erful work going on here! God be workin' here, and He surely has some purpose for this."

While much of Tubman's life is an undocumented mystery, history is certain of one fact. She believed that God spoke to her daily, directly, and meaningfully, so every chance happening, every event that some might call a coincidence, would, for Tubman, have a deep spiritual significance.

Meely along with thirteen escaping slaves, merely stood there, saying nothing, and in only a few moments, Tubman returned from her reflections. "We be getting' de water, now, Meely. You be getting back to whatever you was doin' and bring in de food when you can."

Meely, with the curiosity that only a fifteen year old girl can muster, and still unfamiliar with the ways of the Underground Railroad, couldn't help but ask, "Where is you going next?"

Tubman merely looked at the child with those wise, piercing eyes. She said. "Never you mind 'bout de next Station. You jest get us food for two days. I will tell you they is a Quaker Meetin' house up near Franklin, in Carolina dat help us a lot. Now you get, an' bring back dat food. We' be leavin' well 'afore sunup!"

Thus did Tubman plant a wrong direction on Meely's mind, a direction for men to search, should Meely be caught after Tubman and her passengers left Traveler's Rest. In fact, Tubman had planned to head west to Helen, Georgia, where a group of slaves and free men in the black settlement known as "Bean Creek" often helped runaways. That Bean Creek settlement was known as one of the more important, and frequently used stations on the Underground Railroad in north Georgia, and Tubman was aware that heading in that direction would place her that much closer to the Union Army whom she still believed was in Kingston, GA.

Interestingly one old slave cabin from those distant days still exists in the Bean Creek settlement, near Helen, GA. It has been preserved over the decades by the black families who understood, and understand, its importance; for that cabin represents a to-the-death struggle for freedom for many slaves of the 1850s. It was a light of welcome in the window, a place to rest and eat a hot meal, along the Underground Railroad in those distant, dangerous days. For African Americans today, that lone cabin is a holy place; a place to ponder the past, and even a place of reverence. Such are the rare gifts that history will sometimes offer, if we but take the time to look.

Only six days later, the Union commander of the small force Sherman had left guarding the depot at Kingston was awakened by his subordinate. It seems that overnight Tubman had led twenty-three negroes into the Union camp, requested some food, and then demanded that they be given work for the Union army. Tubman insisted that they could begin immediately to dig trenches to help in General Sherman's holy cause! This woman, like Bickerdyke, Barton, and Dix, would not take no for an answer, and you may rest assured that within four hours, after just a bit of rest, twenty of those black men and women, were digging trenches for the Union army.

## The Dallas Line

After a wait of several days, Johnston began to fret that he'd managed to lose Sherman's entire Union Army. He sent his cavalry out to find the misplaced men, and they soon ran into a hornet's nest of Yankees near Kingston. In the running cavalry fight, the Confederates noticed much movement of Union forces southward from Kingston, into the wilderness to the west, a move that made no tactical sense whatsoever! Johnston simply could not believe at first, that Sherman would leave his precious railroad, but as more reports came in and the evidence mounted, he forced himself to conclude that the wily Union commander had done exactly that. General Johnston had no option but to likewise shift his forces to the west to oppose Sherman. Otherwise, Sherman would merely bypass the Confederates altogether and move on Marietta, or possibly even Atlanta.

Thus once again the Confederates shifted their position, seeking their Union adversaries in the wilderness of west Georgia. Here small streams, some hills, and small, intensely sloped valleys dominate the landscape, and with few farms in the area, it seemed that the whole region was still wooded with virgin forest of oak, hickory, cedar and various other hardwoods. As soon as the cavalry could determine which roads Sherman's armies were using, the Confederate commanders sought out crossroads, intersections, or creeks where they might make a stand against the advancing Yankees. As more and more information came in from the various Confederate cavalry units, Generals Johnston and Hood began to get a clearer picture of where the Union forces might emerge from the wilderness, and that is how the Dallas line emerged as a major axis of defense for the Confederates.

Today absolutely nothing about the small town of Dallas, Georgia would seem to recommend it as a massive battleground. One can count the traffic lights in Dallas on one hand, and the downtown area today is about the same size as it was in 1864! Still, several small roads do cross there in Dallas, and when small roads are all one has to move one's army, that is what both sides decided to use. Confederates, once again abandoned their unused trenches at Allatoona Pass, and like the trenches in Cassville, those ditches saw no major battle. The Confederates managed to arrive in the Dallas region first, led by General Hood's Corps. Not realizing how soon the advancing Union forces might show up, Hood sent out several reconnaissance forces to find out what he might be facing, though each recon unit included only one understrength regiment. The remainder of his 12,000 men, of course, began to dig.

In this manner did Stiggy Stigwell, once again, enter the broad scope of history. His unit, the 23rd Alabama Infantry, happened to be traveling north along a road just east of Dallas, as a "Reconnaissance in force" under General Hood's orders. They were trying to find the Union army once and for all. Stiggy and several of his messmates were doing their turn on the advanced skirmish line, a line of men that spread out and traveled somewhat in front of the moving infantry. Thus, Stiggy was the first Confederate to see the advancing Union skirmish line that day, a line of Union men who, like Stiggy and his companions, were moving in front of the Union advance. On this occasion, Stiggy refrained from showing the Union army his manhood; rather, he merely shouted to his commander, "Here they come" just before he fired his rifle at the first blue coat he saw.

Of course, skirmish lines are merely the first "eyes" on the battlefield, and are not really supposed to slow or stop an advancing army. Once the men with Stiggy fired, they retreated back to their own lines, where Stiggy's commander, gave a report to their superior. That man quickly made the decision to high-tail it back to the main Confederate line only two miles in the rear. He was reflecting the whole time on how fast his men marched when they knew an entire Union army was advancing behind them, and without realizing it, he spoke aloud his thoughts: "God, I hope that those sorry asses in the main defensive line got some defensive positions prepared. We're sure as hell gonna need 'um today!"

Within two hours, those two forces were to meet again, only nine days after Resaca, at a sleepy little place called New Hope Church. By that time, the Confederate defensive line was nearly ten miles in length, stretching from just behind the town of Dallas itself, into the wilderness, and ending near a small grain mill on Pumpkinvine Creek. The fights along this line were to become a single, unified, bloodbath.

## The Battle of New Hope Church

Historians have long debated the name of this conflict along the Dallas line. In particular, they've argued about what would seem to be a simple question. Was this one battle or three? Within only a week, three separate engagements were fought along this ten-mile trench near Dallas, GA, the first of which was the Battle of New Hope Church. In that two day fight, Sherman's advancing Union force attacked the entrenchments of Johnston's line near a small country church—New Hope Church—on May 25 and 26, 1864.

The very next day, May 27, other divisions within Sherman's army attacked the same line at a location only two miles distant, beside a small water-driven cornmill owned by two men, Benjamin and Malachi Travis Pickett—resulting in a fight now referred to as the Battle of Pickett's Mill. On the very next day, May 28, 1864, the Confederates attacked at the opposite end of the same defensive line, resulting in a fight some refer to as the Battle of Dallas. Thus the question, was this one battle or three?

It is a fact that, during this War Between the States, many battles—Chickamauga, Gettysburg, Petersburg, and Vicksburg are examples—took place over two or three days, or in some cases over several months. Further all of those fights involved multiple engagements along extensive, defensive works, trenches that often stretched for many miles. In fact, any one of those battles could easily be "broken up" by historians into several separate engagements, should anyone desire to do so. Thus, many have begun to question how this fight along the Dallas line, a fight between the same armies that stretched over four days along the same ten-mile battle line, came to be viewed by history as three separate battles?

There is no good answer to that question, and one can only note that what should have been viewed as one four-day fight along this Dallas line, is now considered three separate fights by some historians, and thus three separate names are used, as noted above. Of course, as in most battles, every soldier who fought there considered his separate perspective of the fighting as, far-and-away, the most important!

As Sherman's force advanced toward New Hope Church on May 25, they drove the Confederate picket line, Stiggy Stigwell among them, back into the main Confederate defensive line, that stretched into the front yard of New Hope Church. Both the church and a portion of the Confederate trench still share the same yard today, and a historic marker tells the story of the fight on May 25 and 26, 1864.

On the morning of May 25, when Sherman received reports of the early conflict with Johnston's picket line, he assumed, incorrectly, that Johnstons' main army was still sitting at Allatoona Pass, or at the very least, was still moving through the wilderness. He simply didn't believe that Johnston would have, or could have, correctly guessed his intention to shift the entire Union army into the wilderness. In fact, he believed that his forces had been opposed by some small cavalry troop, or perhaps a small Confederate reconnaissance unit. He quickly ordered a forced advance of the Twentieth Corps of the Union army under General Joe Hooker.

Once Hooker received those orders, he advanced the three divisions in his

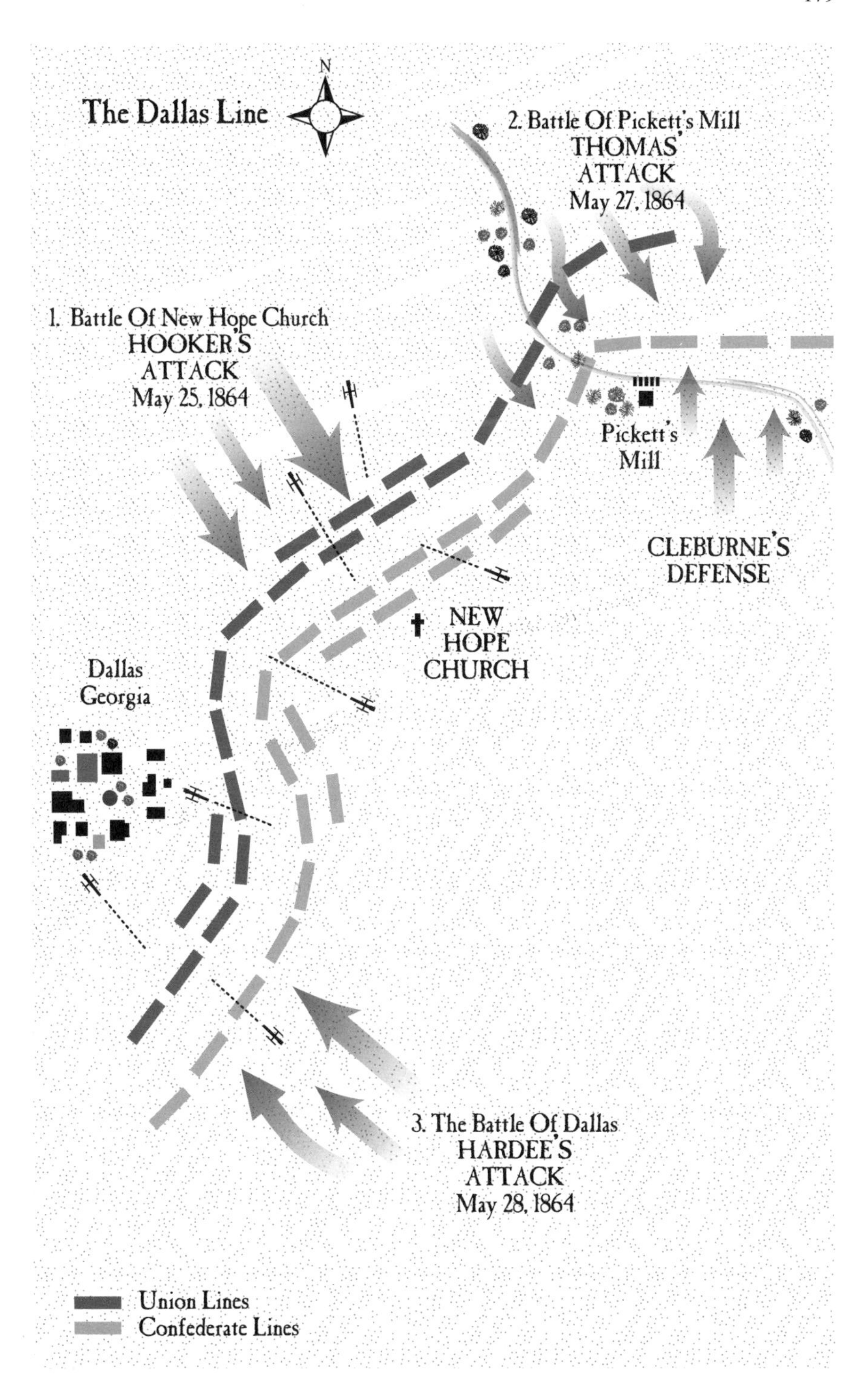

The Dallas Line
N
2. Battle Of Pickett's Mill
THOMAS'
ATTACK
May 27, 1864
1. Battle Of New Hope Church
HOOKER'S
ATTACK
May 25, 1864
Pickett's
Mill
CLEBURNE'S
DEFENSE
NEW
HOPE
CHURCH
Dallas
Georgia
3. The Battle Of Dallas
HARDEE'S
ATTACK
May 28, 1864
Union Lines
Confederate Lines

corps independently along three separate small roads, all of which converged at New Hope Church. Each Union division advanced quickly for two miles or so, but as they emerged into the fields around the church, they saw the prepared Confederate defensive works in the churchyard, not to mention a series of gun emplacements that were absolutely bristling with angry-looking, heavy-bore cannon. Hooker however was never one to worry too much about his men, so he ordered an all-out assault against that prepared defensive line. Each Union division charged into the fight as they arrived on the field, meaning that what could have been one massed advance, was really a series of separate independent charges. Those Union men seemed nearly fearless to the Confederates behind their defensive works, ever anxious to spill their Yankee blood in ill-conceived forward assaults.

Stiggy Stigwell, and the others in the 23rd Alabama had reached the Confederate trench works with the Union advance hot on his tail. He jumped, along with three hundred other men into the Confederate trench just before the Union army arrived, as muskets cracked in the distance, and minie-balls whizzed by overhead. As luck would have it, Stiggy landed right on the back of Mike Wellspeak, who was busy getting ready, right in the middle of loading his rifle. Having bitten into a powder pack to charge his gun, Wellspeak felt something land on his back, and was terrified. He began to scream, even as he wondered, "How did those blue-bellies get here so damn fast?" In the process, with Stiggy's one-hundred and forty-six pound frame atop him, he managed to swallow most of the powder from his powder cartridge, and quickly ended up puking out his guts, a process that continued for the next minute or so. Of course, with the Union forces still too far out for firing, Ten Cent Bill, Batty Prather, Mo Hendon and Duncan Carmichael, all had a good laugh at Wellspeak's discomfort, and most couldn't resist some teasing.

"Dammit, Wellspeak, Cain't you refrain from eatin' before a fight?" Batty said, as he and the other men laughed.

Lee Lovorn chimed in, while he looked back toward the advancing Yankees, still three hundred yards distant. "Never heard of eatin' powder before. Ain't this army got no sow-belly or beans anywhere?"

Even Chad Wilson, the new man, had something to say. "That's okay Wellspeak. I oncted seed a man eat the haunch of a live chicken, 'cause of a bet. You can eat black powder if you want it that bad, and if you like, you can chase 'er down with a minie-ball!"

Duncan, laughing with the rest of the men, decided to bring the focus back to the matter at hand. "Recon they'll actually charge us, across that open field? They sure as hell know what's waitin' on 'um, if'n they do! These cannon 'll blow mosta them Yankee boys all the way back to Ohio!" In that judgment, Duncan was right.

Just then the Confederate cannon opened fire, loaded with canister—an anti-personnel round, and many of the Union men in the first line simply disintegrated. As soon as those cannon fired, both the Union men and the Confederates began rapid volley rifle fire, and while the range was still a bit long, men began to go down in the field before the Confederate trench. Soon, men were dying on both sides. Within thirty seconds the Confederate cannon were loaded once again, and sounding off, but by the second volley, they were answered by several Union guns that had been brought to the field. By then the eye-burning smoke from so many black-powder weapons rendered most of the men on the line blind, but they all kept firing.

The fight lasted most of the afternoon on May 25, with the Union forces trying multiple advances into the teeth of the Confederate defenses, and those massed Confederate cannon. All of Hood's Confederates were engaged, and that corps alone defended approximately a mile and a half of the Confederate trenches. Fighting by the churchyard was so fierce that Batty wondered out loud, "Why in hell can't Sherman attack somewhere else, just once?"

The cannon in particular, showed no mercy at all—they seldom do. Not once did the Confederate heavy guns fail to cut into the Union force, and many times those cannon leveled a massive number of charging men. Grapeshot and canister tore apart men and horses alike on that field, some cut in half; others with limbs torn off, or heads missing. Some men disappeared all-together before those guns.

By nightfall, the fight was winding down, since the Union men simply could not bring themselves to charge into those Confederate positions again. That night, and most of the next day, the remaining Union force moved up into battle positions, as the Union men on the field dug in, carefully preparing their own defensive works. However, when Sherman heard of the devastating losses on the afternoon of May 25, he simply could not issue any orders to advance again, until he found out what he was facing. He still could not believe that Johnston had managed to get into that wilderness first, and entrench. Thus, while shots were fired on May 26, there was not a concerted effort to take the Confederate works at New Hope Church, and men of both sides were quite content to merely sit in their trenches and await the actions of the opposing army.

However the white flags that often appeared on Civil War battlefields did come out at the end of the fighting on May 25, as Union doctors sought to find and help any Yankees that might be still alive in the killing field. That gave the Confederates a chance to advance into the field to assist those doctors, as well as to count the Union dead. By 7:00 PM that night, General Hood reported to General Johnston "The Union army left just over seven hundred men dead on the field in front of New Hope Church. I have also the honor of reporting the capture of an additional three hundred and forty Union men." Confederate losses were much lighter, since the Confederates had fought almost all of the battle from behind their trench works.

In one interesting turn of history at New Hope Church, Owen Collins actually found a wounded woman! He and the others under the white flag were picking up the wounded and seeing no grey coats nearby, Collins and Batty Prather had stopped to assist a wounded Union fighter. There was clearly a serious chest wound, and neither man thought the Union man would survive, but they still decided to give him some water and maybe stop his bleeding. Collins leaned over the man and ripped open his blouse to get a better look at the wound, and got the shock of his life.

"Tits?" Shouted Batty. "Them's tits!"

Collins couldn't figure it. "What the hell is she doing out here wounded?" He quickly checked the soldier's other credentials by roughly fondling the wounded soldier inside her britches, and sure enough he found no credentials at all! He reached the only, the inevitable conclusion. "That man's a damned woman! What is God's name is going on here?"

The answer was fairly simple. Collins had uncovered, along with a reasonably inviting pair of tits, a relatively rare phenomenon, a woman dressed as a man and fighting right beside other frontline soldiers. Historians have estimated that between three hundred and eight hundred women dressed as men in order to fight in the War Between the States, and documents have shown that women were fighting on both sides. A wounded Confederate soldier in the famed Pickett's Charge at Gettysburg was discovered to be a woman when the Union doctors examined her on the battlefield. Other women wrote books about their battles long after the war concluded. It is known that women fought for both Union and Confederate regiments, often without being discovered. As no army admitted women in those days, these women dressed as men and took great care to hide their sex. In some cases they fought out of a sense of pride, or a sense of patriotism. In other cases, they were merely trying to remain with their husbands or boyfriends.

Owen had the good sense to not bring up this discovery with anyone. He simply stopped the woman's bleeding and closed up her blouse. He then pinned a brief note to her chest saying,

"As proud Confederates, we do not use women in war. Therefore this woman, wounded in battle, I return to you." He figured the Union doctors would find her in short order, and they did, along with his note. The note, now famous, is held by the United States Archives.

Batty of course, told that story many times while in his cups, but everyone knew Batty Prather, and only a precious few believed anything he said. No one believed that story. The few times that Collins was asked about it, he merely smiled. After the war, he never spoke of it at all.

## Finding A Fight at Pickett's Mill

By late on May 26, Sherman had observed most of the long battle line, and he quickly determined that an advance at New Hope Church would result in nothing more than a continuation of the terrible Union losses. As he rode behind the Union lines, looking over the situation, he voiced his thoughts to several members of his staff. "We'll have to hit Johnston somewhere else." When the staff heard that, they immediately assumed that Sherman would move his entire army once again, so one gave voice to the complaint of the men. "But, Sir. We've just now completed our defensive works here."

Crazy Billy looked over at the man and grinned. "Don't worry colonel. I didn't mean we wouldn't hit 'um! I just meant we won't do it in this field. I don't want to pay so high a price in blood for any real estate in this wilderness." With that, Sherman turned his horse around to face his staff directly. "Tell me about the northern end of the line, in those trees yonder. I couldn't see much about that terrain, because of the forest."

As the Union high command discussed the northern end of the battle line, Sherman's horse moved a couple more times. Of course, what Sherman didn't realize was that, by turning his horse just a bit, he had managed to expose his back to not only the Union trench, but to the Confederates some four hundred and seventy five yards distant, a fact not missed in the Confederate defensive works.

Duncan Carmichael, ever one to find opportunities where none existed said to the men around him. "Hey boys. Can any of ya'll see that damn Yankee sittin' atop his horse so proud yonder? Let's line up our best shots, and take a wack at 'um!"

Batty was the first to look over the top of the head log, to see what Duncan was talking about. "No Sir-ee! Corporal. That's five 'hunert' yards if'n it's a foot! Nobody can shoot that far and hit a barn, much less a man."

"I'll try it," Chad Wilson said.

"Me too," said Sampson. "I'd like to try that shot."

Wellspeak looked over the headlog and spoke-up next. "I'll give it a go. Do we fire all at once or take turns? That way we can tell for sure, if'n any of us hit 'um!"

Duncan ended that thought quickly. "Hell Wellspeak. When one of us comes close, he'll move! We need to shoot all at once. I ain't even sure we can hit him at all!"

Wellspeak proudly said, "I'll hit him! I'm sure I can hit him, if'n he don't move."

Batty said, "Hell Wellspeak, they always move," as he loaded his rifle.

Within a few more seconds four men were resting their muskets on the headlog before them, and carefully taking aim at Sherman's back. These were the best shots in the Fourth Georgia; Wellspeak, Sampson, Chad Wilson, and Duncan Carmichael.

Ten Cent Bill was giving a vocal rundown. "Don't aim low, now. That's damn near five hun'ert yards and can't no minie-ball carry that far, lessen you aim real high over his head!"

Batty continued the thoughts on careful aim. "There ain't much wind, but it is a blowin' a bit from the northwest. Ya'll have to aim off to the left too, to get a hit at that distance."

Duncan spoke next. "Okay Batty, give us a count."

Batty said, "Yes Sir! Fire when I say three! One, two, three!"

History sometimes changes in an instant. Events taking fractions of a second, sometimes change the entire world. Presidents are killed with a single bullet, hurricanes disrupt naval battles, or generals are blown to bits by cannonfire. Whole ships have exploded and been lost on all of the oceans of the world in a nano-second. All such instantaneous events can change history.

However on this day, no such world changing event took place. While four well-aimed muskets fired at nearly the same time, none of the shots came close to the target. Two fell many yards before the aim point, and one shot actually went high. As it turned out, Sampson had overcharged his rifle, and loaded nearly enough powder to blow up his own barrel. Only Wellspeak's shot was anywhere close to the target, and it tore a trench in the earth about seven feet from General Sherman's horse.

"Damn" Carmichael said. "He's still sittin' there, proud as you please."

"Won't be for long, now that I got the range!" Wellspeak said.

Of course, one of Sherman's staff had noticed the trench, and only a second later, they all heard the shots. "General," one said. "I believe your back is exposed to the enemy, and I'd suggest we move a bit further away."

Sherman turned his horse back around to face the Confederate trenches. "Really? Can those rebels shoot that far, do you think?" Sherman quickly spurred his horse, and shouted to his staff. "To hell with it! I need to see that forest at the northern end of the line again." Off they rode, leaving Wellspeak with a loaded rifle and no important targets in sight.

Batty couldn't resist the chance at one more joke. As he laughed he shouted for all to hear; "Hell Wellspeak. You might as well have eaten that load of powder too, for all the good it'll do you now!"

## The Battle of Pickett's Mill

Sherman apparently liked what he saw in the forest because on the very next day, the Union army concentrated its efforts on the northern end of the Confederate line near Pickett's Mill. Neither Sherman nor any of his commanders could see the actual mill prior to the battle on May 27, but local farmers had confirmed that the forest hid a deep depression that led down to the creek and that a mill had been built there, using water power to grind corn. On that day, Sherman was making two assumptions, only one of which was correct. First he was concerned that his army would quickly run out of supplies, since his massive force was now some twenty five miles from his railroad, and in that belief Sherman was accurate. He needed to attack the Confederates soon, and then get back to his base of supply.

His second assumption however, was not accurate. Sherman still believed that Johnston could not have advanced the Confederate army so far and so fast into the wilderness. In spite of the fight at New Hope Church, Sherman still believed that Johnston could not have moved his entire Confederate force to the field, so the Union command staff quickly concluded that the northern end of the Confederate defensive works might be lightly defended. In fact, they hoped they were attacking an exposed right flank of Johnston's army, hoping to find a Confederate unit that had not had sufficient time to dig in. In this assumption, Sherman was wrong. Still, not realizing that the Confederates were well positioned behind defensive works in the forest, he ordered an attack. However, the communications problems associated with a battle in a wilderness prevented an early attack on May 27.

Rather in the early morning that day, General Thomas, the Rock of Chickamauga, and his subordinates scouted the forest a bit more, and found that the woods contained numerous hills and valleys, any one of which could provide for an excellent Confederate defensive line. By the time, they considered their options, it was somewhat late on that Friday afternoon, May 27, 1864, at which time, the Union forces moved forward for the attack.

Thomas had ordered a Union corps of fourteen thousand men to advance through the dense woods, toward Little Pumpkinvine Creek and the mill itself. General Hazen's regiment was the first to make contact with the Confederates. However during his initial advance, some of his men became confused in rolling hills densely covered with woods, and they turned much too far to the east, removing themselves from the battle altogether. Next, about an hour after the fighting began, the Confederates launched a well-timed cavalry charge that paralyzed Hazen's right flank. Those Union men could not advance at all. Those events left many of Hazen's men stranded in the middle of his line, in one of the few areas of open field near the creek, where they suffered horrible losses from the Confederate cannon mounted on the hill before them.

Another misfortune helped stop Hazen's advance that day. His force had lost a wagon load of ammunition and his men could not be resupplied when they needed it the most. Hazen realized that both his left and right flanks were in trouble, and he sent word to request reinforcements in order to move his advance forward. However, he held little hope that any help would reach him in time, simply because of the logistics of moving large numbers of men through a forest with only one small road. After another hour, Hazen realized he was halted, and he ordered a general retreat.

However Hazen had suffered one more ill-fortune that day. As luck would have it, his advance faced a capable enemy across the battle line, General Patrick Cleburne, CSA. Cleburne was a feisty Irishman, who had briefly served in the British army in the 1840s. Seeing no future there, he had immigrated to the US, settling in Arkansas prior to the Civil War. Most of the rural folk in Arkansas still spoke in an Irish brogue, and manifested the sharp sense of independence of those people. Most had sided with the south when the war occurred, and the south was lucky to get Cleburne in particular.

Cleburne was, in the estimation of many students of war, one of the most effective division commanders on either side during the War Between the States. In particular, his strategic use of terrain often allowed him to hold ground when others could not, and he seemed to have a special talent in foiling the movements of Union troops, who quickly came to hate facing the blue flag of Cleburne's Division. His ability earned him the nickname, "Stonewall of the West." Even the great Confederate leader, General Robert E. Lee referred to Cleburne as "a meteor shining from a clouded sky."

It is an interesting footnote of history that Cleburne was the first senior Confederate commander to see the advantages of arming and training slaves to fight for the Confederacy. Cleburne proposed just that idea, much earlier in the war than other Confederate leaders.

> *"Satisfy the negro that if he faithfully adheres to our standard during the war he shall receive his freedom and that of his race … and we change the race from a dreaded weakness to a position of strength. Will the slaves fight? The helots of Sparta stood their masters good stead in battle. In the great sea fight of Lepanto where the Christians checked forever the spread of Mohammedanism over Europe, the galley slaves of portions of the fleet were promised freedom, and called on to fight at a critical moment of the battle. They fought well, and civilization owes much to those brave galley slaves ... the experience of this war has been so far that half-trained negroes have fought as bravely as many other half-trained Yankees."*

On the battlefield at Pickett's Mill, Cleburne seemed to be everywhere at once. It had been Cleburne himself who ordered the sharpshooters to give Hazen's men fits on Hazen's left flank. He then rode the length of his line, and within a half-an-hour, he ordered the Confederate cavalry to hit Hazen's other flank. At one point, Union men were charging up a ravine directly into the fire of the main Confederate line atop the next hill. That ravine, only a hundred yards or so from Pickett's Mill, was nearly sixty feet deep and had sides that were so steep the Union soldiers had to scramble up on their hands and knees, a position from which it was very difficult to shoot. Unfortunately for those Union men, Cleburne saw yet another opportunity to kill Yankees, and he moved four Napoleons to the head of the ravine. The impact of those guns, in just the perfect position to fire into the Union flank, was devastating. Not a single Union man made it to the top of the ravine, and most died a horrid death, falling to the bottom, only to be stomped on by their comrades or horses at the bottom of the draw. Again it seemed that Cleburne was everywhere at once, and it is not an overstatement to say that the failure of Hazen's initial advance on Pickett's Mill lay in the military genius of Patrick Cleburne.

Still, even as Hazen's battered force withdrew, another advance had been ordered, so after a lull of fifteen minutes or so, more Union men presented themselves as targets for Cleburne's Division. The four Napoleons were still in place at the head of the draw, and once the second Union division reached that killing zone, the impact was the same. Thousands of Union men died, because they had been ordered into the hell of a deadly valley, that any raw recruit knew enough not to enter.

Only one more small advance was undertaken that day, and it was a Confederate advance. The Confederate cavalry having been idle for some time after their first charge, had requested permission to advance and sweep any remaining Union forces from the opposing ridge, as the infantry cleaned up the deadly ravine. Permission was given and that cavalry advance netted several hundred more Union prisoners. In all, Cleburne estimated that three thousand Union men were either dead or wounded, but the actual figure was much lower. Still, sixteen hundred Union men and just under five hundred Confederates were killed or wounded at Pickett's mill, making that fight a devastating loss for Sherman. In fact, Pickett's Mill was one of the most lopsided battles that Sherman lost in the entire advance toward Atlanta.

Moreover, that one day fight raised the stakes in Sherman's Atlanta Campaign. As that battle concluded, Sherman realized that he'd already had two fights along the Dallas line, and had lost both, with terrible casualties. Moreover, his supplies were running dangerously low and he was still twenty-five miles from his supply depot along the distant railroad. He simply had to disengage and return to his base of supply. The only good news Sherman received had to do with the fact that a Union cavalry force had taken the trench-works back at Allatoona Pass, against minimal resistance. This shortened Sherman's supply route by a few miles, at least. Still, he decided that night to disengage and move his army back to the railroad.

## Listening to a Fight

Sitting safely in their trenches by the smoldering ruins of New Hope Church nearly two miles away from Pickett's Mill, Duncan Carmichael and his men looked toward the sound of guns that evening without moving. They listened intently, to the nearby battle. Batty, ever the big mouth of the group, realized that he'd finally gotten his wish. "I'm sure glad some other dumb sons-a-bitches is getting' to fight today. I ain't really ready for something like we seed two days ago!"

Mo Hendon spoke up next. "Don't say that too loud, Batty. Some damn general or 'nother is bound to hear ya, and remember to move us over there!"

As the men looked to the northeast, and without any of them realizing it, the company commander, Major Turnbull, and Captain Collins had walked up behind them. Turnbull's man, Sampson, as usual, was only a few steps behind. Jamie smiled as he heard the comments, then spoke up. "What's the matter, Batty? Don't want to miss any action?"

Duncan turned around to smile at his friend and commander. "It's okay, Sir. I'm sure the boys can just sit this one out, less'n you figure they need us over there. Fact is, I'm sure Batty here and some of the other boys, would love to go join the fun!"

Batty couldn't say anything. Of course, everyone knew of the special relationship between their Corporal Carmichael, and Major Turnbull. Still, no one dared speak so personably to the Major as Duncan. Batty wanted to say that he was just fine where he was, with someone else doing the fighting, but he could not bring himself to say it.

Jamie, noting Batty's unease, put the matter to rest. "Don't worry men. I'm sure Cleburne's men over there can handle things, and we'll have us a day off over here, unless of course, those Union boys across the way get feisty again."

With that statement every head in that trench turned in unison, toward the front of the ditch and the Union force beyond, and each man hoped beyond measure that those Union boys would simply stay put for the rest of the day.

The Major next spoke to Captain Collins. "I don't think we'll see a Union advance here today, Captain, but do keep a sharp eye on the front. I'll get word to you as soon as I find out how the boys did today down by the mill."

"Sir," said Collins. "Is there something we might expect in the morning?"

Turnbull had heard the plans for the fight the next day, and decided that it would do no harm to share them with Collins and the men. "I've been told to prepare an advance for the morning, so every man in this regiment should get a good sleep tonight. Get your men in bed early, but keep a skirmish line out front with their eyes open."

"Yes Sir," said Collins. "We'll be ready in the morning, Sir!"

"Good," said Turnbull. "As I get more information, I'll call for an officer's meeting this evening." With that, Turnbull walked off, along with Sampson.

## Command Decisions

General Johnston, the overall Confederate Commander, was ever aware that his army was badly outnumbered by Sherman's Union forces, and thus, was always on the lookout to catch a smaller part of the massive Union army alone, or in transit. Johnston was, by that point, well aware of the criticisms of his army's performance, not to mention the criticism of his command of the Confederate army. Any idiot with a map could tell that Johnston's force had given up over seventy miles of Georgia terrain during the month of May, and seemed to be constantly retreating toward Atlanta. Thus, on the morning of May 28, after having defeated two attempts by Sherman to overtake his lines, he was seeking a way to attack Sherman's force itself.

As he sat in his headquarters, looking at a large, hand-drawn map of his entire defensive works, he spoke to his subordinates, General Hood and General Hardee, both of whom commanded Confederate corps. General Cleburne was present, along with several other, less senior commanders. Since the armies were not engaged in any fighting that morning, Major Turnbull was present in the command tent, taking notes on the planning, as was his usual task.

"I say," said Johnston. "There may be an opportunity here, on the left flank of our lines. We know that Sherman's men have dug-in around New Hope Church, and likewise on the hills behind Pickett's Mill. He has suffered grievous losses in those two battles. As his strength seems to remain on those fields, he must be somewhat weaker on the end of the line near Dallas. I believe he must now withdraw back toward his supply along the railroad, and thus, we might find his line weakened here." With that, Johnston put his finger on the Union line that extended from the northeast to the southwest, only a mile to the east of the small town of Dallas.

A member of Johnston's staff voiced the thought for all of the men around the map table. "Sherman has thrown two right hooks at us, moving around his right flank at both Rocky Face and Resaca. Perhaps it is our turn to toss a left hook attack back in his direction!"

"Indeed! And I'd like to do it!" said General Hood. Ever the most aggressive of Johnston's commanders, Hood had visualized the opportunity first, so he spoke up before the other corps commanders. "Sir! I can withdraw from my trenches, leaving only a small defensive force there at New Hope Church, and remove most of my corps behind that of General Hardee's force. Then, I shall attack in force the entire right end of Sherman's line. With the artillery support of General Hardee, I believe I can place ten thousand of my men in those Union defensive works by nightfall, if I can begin to formulate a plan of attack by noon."

There was silence in the command tent for a few moments, as all of the senior commanders considered that possibility. Hardee was the first to see the problems with that proposed plan.

"General Hood," he said. "You are a commander of skill, and an attack such as you propose would, no doubt, confound the enemy, and overtake his defensive works. However, why move an entire corps, when my men are sitting immediately before that end of the Union line? Why not allow my men the honor of this attack, and have your artillery, and perhaps one or two of your divisions, move in support of my attack?"

General Johnston was a wily commander, and he could recognize a potential pissing contest among his generals, long before those generals actually dropped their breeches and stepped up to the line. He quickly spoke. "General Hood. I believe that General Hardee is correct, and need I remind you that your boys were in a horrid fight only two days ago, whereas his corps has not faced battle as yet?"

Hood let out a long sigh, realizing that he was not to be afforded the chance of attack, at least not on that day. After a pause, Johnston spoke again. "General Hardee's Corps shall make this attack, but I will support you with two divisions from General Hood's Corps. Also General Hood, if you would be so kind, please remove half of your artillery units from your line, and place them under temporary command of General Hardee's artillery commander for this attack. Hardee will need those guns in place along his line as quickly as possible, as I want his attack to commence at 4:00 PM this afternoon. If Sherman is weakening his lines and is beginning a pull back toward the railroad, perhaps we can catch him unawares."

As the meeting broke up, Major Turnbull heard that his regiment would be among those assigned to Hardee's Corps for this attack. Thus, he spoke to General Johnston as the meeting broke up. "Sir, if I may?"

Johnston looked up from his map, as he stood alone by the map table. "Yes, Turnbull? What is it?"

"Sir, my command has now been assigned to General Hardee's Corps, and I would like your permission to return to that command for this battle. I should lead my men this afternoon, Sir."

Johnston seemed to look somewhat beyond Turnbull for a few seconds, staring out the end of the command tent, and off into the distance. Without realizing it, he gave voice to his reflections. "So many good young men; so many young men who see their duty, and demand the opportunity to do it!"

Turnbull very wisely, said nothing.

"Of course, you may return to your unit, Major. God go with you."

"Sir," said Turnbull with a salute. Then he turned and walked out.

## The Battle of Dallas

Thus did the Battle of Dallas shape up on the afternoon of May 28, 1864. Hardee's Corps, supported by the Fourth Georgia Infantry under Major Jamie Turnbull, along with several other units from Hood's Corps, prepared for the initial attack, which was scheduled for 4:00 PM that afternoon. At 3:30, seventy nine Confederate cannon opened from behind Hardee's defensive works, and they concentrated their fire on a one mile length of the Union defensive line only seven hundred yards away.

Batty Prather, ever present with an opinion shouted to no one in particular, "It's noisy as hell over here when our cannon open up, ain't it?" No one bothered to answer. Batty was lying in a ditch, along with the other men, Wellspeak, Ten Cent Bill, Mo Hendon, Lee Lovorn, Chad Wilson, and Roy Giles. Duncan Carmichael was standing a few yards behind the line, talking with Captain Collins. They had to shout to each other to be heard over the sound of the massed cannon, and Collins shouted first. "I've heard from Major Turnbull. He'll be with us this afternoon during the attack, but I want you, as his friend, to make certain he doesn't expose himself needlessly. You may remember that time he charged way beyond the lines at Chickamauga. He and his nigger Sampson were much further into that deadly smoke than anyone else—they were damn near in Tennessee that day—and I don't want that to happen again. You know that you're the only man alive he seems to listen too, so tell him to get behind his men and not act a fool, you hear?"

Carmichael smiled at Collins and merely said. "I'll watch him, Sir. If'n he does something foolish, I'll be right beside him."

"Good," said Collins, just as Major Turnbull rode up to join the conversation.

For a moment the Confederate cannon paused, so Turnbull shouted loud enough for most of the men to hear. "Gentlemen," said Turnbull. "We'll be in the second advance this afternoon, and will follow along right behind Hardee's men. By that time, General Hardee expects there to be little opposition."

"Good Sir!" said Collins, not believing a single word of what he'd just heard.

Carmichael merely shrugged his shoulders, and smiled at his friend, just as the cannon began to fire again. Turnbull, Collins, and all the other men took a seat behind the trenchworks to wait for the advance.

At 4:00 PM, the Confederate cannon stopped, and the comparative silence of the battlefield alerted well over twenty thousand men to the pending attack. Twelve thousand Confederates stood as one, and climbed from behind their defensive works. They moved into the area just in front of the ditches and formed ranks with the Fourth Georgia Infantry immediately behind a Confederate unit from Kentucky.

The men had not made it far before the muskets and Spenser repeating rifles began to fire from the Union lines. The armies were close enough so that many of the Confederates advancing across that field heard a Union artillery officer should, "Load canister!" Upon hearing that order, the Confederates knew what to do; they charged like crazy for the Union trenches. Every veteran knew that when canister was fired across the field, and you could not get behind your own defensive works, the other place to be, much safer than the field itself, was inside the enemy trench line.

Thus without any official orders, twelve thousand Confederates turned into a massive human wave, running wildly across the field, through rifle fire and concentrated cannon fire. At that moment, the Rebel Yell was once again heard in the Georgia hinterlands. Jamie Turnbull had his LaMat pistol in his hand, and was charging toward the Union lines and firing when the smoke cleared enough for him to see a target. Duncan was running beside him and he was aware of Sampson on his other side working furiously to reload his musket as he ran. At that moment, a loose horse ran past Jamie's front, just visible in the smoke, and when Jamie looked at the terrified animal he tripped over something. As he fell, he realized he had stepped within the thorax of a Confederate soldier who had been blown in half by the cannon only minutes earlier. Jamie's toe had actually caught the exposed floating ribs of the man's chest, and down he went, into a heap on the ground, still trying to extract his foot from the corpse.

That fall over the body of a dead man saved Jamie's life. When Jamie went down, so did Sampson and Carmichael, one on each side of their commander, and at just that moment, a charge of canister was fired from six Union Napoleons, in battery, only forty yards to the left of the Confederate advance. That canister was devastating to the men who were still standing upright on that field, as indeed it was intended to be. The initial Confederate advance was crushed with that single cannon volley, as men went down all across the field. Looking over the ground within only seconds of that battery fire, Jamie saw many of his men falling. Roy Giles was blown in half, and died instantly. Batty Prather took some metal in his side, and Mo Hendon was hit in the leg, and was screaming his head off. Jamie saw that Captain Collins was alright, but then he realized that he himself had been hit in the head—blood oozed down over and into his right eye.

By then both Duncan and Sampson were looking into his face, and as Jamie returned their gaze with his one good eye, he thought, those two sure look strange. Then he passed out.

Just then Captain Collins ran up, and looked down at Turnbull, while speaking to Carmichael. "I thought I told you to keep an eye on him, Corporal! Dammit, he was ahead of the men by fifty feet!"

Duncan was busy examining his friend's head wound. Without looking up he shouted back to Collins. "What the hell was I supposed to do? Trip him?"

Collins knew that his anger was foolish, and he knew Carmichael was no man to trifle with. In fact, if any man could help the Major it was Corporal Carmichael, so he merely said. "How is he Corporal?"

Duncan had by that point examined Jamie's head wound, and was busy wrapping an old piece of cloth around Jamie's head. "Ball only broke the skin—his head-bones ain't soft or nothing. He'll have a headache, I recon, but he'll live."

Collins realized that he would have to take command, so after thinking about it for a moment, he said. "Carmichael, you're a sergeant now. I'll put in the paperwork when this is over. That should help you get the attention you need for him at the surgeon's tent. Now you and Sampson here take the Major back to the field hospital, and don't leave his side. You hear? Even if they tell you too! If he comes to, tell him I led the attack on in, got it?"

Duncan said, "Yes Sir," but as Collins turned away, he shouted out one more thought. "You watch your ass, out there, Captain. I ain't having two officers down in one day in my outfit!"

Collins could only smile to himself, as he turned to lead the men forward.

The Confederates tried to rally and resume their advance over the next hour, but the action was sporadic and disorganized. In two places the Confederates actually mounted the Union defensive works, but in each instance, they were pushed back. While Johnston had been correct that Sherman was returning to his line of supply along the railroad, he was wrong in his other assumption. Sherman had not weakened the right side of his line to any degree, so the Confederate attack had been launched on a fully prepared and well defended position. The attack was over by 7:30 that evening, and with it the Battles of the Dallas Line ended.

All in all, the three fights along the Dallas line accomplished little for either the Union or Confederate forces in a tactical sense. Sherman's Union men had lost substantial numbers in their advances at both New Hope Church, and Pickett's Mill. However, the overall battle ended with the Confederate charge on May 28 at Dallas, and in that single fight, the Confederates were on the losing end. In the days following the fight on May 28, both sides felt they had only one option—withdraw from the field. Overall, the Union lost two thousand and four hundred men along the Dallas line, while the Confederates lost upwards of three thousand—a number that was nearly even, given that two massive armies were engaged.

As usual the Union press told the story differently. On Sunday, May 29, 1864, the *New York Times* reported the "great news" from Sherman's army in Georgia.

> **"Dispatches from Georgia are most positive in character, as recently as yesterday morning. Sherman has driven the enemy back at Dallas, Georgia, and after this victory, his staff officers expect to reach Atlanta by the close of the month. Many report that Johnston has been sending Confederate troops to Virginia, further weakening his army in Georgia."**

Other than the fact that Sherman had won at Dallas, and the non-report of his defeats at New Hope Church and Pickett's Mill, virtually every line of the above report was wrong. Still tactical and strategic results of battles can be quite different, a fact that historians often find interesting. From a tactical point of view, the fights along the Dallas line were essentially a draw. Strategically the Confederates were forced once again, to give ground, and thus the Union forces were again, moving closer to Atlanta. Regardless of who lost more men on the battlefield, if Sherman advanced his army toward his ultimate goal, he had won a strategic victory. All of the senior commanders, as well as political leaders on both sides realized it. By June 3, both armies were on the move, and were heading back to the railroad in the east.

## In The Statehouse in Richmond

It was later that night, around 10:00 on May 28, and once again Jefferson Davis, President of the Confederacy, was having a brandy with General Robert Toombs, a Georgia man who had briefly served in Jefferson's cabinet as his Secretary of State. Davis had just poured two glasses and handed one to Toombs, who was seated at a small table. Davis continued to stand, as he typically did, when tough decisions had to be made. That night, he was in another of his "moods," which meant he was mad as hell at Confederate General Joe Johnston. In his hand he held a telegram from Johnston's headquarters giving the initial details of the fight at Dallas, and Johnston's plans to follow Sherman's army back towards the railroad.

After taking a sip from his glass, Jefferson exclaimed, "Doesn't that damned man know his back is getting closer and closer to Atlanta? How much ground can he give up to Sherman before all is lost?"

Toombs weighed his words carefully, which admittedly, was not his strong suit. "Well Mr. President, Johnston and that Army of Tennessee did give Sherman a bloody nose the other day at both New Hope Church, and Pickett's Mill. Maybe a strategic withdrawal toward the railroad at this time can be to our benefit."

With that Jefferson seemed to explode. "Dammit it all to hell, General Toombs! You're from there! You know the terrain down there! Sherman is already out of the Georgia mountains, and across most of the rivers. We cannot afford to give away any more Georgia ground to Sherman's advance—we'll never get it back! And if Crazy Billy and that damned Union army take the railroads in Atlanta, everything is lost! The Confederacy cannot long survive without those transportation lines, and you know it!"

Toombs merely shook his head, as his president continued to get worked up. He wisely remained silent.

Davis continued in a near-shout. "I should remove Johnston! I should take his command and place the Army of Tennessee in the hands of someone who would advance our cause, and stop Sherman."

Toombs didn't like pleading the case of General Johnston—in fact, he agreed fundamentally with everything Davis was saying, but he felt that he could at least further the discussion, and perhaps help President Davis think the matter through, by being the devil's advocate. That meant, at the moment, being Johnston's advocate.

"Sir," Toombs said. "That is certainly your prerogative, as our commander, but I would urge you to give it some more thought. In fact, I'd caution against it at present." Toombs paused, but seeing Davis turn toward him, as if to challenge his reasoning, he then continued. "Sir, Johnston is adored by his men—they see him as an able commander who does not waste their lives needlessly, and they would follow him into hell if he ordered it. He won the first Battle of Manassas, and every southerner reveres him for that. Also, relieving a senior commander while his forces still face the enemy is never wise, and should be done only when essential."

Davis seemed to struggle to get control of himself, and again, Toombs remained silent for some time. Finally Davis spoke. "I'm sure you are right General. Perhaps it would not be prudent to remove Johnston from command at this time, but I want you to know that if we lose more property to Crazy Billy, I'll string that man up personally!"

Thus, it was up to Toombs to determine which man Jefferson Davis wanted to hang more—Crazy Billy Sherman or Johnston himself!

## A Confederate Hospital

It was late on the afternoon of May 29, 1864, when Major Jamie Turnbull opened his eyes. He immediately heard his friend's voice.

"Well hell, Sir!" Duncan Carmichael said. "You finally decided to wake up, I see." Duncan was grinning from ear to ear, as was Sampson. They stood on either side of the cot where Major Jamie Turnbull lay. Jamie had just opened his eyes, and he thought to himself, I cannot think of two faces I'd rather see than these two. Then, of course, he felt a pang of guilt; why did he not think of his young wife in that same regard?

He wasn't given much time to consider the question, however. Sampson spoke up next. "I sure'nuf is glad to see your eyes open, Mr. James. I sur' is! You can't go gettin' hurt now, and makin' all de homefolks worry like this!"

Jamie's head, as predicted, was killing him, but he still liked the thought of his two friends keeping watch over him. "How long have I been out?" he asked.

Duncan was no longer with his commander—he was with his friend. "Your sorry ass has slept through the night and most of the next day! Hell, we missed most of the festivities when our guys left with the rest of the army. Captain Collins took the boys out yesterday, and left us here with you. We're in Marietta now, and are scheduled to move out in two days."

Jamie tried to concentrate. "Damn my head hurts. Did I get kicked by a mule, or what?"

Duncan said, "It's just a scratch, but it came from a Union cannon, not a mule, you idiot. I've been telling you since Chickamauga to get low and keep low when we're in a fight."

Jamie grunted again, then asked. "What did you say about movin' out?"

Sampson replied. "Like I says, Captain Collins has gone with most of the men, and most of the army. They is following Sherman back toward the east. We's supposed to stay here for another day and then take some prisoners south."

Then Duncan spoke. "You're supposed to lead us, if you wake up and can, and I recon you can! A little headache never stopped a Tugalo River man before, did it? We got forty of the boys from our outfit standing guard, most of'um got a wound, but nothin' too bad. We're supposed to take three hundred prisoners down south."

"I see," said Jamie. He knew of the practice of using the walking wounded as prisoner escorts. The walking wounded could escort Union prisoners, and they clearly would contribute nothing in the next battle, but they could relieve men who were able to fight. "I see." Jamie repeated himself.

Duncan then spoke up again. "Sir, I've got the boys in hand and the prisoners are well guarded. We got a day before we're to march over to the railroad with these men, so you don't have nothin' to do but sleep for the next day or so."

Jamie had one thought. "Didn't they leave an officer in charge here? You're just a corporal."

Duncan smiled. "Hell, Sir. I'm a sergeant now! Captain Collins said so! And as far as an officer goes, I guess you're it!"

Jamie grinned at his friends. "Well, I guess that sounds just fine to me. Keep things straight for me Duncan, until I'm up in the morning. Now you don't need to sit here like I'm a new-born babe or nothing."

Sampson grinned. "We was ordered too, Sir! By Captain Collins himself, before he took off."

Jamie, though his head was still aching, wanted to hug these men, not to mention Captain Collins. When one goes down in a battle, having friends like these means everything. "Well, then, I guess we'll pay some attention to those orders, but may I suggest that Sampson stay with me while you go attend to those prisoners, Sergeant Carmichael? I'd like to know they're secure, if I'm in charge of 'um."

Just as Duncan stood up, hell itself marched loudly into that hospital, and the cursing began immediately. Strangely enough, it sounded like a woman's voice!

"Where are the Union wounded? I saw another load come in here! I know I did! Are they getting the treatment they deserve? We tend Confederate and Union alike in this hospital from this moment forth! Is that clear to everyone! I will take no bullshit on that point! If it is not clear enough, by God I'll have your eyes for my lunch, and your guts for my dinner! Mistreat any wounded man, and I'll rip your nuts off myself! Now, I'll need to see the provisions here immediately, and the bandages."

The loud woman took a moment to shove a terrified orderly out of the aisle, so she could move through. Then she began cursing once again. "Where is the damned store room? I'll inspect every ounce of food these men get, as well as every bandage applied here, and they damn well better be clean, or I'll skin the man alive who brings them into my hospital. Tell that useless shit of a surgeon to stop cutting off legs and arms at least until someone buries that pile of flesh and bone I see outside that window. It is attracting flies, and I do not tolerate flies! And you (here she pointed directly at Sampson) get off your sorry ass and pick up those bloody rags in the other room. I'll have my hospital clean enough to eat off the floors, or by God, you orderlies WILL be eating off the floor! Now MOVE!"

Sampson quickly ran to obey as Duncan sat back down on the edge of Jamie's cot, so as not to draw attention to himself. Jamie looked at the loud, cursing woman, and then glanced at Duncan, and thought to himself, "My God. Duncan Carmichael is scared! I've never seen him scared before!"

The cursing continued in the same general tone, but the volume decreased a bit as Mother Bickerdyke and her entourage of several nurses and two terrified doctors moved into another room.

As the commotion moved away, Jamie had to ask, "What the hell was that?"

Duncan said, "That's the only damned woman on this planet who can out cuss a Carmichael!" She came by the other day, cussin' something fierce then too! He looked in the direction of the other room, "And I don't want to tangle with her, no Sir!"

Jamie, though his head still hurt, had to ask. "Who the hell is she?"

By then Sampson was back at the cot holding an arm full of bloody rags. "She's a nurse, Suh. And a mighty godly woman, Suh, if you can believe that! But she do cuss a lot!"

Jamie looked back at Duncan, who began to explain. "She's a Union nurse, but she showed up over here yesterday, demanding to see her boys and look at their bandages and the food they were given. Our pickets picked her up when she crossed the lines, and the word is that they didn't know what to do with her, so they took her on up to headquarters. Then she just marched into General Johnston's headquarters tent and demanded to see the hospitals."

Sampson spoke next. "She tends everyone alike, Suh! You's lucky to have her checkin' on this hospital where you is."

Duncan nodded his agreement. "Over at headquarters, they say that Johnston didn't know what to do with her either. He asked by what authority she'd crossed the lines. Mother Bickerdyke said, 'On authority of the Lord God Almighty! Have you anyone here who outranks that?' Then she showed him a pass from Sherman, with a recommendation that Johnston should just let her tend to everyone in all of our hospitals everywhere. Then, if you can believe it, she told, not asked mind you but told, General Johnston himself to just keep the entire Confederate army the hell out of her way! Johnston couldn't figure out what to do, so he assigned a Confederate nurse to her as a guide to show her to several hospitals, and then gave her a headquarters pass." At that point, Duncan looked back toward Bickerdyke with a grudging respect. "Right now, that foul mouthed woman is the only person alive that can cross the battle line holding a commander's pass from both armies!"

Jamie said the only thing he could think of. "Well I'll be damned."

Duncan got up to take his leave, but couldn't do so without one more joke on his friend. "You sure will be, Sir, unless you're ready to lead us all south in two days. We've got three hundred Yankee prisoners dying to see the hospitality of the Confederacy. We're headed to some place down south called Camp Sumter.

"Never heard of it," Jamie said. "Does anyone know where it is?"

Sampson merely shook his head, and looked over at Duncan. "Guess I'll go and find out how to get there. Supposed to be a town near there, little place called Andersonville."

Two days later, Jamie Turnbull was up before the sun, and found Duncan getting the prisoners in order. It didn't take long for Major Jamie Turnbull, his selected contingent of forty Confederate guards, and three hundred prisoners to march to the Confederate staging area in Marietta, Georgia, a walk of two miles, which they covered in two hours. There they boarded prisoner trains heading south on June 1, 1864. They got to the main railhead in Atlanta in only two hours, but there they had to wait for several days, prior to boarding another train for the trip to south Georgia. During that time, both the three hundred Union prisoners and their Confederate guards slept in an open field just outside of Atlanta. Once on board the southbound train, they traveled overnight and most of the next day, arriving in Andersonville about an hour before dark on June 6, where they disembarked for the two mile walk to Camp Sumter. When they arrived at the first guard post, a rough looking Sergeant of the Guard directed them to place the prisoners into a confinement fence beside the road, and to guard the prisoners that night. He indicated to Jamie that his three hundred prisoners would be processed first thing in the morning.

## Andersonville: The Death of Hope

History teaches us many things of the human condition, some pleasant, uplifting and hopeful, others less positive. One lesson, shown again and again over the decades is that when all hope dies, men become animals. Where there is no chance of survival, no hint of mercy, no food, no medicine, and most importantly, no hope, men prey on each other to survive. They quickly lose those principles that govern most human behavior.

Examples are numerous. When a frozen wasteland trapped a few wagons in the Donner Pass of California for a winter, it took less than two months before those people began to cut up and eat each other. In Japanese prison camps in 1943 and 1944, American prisoners began to prey on each other, forming gangs by which the powerful and most influential took advantage over the weak and the sick. In Nazi concentration camps, it was often Jews themselves who, at the barrel of a German gun, herded other Jews into gas chambers.

Camp Sumter, most often called simply Andersonville Prison, was one such place. It opened in February of 1864 and like many Civil War prison camps, within a few short months it was vastly overcrowded. Also, it was understaffed and poorly provisioned, and those needs were ignored by the Confederate authorities. Thus, over time it became a death camp. Forty five thousand Union prisoners entered those gates at Andersonville, during the short eight months it served as a Confederate prisoner of war camp for Union detainees. Of those, some thirteen thousand died there. History does provide an occasional example of more deadly locations from time to time—perhaps Europe during the Black Plague where one third of the population died over a ten year period. Maybe certain battles during the Crusades held similar death tolls. Still, few patches of earth have claimed more victims per square foot, more quickly than Andersonville. In a space of just over twenty-six fenced acres, during an eight month period, nearly one of every three men held there died. Andersonville can rightly claim to be one of the most deadly patches of ground on the planet.

The next morning at sunup, Major Jamie Turnbull looked directly into hell. By his side, stood Duncan Carmichael, Sampson, Wellspeak, Ten Cent Bill, and Chad Wilson, and all stared in non-belief at the horror from just outside the north entrance of Andersonville Prison.

The camp was laid out in a large rectangle with a double fence enclosing the prisoner's area. Each end of the rectangle was a hill, with a creek running directly across the camp almost in the middle of the long side of the rectangle, like the centerline of the letter H. There were no barracks for the prisoners—they had to create their own living space by covering themselves with anything they brought to the camp. The whole acreage was covered by makeshift tarps made from thin blankets, a few pieces of wood, or old tents from the first days of the camp. Most men dug caves for themselves on the hillsides at each end, as the earth sloped down to the creek, a creek that was both the water source, and the toilet for the prisoners.

But mere description cannot do justice to the sight they witnessed that day. It is nearly impossible to explain what those men actually saw in their first view of Andersonville. Perhaps we should consider the description of an unknown Union prisoner of his entry into this hellhole.

*"As we entered the place, a spectacle met our eyes that almost froze our blood with horror, and made our hearts fail within us. Before us were forms that had once been men, active and erect men;—stalwart men who were now nothing but mere walking skeletons, covered with filth, excrement, and vermin. Many of us wondered, 'Can this be hell? May God protect us!' Every one of us thought that God alone could bring them out alive.*

*"In the center of the whole was a swamp, occupying about three or four acres*

*of the narrowed limits, and a part of this marshy place had been used by the prisoners as a toilet. Excrement covered the ground and the scent was suffocating. The ground allotted to our ninety men was near the edge of this plague-spot, we wondered how we were to live through the hot summer soon to come, in the midst of such fearful surroundings. It was more than we could think of."*

Jamie and his men, as they stared into hell, knew that they would leave within a few hours, when their prisoners were turned over to the Camp Sumter guards. Still, that did not lessen their aversion to this scene. "I cannot believe this. How can our merciful God allow this?" Wilson exclaimed.

Ten Cent Bill answered slowly. "Ain't no God near these parts. No Sir! Ain't no God near 'bouts!"

After a few moments, Jamie merely turned away and said. "Let's go get our prisoners, and get them processed in."

Over the next few hours, groups of twenty Union prisoners were marched from the containment fence to the prison gate guardhouse where they were listed by name and rank, by the post guard. They were each assigned an area of the camp, but as the limited real estate was already overrun with makeshift tarps, caves, or tunnels where men slept, there was really little new territory to offer for the new detainees. As Jamie's men guarded the dwindling Union force in the containment fence, Jamie and a few of the men continued to watch the prison from the hill just north of the camp. Thus, Jamie Turnbull witnessed the true horror of Andersonville, as each group of twenty men was then released into the camp compound.

First the men passed the outside stockade, a tall wooden fence with guard shacks spaced around it every few hundred feet. Then they walked over a twenty foot space of empty ground; for Andersonville used the "Deadline" system to contain prisoners. Some nineteen feet inside the stockade was another smaller fence of wire—the deadline. Any prisoner caught between that low wire fence and the main wooden stockade was assumed to be attempting an escape and would thus, be shot on sight.

One historic photograph exists of Andersonville prison, showing the sloping northern hill from the southeast side of the prison. One can see the prisoner's tents, a few sleeping caves, and a fairly clear view of the dead-line from that photo taken on August 17, 1864. Men who crossed into that deadline were killed immediately.

It is interesting to note that the term deadline dates from this very practice and this time period. While any office worker today will, occasionally miss a deadline on some work project or another, the term itself dates from a time when crossing a deadline did, in fact, result in one's immediate death. That thought, upon reflection, can put an entirely new spin on the matters which we seem to think are so very important today.

As groups of twenty Union prisoners entered the stockade, they tended to group up just inside the fence outside the deadline; for they could tell that the deadline was the true entrance into hell. Just inside that deadline, stood large groups of Union prisoners waiting to prey on the new arrivals. Forty, fifty, or sixty men, formed on each side of the road leading further into the camp, often shouting to the new arrivals various taunts. "Come on in boys! We've got a surprise for you!" "What ya waitin' for beautiful! Come in and share what you got!"

**Andersonville Prison**

These men, having lost any pretense of humanity, were called raiders throughout Andersonville. They armed themselves with clubs, bones of the dead, makeshift knives, or merely their fists, and they were terrifying. One raider wore the skull of a dead prisoner on a short rope around his neck, just to make himself look more terrifying. By forming raider groups, they knew they could easily overpower any group of twenty new prisoners and steal whatever food and valuables they might possess. As soon as the new men entered the deadline, the raiders pounced and beat the new men senseless, at which point, they quickly stole everything of value, including at times even the clothes the new prisoners wore. Sometimes even buttons and belt buckles would be stolen by the raiders, since they could trade that metal to the camp guards for an extra ration of meal or beans, should another food shipment arrive.

Meanwhile the Confederate guards in the guard towers merely watched, not really caring what the Union prisoners did to each other. In this patch of ground, one may be forgiven if, like Ten Cent Bill, one assumed that God did not exist at all.

Major Jamie Turnbull watched for several hours from atop the hill just outside of the stockade, as his prisoners were processed in groups of twenty. Each group was met by raiders just inside the deadline. At times the beatings would start immediately, while at other times the new men were greeted with handshakes and taken further into the camp, only to be victimized then. Many were completely naked within an hour of entrance, and Jamie knew in his heart there was absolutely nothing he could do.

Still, even in the hell of Andersonville, Jamie soon detected a few signs of humanity, a few hints of mercy and kindness. After the horrid beatings of the newly arrived prisoners, when the raiders were completely done with them, often leaving them bloody and unclothed, a few men would emerge from the tents and the caves, and begin to help the new arrivals. Sometimes they would pick up the new men, and help them away from the swamp where the Raiders usually dumped them. Sometimes those men brought water from their own caves, or fetched some water from the "clean" end of the creek, to share with the bloodied new prisoners.

From his position on the hill, Jamie watched the horror, as well as the occasional kindness. He shared his thoughts with his wife, and we can, via that letter, understand some of his thoughts.

*Ms. Mary Turnbull, Walton's Ford, GA*
*June 8, 1864*

*My Dearest Mary :*

*Today I've had a vision of hell and I must let you, least anyone else know, that my soul aches. I am not in danger, at least not from any battle. In fact, this night I'm riding comfortably on a train headed toward Macon and ultimately back to Atlanta. My men and I delivered some Union prisoners to a prison camp earlier today, and I cannot describe the horror of that place. It terrifies me and, I fear, these visions will haunt my dreams forever. For I would not burden you with the things I saw; I would not wish to burden any man or woman with those frightening images. Still, on occasion, I saw a hint of kindness in that prison camp, and in the degradation of that place, even the small kindnesses seem, in contrast, out of place. The kindness made the horror more terrifying.*

*I can say that I have seen into hell, and it is not on any battle line, or any running skirmish between armies; for at least in battle men have a chance to fight. This hell is, instead, in a prison where men have lost all humanity. I saw men staving, walking dead men, who will not—who cannot survive another week, and at the same time, other men preyed on the weak like a pack of wild dogs; wovles surrounding a wounded deer. It was more than horrible, and I am sparing you much of the vision. If our Confederacy is to keep prisoners in these conditions, I fear that we are no better than the Damn Yankees. You can tell from that last statement how I fear that God himself has deserted that place.*

*And yet, some men were kind to each other, even here, even in the depths of hell. I wonder which of these men I should become if I were to find myself in such a place. I should let you know that I will commit today to not be captured in this war. I will fight a regiment myself, with my sword only, and thus die with honor rather than face a prison like this, for the Union camps can only be worse! I fear God, and have a wonderful wife at home, but still, I truly fear who I might become were I in this place. I, truly, would rather die than find out.*

*To make my mood even worse, I now believe that I shall miss the chance for a weekend pass and will not see you on our first anniversary two weeks hence. We may be going into a fight again soon, and this does pain my horribly. Please forgive me, but I must do my duty to our Grand Cause.*

*Please write to me and tell me of hope! Please speak of things at the plantation. Tell me the news from Walton's Ford and the Tugalo Valley; speak to me of wildflowers growing this spring near the horse pond, or of young boys fishing in the river. How is the tobacco coming along? How does the corn grow this year? Tell me everything, and help me get these visions out of my mind. Your words have always comforted me, so very many times after a fight, and I can only hope they will likewise comfort me now, after this vision of hell. For I need your kind words now, more than ever, and even as I finish this, my men call to me for one reason or another. I'm sorry I cannot even take time to say how very lovely you are, or to let you know that I long for your touch. Please forgive this letter. I must go…*

*Major Jamie Turnbull*
*4th Georgia Regiment, Macon, GA*

## Author's Note: Numbering The Dead

Andersonville Prison was, by far the most deadly prisoner of war camp during the entire War Between the States. During the early years of the war, prisoners tended to be paroled or exchanged, but that practice had long broken down by 1864. Thus as the war progressed, camps on both sides became increasingly overcrowded, and in the Confederacy particularly, both food and medicine became scare. Such scarcity was felt by everyone in the south, as well as the front-line troops. The Union prisoners were last in line for any type of ration, and they often starved to death or died by disease in the many filthy prison camps, throughout the south.

## A Toll of the Dead in Prison Camps

| Prison Camp | Location | Maintained By | Total Prisoners | Total Deaths | Percentage Who Died |
|---|---|---|---|---|---|
| | | | | | |
| Camp Douglas | Chicago, IL | Union | 26,060 | 4,454 | 17% |
| The Stockade | Florence, SC | Confederacy | 15,000 | 2,802 | 18% |
| Point Lookout | Lookout, MD | Union | 50,000 | 4,000 | 8% |
| Salisbury Prison | Salisbury, NC | Confederacy | Unknown | 10,000 | ?? |
| Camp Sumter | Andersonville, GA | Confederacy | 45,000 | 13,000 | 29% |

The commander of Andersonville Prison, Col. Wirz, was the only man tried for war crimes after the War Between the States. Some say he was innocent, arguing that he was doing the best he could to supply his prisoners, given that he received very little support in 1864. He did send one group of Union prisoners, with passes, into Union territory to plead for a prisoner exchange, and hopefully save the lives of the prisoners, all to no avail. At the end of the war, he was tried, convicted and hung, and he remains to this day, the only war criminal, north or south, who was ever tried for actions during that bloody war.

As the grim statistics above suggest, many prisoner of war camps on both sides were scenes of horror, but statistics alone never tell the true tale. Moreover, even within this catalogue of death, the horror of Andersonville stands alone, as a beacon of what men can do to each other. These numbers show that even a bloody, horrifying battlefield is not the purest measure of hell. True hell comes when men have no hope of survival; that is when men truly become animals.

Today Camp Douglas is under several rows of higher-priced condominiums along the lakefront just inside the city limits of Chicago. Nothing exists of the Stockade in Florence, SC, and the acreage of the Salisbury Prisoner of War Camp in Salisbury, NC is an upscale subdivision of private homes. Much of Point Lookout in Maryland has simply washed away into the Chesapeake Bay. Of course, a few mass graves exist near each location, but these, like the prison camps once located there, are largely forgotten, save for a historic marker or two.

However Andersonville is a different story. At Andersonville, the entire camp acreage is preserved, and the deadline has been reconstructed. Visitors can see the camp layout, and the creek in the valley. One can visit the lower creek, long ago cleaned of the sewage from which men drank. One can see tunnel entrances by which prisoners tried to escape, or one might visit the nearby graveyard of over 13,000 Union prisoners. Six of the raiders, the most notorious of the Andersonville raiders, were tried and subsequently hung by their own Union comrades. They were given marked graves in a separate, dishonored, patch of ground.

The whole of Andersonville is a national historic site, and includes a Museum for Prisoners of War from all of America's conflicts. This hallowed ground is worth a visit, perhaps more so than any of the battlefields from that war. Here you can see pictures of the prison ships on which many Revolutionary War Patriots died at the hands of the British. You can see inside a small cell from the Hanoi Hilton—the horrible prisoner of war camp in Vietnam. You can see artifacts from American prisoners of the Japanese in World War II, and of course you can see the horror that was Andersonville. Here you can learn the extremes to which men will sometimes go when faced with the loss of all hope. While those depths of the soul are horrid to contemplate, you can, on occasion, see a small kindness, a small mercy even in the gates of hell. In those kindnesses, one can glimpse the majesty of the human spirit. For once in a long while, even in hell, men can and do show mercy. Indeed, Andersonville, can teach us much.

## Back to the War

As Jamie and his men rode the trains back to the Army of Tennessee during the second week of June in 1864, that force was fighting a few, relatively minor engagements with Sherman's Union force. Both armies were positioning themselves back toward the railroad leading into Atlanta. There were minor cavalry actions at Gilgal Church, Pine Mountain, and Lost Mountain between June 8 and June 16, as both armies moved from the Dallas Line back toward the east and the all-important railroad. Jamie and his men, when they disembarked the train in Marietta, GA, were told that their regiment was preparing trenches only four miles north of town on the steep slope of the last true mountain between Sherman's army and Atlanta. While missing some of the minor fights, Major Jamie Turnbull and the veterans of the Fourth Georgia Regiment were just in time to fight in one of the largest full-scale battles ever fought on Georgia soil, the Battle of Kennesaw Mountain.

# Chapter 4
*Moving On Atlanta*

## A Letter From Home

*Major Jamie Turnbull, Commander*
*Fourth Georgia Infantry*
*Atlanta Station for Delivery to Hood's Corps, CSA*

*My dearest and most loving husband. I know I wrote to you only several days ago, but I am sitting on the porch of Traveler's Rest on this wonderful spring evening, and I was thinking of you, my brave soldier and my husband. I wonder where you are, and what you might be doing. We've heard nothing of any fighting for a few days, so I assume you are well and with the army; I pray daily that you are safe.*

*There is nothing to tell you of the plantation. We still get up each morning and do our chores; cows get milked and the chickens get fed. With coffee so hard to find, we have all gotten used to drinking chicory or even coffee made of peanuts, but I've decided that I'll simply forego the pleasure until some real coffee can be found. Perhaps a blockade runner will bring in some soon! The slaves seem a bit more restless, and one can hear in town about slaves running away to join the Yankees. As yet, I believe that all of ours are still here.*

*There was an interesting moment in Providence Methodist Church this past Sunday. It was a rainy Sunday morning, and church seemed to drag on forever (May a merciful God forgive me for saying so!). Preacher Thompson was going on and on in a prayer, as he so often does, asking the Almighty to keep our boys safe in all of the battles to come. I simply thought it would never end, but just as he asked that God's hand be placed on each and every Tugalo River Valley man, a massively-loud lightning bolt shattered the silence and scared us all to death! It struck the top of the old pine tree just outside the front window (You know the large window near where we sit toward the front of the church). It terrified everyone, and the noise seemed to go on and on! Preacher Thompson jumped nearly out of his breeches, and landed facing the window, while turning the most interesting shade of blue; I thought he was going to have a heart attack and die right there in the pulpit! That massive old tree was right beside the window and everyone could see it! The lighting roared as it struck the tree top, and instantly ran all the way down the side of the tree stripping off the bark in a long blue line of fire and light. Some of the bark shattered the window glass, coming right into the church, and that only added to the noise. It sounded louder than the loudest cannon, and then the light disappeared right under the church window! I think that is what scared everybody the most. It seemed to us all as if God's wrath was coming right up through the floorboards and the broken glass to get us all! Everybody on that side of the congregation began to rush away from the window, even while the thunder continued rumbling louder and louder. It was a most fearsome storm!*

*As we all moved, Mr. Parker stood right up in the front row—he was sitting closest to the window—and shouted, "Oh Hell!" right there in the pew, before he ran down the aisle trying to get away. Old Mrs. Sharpe was playing the piano near the window and as she jumped away from the noise, she tripped on her own hoop skirt, toppled to the floor, and rolled down the middle of the front aisle. Babies began to scream, adding to the roar of the thunder while everybody rushed away from the noise at the broken window. By then we were all on the other side of the church, except for Mrs. Sharpe who was wallowing around on her hands and knees in the front aisle because she couldn't see! Her skirt was over her head, showing the hoops and her unmentionables quite plainly to the entire congregation, and her head was bleeding all over her old white gown with blood dripping down on the church floor!*

*It was chaos for a few seconds, and it took a minute or two to get everyone calmed down, but Preacher Thompson recovered first, and shouted, "God himself, has shown us his power today, and has blessed our efforts in praising him! Mr. Parker, please temper your comments at God's power, and help Mrs. Sharpe get up. Now let us all sing!" With that, he launched into a chorus of "All Hail the Power of Jesus Name" and soon, everybody joined in, singing almost as loud as the thunder! Never in the history of the Tugalo Valley was God's Holy Name praised more loudly, or with more energy, than during that hymn!*

*As you can see, nothing of great import happens in the valley when all the men are gone to war. My Grandfather is still sickly, but is doing as well as he has recently. Meely is fine as are all of my younger brothers. Aunt Fanny has recovered from her death bed once again.*

*I have not very much to tell you, but I did want to write and let you know that I think of you each and every moment. Please take care and come home safely. I have included below another scribbling on the history of Traveler's Rest Plantation. Let me know if these begin to bore you, but as I write, I often think of more things my Grandfather has told me that relate to this never-ending war. At any rate, this should give you something more to read around your campfire.*

## More Scribbling's on Plantation History
### *as told by my Grandfather, Mr. Devereaux Jarrett, Traveler's Rest Plantation written by Mrs. Mary Jarrett Turnbull, May 24, 1864*

Grandfather Jarrett told me of other visits to the plantation by John C. Calhoun. Indeed, The Great Man and his slave Cassius were here again in the autumn of 1849, along with the other fire-eaters. All were sitting in the parlor by the big fireplace, Mr. Edmund Ruffin, Robert Rhett, Mr. Joe Brown (who was elected governor later during the war), and Mr. Robert Toombs. As usual, they were all mad as hell! Grandfather said that Mr. Calhoun was so mad he was pacing all around the room, shouting something when it was his turn or when he took a mind to, and his slave poor Cassius, was following around behind him holding a chair, in case the Great Man wanted to sit. As you well know, when he did sit he never looked back, but always assumed that the chair would simply be behind him!

As usual, Mr. Calhoun was talking more than the rest of them. "We must admit this is one of the wisest attempts at stopping slavery and taking away our property that these abolitionists have come up with! We have to admire their timing, trying to bring in another non-slave state, so that they will hold the upper hand in the Senate. They could then simply do away with slavery by a simple vote of Congress! Our property would simply vanish, along with our wealth and influence!"

Joe Brown then began to shout. "Our friends in Texas want slavery, and already hold slaves. Why can't the damned Yankees just let all of the land that we won from Mexico in 1848 determine the issue themselves? I'm sure most would opt for slavery, as territories like New Mexico or Utah move toward statehood!"

Next Toombs spoke up. "Damn you Joe! That's a fool's dream. Those damn abolitionists in Congress will never allow states to decide the issue for themselves!

Ruffin spoke next. "I don't give a damn what the federal Congress says. They will never take my slaves unless they kill me first!"

"Now now, Edmund," Calhoun said as he grinned at the group. "I fear you'll bust a gut unless you calm down a bit. Perhaps you should have some more port." As the others laughed, Calhoun continued. "I'm not as worried about the slaves as many of you here. If Congress did do away with slavery, there would have to be compensation for those whose sweat and toil had been invested in slaves. I'm more worried about what this would say about our rights as states, under the Constitution. Where would federal power end?"

Jarrett asked, "What do you mean, John? Does Congress have other nefarious plans? Is there something we don't yet know about?"

Calhoun took a sip of his port, as he considered the question. "I don't know of any other confiscation of property, but if Congress can free the slaves, they could also determine that any man's property of any type, should be confiscated, could they not? Just like the damned kings in Europe, Congress is a multi-headed hydra that eats the labor and toil of honest men, and they could decide, like those European kings, to declare any of our plantations forfeit to the government. They could tax anything, even our income. They could do anything!"

As you may imagine, that brought out a series of shouts, and righteous anger like a loud Baptist preacher at a revival!

*"Who do these sanctimonious Yankees think they are?"*
*"How in hell can anyone support such a government?"*
*"It'll be a cold day in hell, when they take my farm."*

## Remainder of the Letter from Mary Jarrett Turnbull

*And there you have it, my dearest husband, my gallant Confederate warrior! According to Grandfather Jarrett, all of the fire-eaters were as angry in 1848 as they had been in 1830. They were really all "in a fiddle" about the Congress moving to bring more non-slave states into the Union without also bringing in an equal number of slave states. Of course, since the Missouri Compromise in 1820, every time a slave state had been brought into the nation, a free state up north was also admitted, so the balance of power in Congress had remained the same. But by 1849, with the large sections of land in the west recently taken from Mexico in the War of 1848, the question had arisen again. Should new states be slave or free? And once again, in late 1849 and 1850, the southern states were considering their role under the Constitution; should they remain in the Union or secede?*

*Well, Grandfather Jarrett says that, just like the Nullification Crisis in 1830, cooler heads prevailed and by 1850, once again, a compromise was reached. In fact, the 1850 version of The Missouri Compromise managed to get through Congress, and it seemed to be acceptable to the abolitionists in the north as well as most of the members of the southern state's congressional delegations. Yet again, a War Between the States, was averted in 1850, when the federal Congress decided to compromise.*

*Of course in that instance, the issue had been expansion of slavery into new territories, rather than the elimination of slavery altogether, as those abolitionists want to do now! Still Grandfather always emphasized that the fundamental question, the question that underlay all of these political conflicts, not to mention this current war, is the power relationship between the states and the federal government, not slavery itself! That was the view of most southerners in the 1850s, just like the 1830s! That explains why so many southerners who don't even own slaves are fighting for the Confederacy. Why don't these damned Yankees see that?*

*We southerners should shout from the rooftops! This is a war for freedom from the tyranny of the federal government! My Grandfather Devereaux Jarrett, was absolutely correct in his view of the politics of the new Union of States. This war is the result of many sectional conflicts. First, the large shipping interests of the north wanted tariffs to protect their shipping profits, and any informed southerner has since viewed the growing power of the federal government with distrust and distain. Still that monkey Lincoln is wise, trying to make this seem like a war about slavery, with his fancy Emancipation Proclamation last year. Grandpa Jarrett has said often that the dastardly proclamation itself may be the smartest political move Abraham Lincoln ever made! With a flip of his pen, Lincoln eliminated any possibility that the Confederacy would find any allies in Europe. No matter how much British mills wanted southern cotton, the British Parliament will not support a Confederacy that allows slavery!*

*I'm sure that is more than enough of my ramblings about my Grandfather Jarrett, and his fire-eater friends, at least for now, so I'll stop. I do hope this letter finds you well. Please know that I love you with every ounce of my being.*

*Can a shameless wife tell her husband such things in these dreadful times? I fear I shall always be shameless in my love for you, and I have no doubt that God himself has placed this love in my heart, a heart that, as always, belongs only to you.*

*Your Mary*
*Traveler's Rest Plantation*
*Tugalo River Valley, Georgia*

## I Need Holes!

After dropping their prisoners in Andersonville, the guard force under Major Jamie Turnbull had traveled back to Atlanta and then to Marietta by two separate trains. One train got them all the way into Atlanta, but they had to detrain and board another for the final leg of the trip to Marietta. Major Turnbull had learned in Atlanta that his outfit was encamped on Kennesaw Mountain, so each man knew when they got off the last train that they would have to march the last few miles to meet up with their comrades in the Fourth Georgia Infantry. When Turnbull and his guard platoon reached the city of Marietta, Turnbull ordered his men to disembark and rest in the town square near the station while he checked in at headquarters.

Before he could even leave the platform however, a Confederate colonel shouted to Jamie from the second floor window of the Kennesaw House, a hotel that stood right beside the railroad tracks. "Hello, Major. May I ask, Sir, what unit are you with, and might I also request a bit of assistance from you and your men?"

As Turnbull looked up at the four story building, he could tell it had been turned into a makeshift hospital. Through one downstairs window, he could see a surgeon leaning over a table preparing to operate on a man, and Jamie wondered to himself, has the battle already started? He shouted back, "We're part of the Fourth Georgia Infantry, Sir, a guard detail just returned from delivery of prisoners to Andersonville. We've orders to report back to our outfit up at Kennesaw. What type of help might you be needing?"

"I'm Col. Ansley Dekle and I need holes. To be more specific, I need a few laborers, you see. As you may know, all of the slaves with the army are building defenses up on the mountain, and I'm at a loss as to what to do."

Jamie didn't understand his meaning, and after a long, exhausting train ride merely wanted to know what the man had in mind. "Sir?"

"I need holes son, holes in the ground, Major. These are usually dug by slaves seconded to my medical group, but all of my laborers were taken up to the mountain."

"You mean graves?" Jamie asked. "Doesn't graves registration..."

"Not graves, Major; holes in the ground. I won't call them graves, just holes. Perhaps if you'd come with me, while your men wait here, I could explain."

"Yes Sir," said Jamie, as the colonel walked back into the Kennesaw House.

Then the colonel spoke a bit more softly. "You may wish to take a breath before we go inside, Major. The smell of a hospital can be overwhelming."

Jamie thought to himself, "Who the hell is this idiot, a man that thought a hospital smelled bad, indeed! He should smell a battlefield!" Of course, that thought changed rather quickly when Jamie entered the premises.

A hospital in the War Between the States, was a singular version of hell like no other environment imaginable. In the days prior to any understanding of microbiology, germs, sanitation, or even infection, most hospitals were deplorable places where body parts were simply sawed off, often with no anesthetic at all. Screams were the order of the day, and most men on the surgeon's table voided their bladders and bowels, as they lay in torment while having their arms or legs, or both sawed off. By 1864, supplies in southern hospitals were few, and if Mother Bikerdyke was a sanitation extremist, most surgeons in 1864, both north and south, were not. As they sawed off arms and legs, such useless appendages were typically tossed out of a window, and frequently created quite a stench as they rotted on the ground, prior to someone taking the time to bury them in the nearest field. However, Kennesaw House was at the center of downtown Marietta, and no corn field was convenient for such a purpose, so no one had taken the time to dispose of the human waste.

It took Jamie less than ten seconds to totally reverse his thinking about the smell. While he'd been in a hospital himself, he had been in a home where wounded men recovered, not in a surgical hospital where men with horrid wounds were operated on. Even the worst, most hellish things he'd seen on the battle line in the last few months were tame, compared to what he saw, heard, and smelled, as he walked through that hospital.

Seven surgeons were quite busy, with wounded from a fight at Kolb's Farm the prior evening. In three of the downstairs rooms, two or more surgeons were operating on patients in each room, and the screams were almost as terrifying as the bloody scene itself. Barrels were set four feet apart, and interior doors from the house were removed and laid across the barrels to form makeshift operating tables. Two or three such tables were placed in each room, with several men around each. The surgeons themselves stood in blood, sometimes several inches deep. The sheer weight of two, or three, or four such operating tables, the patients on them, and the doctors and nurses, all standing in the middle of a room, would often sink the center of the floor a bit, and the blood tended to pool up in the low spots near the center of the floor just under the operating tables.

In most cases, it could not run out between the floorboards quickly enough. The blood, mucus, feces, and pee kept each table top more than moist, as the awful sawing continued, around the clock. As quickly as one patient was moved off the table, another took his place, while the doctors washed off the saws and prongs used to extract bullets in a pail of dirty, bloody water by the door.

Jamie made eye contact with one patient just before the awful saw bit into his upper thigh. The man let out a blood-curdling scream, and then, thankfully, passed out, as Jamie watched the surgeon in horror.

Col. Dekle was watching and spoke up to get Jamie's attention away from the ongoing operations. "Our problem is out back, Major. I need holes badly!" With that the colonel and Jamie walked down the hall, with Jamie careful to not even look into the other operating rooms. As they got out the backdoor, Jamie took a breath of somewhat fresher air while the colonel spoke. "Here's my problem, Major." He gestured to the rear of the house.

And then Jamie saw a sight that he'd never seen before—something more horrible than his worst battlefield vision. Before him was a stack of arms, legs, feet, and fingers that was almost ten feet high! As he watched a man's leg was tossed out of the second story window, hit the top of the pile and tumbled down the side. Jamie thought, "My God! They must have those horrid operations going on upstairs too!"

Dekle spoke again. "As you can see, Major, I need holes to bury these body parts, and graves registration won't give me the men for such work, since these are technically not bodies. Doesn't that sound like a good example of army intelligence to you? God knows the graves people are busy enough this morning. Our own group of ten slaves with the hospital used to dispose of these, but General Johnston has taken those slaves out digging trenches up on the mountain."

Jamie finished the idea. "And you need my guard detail to dig the holes and bury these..." Here he could not find the words, "these things. But Sir? I didn't think the battle at Kennesaw had begun as yet?"

"It hasn't," the colonel replied. "These are merely the result of one charge by General Hood's Corps yesterday afternoon, some fighting near Kolb's Farm about five miles west of here. The wagons began to bring in severely wounded men since about six yesterday afternoon, and they are still coming in, with no end in sight."

After a few moments, the colonel explained further. "We usually just bury these body parts in some field nearby, but we're in town here, and we have no nearby farm. I've even asked the mayor what should be done, and he cannot give me an answer. So on my authority, I'm giving you an order, as you and your men, seem to be temporarily unassigned. You will dig three holes that are eight feet deep, five wide, and twenty feet long, in the town square, just yonder. That is the closest green space to here, and the nearest farm field is nearly three miles away, toward the battle line. When you get the holes dug, you will bury these arms and legs. If anyone challenges you while you work merely send them to me. If they protest too much I'll offer to dig up their own damn front yard for my holes, instead! You'll find shovels and a small cart in the shed, right beside that back door to the hospital."

"Yes Sir." It was all Jamie could say.

Thus upon their return to the front lines, the men with the guard detail found themselves digging once again. Within ten minutes Jamie had rounded up his guard detail, some of whom had actually rested in the town square itself, and started them digging the required holes. Duncan was left in charge to "step off" the outside measurements of each hole, while Hendon, Wilson, Wellspeak and his man, Ten Cent Bill, Lee Lovorn, and the others dug. It took them almost ten hours to dig the three massive holes, and they found that the giant stack of body parts, some nearly rotten, completely filled two of the holes, so those were covered as quickly as they were filled.

As events played out a number of other "holes" were dug in the town square in Marietta, over the next month or so during and after the fight at Kennesaw. Many thousands of arms and legs were buried there, as no place else was a realistic option. There they remain to this day, with no historic marker of any kind, just bones of buried body parts from a long ago battle in a long ago war near the Kennesaw House Hotel. The building itself is still standing on the square in Marietta, and now houses a local history museum, with much memorabilia from that time, as well as surgical instruments used at that very hospital.

## The Fight at Kolb's Farm

As his men dug the holes, Jamie found the opportunity to check in at General Johnston's headquarters tent, where he was greeted, not by his regimental commander, but by General Johnston himself. "Major Turnbull. Do come into the tent. I need your services it seems, as my staff is always out running errands and I need a literate man such as yourself."

Jamie sprang to attention, and saluted. "Sir. I'd be honored to assist, of course, but I've just returned from a prisoner detail to Andersonville, and I must report to my division commander, and see that my men get back into the line."

"Quite so, Major. Quite so. You should send your men forward to rejoin their unit, but I'll need your services here for this afternoon. Also, I'm sure no fighting will take place for a day or so. Crazy Billy is licking his wounds from the fight yesterday with General Hood's Corps. Might I suggest you send your men on up to the line and then report back here to me for just a few hours. I need to get a battle report ready and off to Richmond, and I believe that you've done that type of work summary for me before."

"I have Sir. I'll take just a moment to get my men organized and off to the mountain, and I'll be back here within twenty minutes." Thus Jamie returned to tell Duncan Carmichael to lead the men on up to the mountain once he'd completed digging the necessary holes and burying the body parts in the Marietta Town Square.

"Find Captain Collins and report in to him Duncan," Jamie said. "Sampson will stay here with me, but you take along all of the others. Don't let any of 'um get near the whore's tents, or get into any whisky in suttler's row, at least until you check in with Captain Collins. Also, tell him that I'll follow along in about six hours or so."

When Jamie returned to the headquarters tent, General Johnston was gone, but General Hood, who had led the attack at Kolb's Farm was there. "I understand that you are to write the battle summary for the action at Kolb's Farm, Major Turnbull. Is that correct?"

Jamie sprang to attention and saluted again. "Yes Sir. I'll begin once General Johnston provides me with the battle orders and such."

"It shan't take long, I'd wager," said Hood. "It was a relatively minor action, and I believe you'll find the orders and reports on that desk in the corner. I'd like to see the report once you finish it."

"Of course, Sir," Jamie said, and saluted again as Hood walked out. Thus did Jamie learn of the events in his absence. As Sampson snoozed outside the tent, Jamie read the battlefield notes and orders. It seems that, while both armies were setting up their fighting trenches in the Kennesaw area, with the Confederates atop Kennesaw Mountain, Crazy Billy had ordered another roundhouse punch on June 22, 1864, just the day before. Sherman had sent Hooker's Union Corps of 20,000 men to the west of the Confederate line to get around the end, if possible. Johnston had responded by sending General Hood's Corps to meet the threat. When Hooker heard who was approaching him, he quickly had his men dig in—the aggressive fighting of Confederate General Hood was already well known to both armies. True to form, Hood ordered an attack as soon as he got into position, believing that the Union forces across the field were not yet prepared. Hood's Corps was deployed with Stevenson's Division astride the Powder Springs Road, a road that still winds through that area today. Hindman's Division was north of the road, and Stewart's Division remained in reserve.

Thus did 14,000 tired Confederates charge along the road and across a field on the adjacent small farm, a farm owned by Josh Kolb. However, rather than catching an unprepared Union force, they ran directly into a well-entrenched army supported by heavy cannon.

It was a bloodbath and resulted in over 1800 Confederate casualties in just less than an hour. As Jamie read through Hood's orders, and the written reports from Stevenson and his other division commanders on the field, he understood what had caused the two story pile of legs and arms standing outside the Kennesaw House. Stevenson's Division had been decimated on that field by Union cannon and nearly continuous fire from those damned Spencer repeating rifles! It was the same weapon that had caused such havoc at Chickamauga the previous September! Stevenson's Division was chopped apart, and would not be able to fight again as a unit until several weeks later, after thousands of new men had refilled those ranks.

Jamie wrote up a two paragraph summary report of the action. He added as an appendix, all the relevant information from Hood's stack of orders, observations of cavalry units prior to the fight, and written notes from the division commanders during the fight itself. Once he finished he sent a copy to General Hood, and left the main copy for General Johnston. Again as always, he kept a private copy which he mailed to his wife, as he had done so often before, and that battle summary glazed over the terrible losses.

*To: President Jefferson Davis,*
*Richmond, VA*

*Sir:*

*I beg to report a sharp action on the western end of our nine mile defensive line astride Kennesaw Mountain, just north of Atlanta. At 3:30 PM, on June 22, 1864, using Hooker's Union Corps, Sherman was moving against our western flank, so I ordered General Hood to move his Confederate corps of 14,000 men to that end of the line, and there to entrench opposite Hooker and oppose him. General Hood believed Hooker was not prepared, so an immediate attack was made against Hooker's line. Unfortunately, Hooker had already positioned his cannon so, as our boys crossed a small field on Kolb's Farm, they suffered a deadly enfilade fire. Hooker's Corps was also armed with repeating rifles, and that created more losses than would have otherwise been anticipated. Specifically, our losses were heavy in Stevenson's Division, with just over 1800 casualties. Both armies are now in their original lines, and we anticipate an attack on our front within days. We hope, behind our defensive works, to deliver a sharp blow to Sherman's plans.*

*Your Servant, General Joseph Johnston, Commanding*
*Army of Tennessee, Marietta, north Georgia*
*(Report Prepared by Major Jamie Turnbull,*
*Hood's Corps, CSA)*

Jamie knew that he had glossed over Hood's foolish aggressiveness. Once it had been established that Hooker's men were well entrenched, the attack by Hood should have been called off. Still, no one advances in any army in the world by critiquing the decisions of his commanders, so the report above went from Johnston's headquarters to Richmond later that night.

By that evening Major Jamie Turnbull and his man Sampson had caught a ride on an ammunition supply wagon that was heading up the road toward Kennesaw Mountain. They rejoined the unit at 8:30 that evening. Jamie of course, realized that the fight at Kolb's Farm was merely a precursor, and that the real battle lay ahead. Therefore, Jamie Turnbull and his guard detail had arrived just in time for the big fight.

## Sherman Does The Unthinkable

As Jamie wrote up the Confederate summary of action at Kolb's Farm, another report was being written by the Union Commander Billy Sherman, who was quietly sitting in his command tent only three miles north of Kennesaw. From Sherman's perspective, his options looked bleak indeed. His massive Union army seemed stalled only fifteen miles north of Atlanta, but those fifteen miles held massive fortifications, not to mention the mountain before him. Sherman was contemplating a battlefield reality that had been faced by the commanders of invading armies throughout history. The closer one got to one's objective, the more concentrated one's opposition became.

Sherman didn't think he could continue his "right hook" strategy of sending McPherson's Army of The Tennessee around Johnston's flank. He'd done that very maneuver several times in the Atlanta campaign at both Dalton and Resaca. However because of nearly two weeks of rain, the narrow dirt tracks that passed for roads in northern Georgia were nearly impassable. Worse yet, Sherman's supply line was a dead end, with the last miles of the track dominated by Johnston's artillery positions on the top of Kennesaw Mountain.

Sherman telegraphed his complaint to Lincoln in Washington City. "The whole territory is one vast fort. We move closer to Atlanta every month, but now we face the River Styx, looking into hell. Johnston must have at least fifty miles of connected trenches, defended by significant artillery. We gain ground daily, fighting all the time, and our lines are now in close contact, but as fast as we gain one position the damned Confederates have another one ready. I've never seen so many ditches in my life, and this damned mountain of Kennesaw is the key to the whole country."

Within an hour, Sherman had received Lincoln's reply. "I have faith in your good judgment. Please advance your army with all haste."

Not a lot of ambiguity there, and with those orders in hand, Crazy Billy Sherman decided to do the unthinkable. Rather than send out another right hook, he would break the ongoing stalemate by attacking directly the fortified Confederate position before him. He would do the very thing that absolutely everyone expected him ***NOT*** to do. This time, he would hit the Confederate position in a full-on assault on the slopes of Kennesaw Mountain, and its neighboring hills. Thus he issued orders for an 8 AM attack on June 27, 1864.

## At The Kennesaw Campfire

Kennesaw Mountain is the last true mountain as you approach Atlanta from the Georgia Blue Ridge. It is only some 1700 feet above sea level, and only seven hundred or so feet above the surrounding flatland, but even at that height, it provides a commanding position of the land only fifteen miles north of Atlanta. Further, the Western and Atlantic Railroad ran just along the base of Kennesaw, to the east of the mountain, and Sherman had followed that railroad since leaving Tennessee earlier in the spring. Once the Confederates pulled back from the Dallas Line, they put up some slight resistance at Lost Mountain and Pine Mountain, but they all realized that Kennesaw Mountain was to be the next major line of defense. Every commander on both sides expected there to be a conflict on the "Mountain that guards the fate of Atlanta." However, everyone likewise expected Sherman to ultimately flank the mountain and not attack it directly.

Kennesaw Mountain itself, and its little sister known as Little Kennesaw, run from the northeast to the southwest. A spur of Little Kennesaw, known as Pigeon Hill would soon become a site of horrible, bloody destruction, as would a mountain about a mile to the south, which would from the day of the battle onward, be known as Cheatham Hill, after the Confederate commander who defended it that day. By laying defenses along the tops of this series of hills, Johnston's eleven mile long Confederate defensive line enclosed the northern, western, and southwestern approaches to the town of Marietta, a small railroad town that nestled just south of Kennesaw.

Rain delayed the fight on the mountain, a fight that some had anticipated might begin the day after the fight at Kolb's Farm. Armies in those days moved slowly in the muddy mire of dirt roads rutted by hundreds of cannon and wagons. Thus the Confederates had a precious few more days to prepare defenses. By

June 26, the Confederates were fully deployed and dug in, and the rain, which had been nearly constant for almost two weeks, seemed to be breaking up. The Fourth Georgia Infantry was located atop Cheatham Hill, toward the southern end of the Confederate line. They would be held in reserve behind a Tennessee regiment, and adjacent to a regiment of Missouri men.

That evening around the campfire, the Fourth Georgia Infantry was reunited once again. All of the men were there; Turnbull and his man Sampson, Captain Collins, Duncan Carmichael, Wellspeak and Ten Cent Bill, Lee Lovorn, and Chad Wilson. Around nine that night, in a surprise to all, Lem Davis showed up, now healed from his earlier wound. After a warm welcome, they sat by the fire together and contemplated the fight that all believed was soon to come.

"Recon they'll hit us in the morning?" Wellspeak asked.

When none of the men answered, Jamie Turnbull himself spoke up. "They don't seem to know much at headquarters, 'cept that we'll be hit soon enough." He liked the fact that, at that point in the war, there was really no longer a separate campfire for officers. He wanted to be in and among his men. In the morning he knew that his life would be in their hands, and theirs in his.

"Wonder if most of them Union boys got Henry repeaters, or Spencers now a days?" Wilson said. "I sure don't want to face an army that can load once and fire that many rounds at me!"

Lem spoke up next. "I sure hated what those repeaters did to us at Chickamauga! Don't fancy facing them again."

Ten Cent Bill spoke next. "If'n they got those guns we'll need to keep to our trenches for sure! Can't make no headway when them Yankees can throw that much lead at us!"

The eyes of a few new recruits grew wider, as the veterans among them spoke—a reality experienced by men in virtually every war. At some point every soldier is untested, and ultimately will have to face their first fight.

They were all silent for a few moments, as the campfire seemed to mesmerize every man there. Then Duncan spoke. "I hear they's gonna be a charge down the mountain in the morning. Seems that Gen'al Hood thinks our sorry asses don't seem scary enough behind our head logs. He wants us all chargin' down that damned mountain, screamin' like banshees, and maybe that'll make them damn Yankees think twice about commin' on to Atlanta!"

None of the men believed him. By that point in the war, the veterans on both sides knew better that to think a mass charge would work. Given the accuracy of the rifles, including the repeating rifles the Yankees had, a charging army rarely carried the battle. Rather fights were won by those who remained in the trenches and killed the other dumb bastards who were unlucky enough to charge the enemy in the open.

Captain Collins spoke up next. "I don't think we'll be chargin' down that mountain. Hood ain't no damn fool. Hell, he wouldn't 'a charged at Kolb's Farm if'n he'd a known them Yankees were already dug in."

Jamie thought about that for a moment, wishing that he could believe it, but he kept his thoughts on that to himself.

Mo Hendon, a man who was usually quiet, asked the obvious question. "Why would anyone this side of a pure fool, leave his trenches to face them damn rifles that shoot all week, not to mention all them Yankee cannon?"

Just then a Whip-o-will sounded off just down the mountain slope, and after a moment, Collins spoke up again. "My grandma was part Cherokee. She always said that the Whip-o-will before a battle was a sur' sign of death. If'n you hear one, it might be your time."

"That cain't be right, Cap'n," said Wellspeak. "I figure near 'bouts ten thousand men are close enough to hear that damn bird. We can't all die in the morning, can we?"

A few men laughed at the grim humor, then all was quiet once again, as each stared into the campfire. Every man knew they faced a fight to the death the next day—at that point, most of the Confederates had been there before. There was, surely, more than a bit of quiet reflection that night up on Kennesaw, as well as by the Yankees in the fields below.

Another Whip-o-will was heard in the distance. Then it was Sampson who delivered what he believed to be, the final thought that evening. "Recon whether we charge down the mountain or not, we'll surely need some sleep. Meantime, I'll be sayin' my prayers, and cleanin' my rifle."

Turnbull smiled. "Seems Sampson here, is the wisest man around this fire tonight. Get your weapons clean, then get some sleep! We'll all, for sure, gonna' need the rest."

Another Whip-o-will sounded out down the flank of the mountain; then silence again. Wagon wheels rolled faintly in the distance. The men adjusted blankets and slowly bedded down. After a few more moments, from another fire just down the line, came the sound of one of the younger men, a new recruit who was fifteen years old, sobbing. All the veterans heard it, and to a man, they all remembered the night before their first fight. Jamie lay quietly, thinking that the boy's weeping was, perhaps, the most desolate sound he had ever heard.

No one said anything; no one did anything for a few moments. Terror, paralyzing fear was understandable in war. Every new recruit had heard tales of the accuracy of the Spencers or the destruction of the enemy cannon, and the new men, mostly boys between fifteen and seventeen, had never faced a fight before. One might say they had never really known fear before.

Then as the weeping grew a bit louder, Duncan slid out of his blanket, moving as quietly as the night and disappeared from the glow of the campfire. Within a few moments the sobbing was replaced by the words known by every single man, Yankee and Confederate, on that mountain. Those words were like magic. They held a power. Those words had comforted men at war for thousands of years.

*"Our Father, who art in Heaven, hallowed be thy name. Thy Kingdom come. Thy will be done, on earth as it is in heaven…"*

The two men, Duncan Carmichael and some unknown boy, their arms around each other's shoulders in the dark night before the battle, seemed to be praying for every man on that mountain. The comforting words continued on to the end.

And then two massive armies—over 100,000 men, slept.

## Hell on Pigeon Hill

The morning of June 27, 1864 broke crisp, cool, and clear. Even at sunup, there wasn't a cloud in the sky, but for the first hour or so, nothing happened. Confederates looked down the mountain into the distant Yankee camps, and the Yankees looked up. Still the Confederate commanders, using their field glasses knew. Those Union boys were moving! Then at 8:00 sharp, two hundred Union guns opened in unison, firing up at the mountain summit. Confederate batteries soon responded with counter battery fire, shooting at the guns down the mountain, and the Union men who were clearly massing for an advance. The Union fire did little damage, but the Confederates, firing down on their enemy, were hitting and disabling a precious few of the Union guns. Still, this was one of the most massive artillery duels in the entire Atlanta campaign, and the guns sent fire and smoke all along the line, lasting for a full fifteen minutes.

Even the citizens in Atlanta heard the massive rolling thunder of hundreds of cannon, firing in rapid succession. Many of them began prayers for the Confederates under those guns. One Union officer, looking up at the mountain, later said, "Kennesaw smoked and blazed with fire, like a volcano as grand as Etna. I was sure that nothing could survive on top of that damned mountain!" He would soon be proven wrong. In truth, the cannon fire did little damage to either army, but it certainly awoke everyone in a twenty-five mile radius who wasn't already up. The cannon also had one other significant effect. The smoke cloud from massive amounts of black powder did serve to hide the Union movements initially, as thousands of men moved into assault positions all along the Union line in the fields just below the mountain. More than a few of those

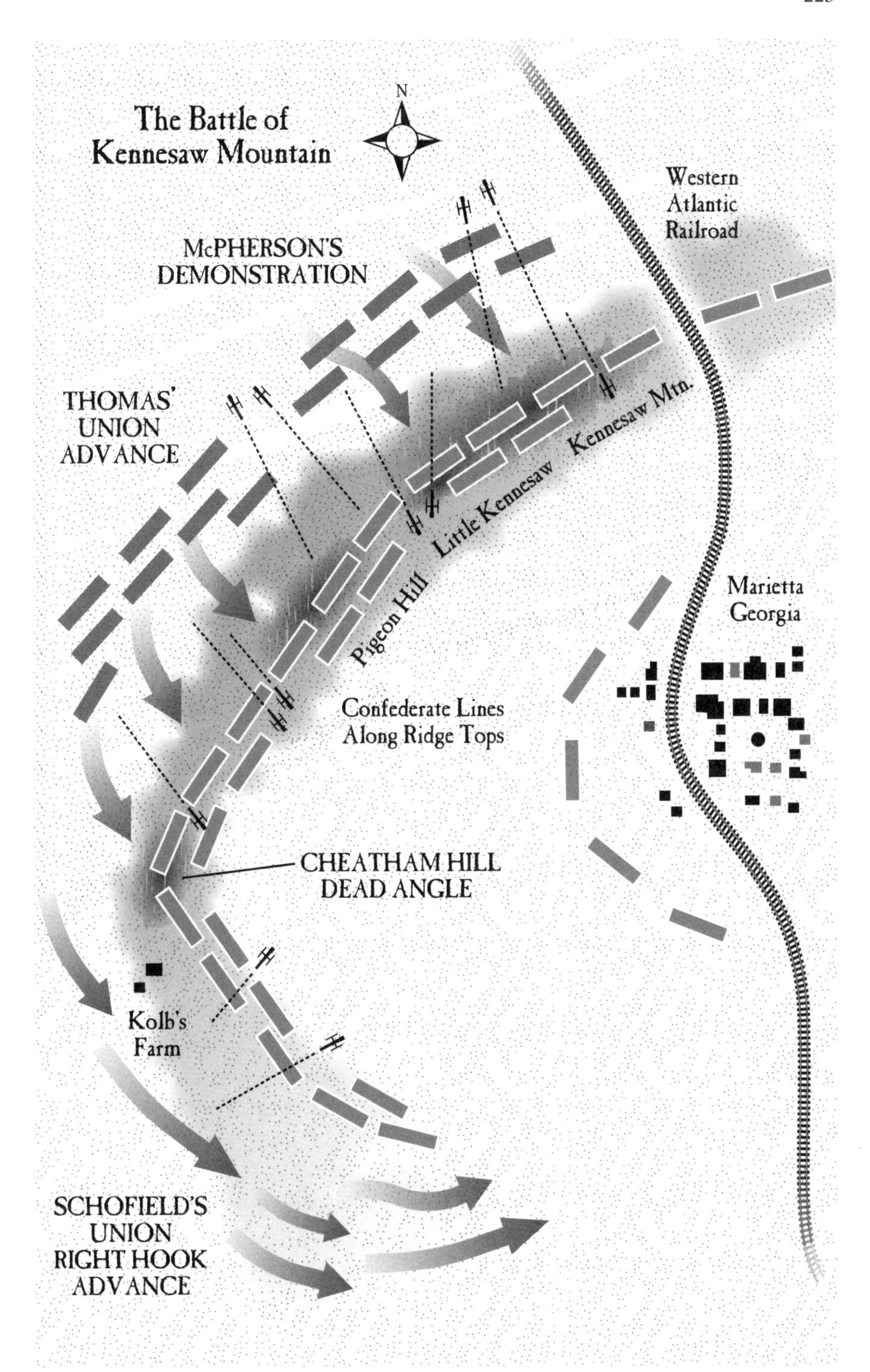
The Battle of
Kennesaw Mountain
N
McPHERSON'S
DEMONSTRATION
Western
Atlantic
Railroad
THOMAS'
UNION
ADVANCE
Kennesaw Mtn.
Little Kennesaw
Pigeon Hill
Marietta
Georgia
Confederate Lines
Along Ridge Tops
CHEATHAM HILL
DEAD ANGLE
Kolb's
Farm
SCHOFIELD'S
UNION
RIGHT HOOK
ADVANCE

Union boys looked up at the slopes of the mountain before them, sure they were going to die within minutes. Many repeated the same prayer that Duncan Carmichael had led the previous evening.

Sherman as always, had planned well. He had ordered two significant attacks, masked by two additional diversionary assaults up the slopes of Kennesaw. The diversionary attacks would begin immediately after the cannon fire ended, one on the extreme right end of the Confederate line, the northeastern end of Kennesaw Mountain, and the other about seven miles to the southwest on the extreme left end of the Confederate line along the Powder Springs Road. That diversionary attack would result in another fight over the same ground as before, Kolb's Farm.

The two major Union attacks would focus on the center of the Confederate line, and the southwestern third of the line, with strong Union advances directed not at Kennesaw Mountain itself, but at two of the more prominent hills to the southwest, Pigeon Hill and Cheatham Hill.

During the artillery exchange, Union men began their advance, under the cover of their own cannon firing over their heads with the smoke hiding their movements. However, by 8:20 or so, the cannon stopped and the smoke all along the line began to clear. At that point, every Confederate atop Kennesaw was in for a sight. It was as if all of the fields before the mountain had changed color from spring green to Yankee blue. Of the 100,000 men at Sherman's command, fully 65,000 were now amassed in row after row of regiment sized units, covering the ground before Kennesaw. No man atop that mountain had ever before seen such a sight. Even veterans in earlier large fights had not seen such a mass of the enemy as that arrayed before Kennesaw that morning, since none had ever before had the advantage of a mountain top perspective over a relatively open plain. The entire earth before them seemed to move, in a seething wave, heading toward their positions on the mountain.

Of course no pictures exist from the actual fighting, but the photograph here (from the Library of Congress Collection) shows a view from the perspective of a Confederate artilleryman, looking down from Pigeon Hill, with the Confederate trenches in the foreground, looking down the slope toward the location of the Union advance. With that entire field covered with Union soldiers, the Confederates must have been glad to have the protection of their trenches.

Just after the 8:00 AM artillery began, Duncan Carmichael jumped to his feet and grabbed his rifle. Then he shouted to his compatriots, "Fourth Georgia, Stand up and render honors!" Of course, Duncan, as merely a sergeant, had absolutely no authority to give such an order, and he probably would not have done so, had any officer been around. Still, Duncan took it upon himself to assemble the men that morning, as he continued. "Men of the Fourth Georgia, stand to attention in place. Our comrades in arms, the brave Thomas Legion, are passing by! We honor our fighting comrades once again!"

And sure enough the Thomas Legion, nearly seven hundred of those brave Cherokee warriors who had been honored by the Fourth Georgia Infantry on the field at Chickamauga were, once again, strolling by. As before, no marching was in evidence as those Cherokee made their way to the fight atop the mountain. In

**Pigeon Hill**

fact, some of the Cherokee that morning were surprised to be so honored. Still, they soon heard the name of the unit rendering the honors, and most of them had been on the field at Chickamauga so they quickly understood. They would take the trenches slightly to the west of the Fourth Georgia, and while their lines did not touch in that fight, men in both units were comforted knowing that a veteran outfit would be fighting somewhere near them when the hell began atop the mountain later that day.

Union forces first came within range of the main line of Confederate riflemen at Pigeon Hill on the southern end of Little Kennesaw, around 8:30 that morning. Using a local dirt track known by the locals as Burnt Hickory Road, 5,500 Union men in two strong columns moved slowly up the heavily steeped slopes along the road and through the trees. Those Union boys were attacking several Confederate units, numbering approximately 5,000 men, as they moved up a hill filled with heavy boulders, many the size of small cabins. Cannon were no longer a large part of the advance at this stage, as once the Union men were lost in the woods on the side of Pigeon Hill, Union gunners could not shoot for fear of hitting their own men. They did, occasionally, answer when Confederate guns fired, by firing directly on the Confederate batteries. Thus, instead of cannon, this fight, for nearly an hour, consisted almost exclusively of rifle fire, as thousands of rifled muskets fired along the mile long front of the advance. While some Union forces on the field that day were supplied with repeating rifles, most engaged at Pigeon Hill were not. Thus, both armies in this small fight, were firing the same weapon—the rifled musket that had been the major weapon for both armies during the war.

By 9:00 AM, Confederate commanders had determined the overall Union plan, carefully noting which Union forces seemed to be making demonstrations rather than truly advancing. This allowed several Confederate commanders to order their men to concentrate their rifle fire, not on the Union men before them at the bottom of the hill—men who were nearly out of range anyway—but rather on the Union forces advancing to their left or right. Thus, a Union boy moving directly up the rocky slope of Pigeon Hill was likely to be receiving fire from Confederate riflemen directly in front as well as from both sides. Such deadly enfilade fire can, most certainly, ruin your whole day!

General Logan's Union men were advancing against Loring's Confederate Corps on Pigeon Hill. If Logan's attack was successful, the Union Army would have isolated Loring's Confederate Corps on Kennesaw Mountain, thus cutting the strong Confederate line in half. While open fields were plentiful at the foot of Pigeon Hill, once the Union men reached the climb itself, all three Union units had to advance through dense thickets and steep, rocky slopes. Some had to advance through a swamp at the foot of the hill, and that was the first unit to stop. They were forced to take cover from a withering enfilading fire from the Confederate breastworks to their left.

The Union men in the other brigades crossed harder ground, full of sharp rocks, cut timber, and boulders, and then they confronted the skirmish line of the 63rd Georgia. Confederates had, quite reasonably, placed a skirmish line and a somewhat stronger line of rifle pits at the base of the hill along a small run known locally as Noyes Creek. It was the first defended barrier the Yankees had to contend with. Behind the creek sat the 63rd Georgia Regiment, along with several other units on forward skirmish duty. Of course, there were skirmish lines all along the Confederate front, and the experienced veteran commanders knew their job was to fire once or twice at the advancing Yankees, and then withdraw. However the 63rd Georgia was new to battle, having spent their entire war up to that point on coastal defense assignments. Their commander was determined to make a good show for himself and his unit, and nothing is more deadly in battle than a commander with his head inserted firmly in his own posterior.

Instead of withdrawing when others fell back, the recently transferred 63rd stayed at the forward skirmish line alone, not really knowing what to do. Six regiments of federals poured out of the forest and over the line held by the Georgians. Brief but deadly hand-to-hand fighting ensued, and the embattled 63rd Georgia never stood a chance. Most of those men were killed within minutes, and five minutes later, the remainder of the regiment ran like rabbits, followed closely by the boys in blue. Punishing Confederate cross-fire from the main line halted the federals, but the 63rd would never serve as a front line unit again. Its commander bravely died along with well over half of his men in a bloody but futile show, without ever once extracting his own head from its dark, moist, if rather unusual position.

Once the Union brigades overran the Confederate skirmish line, and the small rifle pits below the crest of Pigeon Hill, they advanced further, and a few even reached the abatis that had been built about one hundred feet from the main Confederate line. Abatis was common on battlefields in the Civil War. It was constructed using sharpened logs—the best were three inches or so in diameter—that were woven or tied together. The pointed end was then elevated by burying the other end in the ground, such that the point faced the enemy advance. Abatis had been used since Roman times, since armies typically cleared some trees before their lines to provide room for the battle, and with so much timber available, it was fairly simple to create an additional impediment to hinder your enemies' movement.

However abatis rarely killed anyone. Rather, the Union men who reached the abatis that day were cut down by a wall of minie-balls from the Confederates atop the hill. It was rather difficult to miss such a mass of blue-clad men only a hundred feet away, so the Union men quickly took cover and were forced to remain stationary while occasionally firing from behind trees, boulders, or bodies of their dead comrades. Union commanders assessed the situation, and quickly determined that no further progress would be made on that front, so by 10:00 AM they ordered a withdrawal to more defensible terrain, a small gorge further down the slope of Pigeon Hill. Once there, they ordered the construction of breastworks.

Blood ran in torrents down the rocky slope, and as the firing died away, the Confederates peeped over their headlogs to survey the carnage. Screams, smoke, men torn apart, and body parts covered the hill in front of the trenches, and the firing from further down the Confederate line continued. Still, the fight before them was over for the moment, and the Union army had left 1,300 men dead and wounded on the steep, rocky slope of Pigeon Hill, in a fight that lasted just under two hours.

## The Fight At Cheatham Hill

The land to the south of Pigeon Hill falls away in a gentler slope, and then climbs another small hill, a hill that would earn a new name on that day.

General Johnston correctly predicted that Sherman's main attack would come in that quarter, so he assigned his toughest units and his best commanders there. Both Benjamin Franklin Cheatham and Patrick Cleburne commanded men who were battle tested veterans of many rough fights, including some hand-to-hand slaughter at Stones River in Tennessee, and the mountain fights at both Chickamauga and Pickett's Mill. The Confederate defenses in this area were more intricate, since the Union approaches were less encumbered by boulders and timber. Southern slaves had built an interwoven web of deep earthworks rather than merely one main defensive line, and the area atop Cheatham Hill would indeed, see the hardest fighting of the day.

The feisty Irishman Cleburne, has been described previously as a highly skilled, excessively brave commander, but he was, on that day, fighting alongside his equal. Benjamin Franklin Cheatham was born into the antebellum planter class in Nashville, and served with the First Tennessee Regiment in the Mexican War in the 1840s, finishing that war as a colonel. He then headed to the California gold fields in the Gold Rush of 1849, where he, like almost all of the others, failed to make his fortune. He then returned to plantation life in Tennessee where, at the outbreak of the War Between the States, he joined the Army of Tennessee, with the rank of general. That highly varied life of battle, rough frontier, and genteel planter had prepared Cheatham for almost anything, and throughout the early campaigns of the war he acquitted himself and his command quite well. At Cheatham Hill, a small outcropping that would forever bear Cheatham's name, his unit would again be tested by battle.

Across the line from Cheatham and Cleburne lay 9,000 Union troops under the Union General George Thomas, the famous man dubbed the "Rock of Chickamauga." Thomas had no real attack plan, other than to advance his forces as a human battering ram all at once, and overwhelm the Confederate defenses atop the hill before him. He had detected a crook in the Confederate main line of defense atop the nameless hill, so he pointed that out to his regiment commanders and ordered them to concentrate their efforts on that sharp angle in the Confederate line.

Thomas chose that location for two reasons. First, the sharp angle in the Confederate line offered him the option of attacking that point from two sides, rather than from only one direction, and the natural cover near the Confederate salient brought his men closer to the Confederate line than at any other location. Next, Thomas believed that Frank Cheatham had failed to protect his line with adequate amounts of abatis near that point, making that angle an attractive attack point. Thus, he aimed the major thrust of his attack at the jutting angle, the salient atop the hill.

Unfortunately Thomas was behind schedule. He had to amass more Union men and move them into their initial jumping off positions than did other Union commanders, so he didn't begin his fight until around 10:00 AM that morning. The fighting two miles to the north of his position along Pigeon Hill had been constant for some time and was indeed, winding down, before General Thomas gave the order to advance. At his order, two entire divisions began to move, one commanded by General Newton, and another commanded by a Union man who shared the same name as the President of the Confederacy, Jeff Davis.

The movement of so many enemy soldiers was a sight to see, just as it had been at Pigeon Hill only ninety minutes earlier. Once that battering ram began to move, every pair of Confederate eyes atop that hill stared in awe at the mass of humanity advancing on their positions. The Union men advanced in two marching columns rather than abreast, and that only added to the illusion of their might. It was as if they were merely marching into a small fight, where the inevitable conclusion would, of course, be a Union victory. In fact, it seemed that they were daring the whole Confederate army to try and stop them!

Major Turnbull and Captain Collins, along with Turnbull's man Sampson, stood just behind the Tennessee regiment positioned in the angle along the main Confederate trench. The rest of Major Turnbull's regiment was resting as reserve about a hundred yards behind the line, so only Turnbull, Collins, and Sampson had that initial view of the advancing Union battering ram.

Collins spoke first. "With that many damn Yankees commin' we'll be in this thing before too long. I'm not sure any regiment can hold that many blue-bellies for long. Lord, look how many lines there are, and they're still commin' outa those woods yonder!"

Sampson as usual, kept his own council, but Jamie Turnbull replied after lowering his field glasses. "They still got to climb the slope, but I recon, you're right as rain. Them Union boys look determined, and I can't see 'um stopping at this line." Here Jamie raised his glasses again, for a closer look. After thinking a moment, he said, "Let's get back to the boys, but first, let's make a drawing of our line, and guess where we might be needed. It looks to me like them Union men are commin' directly at the forward angle right up here, so I'd guess that's where we're likely to be sent."

Collins once again, looked over the field, just as a few Confederate sharpshooters atop the hill took the range and began to fire on the advancing Yankees. "Guess that's right. I'm thinking that Union strength will be directed right here, near 'bouts on top of us. We'll be fightin' in an hour or so, once them Tennessee boys in the trenches begin to fall, maybe less. You recon the abatis might stop 'um for a while?"

Jamie lowered his glasses once again, without turning his eyes away from the advancing enemy. "Not a chance in hell, Captain Collins! Not one chance in hell. Now let's get on back to the boys and tell 'um what to expect."

Jamie and Captain Collins were, as usual, correct in most of their assessment. The massed Union attack was headed directly for them at the angle in the Confederate line. Newton's Division advanced two Union brigades under Commanders General John Mitchell and Col. Daniel McCook. While both were effective brigade commanders, McCook was especially distinguished. He came from a long line of fighting leaders, with both his father and several brothers serving in the Union army. In fact one McCook or another had served in every American war in history up to that point, from the Revolution right down to the Mexican-American War of 1848. Col. McCook was known to be brave to a fault, and he felt deeply his responsibility to the nickname awarded to his family, the "Fighting McCooks!" It was also widely commented on among Union officers that McCook's pre-war law practice partner was none other than the Commanding General, William Tecumseh Sherman.

The Union men intended to make a simultaneous attack on Cheatham's angled, defensive line at the top of the hill. Mitchell was to hit the angle from the north, while McCook attacked it from the northwest. All of the Union soldiers knew that the fighting would be bloody. By that point in the war the overall futility of frontal assaults on entrenched enemy positions was well understood, and many men predicted forty to eighty percent casualties among the Union units that were to lead the attack on the angled Confederate line. To alleviate some of the pressure, supporting attacks were assigned to units on the left flank of McCook's men, and others would make supporting attacks on the right of the main thrust.

The Union men had received orders to advance silently, capture the Confederate defenses and then send up a loud "cheer" to call for the advance of the remaining Union forces. If one had tried, it would be difficult to create a more ridiculous order, and none of the other orders during the entire war, even came close in the level of sheer stupidity. First, a silent advance is not generally possible, and holds little advantage, when your own cannon have been loudly proclaiming your advance for over an hour. Next, Union commanders could clearly see most of the Confederate defenses, and no "cheer" would be necessary should their men capture them.

Still the Union men under McCook and Mitchell advanced steadily crossing a wheat field, and ascending the slope that would, by the end of the day, be known as Cheatham Hill. They fought their way up the slope and attacked with all their might the Confederate trenches before them. The fighting was brutal with the combatants nearly eyeball to eyeball. Some fighting was hand-to-hand, and while the Tennessee men in the Confederate trenches did well, they needed help. Within fifteen minutes, Jamie received orders to advance his men and support the Tennessee men directly in his front.

## Into The Dead Angle

No one knows who first used the term Dead Angle, or even if it was used on the day of the battle itself. What is known is that General Thomas had selected the sharp angle in the Confederate lines as his target, and that assured many hundreds of corpses on that steep slope at that location. Certainly, by the time Jamie Turnbull received orders to advance his men into the line literally on top of the Tennessee and Missouri units to his front, there were hundreds, perhaps thousands, of dead and dying men all along that open field of fire, just below the Dead Angle.

Jamie raised his sword and shouted, "Move out, double time," with Sampson immediately behind him. Captain Collins advanced about a hundred feet to his right, on the other end of the line, and in between was Duncan Carmichael, Lem Davis, Wellspeak along with Ten Cent Bill, Hendon, Lovorn, Wilson and all the rest. Within only a few seconds, those men hit the line, and dived in beside whatever Tennessee men happened to be right in front of them. Many of Jamie's men had to move dead Confederates from the trench in order to reach the headlogs and take their rifle shots. Men in the Fourth Georgia noted a number of Union corpses in the Confederate trench. Clearly the Tennessee men had repelled at least one assault in a hand-to-hand fight already. The Tennesseans all had black faces from opening powder bags with their teeth, as the powder mixes with sweat, blood, and tears much more effectively in the heat of June, compared to winter fighting.

Most of the Union men under McCook had taken positions behind tree stumps, and in holes about fifty feet from the Confederate headlogs, and anyone whose head was exposed for more than a second or two drew enemy rifle fire. The Confederates would stand and peek out under the headlog, find a target and fire, all in two seconds, quickly lowering themselves behind the protection of the high earth back into the trench.

Just as Jamie's men were loading their Enfields for a second shot, they heard the Yankee commander, Col. McCook, order a charge up the slope. Hand-to-hand hell was about to begin again. Jamie quickly looked to his side, expecting to find Sampson there, but instead looked directly into the eyes of Duncan Carmichael, the best damn knife-fighter in Georgia! Duncan grinned back at him for a split section, and shouted, "Don't worry, Jamie. We all done this before!" While Duncan had found a deep and profound relationship with God over the last few weeks, he was still the best soldier in the outfit, and one of the deadliest. A deepening spiritual belief will, sometimes, make fighting men more committed to their cause, as it seemed to for Duncan.

Jamie drew his pistol and looked up, just as the Yankees reached within twenty feet of the headlog at the top of the trench. Muskets fired, pistols shot, blades sliced the air, and within seconds the Union army was among them, and the deadly fighting was man-to-man. Jamie shot his pistol three or four times at Yankees moving up the slope before him, and then he remembered he should have counted his shots, so he'd know when to reload. Next, he thought, "Hell! I can't even begin to reload in this madness! I'd be dead in a second!"

Just then a Yankee jumped on the parapet in front of Jamie, and looked down shouting, "Surrender, you traitors!" Jamie shot him in the chest with what turned out to be the last shot in his pistol and the blast blew the man backwards off the trench, toward the other advancing Yankees. Only then did Jamie realize the man had worn an officer's uniform, and for a brief moment, he wondered who it was.

The identity of that Union officer was confirmed after the fight ended. Jamie Turnbull had killed Col. Daniel McCook, the last of the "Fighting McCooks!" The location of McCook's death on the Confederate earthworks is marked today with a historic marker in tribute to this brave man. History even records his last words, noted above, which he shouted to the Confederate men below in the trenches.

Knowing that Duncan defended the ground on his right, Jamie looked to his left. As he expected he saw Sampson only five feet away, busily dispatching a Yankee who had been unlucky enough to fall headfirst into the Confederate trench. Sampson stabbed him between the shoulders with a bayonet on his unloaded musket, and then extracted the blade and began to reload, looking up to the headlog for more Union men.

Then there seemed to be a pause—maybe five minutes—maybe ten, in which the Yankees seemed to be regrouping. Firing could still be heard only a hundred yards away to the west, and the fight several miles north was still raging, but for a few moments it was quiet to their immediate front. No blue coats were seen for that spell atop the headlogs of the Confederates, and every man in that southern trench immediately reloaded every weapon he had.

Jamie reloaded then decided to use the pause and move down the line, heading out to the right, with Sampson right behind him. He spent time with each man, making sure they remembered to take a drink of water or two—he didn't need to remind anyone of the need to reload. All of the men knew that the Yankees were only fifty feet away behind a slight rise in the ground, and they could hear the enemy furiously digging their own ditch. They heard bayonets, cooking pots, pans, and even sticks digging into the recently wet earth, as men tried to find any place to lower themselves into the ground and away from the deadly lead that would soon fly overhead again.

Wellspeak, just down the line from Duncan, was grinning from ear-to-ear when Jamie approached. "Look here, Major!" he said with excitement. "After, I kilt that last Yankee, my man, Ten Cent Bill found this rifle, a Sharpes repeater! I've got all of his ammunition too!" Jamie could see Ten Cent Bill standing just behind Wellspeak, grinning from ear to ear, proud of the prize he'd found for his master.

Jamie took the weapon, and looked it over carefully. "Make sure you load 'er up good! I recon we'll be needing all the firepower we can get before this day is over."

Wellspeak, still grinning with his new treasure, said, "Yes Sir! I will Sir!"

Jamie knew he needed to move on, but he wanted to honor Wellspeak just a bit more, so he said, "There's not a man here, 'cept maybe Carmichael, that I'd rather see with one of these! I'm sure, with your deadly eye, you'll put it to good use!"

Again Wellspeak said, "I will Sir! You can bet I will!"

In three minutes Jamie had reached the end of his line and was heading back to the center, not pausing to speak with anyone. At that point he saw Collins coming from the other direction, and knew he'd been doing the same thing in that direction. Collins spoke first. "We lost some men Sir, about twelve, as near as I can tell. I passed you a bit ago, and I've been from one end of our line to the other. The Tennessee men were hit hardest, even before we came up, and most of their officers are down. I told them to hold in place for now. I think them damn Yankees are coming back again real soon! I figured we could worry about getting the units separated out, and replacing officers after this here fight is over!"

Jamie thought for only a moment. "Thanks Cap'n Collins. You are right on the mark as usual. We'll for sure have some more of this in short order, I should think. Why don't you head back down the line about two hundred feet that way, and I'll take charge of this section. Don't charge out of these trenches unless I give the order, or unless you see me do so. You understand?"

"Yes Sir. I'll wait 'til I hear from you. Didn't really like the idea of heading over that headlog anyway!" Collins said with a smile.

"Neither do I Collins! Neither do I!"

Then Jamie found a spot further down the line, and placed Sampson in the line, while he stood in the trench and visually inspected his men. At that point, both the Georgia men and the Tennesseans were his, and everyone in that trench realized it. After a visual inspection in each direction, he took a moment to sit on the backside of the trench, and closed his eyes for a second, saying a quick prayer; "Merciful God. Protect us all through this hell, and let me do the right thing in this fight."

Then a cannon behind Jamie boomed. He had not realized he'd placed himself immediately before one of the Confederate batteries until the concussion wave hit him and seemed to suck the air right out of his entire universe! The wave, and the noise, of several cannon firing above his head shook him and the men near him. In that war, everyone knew that manning the line immediately in front of the cannon batteries assured one of relative safety, and few enemy soldiers at that point in the war wanted to charge directly into the big guns. Still that position assured one of feeling every pressure wave of those massive guns, and a wide range of cursing was offered up after every blast, cursing that no one under those guns would ever hear. In fact, most of the artillerymen on both sides of that war spent the rest of their lives deaf as lumber.

Jamie grabbed Sampson's shirt and made a motion down the line. He would move to find a place where he could at least think, and maybe have his orders heard by someone, should he need to make adjustments in his line. As he moved, he heard the muskets, along with Wellspeak's new repeater open fire in unison, and he realized the Union boys were coming back for more. He was fifty feet or so away from the position directly before the Confederate guns, so he jumped up to see under the headlogs and watched a massive wave of Yankees, shoulder to shoulder, come charging up from the woods heading straight for their lines. Just as Sampson took his place beside him and fired, Jamie jerked out his pistol and shouted to no one in particular, "Let's see how many we can drop from here!"

With that the hell began yet again. Union men from Ohio, Illinois, and New York charged the Confederate lines atop the hill, largely with the same devastating result. They were blown into oblivion by massed cannon and musket fire, often before they could even reach the Confederate trenches. Still some made it far enough to, once again, mount the Confederate's headlogs, screaming wildly, and firing point blank with those deadly Spencer repeaters, into the Confederate trench. At one point, toward the end of the line Collins was defending, the Union men actually cleared the Confederate trench, and Collins, wisely ordered his men to fall back to a secondary, diagonal trench only twenty feet away. From there, they poured a horrid fire into the first trench, now in Union hands. Soon a Confederate artillery commander ordered one Napoleon to be re-directed to fire directly down into the trench, and that massive-bore cannon was loaded with canister. When it fired large gaps of flesh disintegrated with the first blast, and the next, and the next. It took only two minutes for the Union men to realize that they were alone and under direct fire from a massive Napoleon "shotgun" that would soon take all of their lives. They beat a hasty retreat from that horrid fire leaving scores of Union men and hundreds of body parts sticking out at every conceivable angle from the freshly turned earth. The Confederate trench was not discernable any longer—it was merely a field of churned earth with bodies and parts of bodies. One horse ridden by some foolish officer, lay dead in the center of the killing zone just in front of the trench. As soon as the Yankees retreated, the Confederates at Collin's orders, retook the position and began to find every possible depression in the ground that could be used for protection from the incoming fire.

It soon became clear to Newton, the Union division commander, that Confederate counter fire was unbelievably strong. He was afraid he would burn up his entire command trying to take those trenches at the Dead Angle, so once he heard that McCook was down and that McCook's Union men had pulled back from the one section of captured enemy trenches, he ordered his men to "stand in place." Of course, all the Yankees realized that "stand in place" really meant "Dig like you're headed to China!" They all began moving at once, separated from the Confederate trench by fifty to seventy five feet of the most hotly contested ground on the planet.

With that order the Yankees, at least those in the front line, gave up their attempt to take the Confederate defensive works at the Dead Angle. The Union advance had stopped within only a few yards of the Confederate trenches, and the men in blue crouched behind any cover they could find, and as they continued their sporadic fire, they mostly dug.

McCook's second in command probably never realized that he had, automatically advanced to command of the unit with McCook's death. Within ten minutes he was also killed by Confederate rifle fire. Both McCook's unit and Mitchell's Union Brigade lost nearly all of their field officers, and over a third of the men.

Thus the fiercest fighting at the Battle of Kennesaw Mountain, the bloodbath of hand-to-hand fighting at the "Dead Angle," ceased. It had lasted only forty-five minutes, and the Fourth Georgia had been involved in only thirty-five minutes of that fight. Still that can seem like an eternity in a hand-to-hand fight to the death, and all were more than exhausted after such an intense conflict. Of course the fighting continued elsewhere along the Confederate line.

## Mercy Amid the Carnage

About half a mile to the north of the Dead Angle, the fighting, though not as intense, was ongoing. Union men advanced to within a hundred feet of the Confederate defenses but were driven back by Cleburne's men. However, the brush and toppled trees on the slope of the hill had caught fire by 11:30, and some of the Union wounded were unable to escape the blaze. A number of men screamed horribly as they burned to death between the lines, adding more carnage and death to the bloody hell of the battlefield.

Then one of those rare, memorable acts of mercy took place. Confederates all along that section of line were ordered to cease fire, and the battle seemed to pause in that section of the line for a time. Above the Confederate trenches a white flag rose, causing the Union men to hold their fire. They had received no orders to cease fire, but no one would fire on a white flag that day. A lone colonel from the Arkansas Unit in that section of the Confederate trench, Col. Jacob Waller climbed over the Confederate headlog, holding the flag, and bravely walked a few paces out into the dead-man's land, carefully stepping around the bodies and the wounded men.

Once there, he paused and shouted across the bloody field to the Yankees, "Come and get your men, for they are burning to death!" At that point a Yankee Captain stood up behind his own line, and the Arkansas colonel continued. "I propose a cease fire for a time, and invite you Union men to come and rescue your wounded from this blaze. Every man here is brave beyond measure, and certainly no man deserves burning to death. If you accept please leave your weapons in your positions, and come get your wounded before they burn alive. We will do the same."

Without any further ceremony men rushed from their positions on both sides, leaving their rifles where they lay, and began to pull men away from the several fires on the slope of the hill. The dead were left as they were—no help was needed by those men, and no one knew how much time they might have in the cease fire, so attention was given only to saving the wounded. In general, Union men pulled Union wounded from the fire, while Confederates pulled their companions away. However when necessary, men of both sides helped their enemy to escape the certain death of the approaching fires. There was no thought, at that point, of taking prisoners, and when Union men pulled a Confederate away, they carefully helped him back in the direction of the Confederate line, until his comrades in grey could take charge of him. In that way, for twenty minutes or so, a bit of humanity showed up amid the carnage of war on Cheatham Hill. Such things, strange as they may seem, are sometimes seen in war.

Within an hour, the same men who had jointly saved the lives of over twenty Union soldiers, as well as several Confederates, were once again shooting at each other. Both sides continued the fighting but neither charged the other along that section of the line for the rest of that day.

The incident might well have ended there, but for a rather strange occurrence the next day. At 10:00 sharp that next morning, a white flag arose from the Union lines, and the same Union captain stood and shouted out a request to meet with Col. Waller. Waller walked forward and, to his surprise, he was presented with two, matching ivory-handled Colt .45 pistols. The Union men were saying thanks. His Union enemies then offered him three cheers, and as

Confederates along the line realized what was happening, both sides joined in to cheer Col. Waller, and the gestures of goodwill from both their commander and their enemies.

At times even in the hell of war, mercy is shown, and when it is, the gesture is even more telling because of the horror of the situation. Such mercy is the stuff of legend, and it should come as no surprise that those two pistols are, even today, the proud possession of decedents of Col. Waller. They are now owned by his great, great, great, grandson, and namesake, Mr. Jacob Waller of New Bern, NC. They still speak of a day, amid a terrible battle, when a bit of mercy was shown.

## The First Evening

When Sherman learned just before noon, that the Union advance had stopped, he wanted to immediately renew it! He was not overly worried about initial losses, and twice that morning he asked General Thomas to renew his assault at Dead Angle. Thomas merely looked up at the bloody hill in the distance and replied, "I cannot order my men back up there. One or two more such assaults would use up this army."

One of Sherman's staff officers, heard Thomas' comment and realized that such a comment would not make Crazy Billy any calmer. He quickly pointed out the early, and only, Union success of the day. At the extreme left end of the Confederate line, Schofield's "diversion" had born fruit. Schofield's Union army was able to put two brigades across a small creek that Confederates had simply not guarded, believing that it was much too far from the battlefield to make any difference. Thus Sherman had, unknowingly and unintentionally, used the same strategy that had worked for him at both Rocky Face and Resaca—a strong right hook around the left end of the Confederate line. In fact the Union cavalry division on that end of the line was, even then, advancing on the Chattahoochee River, the last barrier protecting the city of Atlanta. They were far beyond the left flank of the entire Confederate army, and were much closer to Atlanta itself than any Confederate unit of any size.

Thus with the fight before him showing no promise, Sherman ordered some additional Union forces to support Schofield's success. With great reluctance, he accepted a halt in the direct assaults at Pigeon Hill and the Dead Angle. Thus, Sherman's frontal assault, an attack plan that had surprised nearly everyone, ended, though the opposing forces would face each other for five more days along that eleven mile Confederate line. At the Dead Angle the main defensive trenches were only fifty feet apart. There the armies would remain, five long days and nights, firing at anything that moved in the enemy works.

That first night, after the Fourth Georgia Regiment had been relieved and pulled back down the slope away from the main-line trenches, the men sat by their campfire once again. Duncan and Wilson were absent, off somewhere looking for prayer meeting, and Ten Cent Bill lay beside Captain Collins—both snoring loudly. Sampson was cleaning both his weapons and those of his master, Major Jamie Turnbull, as Jamie lay on his blanket only five feet away, staring into the dying fire. A few muskets fired occasionally along the line half-a-mile away, but by that point in the war, such random musket fire kept no one awake at that distance. Jamie lay on his side, and using only the light from the fire, he stared at the earth before him.

He watched an ant a foot from his face, struggling with part of a leaf. The ground he thought was not just dirt. It was a living breathing dark earth. He could see other ants between himself and the fire and any infantryman from that war knew of the other critters—lice, chiggers, and dung beetles—that made the earth their home. Jamie watched an infinite pantheon of life in that small fire-lit patch of ground, all very small, but all very present in almost any dirt in north Georgia. He realized that, like always, he was about to go to sleep on any number of unknown critters, and every one of them would bite him sometime before the sun rose the next day.

He wondered for a slit second, if the ground was worth it, worth all the carnage and death he'd seen that day. Was any ground worth it? Why was this mountain so critical, so as to deserve so much fighting? Why had Crazy Billy chosen this ground for a major assault? Didn't he know by now that almost no frontal assault worked, given the modern weapons of war used by both armies? Why here?

He knew there was no answer to that question, as he lay there watching the ants. There was no metaphor there for Jamie; no further analogy between the insignificant life he saw in that dirt, and the thousands of insignificant deaths on the field just up the mountain. He neither sought nor found any hidden meaning. There was no great existential wisdom at all, Jamie thought. There are just the bugs and the dead men. Bugs will eat us all one day he thought, and I have to sleep in them for yet another night.

Then Jamie rolled over on his back, and along with all of the others, he drifted off to sleep.

About two hundred feet away, however, men in blue were whispering, plotting. A group of officers, several from western Pennsylvania, and thus familiar with mining, were thinking on how to advance their cause. They realized that, if they couldn't advance into the Confederate guns above ground, perhaps they could do so underground. They began a tunnel that very night—it would only have to reach perhaps a hundred feet or so, and it wouldn't have to be too deep at all, maybe twenty feet below the surface of the ground. They hoped to place gunpowder into the shaft and blow up the Confederates in the trenches at the Dead Angle. In the subsequent confusion, they planned to charge that position, and then roll up the Confederate line.

While the idea was sound, the digging turned out to be terribly slow. It had to be, since silence was essential least the Confederates sleeping above hear the shovels at work. As a result the tunnel work, ongoing every hour, day and night, progressed slowly. In fact, the tunnel was never used, since it was not ready when the Confederates finally pulled back from their lines at the Dead Angle on July 2, 1864.

The tunnel entrance is marked today on the battlefield, just below the Confederate trenches at the Dead Angle, and while this tunnel wasn't used as planned, the idea was sound. In fact, a similar tunnel was begun on another Union siege line near Petersburg in Virginia, only several weeks later. On July 30, 1864, the largest single blast ever heard on Virginian soil, tore away nearly one hundred and fifty feet of Confederate trenches in what came to be known as the Battle of the Crater. Union men had discovered yet another weapon of war.

Confederate leaders, General Johnston included, soon realized that a major part of Sherman's massive army was moving around their left flank. It took several days to confirm that, but soon General Johnston began to worry, yet again, about the Union's right hook around his lines at Kennesaw. Thus on July 2, 1864, he did what he felt he had to do—he gave more Georgia soil to the Union army, and fell back to his "River Line" along the Chattahoochee River.

It is rather ironic that one of the last Confederate Units to leave the Dead Angle long after dark on July 2 was the Fourth Georgia infantry. Thus did several men, good friends from before the war in the Tugalo River Valley, stand in the trenches just behind the Dead Angle looking out between the dirt and the headlog toward the quiet of the Union lines only a hundred feet away. Duncan Carmichael, Lem Davis, Jamie Turnbull, and Sampson, all peeked at the Union position.

Duncan spoke first, in a whisper. "Some hard fighting in this ditch! Shame to give 'er up without one more good fight."

Sampson spoke next. "Everyone is out, Suh. Maybe we should follow 'um soon?"

Lem merely grunted, but then Jamie spoke up. "I'm damned if'n I can see a good end to this thing! Crazy Billy has more men than he has sense, and he'll sacrifice 'um all anywhere we dig a damn ditch! He don't care how many men he loses! How do you fight somebody like that?"

At that Lem did speak. "We fight 'um until we kill 'um all, or until they kill us."

There was silence for a few moments, then Jamie said, "Doesn't seem like we can do anything but give up more Georgia ground." For that moment, in that ditch, Jamie was alone with his friends. He was not, at that point, their commander any longer, but was merely a friend reflecting on the state of the war. "How can we win if we always pull back?"

No man there had an answer to that question. Perhaps there was no real answer to that question. After a few more moments, Jamie stood up and the men left those trenches to the Yankees.

## The Butcher's Bill at Kennesaw

None of the press like to report defeats, but even the New York Times could not hide the reality of Sherman's loss at Kennesaw.

> **"Yesterday, June 27, an unsuccessful attack was made by our forces on the Enemy position at Kennesaw Mountain. The attack resulted in a loss of between two and three thousand. Diversion attacks were conducted on the Sandtown Road and southwest of Kennesaw. Our main attacks approached the enemy defensive works, and our losses were particularly heavy among our general officers, as well as our enlisted men. I do not suppose the enemy suffered similarly, in that they remained behind their parapets."**

Thus did the fighting end at Kennesaw, with the smell of death still hanging strong over the field. Sherman's armies lost around three thousand men in the fighting along the Kennesaw Line, while Johnston's Confederates lost perhaps a thousand. Sherman, in a subsequent letter to his wife reflected on the fight. "What a horrid war this is. I have begun to regard the death and mangling of a couple thousand men as a small affair, a kind of morning dash. What kind of man does that make me?"

When sharing his thoughts with his staff, he was somewhat more tactical, if less morbid. Only once did he explain his decision to execute a frontal assault at Kennesaw. "I perceived that the enemy and our officers had settled down into a conviction that I would not assault fortified lines. All looked to me to outflank. For an army to be efficient, it must not settle down to a single mode of offence, but must be prepared to execute any plan which promises success. I wanted, therefore, for the moral effect, to make a successful assault against the enemy behind his breastworks, and resolved to attempt it at that point where success would give the largest fruits of victory."

Such are the luxuries of command. Generals can be cavalier about death, they can be reflective about the carnage. The men in the line of battle of course, cannot. It is after all their blood and parts of their bodies on the ground when the fighting ends. Kennesaw was not Sherman's first frontal assault in this advance on Atlanta (he had tried one at Resaca), but it would be his last. In most subsequent battles, the Confederates would take the chore of the frontal advance from him, to their detriment.

Jamie's outfit, the Fourth Georgia Infantry, lost twenty-two men, most of whom were new recruits. However, several of the men that Jamie had gotten to know were also hit. Wellspeak was seriously wounded in his left shoulder toward the end of the fight, though the presence of an exit wound suggested he'd been hit by a shot from a repeating rifle, and not a dreaded minie-ball. That was good news because minie-balls were known to break up inside the body and cause much more damage. Wellspeak would leave the war, and the rest of his life is lost to history. Some say he lived a long life as a fisherman along the Georgia coast, but no one is sure. His slave, Ten Cent Bill, did not accompany his wounded master home, but rather, remained on the Confederate line, as a manservant to Captain Collins, who offered to pay for his services after the war. Thus Ten Cent Bill would fight on, equipped with a brand new Spencer repeating rifle and all the ammunition he could steal.

Mo Hendon was not so lucky. He died at the Dead Angle on Cheatham Hill, shot in the head. Roy Giles was stabbed in the chest, and died a very painful death, within an hour of the battle's end. Both were buried, along with hundreds of their Confederate comrades, in a mass grave in the Confederate Cemetery in Marietta. There they lie today.

No markers testify to these men, and their bravery, witnessed only by their comrades, has been forgotten by history. Today even their names have long been lost, except in a few old family bibles from that time that survive, and the letters of Jamie Turnbull, letters which recorded their fight for the Confederacy, and serve as the basis for this story of the Turnbull and the Jarrett family.

Still one can, on occasion, get an inkling of the fight these men went through. While standing on the battlefield today, atop the Dead Angle, one can quietly contemplate what those men might have seen, what they might have felt, even what they tasted—the mix of blood, sweat, and gunpowder as they bit into their powder bags, just before they died at the Dead Angle. In a quiet few moments atop that hill, one might imagine what it might have been like. Of course in our worst images of blood, fear, fighting and instantaneous death, we only glimpse a pale reflection of the harsh reality of that fight.

Men from Illinois, the very men who had to assault the Dead Angle, were the first to show their reverence for their comrades who died on that hill. Soon after the war, they purchased a track of land on the battlefield, including their assault positions and the Dead Angle itself, in order to preserve some memory of what happened there. Today the Illinois monument marks the hill where so many of their comrades died.

Of course those same Union men had fought in every fight in Sherman's advance on Atlanta. They later fought in the battles around Atlanta itself. Still, when they wanted to select a spot for the memorial to their dead comrades, to a man, they chose the Dead Angle at Kennesaw. It was by far, the worst fighting their unit saw during the entire war.

Thus does the Dead Angle of Cheatham Hill, just to the south of Kennesaw Mountain, take its place among the most fearful battlefields in the western hemisphere. Here the horror is not measured, not scaled, by the total number of deaths. This place did not see the scores of thousands of dead as did other fields of battle in that long-ago war. Rather, here, on this ground, the measure is the sheer fierceness of the fighting. By that measure, as every veteran of the Dead Angle would later testify, that ground rivals and perhaps exceeds, the deadliest locations of that or any other war. The Dead Angle stands amid such horrid, and hallowed ground as the Peach Orchard or Devil's Den on the field at Gettysburg, Custer's Last Stand Hill out west, the Hornet's Nest at Shiloh, Bunker Hill near Boston, or even the Bloody Lane at Antietam. Few patches of ground in the world have tasted the blood, or witnessed the fierceness of combat, as has the Dead Angle on Kennesaw Mountain. Like those other battlefields, this place is now sanctified; it has become holy.

## Reflections Between the Battles

By July 3, 1864, Sherman was camped in Marietta with his cavalry advancing to find the Confederate's next defensive line. Sherman ordered the destruction in that town of any building or resources that were of use to the Confederates. He saved the hospitals that had been established and Union doctors took the place of their Confederate counterparts. That is how the Kennesaw House was preserved for us to enjoy today. A number of other buildings around the town square were also preserved. Many were owned by Masons, a fraternal organization that also claimed Sherman as one of its members.

It only took Sherman's scouts a day to locate Johnston's "River Line," a strong network of prepared positions along the Chattahoochee River. It took even less time for Sherman to order his army to bypass that defensive line. Why attack prepared positions when one doesn't have to? This time, however, Sherman's men advanced around the right end of Johnston's Confederate lines rather than the left, by finding a ford on the river some twenty miles to the north. By mid-July, Johnston had ordered a fall back into the defenses of Atlanta itself.

As Sherman's army was leaving most of Marietta in flames, another of those important conversations was taking place in Richmond. Confederate President Jefferson Davis, always battling his ever-present depression, was sitting in his drawing room with his comrade and former Secretary of State, General Robert Toombs. Davis was holding a report on Johnston's retreat from the River Line, another of the reports written by Major Jamie Turnbull from the Tugalo River Valley.

Davis spoke first. "I told you Toombs! I remember telling you! Johnston plans to give up all of Georgia, and that will cut our throat!"

Toombs was nearly as angry as Davis, but knew to keep his own feelings to himself. "I do remember you saying that previously. Still, what can we do? What can Johnston do?" Toombs expected an explosion from Davis at that statement. He knew how very much Davis loathed General Joseph Johnston, and he thought the anger in the Confederate President was about to boil over. However, when Davis didn't explode, Toombs continued. "We know that Johnston's men love him, nearly as much as Lee's men here in Virginia revere their general. Besides, Johnston is vastly outnumbered down there in Georgia, and Sherman's supplies are endless."

Davis didn't exactly explode, but he did respond rather forcefully. Throwing the written papers back on his desk he raised his voice and said, "Don't talk to me of supplies, Toombs! None of our armies have enough shoes, or belt buckles, or beans right now. It is all our quartermasters can do to provide powder and lead for the muskets. Hell, Lee doesn't have enough supplies, and he is holding Grant's Union army, a much larger army than Sherman's I might add, at bay only thirty miles from here! Why does Johnston have to give up so much southern territory to Sherman? Where is the fighting spirit of the man?"

General Toombs merely looked at his troubled friend. While neither leader would admit it at that time, both were feeling the demise of their beloved Confederacy. In mid July of 1864, Grant's line was wrapped like a snake around Richmond and its all-important southern railhead, Petersburg. Sherman was moving on Atlanta, and his army showed real progress.

Toombs decided to mention some good news. "Mr. President," he said. "That monkey Lincoln has an election coming this November and it looks as if he may not win another term as the President of the Union. I believe, if we can just hold out a bit longer in both Richmond and Atlanta, a new Union government might come to power that will negotiate with us, and leave the Confederacy intact!"

Davis ever the consummate politician, reflected on that. "I've had that thought many times, Toombs! I've had that exact thought since we lost at Gettysburg and Vicksburg last year! Maybe we can reach a compromise, if the Union has had too much of a taste of war! I know there have been draft riots through the northern states."

And thus did these great leaders, leaders in a dying cause, reflect on what remained as their only real hope for any type of victory. With Lincoln's expected defeat, perhaps they could negotiate with a new president who would simply let the Confederacy determine its own fate, and leave the Union. While it is quite difficult today to imagine such hopes, those thoughts were very real in the minds of both the Confederate and Union leadership in July of 1864. Even with a string of major defeats, the Confederacy could still survive as a country, if it could only hold on past the next Union election. In fact, Lincoln sitting behind his massive defenses in Washington City shared that same thought with his cabinet. While no one in 1864 thought the Union would lose the war on the battlefield, few thought they would win there either, so Lincoln's election was really in doubt during the summer of 1864. Therein lay the only realistic Confederate hope.

After some silence in that historic Richmond meeting, Davis announced the decision that Toombs was already expecting. "I'll replace Johnston! I'll have to relieve him and find a commander for the Army of Tennessee that will use that force to drive Sherman out of Georgia as Bragg did last September! I'm sure, with the right commander, that army still has a fight left in it!"

For just a moment, Toombs thought Davis might ask him to assume command, and while he had served admirably as a field command general earlier in the war, he did not seek a battlefield command at this late date. Thus, he was relieved by Davis' next words. "I'll promote General Hood and appoint him Commander of the Army of Tennessee and the entire Georgia department! That man will fight to the death!"

Later that same day, July 17, 1864, two telegrams went out from Richmond to Atlanta. One relieved General Joe Johnston, one of the most beloved of all Civil War generals of his command of the Army of Tennessee. Another went to General Hood, who wasted no time at all, calling a command meeting of all his corps commanders that very evening. Georgia fields would see even more bloody battles, and they would come quickly, with Hood in command.

General Sherman and President Jefferson Davis were not the only ones reflecting on the war as the Army of Tennessee moved into the Atlanta defenses. Mary Turnbull, the young mistress of Traveler's Rest Plantation in northeast Georgia was, likewise, thinking on what the war had come to mean. During Major Turnbull's travels toward the Atlanta defenses in early July of 1864, the following letter arrived, and again, those interested in the exact history of that distant time are lucky to have this letter. It shows the very heart and soul of the Confederacy, just at the point, when the war, though hopeless, still seemed winnable for the final time.

*To Major Jamie Turnbull, Commander*
*Fourth Georgia, John Bell Hood's Corps, CSA*
*Travel instructions via Atlanta, GA*

*My dearest husband:*

*I have heard of a great battle at Kennesaw Mountain, and know that your corps was involved. We have heard that you drove the Yankees back down the mountain, and nearly all the way to Tennessee, but that is clouded by the further news that the army is pulling back, yet again, towards Atlanta. It would seem that the news is muddled, more so than usual. As your loving wife, I do so hope you are alive and may receive this letter in a timely fashion; for I could not bear it, were it otherwise.*

*I write to bring you some sad news. First, my Grandfather Devereaux Jarrett, is down with the flux, and cannot seem to recover. He may have even had a mild stroke, according to the doctor. Of course, his age is a serious concern and Meely is tending him, day and night. She is such a dear member of this family in so many ways, but she is more than she appears, and I'll get to that a bit later. For now, just know that Grandfather seems to be holding his own, and I know not if I shall write in a fortnight, telling you of his death, or of his recovery.*

*While no Yankees have approached our area of Georgia, as nearly as we can tell from the newspapers, everyone here is very worried about the increasing number of runaway slaves. As you know Grandfather had ninety-six slaves at the beginning of the war, and very many of them were highly skilled workers, tanners, coopers, blacksmiths, and such. Since my last letter, I've tried to take a count, and today, as nearly as I can tell, there are only around twenty five still on the plantation. Of course, we've loaned many to the Confederate army in Atlanta, and who knows if those will ever return. I assume they are off digging trenches somewhere. Also, I know that Sampson is with you, as always (and I hope he is well), and several other slaves have been seconded to the army for various tasks in this area with the Home Guard. Armies do require horses, wagons, barrels, and all the other things that slaves make, so many of our skilled help is gone to the service of the Confederacy. Still, I'm sure that other slaves have simply vanished, and such is the case with neighboring plantations also. I know your own family is missing many of their slaves, though I do not know the particulars.*

*Just last week, the slave catchers nabbed seven runaways who were, apparently heading west to try and reach the Yankee lines in Tennessee. Our own Ezra, and his wife Juniper were with them, along with their son Jacob. All were beaten, of course, before being returned to us, beaten in such a bloody, horrid manner, a way that would never have been allowed on our own plantation. I cried when I first helped to nurse them back to health, and it will be quite some time before any of them is able to work again. As you know, Juniper has always had something of an attitude, and at times, a sharp tongue, so I believed it was her that put her family up to the escape. I did not feel I should talk with her, but when I was putting a salve on the lashes on Ezra's back, I pointed out that his family had been taken care of on the plantation, well feed, and never beaten. Then I asked him, why they ran.*

*He looked up at me with those dark pools of his black eyes, and simply said, "Ms. Mary, we wants our freedom. We wants de Jubilee, so we's runned to de Yankees!"*

*Such is the condition of our workers. Even though they are treated kindly, fed, and cared for, they still run, when they can. It has caused me to have grave doubts about what slavery means to these people. Don't they realize that slavery is Biblical? That it is the will of God? I simply cannot understand why a man would run and put his family in danger of a beating when they are never beaten here!*

*I also fear that our own Meely has some involvement with this messy business. On two occasions, I've seen her whispering to other slaves, just before those slaves ran off. Of course, Meely and the others hushed up immediately when I entered the room, as slaves often do. Still, my loving husband, those experiences left me thinking, wondering, if she could have something to do with the run-a-ways. I simply do not know what to think.*

*Still, she tends Grandfather Jarrett as if he were her own flesh and blood. Why would she do that, if she herself intends to run, or helps others in running away? One can never tell what a slave is thinking!*

*Meanwhile, I am well, though of late, I've had some mild sickness nearly each morning. I'm sure it is nothing, and a brisk walk down to the Tugalo River usually clears it up. This river valley is so very lovely; one can only marvel at God's handiwork along that beautiful river bank.*

*Enough of this! I'll write again soonest, and until then, I beg you to communicate with me, letting me know of your situation, and your location. I've not seen you since your quick visit in April. As always, your loving wife misses you more than a lady should, so do come home when you get the chance. As I close this brief note, I'll be bold, and most unlady-like. I love you with all my heart, and cannot bear the thought of missing you for much longer. Please come home soon!*

*Proudly yours,*
*Mrs. Mary Turnbull*
*Traveler's Rest Plantation*

Major Jamie Turnbull received that letter one evening in early July of 1864. As he reread it later that night, lying in his tent alone, he wept.

# Chapter 5
# Atlanta Cannot Fall

## Fortress Atlanta

The message from Jefferson Davis was clear and succinct; "Atlanta cannot fall to the enemy! Defend the city at all costs!"

The recipient of that order, General John Bell Hood, was without exception the single most aggressive commander in the entire war. He fully intended to defend the city at all costs. He could not do otherwise.

As early as the fall of Vicksburg in July of 1863, many Georgia politicians began to believe that Atlanta, rich in factories making war materials and a significant railroad hub, would become a target of the Union armies. Connecting rail lines reached across the Confederacy to both Columbia and Charleston in South Carolina, down to Mobile, Alabama and northwest into Chattanooga, Tennessee. Other lines led to Wilmington, North Carolina and from there up to Richmond, Virginia. With that rich transportation network at its heart, Union armies would no doubt target Atlanta.

Of course the city in the 1860s, with a population of less than 10,000, was much smaller than the city we know today. From the perspective of the 21st century most of the fortifications of that era were long-ago buried under the city sprawl of the last century. Still every citizen in Georgia in those days, as well as most throughout the Confederacy, knew that Atlanta could not be allowed to fall to the Union. The loss of Atlanta would be second only to the loss of the Confederate capital in Richmond in overall importance to the Grand Cause of the Confederacy. This city in 1860 was the 12th largest city in the Confederate States of America, but sitting as it did at the heart of the new nation, it of necessity became a critical focal point of the war. With that in mind, work on the Atlanta fortifications began in August of 1863.

Lemuel Grant, an Atlanta builder and businessman, was charged with the task, and he soon formulated a plan to encircle the entire town with defenses. Over the next months, Grant planned Atlanta's perimeter defenses as a multi-layered bastion. First he would build an outer defensive ring well outside of the city, but that was merely a series of non-connected trenches haphazardly located on high ground and along roads and railroad tracks. Nearer to the city he constructed a much more formidable bastion, a series of seventeen earthwork redoubts laid out in a ten-mile wide circle, encompassing the entire city. That defensive bastion would come to be known as Fortress Atlanta.

That complex line of redoubts along with connecting earthworks and trenches lay over a mile outside the city limits at that time. Fixed wooden platforms with clear fields of fire were constructed for the cannon that would arrive with the Confederate army, and the approaches to Atlanta were all fortified with an earthwork fort or redoubt. The entire circle of trenches and redoubts was protected by abatis and other impediments to enemy troop movement.

Pictures that exist today of Fortress Atlanta were taken by Union photographers after the capture of the city. Still it is easy to imagine a Confederate guard squad living in the dugout bunker below and defending this section of those trenches. Defenses of this nature surrounded the entire city.

Fortress of Atlanta adjoining the Ephraim G. Ponder House

The northern strong point in the line was a redoubt on a hill that is today, the home of the Fox Theater on Peachtree Street. The eastern side of the trenches fell roughly along today's Ashby Street and the southern limit of the fortifications roughly paralleled today's McDonough Drive. The southeastern line ranged across land that today, makes up Grant Park, a park named after the builder himself on land he gave to the city. In fact, one can still visit one of the few remaining examples of Fortress Atlanta in Grant Park itself. Fort Walker was one of the earthen artillery bastions encircling Atlanta. It was named after General Walker, a Confederate hero who died in the Battle of Atlanta, attacking the Union enemy only a few miles to the east.

Ironically none of these Fortress Atlanta defenses were ever utilized for battle. Given the unpredictability of mobile armies during a nineteenth century war, none of the Fortress Atlanta defensive works would be the focal point of a major battle, and most of these trenches witnessed no fighting at all. Such are the vagrancies of history.

## De Cost of de Jubilee!

While Confederates took up positions behind the Atlanta fortifications and Union armies marched to encircle the city, others all across the Confederacy were playing out their respective roles in the deadly game of war. As Jeff Davis fumed against Joe Johnston from the governor's mansion in Richmond, General Robert E. Lee was besieged by General Grant in Petersburg, Virginia. Lincoln fought his battles with Congress to maintain manpower for the ever-growing Union army, and Meely, a kitchen slave from Traveler's Rest Plantation along the Tugalo River in northern Georgia, lay hiding in a muddy ditch bank.

Historians have long noted that no one really knows when or where the term "Jubilee" came to be associated with freedom among the slaves. In Hebrew history, the Jubilee referred to changes in property rights associated with the seven year periods in the Hebrew calendar. Thus, every "seven times seven" (basically every 49 years) property ownership of things such as land, slaves, or indentured servants was to be re-established or redefined by law. This ancient Hebrew tradition did help determine the standard "indenture" period of seven years for many indentured servants coming to the British colonies throughout the 1700s. Further, that tradition may have led one black preacher or another in the 1830s to conclude that "de Jubilee" would result in freedom of the slaves at some point, but again no direct historic reference is available, so this remains merely conjecture. What is known is that, at least as early as the 1840s, slaves both waited and prayed for "de Jubilee!"

Of course this was probably not on Meely's mind as she crouched behind the bank of a small creek in north Georgia. She was serving as the "Conductor" for this particular group of slaves who had escaped from a South Carolina plantation just across the river from Traveler's Rest. Apparently they had decided on their own, to run away from their plantation near Seneca, and try to connect with the Union army that they had heard was somewhere in Georgia. Of course as slaves, they really had no information on how big Georgia really was, and several of them may have thought that if they merely swam across the Tugalo River they would fall into the hands of the Yankee hordes and be free.

They were fortunate indeed, to have crossed just opposite from Traveler's Rest Plantation which by that point in the war was a busy "station" on the Underground Railroad. Fanny Bricebud, as a house servant and thus at the top of the enslaved hierarchy, had been the first to help runaway blacks escape slavery, but as she aged, the actual tasks in facilitating such escapes were passed on to others, including the third Meely to live at Traveler's Rest.

When those seven slaves, five adults and two young children, crawled up on the Georgia side of the riverbank, a young field hand from Traveler's Rest quickly took them to hide in the barn in the nigger yard. He then ran to Aunt Fanny, who immediately sought out Meely.

Luckily Mrs. Mary Turnbull had gone to town—meaning Clemson, South Carolina some thirty-five miles away—to pick up some items, and take in her letters to be mailed directly to her husband. She would probably spend at least one night there with friends, so Meely could slip off from the plantation, leaving Fanny Bricebud (who was then quite old, but still authoritative) in charge of the care of a very sick master of the house, Mr. Devereaux Jarrett. The two women concocted a lie suggesting that Meely needed to go to Clarkesville some twenty miles away to the west, to tend a sickly family member. Meely was a well-known and well respected house servant, and she was not likely to be molested by slave catchers. Of course, she took the time to forge a written "pass" for her travels, complete with Mrs. Mary Turnbull's name, just in case. As this shows, it is a historic fact that slaves throughout the antebellum south were not nearly so ignorant as their owners chose to believe.

The seven escapees had spent most of the first day in the old barn resting up, and just after dusk, Meely and her new "passengers" took off across Georgia to find the Yankees. The first day and night were relatively easy, as the road to Clarkesville was little used. They were fortunate in that a Quaker family in Clarkesville would usually agree to house escaping slaves for a day or so, as long as the slave chasers were not directly on their heels. Thus, did this group of individuals, desperate for freedom, make their escape.

By the morning of the second day, Meely was sure of only two things. First Mary Turnbull had probably returned to Traveler's Rest after only a day in Clemson, so her time was running out. Second, she still had yet to find the Yankees.

Of course, Meely had taken no chances with her seven passengers after leaving the Quaker farm on the second day. Along the much busier road into Cleveland, Georgia, whenever they heard horses or a wagon coming down the road, they quickly hid in the bushes or in the creek bed, parallel to the road. Many mountain roads in those days followed falling water, so creeks could usually be found beside the roads, and they provided wonderful hiding places. Meely knew it was always wiser to hide from everyone, rather than to take the risk that the approaching horses or wagons contained slave chasers. This particular time, after a few moments, a wagon rambled by on the road above them, and Meely looked up. She could see it was merely a farmer taking some pigs to market in town, and in reality they probably didn't need to hide from that man at all. Still, better to be cautious.

Just as Meely stood up, with the wagon already around the next bend in the dirt track, the youngest of the children, a two year old, screamed, jumped up, and ran out into the creek bed a few steps. Meely could already tell the cause. The water snake still clung to the child's arm where it had sunk in the fangs.

By the time Meely got to the child, the snake had fallen into the creek and swum away, leaving the terrified child in his mother's arms, as both of them cried and wailed. Two small blood spots on the child's arm showed where the snake had struck. Meely had an instant fear that the farmer might hear all the commotion and return, so she quickly "shushed" both the child and the loudly wailing mother. It took only a moment for every adult there to realize one certainty. In that day and age, there was little hope for the survival of a small child who'd been bitten by a poisonous water snake. The child's arm was already turning color and beginning to swell.

Meely's task had just become virtually impossible. This would not be an occasion where she would deliver all of her passengers to the next station unharmed. Still she immediately made the necessary, though cruel decision. "I'll be taking de baby back wid' me to Traveler's Rest, and you folks be goin' on to de next station yor' self! It only 'bout two mile further on down de lane, here."

The mother looked in horror at Meely, and was quiet for a moment as the harshness of the plan sunk in. The she said, "I cain't let you have my baby; I cain't do it!" She began to cry in earnest, eyes closed and huge tears rolling down her black cheeks. "I cain't! I cain't let you take my baby. I cain't! I jes' cain't do it!"

Her husband then began to comfort the mother. "It al' right, Sadie. Miss Meely just 'gone comfort de child! When our baby get well, she bring 'um back to us. Ain't dat right, Miss Meely?" He looked at Meely, knowing the reality of the situation, even as he refused to say it out loud—the baby would be dead in less than a day.

Meely played along. "Dat right. You all see yor' baby next week, for sure! I'll bring 'um to ya."

"You see," said the father. "It all right, Sadie. Now you just hand me my chil' and go and clean up yor face. We don't need to let the odder boy see you like dis!" With that the father lovingly took the two year old from Sadie's arms saying, "Go'on now up to de edge of de creek, and clean yor face off. We's got anodder baby just up in the bushes and dat baby scaired! He need his Mama right now! Go on, now."

Then one of the other adults took Sadie's arm and escorted her back toward the roadway leaving Meely, the father, and the stricken child in the creek. The poison in the child's body continued to swell the arm. Meely knew the pain she'd caused; she could see it in the mother's face, but she also knew the reality. The escapees needed to move on, and waiting for a child to die was not an option. She looked back at the father, and spoke. "We's only three miles or so from Cleveland, and you need to get into town just after sunset, so you need to get goin! I'll stay here with de child, and say prayers and such. I'll be buryin' dis chil' later tonight, I recon."

"I know'd it," the father said. "I know'd you will." The father looked into Meely's face at that point. Meely could see he was about to lose his composure, with broad tears running down his cheeks. With an inhuman effort, he managed not to cry out loud, in his agony. He knew his second son was as good as dead, and his face showed that fact. As he cradled his dying, but now quiet child in his arms, he hugged him a final time, and then said, "I know'd der' gone be a price to pay! I know'd it! Dis is it, right here you see? Dis right here is de price of freedom. Dis be de price of de Jubilee."

Meely could only look on, knowing the father was saying good-by to his son in the only way he could. She wept, from the deepest recesses of her soul.

The father spoke again. "Dis it right here, my dead chil!' My baby gonna die here on dis road, an' dis de price of freedom; dis de price of de Jubilee." Again he hugged the child to his breast, tears now rolling down his cheeks.

Meely waited for only another moment, then said. "You need to go on now. Give me de chil, and I say prayers an' bury it here. You still got a family up der, and you need to go on! Day need you, and you need to get 'um to de Yankees."

With that the father looked up to the road toward Sadie and the others in the small group. Meely took that opportunity to take the child from his arms, and continued her instructions.

"Don' you let Sadie come back down here in dis creek! I don't want no long good-byes! You all got to get movin! Move yor' family on down de line!"

Here Meely paused to gage the impact of her words on the father. Seeing both pain and bewilderment on his face, she continued her instructions. "When you get into Cleveland, you got to go to de stables and fin' a black man der named Moses. He work der in the first stables you come to on dis road. Get der before he close tonight right after dark, and he let you stay in de stables, and help you all get to de next station. Tell him what happened. Tell him I took dis baby to de woods to bury him, an' won't be commin' in wid yall. You's gone have to do dis part by yourself! You hear? Now git goin! Go on, now!"

The father looked one last time at his child, and then began to move out of the creek. When he reached the road, he put his arms around Sadie, and began to lead her away, moving down the road to Cleveland. Meely could hear Sadie crying, but thankfully, neither one looked back.

After the slaves had moved around the bend, Meely continued to comfort the child for a few minutes, all the while knowing that when the swelling and the pain of the poison really hit, she would be unable to keep the child quiet. The child's arm would swell to the size of large mellon, then his chest would begin to change color, and his breathing would become labored. He would cry out, shouting in agony, and finally he would die gasping for breath and screaming. There was absolutely nothing Meely could do to prevent it.

Without realizing it, Meely began to do the only thing that made any sense. She started to sing to the child, a hymn of comfort; it was all she had to offer. That particular hymn had become popular of late among the slaves at Traveler's Rest. Like many melodious, comforting hymns this song spoke of the firm belief in God's presence, and his loving will. It was the only comfort that she could offer to a dying child. Meely walked to the edge of the creek, knowing she would need all of her strength, as she sang softly to the child.

And in that moment, along a nameless creek in north Georgia, a black woman's strong voice reached out to God, with a hymn of unimaginable power.

*"Amazing Grace, how sweet the sound, that saved a wretch like me.*
*I once was lost, but now I'm found, was blind, but now I see.*

Meely herself then began to cry softly, as she reached the second verse, but she kept singing. She knew there was no good ending in that situation. She either had to watch this child suffer unbearably for hours and hours, or …

Still she sang, drawing strength from the words of the hymn. She would need all the strength she had for the time ahead.

*T'was grace that taught my heart to fear, and grace my fears relieved.*
*How precious did that grace appear, the hour I first believed.*

As tears rolled down her cheek, she knew she would do the unthinkable. She knew she had to. This world was cruel; it is cruel, so very mean and cruel. Meely faced that reality in that creek bed that night, in a way that few men or women ever have to face it. Still she could take comfort in God's grace. It was, and is, the only real comfort anyone ever has.

Meely laid the child on the edge of the creek bed, and reached for a large rock, as she began the last verse of that beloved hymn. She carefully turned the child's face away from her and sat beside him. It took both hands to move the rock, and tears rolled down her cheeks, as she knew what must happen. She could not let the child die gasping for every breath. Still she sang. She wanted the hymn of God to be the last thing that poor child ever heard on this earth.

*When we've been there ten thousand years, bright shining as the sun,*
*We've no less days, to sing God's praise, than when we first begun.*

With the last word in that verse, the rock came down hard, and mercifully, it completely crushed the child's head. Meely heard a sickening, squishy sound, and a final breath, as the child's body quivered once, for only a brief moment. Meely then tossed the heavy rock to the side, and fell across the body, crying her pain, and saying, "Forgive me chil! You go on to God now, and please forgive me!"

She cried openly for a few moments, then spoke again through her tears. "Go on, chil! You already yonder in Heaben! You already seeing Jesus! Go on now, and forgive me. Dis be it, you see? Dis be de price for your family. Dis be de price of de Jubilee."

Such is the cost of freedom. Sometimes one may fight for it in a desperate, life and death struggle. Sometimes one might even die for it. Sometimes one might have to sacrifice a child to preserve a hope of freedom for others in the family. Sometimes, many times, securing freedom requires the unthinkable as it did that night, in a dark, north Georgia creek.

Meely left the child's body in the creek bed, knowing that wolves and bears would take the remains that night. She would never know if the remaining six slaves escaped or not. She certainly prayed for them, and she never forgot that particular trip when she sacrificed one dying child that others might move further along the Underground Railroad to their freedom.

## Author's Note: Connecting the Dots

As it happened, a Yankee cavalry troop was making a raid throughout north Georgia that very week, so that group of slaves off a plantation in Seneca, South Carolina, was probably one of several such groups that was able to connect with men in blue right after they reached Cleveland, Georgia, on that fateful night. In fact, Union action reports show that this particular Yankee raid resulted in nearly sixty escaped slaves attaching themselves to the Union cavalry. While most Union soldiers considered escaped slaves an inconvenience—indeed, some Union men were openly racist and hostile—Union troops rarely abandoned the slaves. In most cases, the Yankees even shared some of their rations with the hungry escapees, and such was the case that night in the small town of Cleveland, Georgia.

Regardless of the benevolence or lack thereof among Union officers, it is known that some 100,000 slaves escaped to freedom along the Underground Railroad. It is not known how many escaped during the war itself in Georgia. Today most of the "known" stations along the railroad are in states such as Ohio, Illinois, Indiana, or Kentucky. Few such locations are known in the deep south itself, since those stations had of necessity, to remain even more circumspect.

Still Fanny Bricebud and Meely, right here at Traveler's Rest in north Georgia, were among those brave conductors and station masters, and all Georgians today can take pride in such remarkable black women. Bricebud's "slave narrative" recorded when she was nearly ninety years old, shortly after the war, told this story; a story that Meely, no doubt, recounted to her, the story of Meely's group of escaped slaves moving toward Cleveland, Georgia. It spoke of Meely killing a snake-bitten child on that night so long ago.

Knowing the dangers of helping slaves escape, these two black women showed their courage again and again. They never once failed to move their passengers on along the line to freedom. Their bravery, their determination is a lesson for all.

Still among those 100,000 escapees few paid a higher price than the group Meely took to freedom in early July of 1864. Yankees were already in Georgia, and that lure proved too much for some slaves, including that group from Seneca, South Carolina. While today, we benignly quote the old adage that "freedom is never free," few of us today could have felt that reality more than those escaped slaves, as they left their dying child in the hands of Meely, an absolute stranger, along that dark creek bed that night. Perhaps the father, whose name has been lost to history, said it best; "Dis be de price of freedom; dis de price of de Jubilee!"

## Sherman Moves Against Hood

To understand the battles around Atlanta, one must deeply understand the mindset of newly appointed Confederate commander, General John Bell Hood. Since May 6, 1864, when Crazy Billy and his Union armies had left Chattanooga, Tennessee, General Joe Johnston and the Confederate army had been whittling the Union force down to size. By July 17 of that year when Johnston was relieved of command and replaced by Hood, the Union force under Sherman had been reduced considerably, but the Confederacy had paid a stiff price, nearly a hundred miles of Georgia territory. Further, the Confederate President Jefferson Davis thought that price was too high. Thus, Johnston was removed, and General John Bell Hood reached the pinnacle of his military career. His move into command of an army had been his goal since the beginning of the war, but it would prove to be a disaster for the Confederacy.

John Bell Hood was a feisty, thirty-three year old Texan who barely managed to get into West Point, where his limited intellectual capability and generally questionable behavior almost resulted in his expulsion. Still by 1853, he did manage to graduate and served in the cavalry in the western territories, where he developed a reputation for both stark aggressiveness and unquestioned courage. Both of those attributes were obvious in the early years of the War Between the States, and Hood became one of the most rapidly promoted military men in either army. In less than a year from 1861 to 1862 he moved up from Captain to Major General by fighting in scrapes such as the Seven Days Battle and Second Manassas up in Virginia. During the next year, Hood's aggressiveness, some might say his recklessness, began to cost him physically. On July 2, 1863 at Gettysburg, an exploding shell paralyzed his left hand. He should have spent time in recovery, but only three months later, he was back in the war, and managed to catch a minie-ball in his right leg at Chickamauga. He lost both his arm and his leg.

Such wounds could have killed a lesser man but not John Bell Hood. Given his uncanny willingness to lose parts of himself as well as his aggressiveness, Hood was toasted throughout the south as one of the most important of the southern heroes. When he gained command of the Army of Tennessee, there were still 55,000 effectives in that force, and Hood proposed to use them. He intended to attack the Union armies as soon as an opportunity presented itself. The fighting that Joe Johnston had carefully, and intentionally, drawn out over nearly three months, would make Hood's quickness to go into battle seem downright reckless.

Some historians have suggested that the plan for the fight at Peachtree Creek was developed by Johnston himself prior to being relieved of command. Knowing Sherman's tendency to separate his forces into several groups, Johnston expected Sherman to send the Army of the Tennessee under General McPherson in one direction around Atlanta, while sending the Army of Ohio under General Schofield in the other. Johnston reasoned that Sherman had often used McPherson's Army of the Tennessee as his "strong right hook" when facing a strong Confederate line. Such was the case in both Dalton and Resaca. That would leave General Thomas' Army of the Cumberland, a much larger and therefore more cumbersome army, standing alone, so Johnston's plan involved attacking that army while the other Union forces were far removed.

In fact, Sherman did something similar to what Johnston expected. Crazy Billy sent two Union Armies, McPherson's 25,000 men in the Army of the Tennessee and Schofield's 13,000 troops in the Army of the Ohio to the east of Atlanta. Those forces would move toward Decatur, about twelve miles to the east, and there attempt to sever the Georgia Railroad, a rail line that led into South Carolina and on to Richmond. Sherman's main force, General Thomas'

Army of the Cumberland some 60,000 strong, would move directly against Atlanta from the north.

Of course by July 19 Hood had already assumed command of the Confederate defenses around Atlanta, and when word came that Sherman had once again, sent the other armies off into the hinterlands to the east of the city, Hood decided to put Johnston's plan into effect. One of the Union commanders, General Schofield had actually been Hood's roommate at West Point, so the aggressiveness of John Bell Hood was very well known among all of the Union commanders. After all, it had been Hood only the previous month, that had launched the unplanned Confederate attack at Kolb's Farm just prior to the fight at Kennesaw. Thus Hood had shown his true colors, and everyone on both sides expected this firebrand of a general to attack quickly. Hood didn't disappoint. He decided to leave the strong fortifications of Fortress Atlanta, and attack General Thomas' Union Army of the Cumberland as they crossed Peachtree Creek.

In wartime it is frequently the case that plans that might look brilliant can, in retrospect be shown to be sheer lunacy. Why should Hood attack a Union army the same size as his own force, when he could have waited behind the Fortress Atlanta defenses and fought a defensive battle? With the weapons of that day, defensive warfare was much more effective than offensive warfare, and leaving a fortress to attack a similar sized force only seven miles away was simply stupid. Of course, Hood knew that Sherman's armies were separated by several miles, and he wanted to catch Thomas' large Union army as they crossed Peachtree Creek, before they could build earthworks. Thus, at the time, the plan seemed at least plausible, so on the evening of July 19 Hood met with his corps commanders to plan the attack for the next day. As history would show, this singular decision was perhaps, one of the worst battlefield decisions of the war.

Hood's attack plan was only slightly modified from Johnston's original idea. Rather than attack as Thomas' Army of the Cumberland crossed Peachtree Creek, Confederate forces under Generals Hardee and Stewart would attack after Thomas crossed the creek, but before his men could build earthworks. That meant that timing would be critical to success, since those Union men, like their Confederate counterparts, were very experienced with their shovels. In simple terms, anyone can dig a hole quite quickly when one suspects to soon be under fire. Moreover, in July of 1864, Sherman had nearly eight thousand escaped slaves helping his armies by digging defensive works whenever and wherever they were needed.

Confederate General Cheatham was in temporary command of Hood's old corps, and he was to form a battle line northeast of Atlanta along with the Confederate cavalry. He sought to hold the Union forces east of town out of the planned battle to the north. Meanwhile, both Hardee's Corps and Stewart's Corps would hit Thomas' Union army north of town, attacking from right to left in succession along Peachtree Creek, in an attempt to drive Thomas to the northwest. After Thomas' Union force was dealt with, the Confederates planned to turn right to confront the smaller Union forces to the east. The attack was scheduled to begin at 1:00 PM, the next day.

## The Battle of Peachtree Creek

The morning of July 20, 1864 was sunny, and promised to be a warm summer day in Atlanta. One might have expected birds singing on the mid-summer morning as people went about their business in downtown Atlanta. Unfortunately 120,000 men were about to fight for the town itself, so absolutely nothing about that beautiful summer morning was normal. Many citizens were rushing to the train station down on Alabama Street, to catch a train out of town, and many brought wagon-loads of valuables with them. At that point, there were still two rail lines heading south that were open, and as soon as a train bringing supplies to the army could unload, every square inch of space was loaded with family possessions, and the families themselves, and turned around to head south once again. Many dozens of trains were expected on that single day, and their steam whistles screamed every few minutes, all morning long as trains either arrived or left Atlanta.

By noon on that day, the Union forces to the east of Atlanta were in position to shell the town with their longer-range Parrott rifled cannon. At 12:15 or so, two heavy caliber Parrott shells exploded at the corner of Ellis and Ivy streets, catching a family that was heading to the railroad terminal, and killing a young girl who was walking through the intersection. Thereafter, the screams of the train whistles were partnered with the sound of the heavy Union cannon shelling the city.

Hood moved his forces into the planned lines on the morning of July 20, as the trains sounded in the distance. However, he soon noticed that his old corps, now commanded by Cheatham, was much too far to the north to keep the Union forces to the east of town at bay. Seeking to correct this problem, Hood redid his battle orders that morning, sending instructions to shift every corps in the army to the east. Thus, while the three Confederate corps played hopscotch with each other, Union men crossed Peachtree Creek unmolested.

One conundrum of battle command is that, while one hopes to be fluid in battle by quickly responding to changes in the situation, one should avoid relocating one's forces while in range of the enemy. This type of relocation offers the enemy the opportunity to attack while your own force is mobile, rather than entrenched. In this instance, Hood's relocation orders delayed his planned attack by nearly three and a half hours, which was long enough for the Union forces

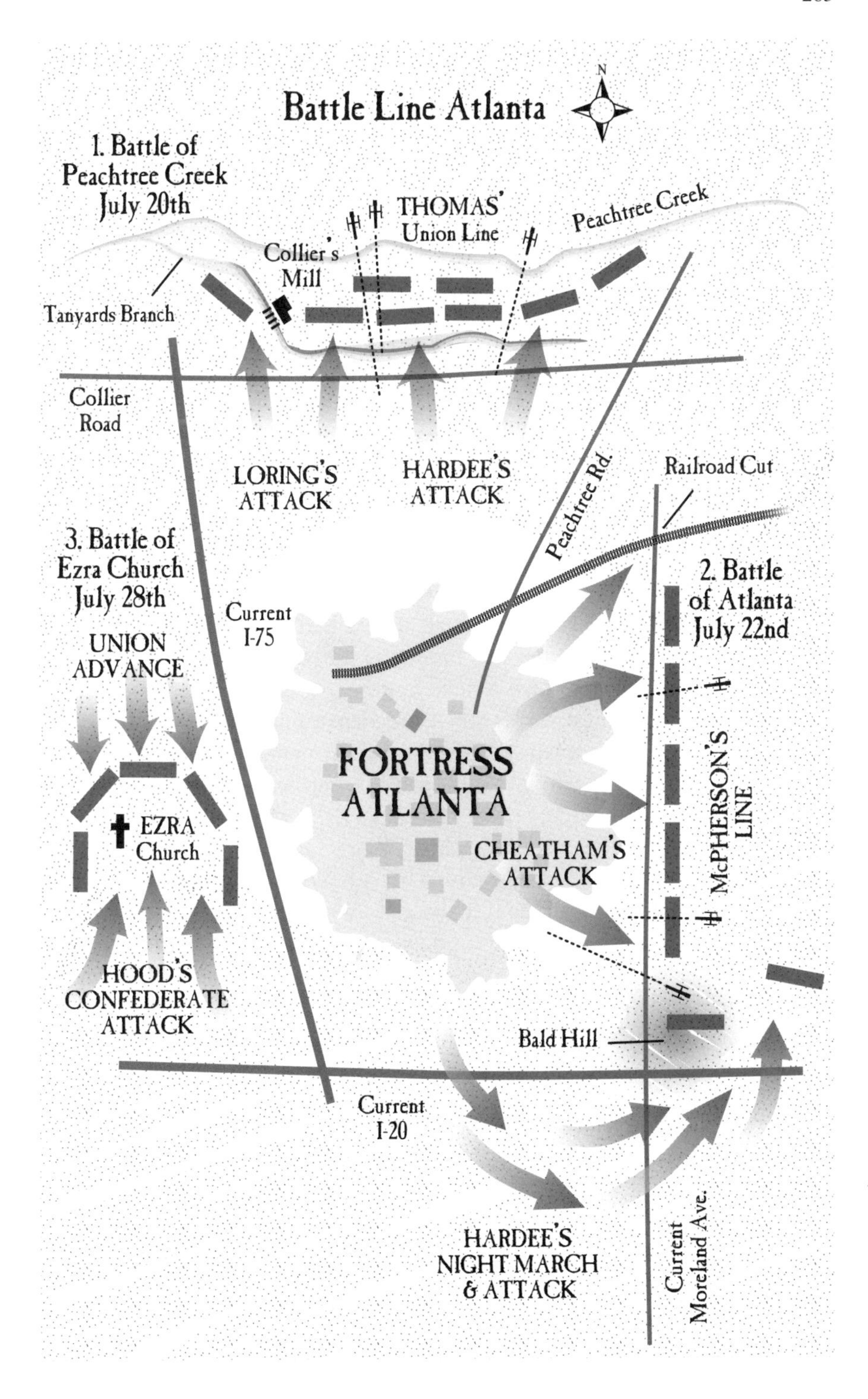
Battle Line Atlanta
N
1. Battle of
Peachtree Creek
July 20th
THOMAS'
Union Line
Peachtree Creek
Collier's
Mill
Tanyards Branch
Collier
Road
LORING'S
ATTACK
HARDEE'S
ATTACK
Peachtree Rd.
Railroad Cut
3. Battle of
Ezra Church
July 28th
Current
I-75
2. Battle
of Atlanta
July 22nd
UNION
ADVANCE
FORTRESS
ATLANTA
McPHERSON'S
LINE
EZRA
Church
CHEATHAM'S
ATTACK
HOOD'S
CONFEDERATE
ATTACK
Bald Hill
Current
I-20
HARDEE'S
NIGHT MARCH
& ATTACK
Current
Moreland Ave.

to capture a few prisoners from the foremost skirmish line. Those Confederates quickly let Thomas know that he was facing a massive Confederate force, equal in size to his entire Union army. Thus Thomas began to entrench as soon as any of his units crossed the creek. By early afternoon of July 20, with the sun beating down on two opposing armies, both time and opportunity for a successful Confederate attack were quickly slipping by.

Still Hood ordered that the attack begin and around 4:30 that afternoon, the men under Hardee moved into battle across from Thomas' Union forces, who were busily digging defensive works across Peachtree Road and roughly parallel to Colliers Road, about three-fourths of a mile south of Peachtree Creek itself. Just like Hood's aggressive advance at Kolb's Farm the previous month, he hoped to attack a moving enemy and instead his men found an enemy heavily entrenched. Of course Hood attacked anyway, with the full force of Hardee's Corps.

Collier's Grist Mill along Tanyards Creek was roughly at the center of the two mile Union line, and the Union brigade at that center location was commanded by a non-descript colonel named Benjamin Harrison. Harrison's command skills were nothing special, though his brigade did acquit itself well in the battle, standing firm against repeated attacks that afternoon. His role in the war would have been forgotten save for one significant fact. Ben Harrison later became the 23rd President of the United States.

Things quickly went wrong for the Confederacy once Hood's belated attack began. Hardee's Corps on the Confederate right demonstrated a comedy of errors, any one of which can, with some justification, be named as a major cause of the ultimate failure. First, one of Hardee's Divisions simply got lost in the thick woods well to the east of Peachtree Road, and failed to attack anyone, while another division dislodged a Union brigade along Collier Road. However, once they had the enemy on the run, those Confederates simply stopped in the hastily constructed Union trenches, and failed to pursue their enemy further.

Another Confederate force marched right into Peachtree Creek well north of the actual battle, and completely behind the left end of the Union line. Of course, that move represented a major opportunity for the Confederates, a chance to turn left and crush the enemy with a well-timed flanking attack, but given the confused, and recently changed orders, that Confederate division commander chose to do nothing. Those men—over five thousand Confederates—did little more than wade in Peachtree Creek for the rest of the day.

Confederates just to the west under General Walker did attack the end of the Union line while the boys in blue were still digging their defensive works along Peachtree Road. As Walker's men burst from the woods with a loud, glorious Rebel Yell, one of them called out "Here they are, boys! By God, there's a million of them!" It seemed for a time as if Walker's attack, alone among

Hardee's entire Corps, might result in a victory, but massed Union guns just behind Peachtree Creek, soon decimated that Confederate assault. Both shot and canister tore men and horses apart. In a fitting turn of history, Piedmont Hospital now occupies the site of that bloody carnage.

In all, Hardee's attack was a complete failure. Hardee's Corps, numbering over 15,000 men, confronted a Union force on that end of the Union line of only 3,200 men, yet failed to dislodge the men in blue.

In contrast Stewart's Corps on the Confederate left had much more initial success than did Hardee's men. One Confederate division, facing what they believed to be the Union left flank, attacked merely a small gap in the Union force. They quickly chased back the Union skirmish line and advanced eight hundred yards. One of Loring's Brigades on the end of that advance, the 22nd Mississippi led by General Featherston, charged the gap in the Union lines, but then got bogged down at Tanyards Branch, near the present bridge along Collier Road. Once out of the creek, they advanced through what was, in those days, open fields to attack the Union force to the front.

All the while, Featherston was looking for a supporting attack by the Confederates to his right, but hearing nothing from that quarter, he assumed there were no Union troops in that direction so he advanced his men anyway. They captured the Union defensive works to their front, but then discovered they had merely attacked a break in the Union line, and not the end of the line. They were quickly enveloped by enfilade fire from Union men on both sides. Featherston reported that Union "musketry and the artillery cut down many of my bravest and best officers and men." The unit was unable to reform so they retreated to the branch itself and, at one point those Confederates were shooting at Union troops to their front, their right, and even in their rear. They abandoned that position after only thirty minutes, and were driven back with substantial losses, taking positions along the "sunken road," which is today's Collier Road, near Tanyards Creek Park.

Virtually the same events played out all along Loring's Confederate advance across Tanyards Branch and toward Peachtree Creek. Men in grey and butternut would shout the Rebel Yell and advance, many times on unsuspecting Union brigades, and take some territory. Walthall's Confederate division moved way beyond other Confederates in the vicinity of today's Howell's Mill Road, to the north of Collier Road. To their front, the 123rd New York men were napping and playing cards, completed exposed. They had been told they had no enemy to their front, but they would soon learn one of the fundamentals of battle—things can change rather quickly. Those Union men were congratulating themselves on their great luck when they heard a rifle shot, followed by the fearsome Rebel Yell. They quickly formed a defensive line and returned fire, but were overrun by advancing Confederates within ten minutes.

Another Confederate unit was passing into a deep ravine to the east of Howell's Mill Road, with those Mississippi and Alabama troops yelling like demons. Their advance resulted in hand-to-hand fighting on the high ground. However, more Union forces arrived and soon the Confederates were forced back into the ravine by men in blue who now held the ridge top. Only a bit later, those Confederates, like the others, had to retrace their steps.

While rifle and cannon fire continued until dark, the battle had all but ended when all the units in Loring's Corps withdrew. As darkness came, the Confederates counted their losses, and realized they had very little to show for their effort. Confederates early in the advance, had captured most of the 33rd New Jersey Infantry, along with their battle flag, as well as a four gun Union artillery battery. However, no territory had been taken and held. Featherston's advance, at around 5:00 PM on June 20, 1864 marked the highpoint of the Confederate achievements that day, and those men, like the other Confederates had fallen back to their original lines.

Like many fights, historians have played out different potential outcomes for this battle. According to some, it was possible that the battle could have been a great Confederate victory. Had other Confederate units in Hardee's Corps supported Featherston's advance, it is quite possible that the Union front may have been broken in the middle with each end of the line destroyed before dusk on that summer day long ago. However history documents no such support from Hardee's Corps and for that, Hardee's leadership has been justifiably criticized, along with Hood's decisions to keep moving his lines to his right immediately prior to the battle. The result was that the Union line held, and Thomas' Army of the Cumberland was not destroyed. Further, General Hood soon needed his Confederate forces to confront other threats to Atlanta, so no follow-up fight the next morning was possible.

Because of Hood's aggression, coupled with his and Hardee's leadership decisions, the Confederates lost approximately 4,800 men in this fight, compared to only 1,780 men for the Union, and the Confederacy gained absolutely nothing. Of course, the Confederates could not sustain such losses, whereas, by that point in the war, men available for the Union cause seemed endless. In the end the dead and wounded lay everywhere, and one Union officer commented on the fierceness of the fight. "Few battlefields of the war have been strewn so thickly with many dead and wounded as they lay that evening around Collier's Mill."

While walking today in a beautiful residential area, one can see mothers with strollers in the small park at Tanyards Branch. Joggers use the greenway beside the gurgling creek, and trees, yards, and homes now cover the entire battlefield. Still it is interesting to contemplate the long-ago afternoon here that was anything but peaceful. Nearly sixty-eight hundred men, either dead or wounded, fell on this field during the Battle of Peachtree Creek. Like almost all of the battlefield sites from that war in the Atlanta area, the field itself is now gone, covered under various commercial businesses and housing subdivisions in Buckhead, a stylish area of northwest Atlanta. The site is marked by one park, Tanyard Creek Park, along Collier Road. There one can review many historic markers that provide some detail on the battle. Further, Piedmont Hospital in northwest Atlanta, now sits exactly astride the Union line at the corner of Peachtree Road and Collier Road. Hundreds of men died on what are now the hospital grounds.

## Continuous Battle: The Fight For Atlanta

If it seems that one battle followed immediately behind the next throughout the spring of 1864, that is accurate. Moreover, the pace of battle got worse as the armies neared Atlanta. The fight that has come to be called the Battle of Atlanta, took place only two days after the Battle of Peachtree Creek and as that timeframe indicates, the Confederates under General Hood were hard pressed to confront every threat to the city itself. Even as the fight at Peachtree Creek was ongoing a mile to the north of the Atlanta defensive works, Sherman's other Union armies were advancing on the city from the east against little to no Confederate opposition.

In fact, it is interesting to consider the situation of our fair city on July 21, 1864. The entire city was ringed with heavy Confederate defensive works, though each of the several battles in this continuous fight for the heart and soul of the city was fought outside of those works with the Confederate forces attacking the Union armies. At that point, the largest of the Union armies, the Army of the Cumberland under General Thomas, still faced the town from the north. Meanwhile, two Union armies, the Army of the Ohio under General Schofield and the Army of the Tennessee under General McPherson, numbering nearly fifty-thousand men together, were moving toward Atlanta from the east. That force alone was nearly equal to Hood's entire Confederate command.

Late on the night of July 20, after the futility of the Peachtree Creek fight was known, Major Jamie Turnbull was working on an after action report in Hood's headquarters. Therefore, he and several other lower ranking men heard the shouted, accusing recriminations among the Confederate commanders. All of Hood's commanders, Cheatham, Loring, and Hardee, were present, along with General Joe Wheeler in command of the Confederate cavalry. Both Loring and Hardee were blaming the other for the failure that afternoon at Peachtree Creek, and this did not make for a harmonious chat, as one might imagine.

After long, acrimonious discussions of who had done what wrong, Hood finally decided to change the topic to the next action, which was anticipated all too quickly. Thus began the highest level discussions of how Hood planned to continue the defense of Atlanta.

As Jamie pretended to write up the after action report at one end of the tent, he listened to Hood open the discussion around the table only fifteen feet away. "Gentlemen. Let us now consider our next action. I have been thinking of an action similar to Stonewall Jackson's victory at Chancellorsville several years ago. You gentlemen recall, of course, General Jackson's midnight march of fifteen miles around the end of the Union line, and the successful attack on the open Union flank. Jackson's Corps captured nearly five thousand Union prisoners in that fight, and I'm wondering if something similar might work in our situation."

Loring spoke up next. "My men, Sir, are still in those damn ravines and that wilderness up near Tanyards Branch just south of Peachtree Creek. We are still collecting our wounded. I do not believe I can undertake such an action within the next forty-eight hours at the very least. We must be nearly twenty miles from the lower end of the Union line southeast of town."

Cheatham spoke up next. "Perhaps we can shift my corps to the south and flank the lower end of the Union line. If General Hardee could move his men into my positions to hold that line, I think we have an opportunity to attack Schofield and McPherson before they receive any reinforcements from General Thomas. We could crush them, if we move immediately."

Jamie Turnbull watched the discussion at this point, as did every other man in that tent. There was nearly a minute of complete silence as General Hood gazed off toward the tent flap and reflected on his options. Hood was quickly learning a fundamental lesson learned by all battle commanders; command decisions take on a whole new dimension when you, yourself are in charge. When it is your own decision sending men into harm's way, indeed when your decision could win or lose the battle and perhaps the war, one tends to be somewhat more contemplative.

Meanwhile General Hardee felt a need to speak up. He knew that he was, inevitably to receive the lion's share of the blame for the failure at Peachtree Creek. After all, he had held an entire division in reserve in that fight and as it turned out, that division probably would have made a decisive difference. While that caution was based in part on Hood's shifting everyone's position on the field just before the fight, Hardee realized that no one ever advanced in an army by criticizing one's commander. Such criticism of high command must, of necessity, wait for the history books. In short, his failure at Peachtree Creek would be magnified, so in simple terms, it was his responsibility to do something.

In that frame of mind, Hardee spoke up. "General Hood. General Cheatham's Division is in a strong defensive position now with the enemy to their front. There is no need to sidestep this entire army. Rather, with some time, I can remove myself from the position north of town, and move through the downtown area. Within twenty-four hours, I could march south of town, and when I'm well off the field, I can turn my corps to the east and flank the Union position. Perhaps I could even get behind them."

Hood spoke up next. "You believe you could remove yourself in such a way that the enemy to your front doesn't realize you are gone?"

Loring spoke next. "That is possible, General Hood. I can extend my lines to take the place of Hardee's Corps in the line to the north, since that is a much shorter distance. We gave General Thomas a bloody nose yesterday, and I don't believe we will see any aggression from him. If we do, I'm sure my corps can, most certainly hold the northern line."

Hood was the next to speak. "I believe you are correct, General Loring, but I shall need more from you. I'd like to take your reserve forces, those regiments that did not fight at Peachtree Creek, and second them to General Hardee's force. I'm sure we'll need those men and their rifles in the coming fight."

Next General Hood turned in the direction of his cavalry commander, saying, "General Wheeler."

"Sir!" Wheeler said.

"You will take your cavalry to the south and precede General Hardee's Corps in this move. I want your horsemen to advance all the way into Decatur with Hardee's Corps following close behind, but you should move freely out to his front, rather than maintaining contact. With your four thousand cavalry, Hardee's Corps of thirteen-thousand men, and those additional regiments, we shall have a very large hammer and we shall strike a mighty blow on the left flank of the Union army in two days. That is a long march for your men, General Hardee, but you will not need to deploy a skirmish line, as you will be preceded by General Wheeler's men."

Hood paused for a moment, and then continued. "Yes indeed! We'll hit the damn Yankees just like Stonewall hit Hooker at Chancellorsville! And we shall anticipate the same result! God willing gentleman, we shall use this move to drive the damn Yankees away from Atlanta!"

Then Cheatham spoke once again. "General Hood. When that flank attack begins against McPherson's Union army I believe I should likewise advance my men. Perhaps we can break the back of Schofield's force at the same time General Hardee attacks McPherson's Union force. That will give Crazy Billy a severe headache at the very least!" All of the commanders smiled at that. To a man they truly believed that General Billy Sherman was, at least somewhat crazy, and like their men, they often referred to him as such.

General Hood then added the final important element to the battle plan. "Gentlemen, I believe we should constrict the area somewhat, so on the evening of July 21, I shall order General Cheatham to withdraw from his outer defensive position, and locate himself behind the inner defenses of Fortress Atlanta. In that fashion we shall have better communication, and perhaps we might confuse the enemy a bit in the process."

While there was some discussion of that idea, Hood wanted that withdrawal, and of course, he was giving the final orders. Other discussions continued for some time after that on various aspects of the attack, but the plan devised by Hood and fleshed out by his commanders, was ultimately set. Hardee's Corps, along with Wheeler's Cavalry, would march through Atlanta, swing wide to the south and leave the area by at least five miles. They would then turn to the east with the goal of flanking the Union army, or attacking that force from behind. At the same time, Cheatham would attack that Union force from the front. If they could destroy Schofield's and McPherson's Union armies, they could deal with Thomas' force to the north later.

## Continuous Battle: The Long Night-March

And that is why the Fourth Georgia Infantry, Major Jamie Turnbull commanding, found itself marching all night, along with the rest of Hardee's "attack hammer." On that day forty men (out of an original eighty nine) were still reporting for duty in the 34th Georgia Rifles, and only six hundred and forty-two (out of an original nine hundred and thirty) for the entire Fourth Georgia Infantry regiment. Still both the company of the original Tugalo River Valley men, and the regiment were considered very experienced, combat-ready units. While normally a part of Hood's Corps (it would always be known as Hood's Corps, thought it was now commanded by Loring), the Fourth Georgia Infantry had been held in reserve at Peachtree Creek and had never been committed to that battle. As a result, they were ordered to form ranks at 3:00 PM on July 21, and later that evening, they found themselves marching in the dark along with many other reserve units, that had been "seconded" to Hardee's Corps.

They had marched right through the center of Atlanta just before dusk on July 21, and for many of the Tugalo River Valley men, it was the first time in their lives that they had seen the city, a city which they had been defending for nearly a year. History records that few people, prior to that war, ever traveled further than the nearest large city. Many never traveled further than the nearest grist mill or tannery. Such was the life of the farmers turned soldiers in 1860.

By 4:00 AM they were well past the city, and to a man, they knew they were headed into a fight, but they had no understanding of the role they were to play in the coming battle to the east of the Atlanta perimeter. Only Jamie Turnbull, riding in front of his men, and nearly asleep astride his horse, understood the overall plan.

"Major Turnbull, Sir!" Duncan said to his commander and friend riding just ahead. Duncan was tired of walking, and apparently wanted a bit of "play" to keep himself awake. "Would the Major mind telling us where in hell we're a'goin? Fer as we've marched, I think we might'n be a commin' near to Savannee! Or are we marchin' all the way to Washington City?"

Several men laughed and none took offence. Still Collins wanted to protect his sleeping commander so he felt he should say something to the exhausted men behind him. He rose to his commander's defense. "Just you 'll never mind where we 'r a' going! I'm sure they'll be plenty o' Yanks for you to shoot at when we get there! Let the Major sleep, best he can, and keep your ideas and your damn questions to yourself, Carmichael!"

Duncan merely increased the volume of his voice. "Sorry, Cap'n. I was just a wonderin' if'n we might rest, an' maybe even sit a spell. Must be damn near ten thousand men walking through here tonight, and I promise you, every damn man in this line needs to take a piss!"

With that, many more men laughed and Jamie was, by that point, slightly more awake. As he smiled at the laughter of his friends, he decided a bit of humor and maybe even a small break were good ideas. He spoke up next. "Cap'n Collins. It has been my experience that two animals never seem to know where in hell they are. Both of 'um get lost all the time, unless you really watch 'um. It is a natural born fact; you can't plough a straight row with either a jackass or a Carmichael. Neither one pulls a plough too well, 'cause they never know where they're going!"

Even more men were laughing and smiling at that point, including Duncan Carmichael himself. Men heading into battle always seem to want two things; a tested and proven battle commander, and a few jokes to relieve the stress.

"Yes Sir!" replied Collins with a grin. "Both are stupid and neither 'll follow a plough worth a damn!"

Everyone in the first company in the line behind Major Turnbull heard the friendly banter between their commander and the sergeant of the first company. All understood that to be chatter between pre-war friends, and to a man, they were glad, once again, to be commanded by Major Turnbull.

After the laughter died down, Jamie said, "On the other hand, Cap'n Collins. Once in a while a Carmichael will have a good idea. Let's take a fifteen minute break in that next field up yonder." I don't think General Hardee will mind too much. He knows we had four extra miles to walk tonight compared to most of his corps, since we had to come all the way from the west end of Peachtree

Creek. These men do need a break." Jamie was sure of that last statement. He was completely exhausted, and he'd been riding all night and not walking like his men.

That extra marching distance had resulted in the regiment being located behind Hardee's Corps on the long trek. Even if the few regiments behind Turnbull's men took a break, the main force out front would not be delayed at all.

Collins smiled and shouted. "Yes Sir! A break it is! All companies. Fifteen minute break when we reach the field up yonder. All men to remain with your companies." Collins knew the last part of the order was almost meaningless. At least half the men would take a bathroom break over in the edge of the woods, and some would linger and talk to friends. Still, the final order might cause most of the regiment to relocate with their own company after attending to their needs in the woods.

As Major Turnbull reached the far end of the open field, he dismounted, as did Sampson, who quickly took the reins of both of their horses. Collins was left on his mount, and Jamie spoke to him. "Let's see if we can get 'um up and moving again before we get cursed at by someone important. Give 'um thirty minutes here, then we'll move again. Now get down to the end of the field, Mr. Collins, and make sure no one is blocking the road. Those units behind us may not need to stop."

"Yes Sir. I'll see to it. Now you rest a bit!" Collins replied.

When Captain Collins returned, Jamie was sitting with his original outfit, the 34th Georgia Rifles. Most of those men were his childhood friends, Lem Davis, Sampson, and Duncan Carmichael, sat in the same circle, along with others they had gotten to know during the war, Lee Lovorn, Ten Cent Bill, and the others. This time, the men's questions were a bit more serious. Lee Lovorn spoke up first. "Major, can you tell us what we might be expecting ahead?"

Turnbull, once again among friends and battle tested veterans, knew that whatever he said would spread throughout the regiment in less than half an hour. On the other hand, it didn't make any difference, since it was no secret the unit was advancing into an attack position. "We're going up the road yonder, and see if we can catch the blue-bellies sleeping! We might try and get around the end of 'um and attack their flank or raise a little hell with their supply lines."

Lee spoke next. "Might be a good time, if'n we can get behind 'um. Do you recon we've marched far enough?"

Collins answered. "Not by a long shot. I sometimes think Crazy Billy's army just goes on and on!" At that all the man smiled. Many had suspected that the supply of Yankees was endless in many previous fights.

Turnbull then added a comment. "If anybody can do it, I recon General

Hood can. He is one impressive man, what there is left of him." All the men smiled, realizing that Hood had been wounded a number of times, and seemed to lose body parts with each succeeding battle. After a moment, Jamie continued. "Now let's rest our eyes for just a few minutes, before we have to move again."

Immediately after he finished that sentence, a loud snore was heard, and several men smiled. Off to the side, Duncan Carmichael was sleeping like a new-born babe!

## Wheeler's Attack in Decatur

On the morning of July 22, 1864, General Sherman had received reports that the Confederates were evacuating the city of Atlanta. In that fashion, did a part of General Hood's plan work. Hood's retreat from the outer defensive line to the inner line did cause some early confusion among the Union commanders. Sherman ordered his men to hold in place until their cavalry could find the enemy. However, this illusion was quickly shattered when everyone heard a major fight developing out to the east, well behind the Union lines.

Thus the opening of the Battle of Atlanta actually took place in Decatur, Georgia some ten miles to the east of the city. That is where McPherson's Union supply train had been located, so that is where General Joseph Wheeler's Confederate Cavalry hit their enemy. Wheeler's Cavalry had left Atlanta just before Hardee's Corps had marched through town, with the express orders to capture the Union supplies if possible. Wheeler was then supposed to fight his way back into the city, assisting with Hardee's assault on the Union left flank. Just as Major Turnbull ordered his men to resume their march in the early morning hours of July 22, 1864, the sound of an intense battle was heard somewhere up the road. Both rifle fire and cannon were heard, as the men in Turnbull's regiment marched along toward the sound of the fight.

General Joseph Wheeler had taken the old Fayetteville Road out of Atlanta, while Hardee's column took the somewhat shorter, Flat Shoals Road. With his men mounted, Wheeler had reached his objective, the town of Decatur, first and he immediately attacked the Union men guarding the supply trains. The Union men saw the attacking horsemen streaming into the city, and realizing they were outnumbered, those blue-bellies put up only token resistance for thirty minutes or so and then fled in mass, back to the north. After all, who expected any Confederates to attack this far away from Atlanta?

However those Union men did fight just long enough to reverse the train engines on the two loaded supply trains along those tracks. For that reason, General Wheeler and his men watched as their quarry escaped back to the north. He had failed in his mission to capture the Union supplies of food and munitions. Still Wheeler had his men dismount and entrench around the town square and the old courthouse, to await further developments. At that point, there was no sound of battle behind him so he rightly surmised that Hardee had not yet reached his attack point, and it would have been suicide for his entire force to attack the entire Union army alone, with no infantry or cannon support.

In fact Hardee's march had been very slow. Several of Hardee's units had just left a major fight at the east end of Peachtree Creek only one day previously, and those men were desperately tired. Of course, men on both sides in that war were by that point, very tough, lean men. While large units could normally march fifteen to twenty miles in a day, no commander would normally contemplate such a move only one day after a major battle. Still Hardee's men, while exhausted, managed to march with their fellows the fifteen miles around the end of the Union line, but it was very slow going.

## The Battle of Atlanta

The joint attack by Hardee and Wheeler was originally scheduled for the early morning of July 22, but the slow advance of Hardee's Corps resulted in significant delays. Of course, General Hardee knew he was behind schedule, and he had heard the fighting up toward Decatur begin and end earlier in the day. While he knew he was not nearly far enough along to totally encircle his enemy, he decided to turn north anyway where he hoped to catch the Union left flank un-entrenched.

They succeeded! When Hardee's Corps reached the Union position, they quickly became aware that they were attacking the open flank of the Union line. While the Union men had dug some entrenchments, they were all facing the city of Atlanta and not in the direction of Hardee's Confederate attack coming from the southeast. One end of Hardee's force had, luckily, hit a half-mile gap at the end of the Union flank.

Still not every Union commander was a fool. While Crazy Billy was sure there were no Confederates to the south of his position, General McPherson was not nearly as confident. Thus McPherson had ordered one of his Union corps, led by General Granville Dodge, to encamp about a mile behind and slightly to the rear of the main Union line, as a protection against just the sort of flanking move the Confederates were attempting. This created a gap between the open Union flank and Dodge's Union Corps, and while that small Union corps was hopelessly outnumbered by Hardee's massive force, they did put up an intense rear-guard type of action.

Turnbull's men had been the last to reach the fight and were thus, placed along the far end of the line, where they came directly up against Dodge's Union force. As soon as the men in Turnbull's regiment broke through the woods, they came under fire from a regiment of Yankees who only ten minutes previously, had been in the process of making and eating a late lunch. The fighting began in earnest around 1:30 in the afternoon. The unit had flushed three deer from the woods, and those terrified animals fled the field to the east. As Turnbull's men moved forward in two lines, the Union men scrambled to find any cover they could. Once in the open, Turnbull himself shouted, "Okay boys. Let 'um hear that yell like they never heard it before! Charge!"

Thus did over seven thousand Confederates in the Fourth Georgia, and all of Hardee's other units charge into the Union line. After firing one volley, the Confederates continued to move forward with the Rebel Yell tearing out among them like a battle wind. While many Union men responded with fire from their repeating rifles, all were terrified and their line began to give way. Because that Union line was not grounded by entrenched positions, the battle became fluid quickly. The sound was nearly overpowering, the cannon loud and continuous, and the fighting soon dissolved into hand-to-hand confrontations. Both Confederate and Union cannon fired nearly point blank into their foes, when such shots were available. At other times, the armies were simply too close to fire at all.

The fighting was as intense as Jamie had ever seen, and it seemed to last forever; ten minutes, twenty, thirty? Jamie couldn't tell, but time seemed warped somehow into the reality of a deathly fight. A brown mare tore by with blood on its hindquarters, its eyes showing the terror that every living entity on that field felt at that moment. Jamie and Captain Collins were mounted, and both were surrounded as usual, by Turnbull's man Sampson, Lee Lovorn, Lem Davis, and a few others. Jamie fired his pistol whenever a target presented itself, but the others wouldn't let him engage hand-to-hand if they could prevent it. Twenty feet to the right, Lovorn had just broken his rifle stock against the head of a man from Michigan, hearing both the crack of the wood, and a satisfying squish of the cracked skull. Men in any to-the-death fight think of such things as sounding sweet, but they don't dwell on such thoughts for too long. Ten Cent Bill calmly fired his repeating rifle then paused to frisk a dead Union man at his feet, for more ammunition. That man never missed a chance to steal something from a dead Yankee.

Jamie shouted to Collins, "Get yourself toward the other end of the unit and take charge there. Keep the men moving forward and don't waste too many men guarding any prisoners. We need 'um all. Make sure you don't get too far ahead of that Louisiana Regiment on our right flank either. We damn sure don't want to fight this one alone!"

"Sir," was all Collins could answer, while tearing into a powder bag with his teeth. Still, when he finished reloading his pistol, he galloped off to the other end of the regiment.

Jamie's rank of major did not yet allow him to have an adjunct officer, but every man in the regiment knew that the best knife-fighter in either army was Turnbull's personal body guard. Carmichael wouldn't be too far from Major Turnbull and sure enough, Duncan was fighting with his knife in one hand and an axe in the other. He'd discarded his rifle after hooking his long bayonet into the spine of a Union man only a few minutes before. He left it there when it proved too hard to extract, since the fighting nearby demanded his immediate attention. God only knew where Duncan had come up with an axe on that battlefield, but God was probably smart enough not to ask any Carmichael where he got his weapons. Jamie smiled in the middle of the fight at that thought, and then he figured that he wouldn't ask either. Then just for moment, Jamie was reminded of the fight at Chickamauga when a Cherokee warrior with a battle axe had saved his life. Sometimes history does repeat itself.

Wilson shouted then, bringing Jamie back to the fight before him. "Looks like they might have had enough for now, Sir!" When Jamie turned to Wilson, the young man was grinning from ear to ear, but his mouth was covered with black powder, making his teeth shine all the brighter. He was smiling and pointing to the north.

Jamie looked across the field and, at least in his area, the Union men were disengaging, and moving quickly back toward the next tree line nearly a hundred yards away. Many of those men paused long enough to grab a wounded man from the field, if they happened to pass near one. The cannon continued to roar and pour their blue-grey smoke onto the battlefield, making the retreating Union men seem like ghosts moving across some swamp in the early morning.

Then Jamie saw a lone figure, a Union officer, atop a white horse ride purposefully onto the field about two hundred yards to his left. The man road directly into a group of Confederates, and then seemed to instantly realize his mistake. When the Confederates demanded he dismount, the officer tipped his hat, reared his horse, and then charged like a banshee back toward his own men. Jamie actually spoke out loud to himself. "Brave but stupid. He should have surrendered. That idiot won't reach the tree line alive." Even before Jamie heard the collection of rifle shots, he saw that officer fall dead in the no man's land between the two armies. Several Union men rushed out to grab the officer, and Jamie took a second to wish him well, thinking that maybe he was just wounded.

Thus General McPherson, Commander of the Army of the Tennessee, died. He had ridden directly into the gap in the Union lines, thinking there was a solid line of Union men in front of him. He paid the ultimate price for that mistake. Of course, this was the very same Commander that General Sherman had used so often as his strong right hook against the Confederate army in north Georgia. At both Rocky Face and Resaca, Sherman had ordered this man to move scores of miles away from the battle in order to force a Confederate retreat. Even here on this battle line in Atlanta, McPherson's army was the end of the Union line, but there is always some confusion toward the end of the battle line and in this case, that confusion cost McPherson his life. Within an hour word had been delivered to Sherman himself of McPherson's death. Crazy Billy sat down, then and there, and cried.

The Confederate regiments near the right end of the Confederate advance were almost indistinguishable. Confederates were mixed in various groups, but they had overrun several Union positions and captured a few of the Union Parrott rifled cannon, which they quickly turned on the retreating Union troops. However only five hundred yards away, a portion of the Union line still held, though they were now surrounded on three sides. Such was the fighting in the Battle of Atlanta; confused, dangerous, and fluid. Few commanders who were not on the battlefield had any clue as to what was happening, and Jamie soon realized it would take some time to sort the men out into fighting units once again. Meanwhile they had to expect a counter attack by the boys in blue who were, even at that moment, in the tree line across the field, busily sorting out their own units.

Suddenly realizing that he was a sitting duck for any Union sharpshooter who might be around, Jamie nevertheless decided to remain mounted and take a quick look over the entire battlefield as the fighting nearest to him died down a bit. It was by then midafternoon, but Jamie was under no illusions that his day was over. Cannon on both sides were firing in the distance, and Jamie could hear firing all along a line that seemed to go on for miles out to his left, as he faced the retreating Yankees. The main lines of battle had formed into an L shape, with Hardee's advance forming the lower part of the letter, and Cheatham's attack forming the upright of the letter L off to Jamie's left. Jamie knew that Cheatham's Division was attacking all along that line, and he could see a fierce hand-to-hand fight taking place on a rise above him about a mile away. The fiercest fighting was centered at Bald Hill, a small rise several miles east of the city that sat at the lower corner of the L shaped battle line.

Further to the north Cheatham's troops had broken through the Union lines at the Georgia Railroad tracks by fighting their way along a "cut" or depression in a hill through which the tracks ran. As elsewhere the Rebel Yell seemed to carry the Confederate line forward, even in the face of deadly Union fire, until the men in that section of the field were, like those to the south, fighting hand-to-hand. The Confederates had won the territory around the railroad cut for a time but then General Sherman himself, who had camped behind that end of the Union line, assembled twenty artillery pieces and fired on the Confederates in the railroad cut. Sherman himself commanded the Union bombardment for some time, while his staff prepared a counter attack against that position. In the face of such devastating bombardment, the Confederates could not hold and by nightfall, the railroad cut was once again in Union hands.

At 4:45 or so the Union forces emerged from the tree line in front of Major Turnbull and the Fourth Georgia Infantry, who had spent the best part of the last hour, busily digging. While the defenses weren't deep, they did provide a place to hide while his men returned fire and there were, by then several more Confederate cannon on the field arrayed just behind the line. Captain Collins, ever the forward thinking commander, had made certain that every man had replenished his ammunition and that any captured rounds for the repeaters were provided to Confederates who'd been lucky enough to find one. While the firing lasted for nearly an hour it was, at best, only a half-hearted attempt by the Yankees to retake their positions, and as darkness approached, the Union men once again, withdrew to the north. However, the Bald Hill had changed hands once again, and as the sun set, Union men were atop that rise in the middle of the battlefield.

Fighting all along the battle line died after dark, with each army remaining in place for a time. While Confederates had taken some Union cannon and several Yankee positions, the Union forces had retaken both Bald Hill and the railroad cut to the north. Only in Hardee's section of the battlefield had the Confederates gained and kept any ground. Still that was no real victory. Hood's intent had been to totally destroy McPherson's Union Army of the Tennessee, and perhaps the Army of the Ohio to the north as well. Neither had been accomplished, leaving Hood still facing three massive Union armies that outnumbered his Confederates more than two to one. By midnight, Hood had recalled all of his forces, including Hardee's Corps from the south and Wheeler's Cavalry from Decatur, leaving nothing to show for the fight, save the dead and dying.

## Author's Note: Another Buried Battlefield

Like the battlefield at Peachtree Creek, the field for the Battle of Atlanta has been buried under the ever expanding city. The upright of the L shaped battle line reached from just south of the current location of the Carter Presidential Center and roughly follows today's Moreland Avenue to just below the intersection of Moreland Avenue and Interstate 20. Then the line turned in a slow arc to the east, with Glenwood Avenue roughly representing the bottom of the L shaped field. The railway cut that Cheatham's men attacked was near the present Metro station just south of the Carter Presidential Center, and the rail line in that location still follows the general route it followed during the Battle of Atlanta in 1864.

Two miles further south, the Bald Hill was the prominent feature at the bottom of the L shaped battle line. It was renamed Leggett Hill, for the Union General Mortimer Leggett, the man who defended it during the fight. The hill was once part of a ridge along which the present day Moreland Avenue runs, but the hill itself was partially taken down with the building of the interchange of Moreland Avenue and Interstate 20. Part of the ridge is located slightly north of I-20 and a few feet east of the present-day Moreland Avenue. While the remaining rise today is non-descript and covered with the I 20 interchange and strip malls, the spot is still worthy of some reflection. On that very spot under that very busy, modern day overpass, men once engaged in a desperate hand-to-hand fight, and over two thousand men died.

Today Alonzo Crim High School on Clifton Street is located where Hardee's Confederate Corps initially emerged and confronted Dodge's Union Corps. That locale today abounds with historic markers about the battle. Still since little was accomplished here, nothing remains of the hasty defenses that were once scattered through those woods and rolling hillsides.

The Union lost approximately 2,600 men in the battle while Confederate casualties were much higher. Confederates at that point, were less exact in counting losses but most historians suggest that nearly 5,500 boys in grey were lost in the Battle of Atlanta. However, even those one-sided figures do not tell of the real failure for the Confederate cause. For the second time in two days, General Hood had launched a massive attack against an entrenched foe and suffered horrendous loses, men whom he could not replace. Further, he had failed to destroy either wing of Sherman's giant Union force, so he still confronted three, tested, battle-ready Union armies.

General Sherman, known to be a man who rarely commented on casualties, seemed unconcerned with those ghastly numbers. Still he did actively mourn the loss of his young protégée, General McPherson. It was more than the fact that McPherson was the highest ranking Union officer lost during the entire war. Sherman's despair was deeply personal. In his official report he spoke of McPherson, and his respect, even his love for the man was obvious.

*"McPherson's enemies, even the men who directed the fatal shot, ne'er spoke or wrote of him without expressions of marked respect; those whom he commanded loved him even to idolatry; and I, his associate and commander, fail in words*

*adequate to express my opinion of his great worth. I feel assured that every patriot in America, on hearing this sad news, will feel a sense of personal loss, and the country generally will realize that we have lost, not only an able military leader, but a man who, had he survived, was qualified to heal the national strife which has been raised by designing and ambitious men."*

Never before or since did General Sherman so praise anyone, including his own mentor and close personal friend, General U. S. Grant.

In one final historic irony, the Battle of Atlanta as that fight came to be known, was ultimately misnamed. It was fought outside of Atlanta, and not in the city or even near the Atlanta defenses. It was neither the first nor the last fight around the city, and it didn't result in Atlanta falling to the Union. In fact, there was no mention of any significant victory noted by the Yankee press relative to that fight, since the Union forces had failed to dislodge Hood's Confederate forces. Still today the name stands in history suggesting that this desperate fight actually accomplished something. It didn't.

## A Letter from Home

*Major Jamie Turnbull, Commander*
*Fourth Georgia Infantry*
*Atlanta Station for Delivery to Hood's Corps, CSA*

*My dearest husband. I've been feeling somewhat ill of late, as I told you in my letter several days ago, and it was Aunt Fanny Bricebud, that marvelous woman of ours, who finally told me what was wrong! We are to have a child! You will be a father sometime next winter, perhaps around Christmas!*

*Apparently, when women are in a family way, they begin to have some mild feelings of sickness each morning of which Aunt Fanny was aware. She giggled like a child when she told me that she had "reckoned on" my having a baby. You should have seen her grin!*

*Of course, I feel that we have certainly been blessed with this wonderful news, and I so wish I could share it with you in a more personal moment. I do miss you so. Still you are wherever you are, and I am, as always, at Traveler's Rest.*

*Now I do not want you worrying about this one little bit! I will be fine, here in the care of my family. I have summoned the doctor, and all is well. He ordered me to do less work around the house so I guess I'll read more, and perhaps write a bit. As you might guess Meely and Aunt Fanny are both bending over backwards to take care of me, along with tending to Grandfather.*

*Alas, Grandfather Jarrett seems to grow a bit weaker each week, and he can no longer control the movement of his right arm or his leg. He spends most of his time in bed, but does occasionally sit in the rocking chair on the porch in the evenings. He is slurring his words when he speaks, and I understand him only with some difficulty. To make matters worse, he seems to get quite frustrated when he cannot make himself easily understood. It is so sad to watch a once commanding man such as Grandfather Devereaux as he weakens. He cursed openly the other evening as we sat on the porch after dinner, but would not say why. He then insisted on going to his rooms, and only the next morning did Aunt Fanny say that he'd "lost control of himself," (in his bowels).*

*I continue to speak with him some each afternoon, and read to him some poems or a few Bible verses. I do not tell him much of the news at this point, since so much of the news is not good. He gets so angry if I read the news about the war that I've taken to pretending that we have no recent newspapers, and I really think that is best, at least for now.*

*I did ask him last week if he had other things to share about the fire-eaters, or things that he would like me to understand about the war. He looked at me for some time and then, while he slurred his words, I believe he said, "Just tell them. Tell the damn Yankees the truth about why we are fighting!" Then he turned his head away, toward the wall, and I believe I saw him crying a bit. He then said he wished to sleep and ordered me out of the room. I didn't want to inquire any further, since he seemed to get so agitated. Still, I think, I truly feel that he wants posterity to know that the fire-eaters truly fight for their freedom from a tyrannical government in Washington City. In his mind, that is what this terrible war has always been about; whether to live as slaves under a government that takes one's property, or to live as free men. Perhaps I'm reading more into his mood than I should, but he knows that I've been sending you my scribblings, and that seems to make him happy. I do believe he wants that story told.*

*Again, I do not know how well he will recover, or if he will, but he is still among the living today, on July 21, as I write these lines. I thank our most merciful God for that. I will certainly keep you advised of any changes. I do love him so, and I know you feel the same.*

*I've had increasing concerns about Meely, since my last letter. I went to shop over in South Carolina for a couple of days and when I returned, I learned that Meely had been gone for three whole days, apparently with no pass for her travel at all! She was supposedly visiting a sick aunt in Cleveland. She was back at Traveler's Rest when I arrived, and she has certainly been keeping up with her work since then. She tends Grandfather so lovingly! Still, I begin to wonder more and more about that young gal. Does she have a lover somewhere off the plantation? Is that the reason for her absence? Is she helping slaves escape? How can I ever find out?*

*Of course, that is my concern and not yours. I want you focused only on the job at hand. For I am sure that no soldier who is overly concerned about an expecting wife or possible trouble with his house slaves can keep himself safe in the midst of a battle, and you Sir, must remain safe! You now have not only a wife to be concerned with, but a new and growing family as well! God is indeed most generous in his blessings to us!*

*Meanwhile do remember to write, and let me know of your safety. Alas, I know not where my husband is on this night! I have heard that Hood's Corps has moved into Atlanta after a great victory at Kennesaw Mountain outside of Marietta, but why would Johnston move the army if he won? Beyond that I know very little. There was some rumor that General Johnston had been replaced, but I'm sure that this could not be the case! Anyway, I do hope that General Johnston can keep the damn Yankees out of Atlanta, as all of our mail seems to come from there. I would be afraid that I could not write to you should Atlanta be lost.*

*I always seem to await the very end of my letters to thee, before I tell you of my deepest love for my wonderful, gallant husband! If anything could make me any happier to be your wife, or any prouder to be carrying your child, I'm sure I do not know what that might be! I would so treasure a touch of your hand on my shoulder, or a soft kiss on my neck on this night!*

*Be most careful my love, and come home to me soonest.*

*Your Mary*
*Traveler's Rest Plantation*
*Tugalo River Valley, Georgia*

## At the Campfire, Fortress Atlanta

Jamie was sitting around the fire, reading his most recent letter from Mary. He hadn't even told his friends the big news about his wife's pregnancy. While men who face battle repeatedly together always seem to know each other intimately, somehow Jamie wanted to hold that news for himself, at least for a day or so. He thought of it as his personal treasure, and he felt himself smiling deep inside, as he lay by the fire listening with one ear to the usual campsite banter.

As the pans and plates were taken up from their communal supper of beans, Duncan farted loudly, and giggled like a schoolboy. As the others cursed him, he just replied, "Awe, just shut up, and let's talk about something important. I wonder how long General Hood might let us rest this time. I mean, maybe we could march twenty or twenty-five miles tonight too, and then hit them Yankees again in the morning!"

Most of the men laughed, as they sat around the fire near Fort Walker, in what is today Grant Park. They were manning the Confederate defensive works to the southeast of the city, having moved back into the works from their attack point the day before. It had been three days since the Battle of Atlanta, and neither army seemed to want to be too quick to do anything.

Lovorn spoke up next. "Say, Sarge! Don't go givin' the good general any ideas now! He might just make us do it!"

Ten Cent Bill tossed back a shot of the home-made liquor that he'd gotten somewhere in town, and then spat a bit toward the fire, causing something of a flame-up, as the alcohol caught the flames. "Don't want to be too quick to move into a fight again. Dem damn repeating rifles are hell to face in a fight. Some of dem boys in de First Alabama said they could' a held that Bald Hill a few days ago, if'n dem damn Yankees didn't have dem repeatin' rifles."

Lem spoke up next. Ignoring Ten Cent Bill's comment he responded to Carmichael. "Lovorn's right, Duncan. Don't go givin' any ideas to Gen'l Hood, lessen' you want to march all night again tonight!" They all laughed.

Captain Collins spoke up next. "I wonder what the good general might have in store for us, all the same. We can't just spend the rest of the war sittin' here, with them damned Yankees out there sittin' comfortably around their campfires. You boys seem to worry about the repeater rifles, but for me it's the damn Union cannon. Those Union Parrott cannon are accurate to damn near two miles, and they shell us every damn night! Half of Atlanta is living in their root cellars, and them city folks ain't used to living underground like that!"

Such were the reflections of the war-weary men of the Fourth Georgia Infantry, reflections that were no doubt shared by men on the other side of the

Fortress Atlanta defenses. Like all warriors between battles, they simply rested, played cards, raced their lice, prayed, visited the whores behind the lines, or merely joked with each other, as they waited for the killing to begin again.

## Continuous Battle: Ezra Church

By July 26 only four days after the Battle of Atlanta, the Union lines around the city had taken the shape of an inverted U. General Thomas' massive Army of the Cumberland, still to the north and reaching downward to the northwest of Atlanta, had joined the Union line with Schofield's Army of the Ohio east of Atlanta. Schofield's small army, in turn, connected with McPherson's Army of the Tennessee, which was now commanded by General Oliver Howard. In that fashion, some eighty-five thousand Union men looked directly down on the defensive works of Fortress Atlanta, a city guarded by only forty thousand Confederates. Even as the bulk of the armies remained stationary, the Union army brought in its biggest guns and shelled the city daily. But that was not Crazy Billy's only strategy. Sherman soon began to extend his hold around the western side of the city.

Unlike Sherman, General Hood was always ready to launch a brave, frontal attack on prepared defenses, and therein lay the reason for the vast disparity in armed men in each force. Hood had used up nearly one fourth of his entire army at Peachtree Creek and the Battle of Atlanta, launching nearly suicidal attacks on entrenched positions. He had accomplished absolutely nothing.

Meanwhile Sherman was considering his next move, and reluctant as always to even consider a frontal attack on Fortress Atlanta, he decided to starve out his enemy. If he could cut the few remaining railroad lines leading into Atlanta, Hood would not be able to feed his forty thousand men, not to mention the ten thousand or so citizens that were still in the city.

Thus only several days after the Battle of Atlanta, Sherman gave his orders to his newly appointed commander of the Army of The Tennessee, General Oliver Howard. Howard was instructed to take his army, which was still encamped to the east of the city, pull away from his entrenchments, and head to the north. He would circle behind the entire Union line to the north of Atlanta, and then extend the inverted U of the Union line down the west side of the city, reaching one of the two final railroads that supplied the city of Atlanta and Hood's Confederate army. Howard was ordered to cut that railroad somewhere between East Point and Atlanta.

Of course moving any horse drawn army took some time, and these fights took place at least one hundred years before anyone ever considered building a perimeter highway. In those days, every road led directly into Atlanta rather than around the city, so Howard was forced to use side roads and even single-cart dirt tracks in a haphazard pattern to move his army. Still, his route roughly traced today's perimeter highway, Interstate 285. Over a four day period, Howard moved up the east side of Atlanta, then moved west and finally, south on the west side of the city. Meanwhile, Schofield's Union force extended their lines to replace Howard's men on the east side of town.

Hood heard of the plan within two days and quickly realized he had to protect his last rail lines at all costs. Thus did the Battle of Ezra Church, just to the west of Fortress Atlanta, take shape. The fighting began in the afternoon of July 28, 1864. However, the Fourth Georgia Infantry was not involved in that fight, so Major Jamie Turnbull would only learn of the fight the next morning, when he wrote the after action report at General Hood's headquarters.

*To: President Jefferson Davis,*
*Richmond, VA*

*My Good Sir:*

*I beg to report a sharp, successful action on this day, July 28, 1864 on the western side of our Atlanta defenses, approximately two miles beyond our defensive perimeter. As reported earlier, the Union force under General Howard has been moving down the western side of town for some time, and was attempting to reach the East Point and Macon Railroad which currently supplies my army. I determined to oppose this move and sent two corps under Lt. Gen. Stephen D. Lee and Lt. Gen. Alexander P. Stewart, to stop the Union advance. We had the advantage of using the rail line to get our troops into the field more quickly, while the Yankees had to use back roads around the north of the city. Our forces met the enemy at 2:00 PM and fought until darkness ended the action. The enemy was by then entrenched, but through multiple advances, our men were able to stop Howard in his tracks. Unfortunately our losses were heavy, with just over 4,100 men dead or wounded, one of which was General Stewart, who was wounded most grievously in his chest. We spent the evening removing our wounded into our hospitals in Atlanta.*

*Still our objective was accomplished. We stopped Howard, protected the rail line, and captured four Parrott rifled cannon, and nearly four hundred prisoners.*

*I'm also sure we inflicted many additional losses on the Union army, though I have no count to present to you. Howard is now entrenching in place, and his lines are some five miles removed from the railroad. He cannot shell the railroad from his position. Of course, I will keep you posted of further advances, but I anticipate no further action in this quarter any time soon.*

*Your Obedient John Bell Hood, Commanding*
*Army of Tennessee, Atlanta, Georgia*
*(Report Prepared by Major Jamie Turnbull,*
*Hood's Corps, Army of Tennessee, CSA)*

## The Siege of Atlanta

And that is when the "waiting time" began, a month long siege of Atlanta. For nearly four weeks from July 28 until the end of August, both armies and over ten thousand civilians in Atlanta simply waited.

Of course, the Confederates under General Hood had no other option but to wait. Hood could take no further action since each battle depleted his forces even more. In just over ten days, he had managed to cut his army from 55,000 men to 40,000. In the three fights, Peachtree Creek, the Battle of Atlanta, and Ezra Church, Hood had lost 15,000 men, nearly one third of his entire army!

As they awaited further developments, the civilian population of Atlanta not to mention the entire Confederate army, continued to move underground. Crazy Billy and his Union artillerymen were shelling the city day and night from cannon batteries all along the lines, so no location in the city was safe from cannon fire. While Hood became concerned with supplies for his army—beans, hogs, ammunition, cannon shot, Sherman seemed to have ammunition to waste, and he intended to use every bit of it! Within only two weeks, rations for the Confederates had been cut five times, and many citizens were forced to eat their horses, cattle, and even their pet dogs. Sugar, milk, fresh bread, coffee, and even chicory coffee were all considered luxuries by August 20 in Atlanta, though many of those items had been scarce long before the siege.

To make matters worse, if one was seen on the Atlanta streets, cannon fire soon followed. By mid-August, nobody moved about the city during the day, least they draw attention of the many Union observers in large observation balloons that surrounded the entire city. No citizen could look in any direction around the city and not see large balloons tethered at three hundred feet in the sky. Any movement around town was for that month, done at night. During the day everyone in Atlanta went underground and simply waited.

This month-long waiting time did have one significant impact on the war. Ironically, it raised a slight possibility of a Confederate victory! By that point in the war, it seemed to many in the north that the War Between the States was becoming unwinnable. In August of 1864, no major Union army seemed to be making any progress anywhere. Up in Virginia, General Grant's massive Army of the Potomac was stalled in their attack on the Confederate capital at Richmond, Virginia, with no end in sight. That fight had resulted in a forty-mile siege line beginning just north of Richmond and ending well below the Confederate railroad hub in Petersburg, Virginia. Everything along that line seemed to be frozen with no progress for the Union at all.

Therefore when Sherman's siege of Atlanta began, the northern papers loudly affirmed that the war was a total stalemate, since no Union army was making progress. Further, that assertion threatened President Lincoln's re-election hopes that following November, only three months away. Many in the north were tired of the never-ending war, and wanted to simply "let the south go!" Even Lincoln himself didn't think he would win the presidency, and his opponent had openly advocated for a negotiated end to the fighting.

To the leaders in Richmond, those possibilities suggested that the Confederacy might negotiate to keep its independence from the Union! In that fashion, the siege of Atlanta, if it could be prolonged for four or five months, might actually result in a Confederate victory!

While leaders in both Washington City and Richmond pondered that possibility, soldiers simply did what soldiers often do. Almost all of the Confederates encamped in Fortress Atlanta wrote letters home. Even the unlettered men wanted to let their families know they were still among the living, so they quietly asked one comrade or another to help them write a letter to a mother, wife, or sweetheart. Jamie Turnbull was no exception.

*Ms. Mary Turnbull,*
*Traveler's Rest Plantation, Tugalo, GA*

*My most beloved wife, I cannot tell you the joy your news brings to me! Since I recieved your last letter, I have been so very happy. I seem to walk on a cloud each day, hoping that my men do not find me giddy with joy, as we still face a determined enemy. It has been quiet the last two weeks all along the battle lines and at those times, I imagine myself playing with my little man as he grows, year by year, at our home in the Georgia Blue Ridge. I cannot imagine a more pleasant thought than you and I, with our growing child at four or six years of age. We'll sit on a blanket in some green, flower-lit valley on a Sunday picnic in those wonderful mountains in the spring, as our child chases butterflies. Perhaps by next Christmas, all will be well once again in our land and maybe this ghastly war will be behind us. I do so hope I can join you for the blessed birth of our son.*

*Of course a daughter would, likewise be a blessing from God, particularly if she has the fair countenance of her mother. I would wish to see her face, as I imagine it, right beside yours. I pray daily that you are safe, and that all goes well with you and with our baby.*

*There have been three fights here just outside of Atlanta within the last few weeks or so, and our Tugalo River men were in the first two of them. In each case, we attacked the Union army, but did not drive them from the field, so alas, we still face a determined foe. I've included those battle summaries herein. Please do place these with the others, if you will.*

*God willing, we will certainly fight again, and the damn Yankees will not take Atlanta. For now, we all live in our bomb-proofs just behind our defensive works, and I'm told that most of the remaining citizens in the city are camping in their cellars or spring houses. The Yankees shell us repeatedly but do little damage, since most are underground. We move only at night.*

*I do not understand why those damn Yankees would rain shell and cannon on civilians here in Atlanta—it is a barbarism that is unheard of in the annals of war. Civilians do not fight battles, and cannot influence this fight in the least, but Sherman and his monsters seem to take great relish in killing innocent women and children with their cannon. That is one of the many horrors of the Yankees that we fight against I suppose.*

*Meanwhile, the men gamble, drink, write letters home, race lice and then drink some more. Each evening, as we emerge from our caves, some of the men are off to downtown Atlanta. There seem to be more houses of fallen ladies here in Atlanta, just along Alabama Street, than there are men in the whole damned army! Of course, I hesitate to mention that to my fair wife, and do rest assured that your husband hasn't seen these places from the inside. I long only for you, and these houses hold no interest for me. During the day, I help out some at General Hood's headquarters, and in the evenings, I usually just join the remaining men as we get together to sing a few rowdy songs around the campfire.*

*Last evening, I went to a prayer meeting with Sergeant Carmichael, and one of our younger men, Chad Wilson. Wilson is but a boy, though he has always been godly, but who would have thought Duncan Carmichael would ever become such a devoted Christian? You know that filthy Carmichael clan down river. Certainly you've heard of the drinking, the cock-fighting, the bear-baiting, and their other sinful proclivities. Yet there was Carmichael himself, my friend and childhood companion, Duncan Carmichael, right there leading the hymn singing in the meeting last night. To note that God works in mysterious ways is the grossest of understatements!*

*I do not know what to advise you as to Meely. If this war is lost (and I can say that openly now, to my loving wife) I suppose she, and Aunt Fanny, and all the others will be free one day. Meanwhile keep the plantation together and running as best you can. At this point, let us prepare for the worst. By all means, slaughter only the pigs and cattle you need, and rather than harvesting the cotton, use the slaves to plant late vegetables, collards and anything else that you can grow in the short time between now and winter. By all means take care in canning as many of the vegetables as you can this year. Make certain the apples are dried, and the corn is well preserved in the corn bins. If this war does turn against us, we shall need all the food we have.*

*I need to go to Hood's bunker now, and no doubt copy some dreary order for beans or some other meaningless task. Still, I do not wish to end this communication without letting you know again, of my love for you. If ever I fail to speak to you of the esteem in which I hold your love and the memory of your face, I shall have then failed in my one true purpose in this life.*

*Let me then merely say, I love thee. I love thee completely, utterly, and without a care for my soul, a soul now lost within that love and that longing for thee...*

*Ever devoted to you,*
*Major Jamie Turnbull,*
*Fourth Georgia*
*Atlanta*

## A Railroad Race to Jonesborough

Historians have long known that Billy Sherman was often manic in his emotions. He was frequently talking, sometimes to himself, and often sleeping only three or four hours per night. His staff had to divide their time such that someone would be available for the general nearly twenty hours each day. That constellation of strange characteristics is how this man earned the name Crazy Billy, to begin with, and he even called himself crazy from time to time. As hyperactive as he was, one thing Sherman absolutely could not do, in any sense of the term, was wait.

Therefore while others waited in August of 1864, Crazy Billy was doing anything but waiting. Rain hampered the movement of his armies during August of that year, but Crazy Billy still sent his cavalry to break up the Confederate supply lines south of Atlanta, and each time he drove his staff nearly crazy, waiting for the results of the raid to be reported back to him. On several such raids, Union cavalry would capture a small Confederate garrison near a rail head, occupy the town for a day or so, and destroy one or two miles of the railroad track. However, Joe Wheeler's Confederate Cavalry would soon show up, and chase the Union horsemen away from the rail line. Within a day hundreds of slaves, working as repair crews for the Confederacy, would once again have the supply trains moving into Fortress Atlanta to supply Hood's army. With each raid, even though they were successful to some degree, Crazy Billy merely got more frustrated!

Perhaps initially Sherman thought that by breaking a rail line, even for a brief time, he could bring Hood to his knees. However, after several such cavalry raids even Crazy Billy had to admit that supplies were still getting through to Atlanta. Thus around August 20 or so, Sherman had determined that something else would have to be done to capture the city, so he decided to take a chance. While understanding Hood's natural aggressiveness very well, Sherman determined that Hood was no longer capable of mounting a significant offensive move, and that gave Sherman an option. He began to pull his Union forces away from the U shaped line around the west, north and east of Atlanta. He ordered six of his seven corps, to move south and hit the two rail lines that were still open south of Atlanta. He wanted one staggering blow, a battle to sever the Confederate supply lines once and for all. Meanwhile, he would continue to use his other men in the one remaining corps to protect his own rail line to Tennessee.

While Confederates had no observation balloons in Atlanta, they did have numerous observation towers around the city, some of which rose a hundred feet into the air. While much lower than the Union balloons, someone on those towers, even at that lower height, could detect enemy movement. It didn't take a genius to determine that only six Yankee heads were now sticking up behind the Union defenses whereas, yesterday, that same section of the line had held over fifty Yankee noggins! In fact, by the morning of August 26, most of the Union lines around Atlanta were empty altogether, and later that day, General Hood knew it!

By the afternoon of August 26, Hood received word that Sherman's Union armies were gone, though some Union forces still guarded the bridges across the Chattahoochee River north of town. Given Sherman's repeated attempts to cut the Confederate supply line to the south, it took very little thought to determine Sherman's final destination. Clearly there was to be another major fight for the Confederate supply lines south of town, and both Sherman and Hood expected that fight to determine the fate of Atlanta.

## The Battle of Jonesborough

Early on August 28, Hood gave orders for Hardee's Corps, his most powerful corps, to head south along the rail line and prepare for an attack against the railroad somewhere near the crossroad town of Rough and Ready, or perhaps further south at the somewhat larger town of Jonesborough, Georgia. Like the fight at Ezra Church, the Confederates could use the rail line for quick movement to the south whereas, Sherman's six corps were, once again, using a mix of wagon roads, farm tracks, and paths through the woods to head south. It took nearly a week for Sherman's men to arrive outside at the small town of Jonesborough.

While Hood knew many Union men were heading south, he could not know exactly how many, and by sending Hardee's Corps and a few additional divisions and scattered regiments, he had placed only about half of his strength in Jonesborough. Thus, Hood played it safe by keeping half of his strength in Fortress Atlanta. In contrast, Sherman shoved nearly all of his chips in, by moving virtually his entire force. In that sense, both generals were acting against their own natural inclinations. Hood was widely known for his "all or nothing" attacks, while Sherman typically avoided major risks whenever possible. Both were doing the opposite, as each side prepared for a fight at Jonesborough.

Thus the Battle of Jonesborough began with Howard's Union Army of the Tennessee taking strong defensive positions on a series of ridges on the east side of the Flint River, overlooking the Macon and Western Railroad just west of Jonesborough. That line split off from the main north-south rail line, which meant the Confederates could still utilize the rails to get men into the battle area. Some Confederate cavalry were there to provide some opposition when Howard's force arrived, but those few southern horsemen could not stand long against an entire Union army. However within a few hours, Confederate infantry and cannon began unloading from the trains at the depot in Jonesborough. They were immediately marched to the west of town. Union forces continued to arrive haphazardly from any road or one-cart track they could find. The armies first came within sight of each other on August 31, and after some repositioning, the killing began at 3:30 or so with a strong Confederate charge into the prepared defensive works of Howard's Union army.

Hardee had organized his men into two attacks. General Cleburne was ordered to attack the Union army to the south and west of Jonesborough, while Hardee himself would lead the Confederate attack further to the north. However, as Cleburne moved his men forward to the southwest, they were hit by sharp fire from a dismounted Union cavalry regiment much further to the south. Cleburne's men responded well to that attack with a massed charge in that direction and they quickly broke the back of that Union attack. However at that point, Cleburne made his most serious battle-command mistake of the entire war. Rather than stop his men from their pursuit, he let them "chase the damn Yankees" for a mile or so, all the way back across the Flint River. That decision effectively took his entire command away from the main battle.

Thus while Hardee expected Cleburne to cover his left flank, there was in fact, nothing on that flank of Hardee's main attack. Of course, an open flank is one of the most dangerous situations on any battlefield, and by the luck of the draw, some might say a curse from the gods of war, that is exactly where Jamie Turnbull, Sampson, Ten Cent Bill, Wilson, Duncan Carmichael and the rest of the Fourth Georgia Infantry found themselves.

At 3:45 that afternoon, all of the men of the Fourth Georgia were marching forward in their battle line, heading toward the Union lines before them, and moving directly into thick cannon smoke. They could catch only an occasional glimpse of the enemy, which was good news since it meant that the enemy could not really see them either. When they reached a point just over three hundred yards from the Union defensive works, a runner arrived shouting, "Halt! Wait for the unit on the flank to move up!"

Of course there was no unit on that flank, so not a single man in the unit could believe the sheer stupidity of that order. Duncan was the first to shout back. "Are we supposed to be invisible? Don't that bone-head general know we're facing some pissed off Yankees up there? And they got guns!" Even as he shouted he, along with the others, fell behind whatever cover they could find, downed tree stumps, cannon craters, or any other slight depression in the ground. The last thing any of them wanted to do was remain standing and completely exposed in that open field, hiding only behind smoke.

Neither Jamie Turnbull nor Captain Collins wanted the men that exposed either, but there was little either could do to countermand a direct order. Collins came up with an idea first, and it is a tribute to his and Turnbull's working relationship that he merely shouted an order, rather than finding the Major and clearing the idea with him first. "Find whatever cover you can, but look to the colors and be prepared to advance as the flag advances!"

Meanwhile Major Turnbull was busily dismounting, only ten yards or so behind Collins, and both men tossed the reins of their horses to Sampson without even looking in his direction. Within a moment Collins and Turnbull were huddled together on bent knees to be less visible. Each was trying to think of some way to save their highly exposed men. Even with the entire field covered in smoke from the Union guns, both cannon and rifle fire could kill any man unlucky enough to get in the way.

"Collins!" shouted Major Turnbull. "Have you seen anyone out to our left? Is there someone on our flank in that direction?"

"Haven't seen a damn thing move over there, Sir. Smoke's too thick. It's dead as a whore's heart in that direction, as far as I can tell. Want me to ride that way and take a look?"

Just then the big Union guns sounded off again, and each man flinched a bit from the horrific noise. A moment later a massive pressure wave hit them. "We're too close to those damn guns! They got to be shooting over our heads. Maybe they'll at least keep some smoke around us for a minute or so." Jamie said. "I'd hate for the men to be out here if them damn Yankees get a clear shot at us!" Rifle fire was only sporadic at that point, since the distances were still great unless one could directly and clearly see one's target.

Just as the men mulled their situation, a rider charged up with another message from Hardee himself. He saw the horses held by Sampson, and quickly recognized Major Turnbull nearby. That man, a captain on Hardee's staff, a man that Jamie recognized from headquarters, saluted Jamie and said, "Sir. General Hardee sends his compliments, and suggests that you advance your regiment full into the Union defenses to your front immediately. He is unsure where the previous order to halt originated, but he is confident that our current force can take the higher ground from the Yankees, even without the support of General Cleburne on our flank. General Hardee did recommend that you refuse your lines somewhat to form a flank to our left. General Cleburne's action has seemingly taken him somewhat far afield." With that, the man finally shut up long enough for Jamie and Collins to think.

Collins spoke first, with some disbelief. Looking at Turnbull he said, "Captain, does the general want us to be our own flank and still attack? Are we now the flank for the entire corps?"

The man didn't answer those questions. He simply didn't know either answer, so he said nothing.

Jamie didn't think the orders made sense either, but he could see no option but to obey. At the time, he thought it might be suicide for him and his entire unit, since anything could emerge from the smoke on his open left flank. Jamie finally realized he should return the courier's salute, so he did so, and said,

"Compliments to General Hardee, Captain. Tell him the Fourth Georgia will advance in ten minutes after I've reorganized my men." Here Jamie turned to Collins. "Captain Collins, please assemble company commanders, sergeants, and any other officers on me."

Within a minute, four company commanders, five veteran sergeants, Collins, Turnbull, and Sampson stood together behind a few trees that, for some reason, had yet to be chopped down. For a moment, they were out of sight of the Yankees. Turnbull then addressed his company commanders. "We advance in five minutes. I want Carmichael and his men on my left, and I'll fight from that end of our line. If we are to have trouble that is where it will be. Collins will command the advance on the other end of the line, but each of you must keep your men in tight. We'll all move forward fast, only on my command. Understood?"

His men all nodded their understanding.

Then Turnbull paused for just a moment, as he looked toward the Union line. Every face in that circle of men was staring at their commander, with few believing those orders.

Jamie continued. "We all know it'll be hell gettin' up there, and we all know what to expect when we reach those works, boys. We've all done it before. But this time, I want you to fight like hell, just like old Carmichael here in one of his knife fights!" Here a few of the men smiled, as Jamie continued, getting louder, and more forceful with each word. "We'll make those bastards pay for being on Georgia ground. You all know that we cannot afford to lose this railroad. You know what it means if we do, so tell your men to fight like never before, and we'll chase those bastards all the way back into Tennessee!"

By then the men were all nodding, and looking confident. Several shouted, "Yes Sir!"

Jamie merely smiled, and continued, louder still. "God bless every one of you boys today, and bless your men. When we move, I want to hear a Rebel Yell so loud that it'll scare the hell out'a that monkey Lincoln all the way up in Washington City!"

The men were standing, and shouting. "Damn right, Sir!" said Carmichael. "We're there already!"

Seeing the sheer emotion on his commander's face, Collins then took up the slack. "Get back to your companies, men. Tell 'um to fix bayonets, and make sure they know what to expect. You'll hear the order to charge in five minutes."

Jamie, Collins, and Sampson were, within a minute, all mounted. As Jamie saw his battle lines form, he shook Collin's hand and nodded his head toward the other end of the line. Collins looked deeply into his commanders eyes, and shook his hand one final time. At times, men in battle need say nothing, so after a moment, Collins turned and rode off, without another word. Jamie waited a couple more minutes, and he could see that his lines were fully formed, with his color bearers in the center. He drew his sword and shouted. "Fourth Georgia, Charge!"

And that is when it happened. There on that do-or-die battlefield just to the west of Jonesborough, Georgia, those fighting men charged into battle riding atop the loudest, and the last Rebel Yell ever heard on Georgia soil!

Into the smoke the men ran, with Jamie and Collins riding at a trot in front of the lines, just as the Rebel Yell arose. For the New Jersey, Ohio, and Wisconsin men behind those defenses atop the rising land, it must have seemed ethereal somehow. With the big cannon firing just behind them, struck by the nearly constant pressure waves from those guns, those Yankees now heard what all Union men feared above all, the famed Rebel Yell. It arose a fearsome mystery, the sharp yelping sound of thousands of voices, as if springing from the mist to their front, or out of the battle smoke, or even coming from the very ground before them. For a moment, they had nothing to do but experience their palpable fear—there was even then, nothing in front of them to shoot at but smoke. Still, that horrendous sound—sharp, angry, nearly as loud as the cannon —now tore at their very souls.

And then the shapes took form in the smoke, horses, steel bayonets, and men, screaming like banshees and charging for the Union defensive lines. Of the four thousand Union men arrayed along the high ground, one in ten peed in their pants at that very moment. That urine would soon mix with blood, guts, brains, and other body parts, as Confederates attacked those trenches. Still, the Union officers and veterans, men who knew war, marveled at the magnificent charge before them. Nearly to a man, those Yankees wondered, if they got those same orders, would they do the same? Would they charge into a near certain death?

On came the boys in grey, charging forward, rifled muskets at the ready, screaming row by row. As more lines of Confederates emerged from the smoke, the screaming only got louder. Several officers were clearly visible now. While Collins had allowed his end of the line to bypass him, Jamie had not done so, though by order, he was supposed to move behind his charging line when they reached two hundred yards from the enemy. Still, there he rode, sword raised, right in front of the line near the unit color bearer. Sampson rode atop his horse, not too far away.

As more Confederates emerged from the smoke, the lines were only one hundred and twenty yards apart. The Union men put aside their awe and took aim. Without any order from a single Union commander, the entire line opened fire on the advancing Confederates. A few of the Union artillerymen had realized what was about to happen and had lowered the muzzles of their guns, and loaded them with canister. Cannon shot, canister, and rifle fire tore into the Confederate line, and some bodies in grey simply ceased to exist in a momentary flash of fire, many others tumbled to the earth dead. Legs, arms, and heads flew through the air, and many men in grey died without having fired a shot on that field. Jamie was hit in the shoulder, and his horse was hit several times—a mounted regimental commander was hard to miss at a hundred yards, and more than a few of those veteran Union men wondered why the hell that man was mounted and in front of that charge anyway.

Sampson had been riding "low" astride his horse to make himself less of a target, and he saw Jamie go down. He jumped toward Jamie, and was able to pull him behind the wounded horse, and thus those two had some protection from the hostile fire. More shots tore into all of the Confederates on that field, but by that point, the men in grey were close enough to fire back. Men all along the Confederate line took cover—any cover, even it if meant hiding behind a wounded man—and fired at the Union heads in the defensive works to the front.

For some reason, the men at Collins end of the line were spared the canister shots that had so decimated Jamie's end of the line. Such are the imponderables in battle. Collins by then was just behind his men, and from that position, he was able to keep them moving forward. Jamie, looking in that direction, saw some of those men mount the defensive works, and begin the hand-to-hand fighting, which at that point, was the only Confederate hope for victory.

Within only a minute, the boys in blue began a terrified run toward the rear with the Rebel Yell fresh and biting in their ears. Collins' men had captured a section of the Union trenches and one artillery battery of four guns.

Jamie was suffering from shock, but he knew his wound was not mortal. As he saw one group of his men begin to turn the Union cannon toward the retreating Union troops, he moved to get up, but a vice-grip of muscle, bone, and sinew clamped down on his good shoulder and put him back on the ground. Sampson said. "Suh! You is done for dis day, and you needs to jus' stay still here behind dis horse! Cap'n Collins, he know what to do down der!"

Just then the wounded horse in front of Jamie arose, as if regaining consciousness somehow. It whinnied loudly, and began a terrified run parallel to the Union lines, with blood flowing freely from no less than four separate wounds in its shoulders and flanks. With no cover to his front, Jamie said. "Thank you for keeping me safe, Sampson, but I need to get up there and see what can be done."

Sampson gave up, and merely said, "Yes Suh,"

However, as Jamie stood, he saw that his own end of the line was still short of the Union trench. Many men near him were still firing—Ten Cent Bill, Lee Lovorn, and the others. All had black faces and were, even then, tearing into powder bags, loading, and firing as quickly as they could. When Jamie looked to the front again, he saw a massive wave of Union blue advancing on Collins and his men in the Union trench. It had taken the men in blue only ten minutes or so to organize a counter attack, and it seemed the entire field behind the Union trench was covered in Union men moving forward.

Then he heard Collins shout the order, "Fall Back!"

It only makes sense, Jamie told himself. We cannot stand with our numbers, against that counter attack, even with the enemy cannon. Collins has done the right thing, and I'll have to remember to tell him that. Then Jamie looked back at Sampson. "Help me up, Sampson. It seems we need to retreat with the rest of our men. Meanwhile, shout out for me. Call the retreat."

As Sampson lifted his master, he shouted, along with several others, "Retreat!" The cry was taken up by others, and the rifle fire and cannon fire seemed to die away, as the Confederates fell back.

Sampson, with Jamie's arm around his massive shoulders half carried his master to the rear. Jamie was only able to support some of his own weight, and they moved slowly for what seemed like an eternity. Both were thankful when they entered, once again, the smoke of the battle, but at that point the frequency of the firing decreased again, at least in their sector. With their eyes stinging from the smell of burnt powder, they walked through the blue, biting smoke, following other shadows of men, as other Confederates likewise retreated all around them. Somewhere to the south the fight continued with heavy rifle fire and cannon blasts, but in their sector the fighting was over.

As they retreated they passed others, wounded in the initial charge. Some of those men begged for water while others crawled toward the rear. Retreating Confederates who could, helped the wounded during the retreat, picking them up, or helping them hobble toward the jumping off point for the Confederates back toward the town itself. Some men picked up rifles or ammunition from the dead. Every man knew that they had no real defensive works in Jonesborough, since they'd headed into the fight as soon as they got off the trains only a few hours ago. In short, if the Yankees charged at that moment, the entire Confederate army was wide open and very vulnerable.

Jamie was in and out of consciousness, held up by Sampson's massive arms, as they stepped around the wounded and the dead. They passed many wounded and dying men. As they came up to another Confederate body Jamie saw that it seemed to move a bit, so he looked more closely. The man lay on his side facing the other way and he was breathing, but a horrible sound was coming from his chest. Jamie could see an exit wound in the man's lower back. He said, "At least he wasn't hit by a minie-ball; he'd be tore up and deader than hell, if he was." Then after a bit of a pause, he continued. "Let's help him. I think I can stand here by myself, and maybe even walk a bit on my own now, Sampson. Turn this man over, and you can help him to the rear."

Sampson, reluctant to let go of Jamie, nonetheless complied. Making sure that Jamie wouldn't simply fall, he let go of his master very slowly, and then bent down beside the wounded man. He gently turned the man over on his back, and got the shock of his life.

"Good God!" said Sampson. As he rolled the man over, he recognized him. "Oh, my good God!" Sampson said again, as he looked into the filthy face of Duncan Carmichael. He knew he was looking at a dead man, though Duncan had not had the courtesy to stop breathing as yet. Duncan's eyes were unfocused, and he had a chest wound—just a small hole really—in the lower right of his ragged butternut blouse. The injured lung in his abdomen made a sucking sound with each breath, and a little blood gurgled at the wound as air passed with each exhale.

Seeing Duncan on the ground, Jamie let out a yell, and then fell, landing heavily on his knees. Sampson thought Jamie might reach to help Duncan, but he didn't. Instead he merely looked at his childhood friend, and then looked up, as if beseeching the heavens for some reason, some explanation. At first a small scream came, then Jamie's face contorted, showing horror and then pain. At that point, Sampson saw something in his master than he'd never seen before—a whole, consuming, and complete agony, a crushing pain that no man should ever have to tolerate.

Jamie drew a large breath, opened his mouth wide and then screamed at the top of his lungs, a heart wrenching scream, as tears flowed down his cheeks. Then he drew another breath and screamed again, louder still, and then again with each new breath. As sporadic rifle fire could be heard in the distance, others on that field called for water, or mother, or for a quick death. Jamie, wearing a face of agony, screamed repeatedly for his dying friend. Sampson could say nothing. He merely sat beside his master and wept.

## Giving Too Much

The evening dusk-colored sky showed a few clouds, and the firing stopped a few minutes later. Captain Collins came by at some point, even as Jamie continued to shout his pain, wailing at the top of his lungs, still on his knees and rocking back and forth, with Sampson's massive arms around him. Duncan had passed out, but the blood on his chest still gurgled with each breath. Jamie had been shouting just like that for nearly half-an-hour, but to Sampson that time seemed like an eternity. Chad Wilson now sat on the other side of his dying friend. With Duncan's head in his lap, he prayed softly, the holy words punctuated at every sentence by Jamie's mournful cries.

Jamie didn't even look up as Collins approached. He just continued his screaming for his dying friend. With only one look at the scene, Collins took it all in. He knew in an instant that Major Turnbull was finished. Clearly, the Major was completely exhausted as well as seriously wounded. Collins could see that these men had lost a childhood friend. Collins knew that Major Turnbull had, at that point, given everything he could give. Jamie had nothing left. He was no longer a weapon in war. He was done.

Looking more closely at Turnbull's shoulder wound, Collins merely ordered others to come and get their commander, and the other wounded man. He then announced to several nearby that he himself would assume command of the Fourth Georgia Regiment, until further notice. Collins could see that Carmichael was still breathing—that seemed like a miracle. Still, every single man in that war knew that almost no one survived a sucking chest wound. Collins didn't like the fact, but he did admit it to himself. Duncan Carmichael would be dead before the next sunrise.

The Fourth Georgia was pulled back into the town of Jonesborough that night, and the retreating men saw that other units were busily digging a defensive trench. More Union men continued to arrive on the field all night long, and the fighting to the west of town would resume the next day. However, any chance of a Confederate victory in that fight was lost on the first day. By the morning of September 1, 1864, the Union forces in Jonesborough outnumbered Hardee's men by five to one, and cannon bristled from their defensive works.

The Confederates held to their own lines that day, but from early that morning until dusk, men in blue charged across those fields, with the Union forces probing each section of the Confederate line. There was sporadic cannon fire but the Fourth Georgia took no part in the fight. The battle had already been decided. By the early evening of September 1, Hardee finally recognized his own defeat and withdrew his men. The Battle of Jonesborough ended on the evening of September 1, 1864. It had cost the Confederates another 3,000 men, while Union losses were a mere 1,200.

Thus on September 1, 1864, history rendered her harsh, unyielding verdict, a verdict that impacts us all even today. On that battlefield just to the west of Jonesborough Georgia, the Confederacy lost the Civil War.

Some have argued that the Grand Cause was doomed after the Confederate losses in the summer of 1863. Gettysburg and Vicksburg were both harrowing defeats. However, at that point, the Confederacy still held a transportation system and several open blockade-running ports, not to mention two massive armies.

In contrast, by September 1, 1864, the Confederacy lost its main transportation hub in Atlanta, and the Army of Tennessee. Further, the Confederacy was split for the second time on that day. With the defeat of Atlanta, both Mississippi and Alabama were taken completely out of the war. Only one port, Wilmington up in the Carolinas, was still receiving blockade runners, so few supplies reached any Confederate army. Again, with the fall of Atlanta, the south lost any hope of victory.

Of course, the leadership on both sides knew it, though southern leaders continued to refuse to face the inevitable. Still, the pieces fell apart quickly for the south. When Hardee's men lost control of Jonesborough, and the last open railroad into Atlanta, the city itself was doomed. Thus, the fight for Atlanta was, in effect, lost some fifteen miles south of the city. General Hood could no longer feed his Confederate army in the town, and he knew he had to leave the city to Sherman and the Yankees. That evacuation would give the citizens in the Union states tangible evidence of real progress in that war. In fact, the fall of Atlanta ultimately resulted in Lincoln's reelection only three months later.

On September 1, General Hood ordered the destruction of his ammunition trains, as he prepared to evacuate. It must have been a sight, late in the night on September 1, 1864, to see no less than five separate ammunition trains—eighty two boxcars in total, all loaded with high explosives—go up in one massive blast at the railroad depot along lower Alabama street in Atlanta. Never before or since in the history of Georgia, has a singular explosion so shaken this land. No other explosion in the history of the state has ever come close.

The massive explosion and the following fires tore the guts out of the city, destroying the very rail lines that had been the focus of the entire Atlanta Campaign. Much of downtown Atlanta was destroyed that evening, as thousands of citizens watched the heart of their city cease to exist. Men and women alike wept openly as Hood's Army of Tennessee, now reduced to a mere thirty thousand men, withdrew from the city heading to the west and north. Union forces entered Atlanta on September 2, 1864.

Even as Major Jamie Turnbull had given too much, one might say the city of Atlanta had likewise given too much. It had given itself over to the dreaded foe, with one last massive gasp of indignation, as if that giant explosion was the final breath of this great antebellum city. Atlanta was almost completely destroyed that night, ironically, at the hands of the Confederates who were, to a man, sworn to defend her.

Of course, perspectives differ depending on which end of the rifle one holds. While every southern soul bled for that horrid scene in Atlanta, Unionists around the nation were celebrating on September 2, even as the heart of the great city still burned. Sherman telegraphed Lincoln as soon as his men confirmed Hood's absence from the city. "Atlanta is ours, and fairly won!"

With that news trumpeted in every northern paper, Lincoln's election was assured. Moreover, with that man in the White House in Washington City for four more years, there would be no chance for any negotiated peace.

Thus the War Between the States would continue to its bloody conclusion. Thousands more would die in a meaningless struggle, and all to no avail. After Atlanta fell, there was not one chance in hell of a southern victory in that long-ago, long-forgotten war.

# Epilogue

Major Jamie Turnbull became dimly aware of the hard wood beneath his head, as the wagon hit a bump in the narrow dirt track. His head bounced on the wood, and his eyes opened just a bit. He could see the underside of the wagon seat above him, and that board covered the bright sun, mercifully keeping his face in the shade. Above the wagon seat, he could see the strong back of a large black man, so he knew Sampson was taking care of both he and the others that he sensed were in the wagon. That thought brought him some degree of comfort, but the wood was hard, and the wagon road was rough. His shoulder was on fire with every bump.

He turned his head then, and saw several more wounded men in the wagon. Some, like Jamie were on the wooden floor, while several were on narrow benches held up by stout wooden legs. He recognized it as a hospital wagon.

Jamie's shoulder hurt horribly and everything around him seemed to stink. He then remembered that he took a shot in his upper arm, and thought about the pain in his chest. He wondered if he'd lost the arm, and thought for a terrifying second about that horrid pile of arms and legs outside the hospital at Kennesaw Mountain. Then mercifully, his eyes closed, and he drifted off once again into a deep sleep.

When he next became aware, he heard voices. Strangely some were women's voices, and he wondered if he was in a hospital. He could not get his eyes to focus but he felt himself moving, as hands picked him up off the hard wood of the wagon bed. Then several people were holding him in a blanket and moving him up a set of stairs. He recognized Sampson and thought he saw Meely, but he closed his eyes and knew that couldn't be right. She wouldn't be in a hospital near the fighting. Then he passed out again.

Horrid dreams came, swirling images of dead men, mutilated horses, cannon fire, and parts of bodies flying from cannon blasts. Those pictures were real, though only in his mind. Aunt Fanny's face hung in the air over him, and she seemed to be mopping his brow with a damp cloth, but again, that couldn't be right. He must be dreaming.

Sometimes it was Meely beside him, and sometimes even his wife Mary appeared. Each time he shut his eyes to the pain, since he knew he was dreaming.

He could feel the fever, the white hot pain taking over his body. He was drenched in sweat until his bed sheets stunk. His whole chest and shoulder felt like it was on fire. He screamed when the hot blast tore into his arm, and then he passed out again. He kept telling himself none of it was real, none of this hell could possibly be real.

Sometimes he felt himself approach consciousness, but he knew the pain would come to him then, so he fled back to the dark places in his mind. He didn't want to live if it meant going back into the pain, that white hot, burning pain. He remembered seeing Duncan die, remembered exactly the look of that horrid wound, that sucking hole in Duncan that would bubble with each breath, as it sucked the life out of his childhood friend. That pain was worse than the burning stink, and the rot, of his shoulder.

He saw his long-dead mother telling him not to play with "those Carmichael boys!" She never wanted them around. Even those many years before the war, the Carmichaels had a bad reputation and his mother always said, "Good little boys don't play with Carmichaels," as if that ended the matter. He ignored her, of course. Duncan Carmichael, even at ten years of age, was the best hunter and fisherman in his age group, and all the boys wanted to fish and hunt with him. Jamie's Mom lost that fight.

Now Duncan was gone, dead with a sucking chest wound, and Jamie knew he couldn't live with that. He felt he should be dead too. His flesh was rotting even as it clung to his body. The horrible sucking wound had taken his friend, and Jamie knew he would soon follow so he ran away from consciousness. Consciousness hurt terribly, with one's own shoulder aflame with pain and his childhood friend dead. Sometimes when Jamie felt himself coming around, he simply went back to the dark place to escape the pain. He ran to the darkness.

Other faces would come in his dreams. Faces that Jamie knew could not be there, not in a hospital, and not with him in the hell he'd created from the darkness. Aunt Fanny was there sometimes, and even Grandpa Jarrett showed up once in a while, looking down at him as Aunt Fanny wiped his face. There was Lem Davis and Sampson, looking on—faces that could not be in the dark hell that had become Jamie's chosen world.

He came to the edge of consciousness many times, and always some of the faces would be there. Sometimes they were wiping his brow. At other times they moved him, rolling him from one side to another, as they changed the wet sheets beneath him. Sometimes they burned his body away, and the pain was horrible, so he ran to the darkness once again. Always, there was less pain in the darkness, and no sounds of war. No one else died as long as Jamie could keep himself in the darkness. His shoulder didn't burn when he stayed in the darkness.

Then one morning he awoke completely. Barely able to move, he could still sense that someone was in the room. For the first time he kept the darkness away and spoke, "Water."

"Yes, Suh! Mr. Jamie, Suh! Yes Suh! I'll get you some water right now, Suh!"

Jamie thought it was Meely's voice, but she wouldn't be in a Confederate hospital, so he knew it had to be someone else. Without opening his eyes, he wondered where he was. Maybe he was in a hospital in Jonesborough, maybe Macon. He thought that was where the army had been moving the wounded after Atlanta fell to the Yankees. His shoulder was still painful, but the pain seemed a bit softer somehow; not as all consuming.

"Here's yor' water, Suh!" said Meely. "I'm mighty glad, powerful' glad to hear you ask for water, like dat!" Meely held a small cup to his lips, and with her other hand, she helped Jamie lift his head so he could drink. When he moved he felt again the sharp pain in his shoulder, and he could tell that his arm was strapped firmly, unmovable, across his chest. He knew then that he'd kept his arm somehow. He sipped the water and lay back down, as his eyes closed from exhaustion. He soon slept again.

Again he seemed to be coming out of the darkness, and then he heard. "There you are, Mr. Turnbull! It is about time you showed up, and came back to us!" Mary walked into the room talking, just as Jamie shut his eyes again. Still she spoke all the more loudly. "Oh no you don't! I will no longer stand for you to lie there as if the world had simply stopped turning. It is well past time for you to get better. I've been very concerned, very concerned I must say, about you, but I see that you do seem to be getting a bit stronger now. You will open your eyes this instant, and talk with a wife that loves you more than she could ever say."

Jamie opened his eyes, knowing that Mary could not be there, believing, fearing that her voice would dissolve as soon as he opened his eyes.

Then suddenly the awareness came. There was Mary and Meely. Aunt Fanny was rushing into the room behind them, as Mary sat down by the bed. Meely continued to wipe his brow, and the damp cloth felt good on his skin.

Jamie could not understand what he saw, but for some reason, he knew this was real, and he understood that all of the dreams had been real. He managed to say only a few more words, on that first morning after his re-awakening. "How long?"

Mary leaned in closer, putting her ear near his lips.

"How long?" Jamie said again, a bit more loudly. The effort of speaking even those two words seemed to exhaust him completely.

"Don't talk, my dearest." Mary said. "I love you so and have missed you so. I do want to talk with you but for now, don't talk. There will be time for your questions later. Now the doctor says you just need to rest and get stronger.

Nothing else should matter. We are all here, and we will keep you safe and comfortable."

Jamie's eyes were closed now, and Meely lay his head back on the soft pillows. Still, he had to understand the dreams, the darkness so, once again, he repeated himself. "How long?"

Mary realized then that he was most determined to get some type of answer, so she chose her words carefully. "My love, you're at home now. You've been in a fever for over three months, my dear, and we've been caring for you. It's almost Christmas time, now, but you're home with your family, and we're all going to take the best care of you. Now sleep, please. Just rest and get well."

Jamie closed his eyes as he cried, and the pain came again, the darkness overtook him. Mary could only look on as tears ran down her husband's face from his closed eyelids.

Then she whispered softly. "Do come back soonest, my dear husband." She began to cry herself. "I need you so badly, and I love you so much. Do come back to me soon."

The next time he awoke Jamie didn't know if it was the same day or not. No one was wiping his brow that morning, but when he turned his head, he could see Meely sitting across the room from him. Strangely, she seemed to be reading a book, the Bible.

"Water please, Meely," Jamie said.

"Yes Suh! I'll get you'll a cup right now, Suh! I know'd that Mrs. Mary wants to talk wid you too, so I run gets her jest soon as I get yor water, Suh!"

Jamie had shut his eyes again, but as she fetched his cup of water he realized he was curious. "Did I see you reading the good book, Meely? Do you read?"

Meely knew that the Major might be mad about her reading, and she certainly wasn't going to tell him that she'd been reading even prior to the war. Still she could let him know about Mrs. Mary's decision to teach the slaves to read. "Yes Suh! I's reading de Bible. Mrs. Mary, she teach all o'us to read de good book. She say, if'n de Jubilee come, we all gonna need to know how to read! She be teachin' us for some while now."

Unconventional, but that did make sense, thought Jamie. Slaves will need to earn their keep in totally new ways, if the Yankees come. He simply said, "Reading the good book is always pleasing to God, I suppose." Then he closed his eyes again.

"Yes Suh! I believe dat God does want everybody reading de Bible!" said Meely. "Now you rest, and I'll be getting Miss Mary. She say she want to see you, if'n you wake up again. I'll go get her." With that Meely left the room, and Jamie closed his eyes again.

Mary was in the vegetable garden out behind Traveler's Rest, when Meely came to fetch her. She hurried upstairs into the bedroom, but she could tell that her husband was already sleeping again. She so wanted to awaken him, but the doctor had been very specific in his instructions; "Sleep is the body healing itself. Do not awaken him for any reason when he is asleep, and let him sleep as much as he can!"

The next time Jamie became aware, it was dark, but he could hear voices. In fact, he could hear singing. He didn't understand why but he recognized the song.

*Silent night, holy night, all is calm, all is bright,*
*Round yon virgin mother and child,*
*Holy infant so tender and mild,*
*Sleep in Heavenly peace, sleep in Heavenly peace.*

He opened his eyes, and looked across the room. As he expected, there sat Aunt Fanny. He smiled, knowing that she or Meely had been there for months. He spoke more loudly than he had previously. "I'd like some water please, Aunt Fanny. Would you mind?"

"Oh, praise GOD! Suh! It shor is good to see yor eyes clear as a bell," Said Aunt Fanny, as she scurried across the room to grab a pitcher from the bath stand. "Here's yor water, Suh! I'm gonne get Miss. Mary, Suh! PRAISE GOD FO' YOU COMMIN' BACK TO US! PRAISE GOD, ON DIS HOLY NIGHT!" With that, she ran out of the room.

Jamie realized that someone had put more pillows behind his head, so he was partially sitting up. When he heard the noise, he looked toward the doorway, and they all came rushing in at once, his beloved Mary, Aunt Fanny, Meely, Sampson, Mary's younger brothers, even the local preacher all crammed into the bedroom, all talking at the same time, too many voices, and too many congratulations. All the while, Aunt Fanny continued her overly enthusiastic praises from the doorway; "PRAISE GOD, FO' HIS BLESSIN'S! PRAISE GOD FOR MR. JAMIE COMMIN' BACK TO US, EVEN IN DIS DARK TIME! PRAISE GOD DIS HOLY NIGHT!"

Jamie thus received his family and friends, for the first time after his wound, on Christmas Eve, in 1864. There was much talking, but given his injuries, Jamie didn't shake hands with anyone. After some time, however, he grew tired, and Mary ushered everyone out of the room. For the first time, she and her husband could talk for a bit.

Jamie spoke first as he sipped a cup of water. It was the first time, he'd held his own cup in months. "Is it really Christmas Eve?"

Mary smiled. "My dear, dear, husband. Your lost much blood with your wound, and passed out before Sampson could even get you to a hospital. You owe your life to your slave, I can tell you! Within a week, your arm infected while you were recovering at Jonesborough, and the doctors had given you up for dead. By the time Sampson could get you back here, gangrene was in your shoulder, and you've been in a fever for months. A part of your arm rotted. You were delirious with fever most of that time, and the doctor was sure that we would lose you. About three weeks later, your shoulder became red and inflamed. Each time, the doctor would come and cut out the rot, and then use a branding iron to burn your flesh and cauterize the wound. His care saved your life, but I must say that the whole of Traveler's Rest smelled like a hog killing!"

Jamie smiled when she said that, knowing what the first-frost hog killing smelled like each year! At times, Traveler's Rest would butcher thirty hogs over a two or three day period at the first cool spell in the fall, and that slaughter house smell covered the whole plantation!

"Do I understand that you are teaching our slaves to read?" He asked.

"My dearest, there are so many things to tell you, but the doctor has said to make you rest now. There will be time for talking in the morning, and it shall be Christmas Day! We'll talk then. For now, we shall pray, and then you shall sleep." Then they all closed their eyes, as Mary prayed.

> *"Dear God, We thank you for bringing Mr. Turnbull back to us, and we welcome your blessings on this family on this Christmas Eve. Thank you for his strength, and do give us all strength as we move into an unknown world this year. Most of all, thank you for your son who came to us on this holy night so many years ago. Thank you for your presence in our lives, and for this holy season to celebrate it. We thank you for the power to soldier on and to move forward in whatever world comes next. Grant us your peace, even as we realize and freely admit that we are unworthy of your grace. In Jesus' holy name we pray, on this Christmas Eve, Amen."*

Mary looked back at her husband and then realized he was, once again, in a deep sleep.

The next day, Christmas Day, everyone seemed to come by to wish Jamie well. In the morning everyone on the plantation came in to talk briefly with him, but by that afternoon others in the community were coming to welcome him back. All of them had assumed that Jamie would die given his wounds and his fever, so all wanted to welcome him back. Of course, Mary made certain that few stayed very long. Jamie still needed his rest, and Mary was determined to jealously guard his time.

Jamie meanwhile, welcomed all of his visitors, sitting up in his bed. His shoulder was still strapped tightly to prevent movement, and Jamie had not tested his arm. He was merely glad to still have an arm attached to his shoulder.

The visitor on that Christmas Day that most surprised Jamie was a dead man. As Meely handed him a cup of water early in the afternoon, Mary ushered in none other than Duncan Carmichael. Duncan was considerably cleaner than Jamie had ever seen him, though his hair was still long. He was clean shaven but was limping. He leaned heavily on a cane, but there he was, grinning from ear to ear. Jamie had not even asked about Duncan, since he thought he knew the answer. He'd merely assumed Duncan Carmichael was dead and gone.

Duncan spoke first. "Glad you made it, Sir! I knew when I went down that you probably wouldn't keep yourself safe, not even for one little fight!"

Jamie smiled, as Sampson came in right behind Duncan, bringing a chair for Carmichael, and taking a seat along the wall for himself. Just then Lem Davis arrived, bringing his own chair. Mary stood in the door and looked worried, concerned about how much time this visit might take, but Jamie soon put her concerns to rest.

"My dearest wife," Jamie said. "Please don't rush these men away. I'm alright and we have much to discuss. Please leave us for just a few minutes, while we talk."

Mary, looking quite worried, nonetheless, left the room.

## Catching Up With the War

"And that's about it," Duncan said. "Sherman has marched his damn Yankees all the way across Georgia with nobody fighting against him at all. He stole whatever he needed, and burned damn near everything else. A few Home Guard units attacked him but he swatted them away like flies. There was just nobody left to fight him!"

Jamie asked, "Where is General Hood? Where's the army?""

Duncan looked at his feet as did Sampson, leaving Lem to answer the question. "General Hood took the army all the way up to Tennessee. There were two fights up there in Franklin and Nashville. Hood charged a fixed defensive line loaded with cannon both times. That idiot got our boys in the Fourth Georgia slaughtered up there. Nobody even knows who lived and who died, for sure. Hood's army is done for."

"Now Sherman's captured Savannee, and is sittin' tight right there in the center of town, drinking and goin' to parties, I expect. General Hardee was supposed to defend the place, but he moved his division into South Carolina without firin' a single shot, just left the city to Sherman."

Jamie then asked the inevitable. "Just ain't no reason to hope for the Grand Cause any more, is there? Ain't we already lost the war?"

Lem was silent this time, and Sampson continued to hang his head. Then Duncan figured he owed the harsh truth to his friend. He took a breath, and then spoke up. "Yes Sir, we have. I recon the Grand Cause is finished. We ain't got nobody to stop Sherman in the Carolinas, and Grant has almost starved Lee out of Richmond. There just ain't enough men to fight 'um."

The four comrades, warriors in arms, were quiet for some time after that. When a war is lost there is little left to say.

Then Jamie looked up and spoke directly to Duncan. "How in the hell did you keep breathin'? I saw a sucking chest wound at Jonesborough, and I figured you were done." That was, indeed a rare, and very personal question. Only a man who has given it all can really ask that type of question to another man, a man who, likewise had given everything.

"I don't rightly know, Sir. I woke up in a wagon, with Sampson here driving down the bumpiest damn roads in Georgia." Here he grinned at Sampson, as he continued. "You were on the floor, or one of the benches and it's a damn wonder Sampson didn't kill us all with that ride! Instead, he brought us home, and for some reason, I got better."

Jamie thought on that a moment. "Duncan, you had a sucking chest wound. Nobody survives that."

Duncan realized then that he was talking as intimately as he ever had to anyone. He wanted to say some things that he could never say to anyone else but these few men, men who had been there and seen what he'd seen. So he began for the first time in his life, to open up. "I'm a knife fighter, Jamie. I'm a drinker, a chaser of whores, and a soldier. I'm pretty good at all o' that, but I'm not a good man, not by a long shot, and I don't know why I got better. I don't know why God wanted me to live. All I know is that he did. God wanted me for some reason, and I found him. I found God right there in the middle of all o' that blood and death; right there in the middle of that damn war."

Duncan then paused, and wondered again if he should continue. Should he even share these thoughts with anyone? He'd reflected many hours on why he had lived when he shouldn't have, and he had no answers. But he did have things to say, things that, again, could only be said to these friends. So he spoke again, softly, looking deeply into the eyes of Jamie Turnbull, his commander and wounded friend. "I don't know why God let me live. I don't know why God wanted me to live." Here he hung his head to his chest, and began to cry, without looking at Jamie. "Maybe God has found a purpose for a worthless man, a useless drunken man."

More tears rolled down Duncan's cheek, and after another pause, he continued without looking up. "God has something for me to do is all I can figure. I don't know what yet. I cain't understand it. I just don't know. I cain't even say why I lived, or what I'm supposed to do. Hell, Jamie. I was in a fever for two damn months, and just like you I was outta' my head, just not quite as long. I don't remember nothin' from then. But all of a sudden one morning, I wake up and I'm home at Mama's, and I'm still breathin' and I wonder why I'm still alive." Here he paused to gather himself, then said, "God has something for me, I think. That's all I can guess."

There was silence in the room, and Duncan continued to sniffle softly. After a time, Sampson spoke. "I guess we's all got thinkin' to do now. Don't know what's commin' wid Yankees all over Georgia now. Nobody does."

Duncan made an effort to recover himself, and he spoke up next. "You know, Lem here made it home from Nashville. He's the one tol' me about Hood's foolishness up in Tennessee. When Hood lost his army at Nashville, he simply resigned, left 'um all hanging out in the wind."

Lem then spoke up. "It was a sight to see, Jamie. Nobody knew who was in command, and many of the boys just started to walk away after that last fight. Winter was coming, and they jest wanted to get home. Some of the boys stayed up there, but I figured it was time to come on home too, so I left. Most of us had heard about Crazy Billy burning everything in Georgia, and I was worried about my family, so I jest left and come on home."

Jamie then asked Sampson the obvious question. "Sampson, how in hell did we get home?"

Sampson didn't want to get into particulars, so he just said, "I brung you, Mr. Duncan here, and a couple other local boys home from de hospital in Jonesborough. Day was gonna' send you to Macon on de train, and day was burning hospital wagons, so I jest got one and I brung you home."

Sampson then grinned at the two men he'd saved. He never told his master the real story. He'd simply stolen a wagon and two mules right from the Confederate hospital in Jonesborough. Then he'd loaded his master and his friend up, along with two other local men wounded at Jonesborough. He'd stolen some bandages for the trip, and took a ham he found at the mess wagon, and then he hit the back roads up through Athens, GA and on to the Tugalo River. Many years later, he told that story to Mary Turnbull and those details ended up as a part of her written work after the war.

There was another pause and then Duncan spoke again. "What do we do now Jamie, once you get better and all. Are you goin' back to the army? Is that what we should do?"

Lem, Duncan, and Sampson all looked to their leader, and Jamie quickly realized he had no answer for them. He didn't even know if there was an army nearby for them to return to! Jamie merely said, "I don't know Duncan, I just don't know."

## Rejoining The War

Their new baby came in January. It was a bouncy baby girl, who was named Mary Jarrett Turnbull. She was called Mary, after her mother. She cried little, and slept nearly all night at only three weeks old, so she soon became a delight to all on the plantation. She often slept on the one good arm of her recovering father, and he rocked her nearly every afternoon in a large chair on the porch of Traveler's Rest Plantation. At times, Jamie Turnbull looked into her eyes, as does every new father, and wondered what life may hold for this, his precious child, a new baby, a baby with such promise, born into a changing world.

By early April of 1865, both Duncan Carmichael and Major Jamie Turnbull were well enough to be able to return to service. However, all of the Confederate armies had moved out of Georgia by then, and as Jamie had feared, there was no Confederate army to report too. Still, the Home Guard was active in the area, and offered one option. The Home Guard had, throughout the war, been made up of young boys and men who were too old to fight. In some cities, they took guard duty over armories or essential factories, but in most communities they merely marched around town a bit and tried to look important.

Still in other cities, they did serve a policing type of function. With the war soon to be over the Tugalo River Valley would need some type of authority, and no one in the south expected the Yankees to do anything other than what they had been doing—stealing anything and everything. So Jamie, Duncan, Lem, and Sampson had joined in the twice weekly meetings of the Home Guard in Franklin County, Georgia. Those men patrolled the local roads and the river trade routes keeping thieves at bay. There were many former Confederates coming through the area at that point. Just as Lem had done, they were trying to get home, and they stole worse than the damn Yankees. After all, they had to eat something. The Home Guard would offer them a meal, a few beans for their future travels, and then move them on down the road.

The slavery issue was more complex than which army unit to join. No Yankees had as yet, showed up in Franklin County, nor had anyone locally announced that the slaves were free. To make matters even less clear, Devereaux Jarrett had died at the end of March, and so his granddaughter, Mary, and her husband, Major Jamie Turnbull, now owned Traveler's Rest.

Of course, no one could be sure of exactly what that meant. Much of the plantation wealth was tied up in the slaves, and because their status was unclear, the inheritance was unclear as well. Jamie and Mary had merely decided to ignore the legal complexities, and continue to farm and run the plantation as best they could, using those who wished to work.

Many of the slaves had already disappeared but others remained, and most of them seemed quite content to do the same jobs they had done for years. Aunt Fanny and Meely kept the house and worked with Mrs. Mary to tend the vegetable gardens. A few of the older slaves had likewise remained, working on the vegetables that Jamie insisted be tended. He focused only on edibles, peanuts, beans, and seed corn, with no concern whatsoever about the cotton. He did have his workers tend the tobacco, since that commodity was still quite valuable. For a time, tobacco even became the medium of exchange in the spring and summer of 1865, certainly in north Georgia and all throughout the Carolinas.

Word came in late April that both Lee in Virginia, and Joe Johnston in the Carolinas had surrendered their Confederate armies, so it seemed to all that the war was over. And that was exactly when Harriet Tubman, that powerful woman, that giant of history, marched up the steps and banged on the front door of Traveler's Rest Plantation. Not being prone to great patience, she knocked loudly on the front door again, and shouted. "I hear Major Turnbull is here! He need to come out and talk to me. I's been sent by God to this house to tell de slaves de Jubilee has come! Praise God!"

This shout terrified the few slaves that heard it. While quite excited, Meely and Aunt Fanny could see that no Yankee army came with Tubman, and thus her announcements were not backed up by force. Why had she merely marched in with such an announcement?

Jamie and Mary soon arrived on the porch and looked out at this strange black woman whom they had never seen before. Tubman continued. "I's been sent by God to tell de slaves dat they are free! Jubilee has come to Georgia, Praise God!" She looked at the bewildered white plantation owners as they stood on the porch, not knowing what their reaction might be, but certain, as always, in her mission.

Jamie was thinking he should just have Sampson escort this crazed woman off the plantation, but her next words shocked him. "Major Turnbull. I seed, before God, dat you is a good man. I seed you let a slave go and not kill her when she stole from you last year in de forest. You is a good man, a Godly man. You know in your heart, God put it in your heart, to LET MY PEOPLE GO!"

Jamie was shocked. He looked at this woman and could only wonder. How could she possibly know I let a slave girl go that night so long ago?

Tubman continued. "You know God put dis in yor heart, Mr. Turnbull, 'caus God talks to me, and he tol' me to come on here, and to tell you to let your slaves go! Jubilee is here, Praise God!"

Of course, Jamie and Mary had discussed this eventuality several times, and they knew this time was coming. Still they had expected a Yankee patrol to arrive with this announcement, not some old black woman. As they stood there bewildered, Meely made a suggestion that bought them some time to think.

"Maybe we can offer this woman a bit 'o water, while you think about this Mr. Jamie. That alright?"

And that was how the Jubilee arrived at Traveler's Rest. Within an hour, Jamie had called all of the remaining slaves to the porch, and with Tubman looking on, he announced that they were now free. However, not wanting to merely turn them out, he offered an option to his newly freed slaves. He suggested that they work on the plantation for the next summer and the next planting season for which they would each receive one half of what they produced. They would also be provided their own shelter and food. No one would receive any cash pay until some type of economy could be reestablished.

Of course, that very system was the only solution anyone could think of in 1865, since no currency was circulating that had any value. The system became known as sharecropping, and it was practiced throughout the south until the 1940s.

In late April, through the Home Guard, Jamie received word that he was to meet an "important man" at the river crossing by Traveler's Rest Plantation, on the night of May 1. So Major Turnbull and his men Lem Davis, Carmichael and Sampson all rode to the river crossing behind the plantation, and soon saw a carriage begin to ford the Tugalo River from the South Carolina side. As it came up the bank on the Georgia side of the river, neither Jamie nor his men knew what to expect. When the carriage door opened General Robert Toombs emerged, followed closely by Jefferson Davis, President of the Confederacy, and several other members of the Confederate Cabinet. Four baggage wagons followed closely behind.

After a quick greeting, Turnbull and his men were ordered to escort the remaining Confederate government some sixty miles south to the Toombs estate in Washington, Georgia. That is how Major Jamie Turnbull of Traveler's Rest, attended the last official meeting of the Confederate Cabinet in Washington Georgia in May of 1865. At that point, Major Jamie Turnbull could see no reason to try and continue the war, but he'd received orders directly from President Jefferson Davis himself, and as a man of honor, he would make every effort to follow those orders. It became his job to transport the Confederate gold to the final remaining Confederate army down in Texas, as soon as an opportunity presented itself.

## At Devereaux Jarrett's Grave, May, 1865

Duncan tossed down his shovel, just as Sampson lowered his. They had just finished the second interment of Devereaux Jarrett on a hill near Traveler's Rest Plantation, beside the Tugalo River in northern Georgia. A few feet under

Jarrett's coffin, they had likewise buried just under a ton of Confederate gold.

"What does the good Major recommend now?" Lem asked. "Ain't no way we'd get through them damn Yankees and make it all the way to Texas, certainly not with two wagons loaded with gold."

Jamie looked up in contemplation. After a moment, he said. "I'd guess you're right Lem. Ain't no way in hell to follow our orders, right now. I figure we'll just leave it here for the time being, and maybe in a month or two, things 'll clear up a bit. Then we can dig it up and move it down to Texas, once President Davis gets himself set up down there."

Duncan then asked the obvious question. "So what do we do now, Jamie? I mean, ain't no army to go back too, now, and the Home Guard here in the county is disbanding. Most of them are taking the loyalty oath to the Union."

Jamie looked again into the faces of his friends. "Tonight we go home boys. We all just go on home. It's May and we all got planting to do. God knows, we're all gonna need the food. Besides, there just ain't nothing else we can do, not right now." He paused another moment then repeated himself. "Go on home, boys. Just go on home."

## When Does It End?

And that is how the war ended, at least for those men from the Tugalo River Valley. They left Jarrett's grave on the mountain that night in May of 1865, and simply went home. Of course, that isn't quite the whole story, is it?

This book opened by asking when did the War Between the States, that Great American Civil War, really begin? Did it start in 1861, with the cannon fire on Fort Sumter, or did it start in 1828, with a bloody duel right here in Franklin County, Georgia during the Nullification Crises? Since there is no clear answer to that question on when the war began, one might also be inclined to ask, when did that war actually end? Does a war end when the last soldier goes home, or with the last battle? Did it end when the Confederate treasury was buried?

What about the dreams, the night terrors that soldiers in every war experience? They continue for years. Is that a part of the war? Do they ever really end? Were all the questions in that war settled in 1865, or does the war continue until all those issues are addressed? Perhaps the war must, of necessity, include the extended lives of the survivors, how the battles impacted the men who fought. How did it influence them later in their lives, or even influence the lives of the women they left behind?

So many good men died in that war. Dewey Snyder fought only one fight, sacrificing his life at Chickamauga, and Jake Lovorn died early on as well. Batty

Prather, in contrast was along for most of the Atlanta Campaign, but got killed toward the end. Mo Hendon and Roy Giles both died at the Dead Angle on Cheatham Hill. Peter Wood simply faded from history. Captain Owen Collins led men bravely throughout the fight for Atlanta, but died when General Hood foolishly attacked a strong defensive line much later up in Nashville, Tennessee. Lee Lovorn was wounded in that fight, and later died in a hospital tent under Union guard. Neither of the Lovorn brothers returned home after that war. All of these lives were snuffed out with no future, those men making no contribution at all to our society, other than giving their blood on long forgotten battlefields.

More Americans died in the War Between the States than in all other American wars combined, save World War II. Nearly six hundred and fifty thousand men perished in the Civil War from 1861 through 1865, but those loses were much worse than they would seem today. At a time in history when the entire population of the county was only twenty-five million, every single American knew someone who had not survived, and many in southern communities knew scores of men who failed to return home to their families.

Many of those that did return from the war had left a leg or an arm behind on some forgotten battlefield. Chad Wilson was one of those severely wounded men. He left his right leg on the field in Franklin, Tennessee, where he nearly bled to death. However, with the support of a devilishly loud, often vulgar Union nurse, none other than Mother Bickerdyke, Wilson survived the amputation of his appendage. He would never farm his family property, but, as he could read and do some math, he found a role in life as a shop keeper. He died in the 1890s, a wealthy, well-respected man in his community. To his dying day, he never missed a church service, and he often visited with his closest friend Duncan Carmichael. Further, he prayed for Duncan Carmichael's soul until the day he died.

Others survived the carnage as well. Wellspeak was shipped home wounded after the fight at Kennesaw. He lost the use of his right arm, and wore that arm in a sling until the day he died, but he did survive to live a long life after the war. Lem Davis was wounded early on, but returned to the war and lived to tell about it. Jamie Turnbull was wounded several times, but survived, and his man Sampson fought the entire war for the Confederacy without a scratch.

Records show that Sampson took the name of his original master. He became Sampson Prather and within the year, he had married the young girl, Meely from Traveler's Rest Plantation. They farmed a section of land that was a gift on their wedding day from Jamie and Mary Turnbull. Sampson and Meely had more babies than anyone could count, and became leaders in the local black community. The descendants of those Prathers live in the Tugalo River Valley today. Like many southern towns, both black and white Prathers live in that area, and the community has been enriched by both of those fine families.

Fanny Bricebud and Cassius, both were interviewed during the late 1860s by reporters from northern newspapers about their lives as slaves. Both were then very old, well into their eighties, and thus emerged two of the most interesting slave narratives known to exist. Even then, Aunt Fanny was very careful about providing any hard information on the Underground Railroad. She did tell about a few of her own and Meely's adventures, on condition that that particular information would be published only after she had died.

Thus we ask again, did that war end with the men who fell in battle? Did it end when the last shot was fired? Did it continue in the minds and hearts of the men who never again slept quite as well, men who refought that war every night for the rest of their lives?

Maybe the end of the conflict rests in the success of the men who, like Sampson, survived. Turnbull and Davis both farmed in the Tugalo River Valley for years after the war. Major Turnbull built a wonderful plantation home near Traveler's Rest because he wanted a home of his own. It was a very modern brick home, and that house, the Turnbull place as it was locally known, was standing as late as the 1970s. Then a spark from a fireplace caught the home ablaze and burned it to the ground. The brick remains still stand along the upper Tugalo River.

Lem Davis was not nearly as wealthy as his friend Major Turnbull, but he did raise a family on his small farm in Eastanollee, Georgia about two miles from the river. Many of Lem's descendants are still in the area today.

Ten Cent Bill, another black Confederate, survived the war, and surprisingly his life after the war is fairly well documented. After the fight at Nashville, he took his owner, Captain Owen Collins, home to be buried by his family. After the war, he married, had a family, and worked as a barber in downtown Atlanta, where he cut hair for many senators, and a few governors of Georgia, since his shop was near the Capitol. He also attended virtually every meeting of Confederate Veterans in Atlanta over the next forty years.

Ten Cent Bill died a very old, proud Confederate, in 1912, having lived in the home for Confederate Veterans in Macon Georgia, during his final years. Government records in Georgia show that he drew a pension for his war service with the Confederacy, and many of his personal belongings have been preserved in the Cobb County Historical Museum. Thus, Ten Cent Bill's Confederate service is well documented, and is on display for all to see. Ironically, that museum is housed in the same building where Ten Cent Bill and the others buried legs and arms during the fight at Kennesaw Mountain. That old building is the same building as the old hotel, used as a hospital, and still sits by the railroad tracks in Marietta, Georgia. It is now known as The Kennesaw House.

Harriet Tubman continued to help the newly freed slaves, moving across the states that had made up the Confederacy, helping them get to the new

Freedman's Bureaus, helping them learn to read. Her ongoing conversations with God provided both her instructions and her motivation, and she never once, for the rest of her life stopped her efforts to help her fellowman. Much later in life, she began a new chapter, fighting in a new cause. She became one of the first women in America to champion women's suffrage in the late 1890s. Of course, she is, today regarded as a leading historical figure from those times, having led so many slaves to freedom. She was a woman of conscience, a woman of courage, who spoke with God directly, and she never failed to follow his instructions. She is, and should be, an inspiration to all.

Perhaps the most interesting story is that of the drunkard knife-fighter, Duncan Carmichael. By all historic accounts, he did find a true calling to God in the midst of that horrible war so long ago. When he returned home, he quit his rough ways, and really began to question much of his life. Finding that his mother had never bothered to marry his father (such were the ways of the Carmichael clan in those days), he decided that it was more honest to own his disreputable past, and so he began by taking her name. Thus, Duncan Carmichael became Duncan Carmichael Wilkes, in 1866.

Duncan spent the next few years farming. He married and by all accounts lived a very upstanding life for a couple of years. He even began to educate himself at that point, but something was still missing in his life. God had brought that man home for some reason, and Duncan was by that point even more determined to understand what that truly meant.

He continued to go to church after the war. He even led hymn singing from time to time, as he'd done at so many prayer meetings during the war. Within five years he was actually preaching in churches in these parts. By 1872, he decided that God wanted him to build a church, in the new railroad town that was just beginning only six miles away from the Tugalo River. Thus, D. C. Wilkes, as instructed by God himself, formed a church that soon became the First Baptist Church of Toccoa, Georgia.

Indeed, some might say that God did save that man for a higher purpose. That church thrives today as a true servant of the local community, with well over seven hundred members.

## The Confederate Gold

Some things from those distant days, remain a mystery. No one today knows where the Confederate gold was hidden, or if it may have been recovered and dispersed over time. Rumors started after the war suggest that the gold was buried a few miles outside of Washington Georgia, over in the very next county. Even today, various gold seekers are still digging holes in Lincoln County, Georgia, looking for the lost Confederate gold.

Historical records show that a black Union cavalry unit attacked several wagons carrying gold in May of 1865 in Lincoln County Georgia, and they captured one of the wagons loaded with gold. Alas, those funds also seemed to have disappeared for decades, but they finally turned up in the records of James City, North Carolina. That Confederate gold funded churches and schools for former slaves, in and around New Bern, North Carolina. Still, the majority of the Confederate treasury seems to have simply disappeared somewhere in Lincoln County.

But the treasury was more than merely gold—it was history. One non-monetary part of that treasury did show up recently. In 1988, a janitor at the courthouse in Washington, Georgia was cleaning out an old cabinet in the attic, when he found a very old document. Thankfully, he took the time to see what it might be. Later that day, historians at the University of Georgia received a strange, rather disjointed call from a local magistrate judge, and they were told to "get your ass" up to Washington, Georgia. The find was confirmed the very next day. The janitor had found the one remaining original copy, a hand written copy, of the Confederate Constitution.

That "treasure" confirmed the local historical rumor relative to that last meeting of the Confederate Cabinet at Robert Toombs' home in Washington Georgia those many years ago. That most rare copy of the Confederate Constitution is now held in the Heritage Collection of Rare Manuscripts, at the University of Georgia.

Still most of the Confederate gold was never found. It may be buried still down in Lincoln County. However, it was known that a number of local men from the Tugalo River Valley used gold to pay their taxes for decades after the war ended. Some even suggest that four Confederate veterans used the gold locally, to rebuild various Tugalo River communities. For example, the Traveler's Rest Plantation paid taxes and retained most of its land holdings, in a time when no cash was otherwise available. Taxes for the Davis farm just down river were paid in gold for the next twenty years, as were the taxes on a small place owned by Sampson Prather.

When he was questioned about his gold one day in 1884, Sampson claimed he found his gold flakes along the edge of his farm on the banks of the Tugalo River. Of course, many Georgia gold mines were still operating as late as the 1880s and 1890s only twenty miles from the Tugalo River itself, and in those days gold was one local medium of exchange. No one thought it strange that Sampson had found a few flakes in the river by his farm.

Moreover by late May of 1865, there was no Confederacy to take charge of that gold anyway. By then, the Confederacy had ceased to exist. The Confederate government had not met since that fateful meeting in Washington, Georgia in early May, and most cabinet members were still in hiding. The Confederate armies, including the small army in Texas, had all surrendered. President Jeff Davis had been captured by the Yankees in southern Georgia, while he was still trying to make his way down to Texas.

General Robert Toombs, in contrast, never made it that far. He hid from the Yankees one afternoon in an upstairs closet of the Prather Plantation house right beside the Tugalo River in northern Georgia. He later escaped to Europe for several years, and died many years later as an "Unreconstructed Rebel," totally unrepentant over his role in the war, and never having taken the required oath of allegiance to the Union.

Thus if several local Confederate veterans did have that gold, they had few reasonable options for turning the gold in anywhere. Yankees were running the governments of the states in the south at that point, and the Confederate veterans would certainly have never turned the gold over to them. Thus, it was not unreasonable to use the gold locally. Further, a number of groups did seem to spring up from nowhere, to help Confederate veterans who were wounded, as well as widows of the dead. Funding for several "Old Soldier's Homes" throughout the south also seems to have involved some funds in gold. One can only hope that the Confederate gold was put to good use.

It is known that gold was used to fund the building of the First Baptist Church of Toccoa, Georgia. Records show that gold also paid for the construction of Bethlehem Church, a small church for a growing black congregation, six miles from town along Prather Bridge Road near the Tugalo River. Mr. Sampson Prather was the first minister in that small church, and once again, one can only hope the Confederate gold was put to good use.

## The Dead Angle, June 27, 1914

Still the question of the end of the war is a perplexing one. Perhaps we should mention the event at the Dead Angle, exactly fifty years after the Battle of Kennesaw Mountain. The newspapers of the day had published many stories all across Georgia, marking the fiftieth anniversary of the Atlanta Campaign. Stories of various battles were told and retold across the state, and everyone was celebrating at the same time, since the entire campaign took place between May 6 and September 2, 1864, exactly fifty years earlier. Events were held from Rocky Face near the Tennessee line all the way down to Jonesborough, Georgia, fifteen miles south of Atlanta. Every local paper in that area covered the story. The governor of Georgia marked the occasion at the Kennesaw Battlefield with a speech where hundreds of very old veterans were expected.

Few men however actually went up Kennesaw Mountain that day, since most of the celebrations that year were held in a large field at the base of the mountain. After the several speeches and a closing prayer, the men who had fought in both blue and grey dispersed. Some headed back to their hotels for a much needed afternoon rest, as they were, by then well into their seventies. Still, others went off to see various sections of the battlefield where they had actually fought, or where their friends had died.

Old men don't climb mountains very well, and with several of the attendees in wheelchairs, the going was slow indeed on the climb up to the Dead Angle on Cheatham Hill. The Reverend D. C. Wilkes was making that half-mile walk as was Lem Davis, both were very old men by that time. An old black man, Reverend Sampson Prather, slowly pushed a wheelchair up that mountain, with his elderly wife Meely walking by his side. Those men wore old grey caps, the faded remains of what had passed for uniforms fifty years before.

As they neared the large monument atop the hill, they saw men from Ohio, New Jersey, New York, and Illinois across the way. Those Illinois men who fought at the Dead Angle had long ago, purchased the land as a memorial to their dead, and theirs was the first monument on that hill. They chose to mark that location, since it had been the fiercest fighting they had seen in the entire war. The monument rose some thirty feet in the air, and stood only fifty feet from the worn-down earthen trenches of the Confederate line, and that distance accurately suggested the ferociousness of the fighting at the Dead Angle.

At first the men merely looked at each other across those fifty feet, as they had exactly fifty years before, each of them sensing the blue and grey tensions once again. There was silence for a few moments. Then Reverend Wilkes took a few steps toward the Union men and issued his invitation. "Would you men care to join us in a prayer for all of our fallen brothers?" The veterans on both sides instantly accepted that as a worthy idea, so they gathered together and formed a circle between the lines, and bowed their heads. Duncan's voice arose in the still afternoon air, beside the trenches where so very many had died.

*God, we ask you to come to us today as we remember our struggle here, and honor those who died fighting for what they believed was right. You have rendered your judgment on them, as you will one day render it on we who stand here today. We ask that you grant us mercy and the loving embrace of your forgiveness, as you did these, our fallen friends. We know that those of us still living, like those who fell here, rely only on your mercy. We know that our only hope is your love, your grace, and we ask for your forgiveness.*

*Spread healing today among us, oh Lord. Spread your blessings of peace on us, as we stand here on this holy ground. May our words together honor our fallen comrades, even as we likewise seek to honor you on this memorable day. May our lives be worthy of the time you gave us, even as we realize that those who fell here were given no such time. Let every man who fought here be humbled by that gift of a long life, a gift from thee alone.*

*Most of all, Lord, we thank you for this day to honor them, and for the opportunity to honor our enemies, men whom we now embrace and greet as friends, men who like us, survived the hell of that long-ago war. May our memories be blessed by you, and may you bless our new friends as we gather together here, in a time of humble remembrance. In Christ's name, we all pray together. Amen.*

Over thirty veterans were gathered that day at the Dead Angle. Some had been wounded, others had lost an arm or a leg. All had been terrified. Still, Duncan's prayer was all it took, and as he finished there were few dry eyes on that mountain. The men shook hands with their former foes, some embraced, and one or two pulled a flask from their coats, and offered up a toast to all the dead and wounded of the Dead Angle. Memories were joyfully shared, as they asked questions of each other, about their role in the fighting.

One man from Illinois was heard to say, "There was one of you boys that scared us nearly to death! He wasn't real big, but he moved like a ghost, quick as lightening, and he fought like hell with his knife every time we got up here in these trenches and mixed it up with you boys." The man then paused, as if searching his memory for just a bit more. "I remember that he had long hair and a dark beard. Hell, I guess we all had beards and we all knew how to fight pretty well by then. Still, this man was something. He was wild, different, somehow. It was as if the devil was in his eyes, like he could kill you with a look, and he sure knew more about knife-fighting than any man I'd ever seen. He scared the living hell out of us, and we talked about him all the time we were here. Nobody wanted to see him in the bottom o' your trenches! Nobody wanted to fight him. Do you know that man? Do you know who that was?"

In a flash Lem and Sampson caught each other's eyes. They knew exactly who the man referred to but neither spoke. Duncan merely looked to the ground and shook his head. Then he spoke up, having found just the right thing to say. "That man died many years, ago, Sir. May God forgive him for the life he led."

With no further information coming the man from Illinois dropped the matter, just as another Illinois man asked another pointed question. "Do you men know who might have killed General McCook? He was our company commander and I watched him fighting one of your officers right there on the rim of your trenches. He was a brave man, and we were sure sorry to lose him."

Several of the Confederate veterans could have answered that question, and Duncan started too, but just then, the woman in the wheelchair spoke up. "I believe that your man McCook may have been fighting with my husband, Major Jamie Turnbull. My husband said he believed he had killed a Union officer here, but he wasn't sure." She paused for a moment, then continued. "I questioned my husband rather closely, you see, as I'm writing a memoir of his role in the war. Major Turnbull did not reveal much about the specific battles unless I questioned him most directly, but he did once say he believed he'd fought with a general officer at the Dead Angle."

The Union man reached out to shake her hand, and then responded. "McCook was a good man, and I'm sure your husband was too. We were sorry to lose McCook, and we'd have followed him into hell and back if'n he'd led us. Well, I recon that's exactly what we did right here at the Dead Angle, ain't it?" He paused then, before asking his next question. "And your husband, Mam? Did he survive the war?"

"Thank you for asking, Sir. Major Turnbull did survive the war by many years, though his arm was rendered useless at Jonesborough. He passed away nearly fifteen years ago, but I'm sure he would want me here with his friends for this important day," replied Mary Jarrett Turnbull, the sole owner and Grand Mistress of Traveler's Rest Plantation.

Then to everyone's surprise, Mary continued. "You see, Sir. I've wanted, in my writings to tell the story of that war, and of the south before the war, from the perspective of the southerners. I want the truth of that war out, for all who would care to read it. My husband asked me to do so during the war itself, and I continue to do so. Unfortunately, I've found little interest in publishing that work, but I've kept writing all these years, and I will continue until I die. My husband asked me too, you see? Perhaps someday, the world will listen to the true story of the south."

There was silence then, as men who once wore both blue and grey thought on those words. They all thought on what had been won, and what had been lost, and without exception, even they realized that they did not know the whole truth of that war.

It is a fact that the truth of history only rarely coincides with the politically correct version of history, as written by the winners. Indeed, how could those men, men so involved in the thick of it—in the death of it, how could they know that truth? Does history have some responsibility to at least acknowledge perspectives of those who are defeated, as Mary Turnbull was trying to do, or is history simply a meaningless, propaganda-filled chronicle of those who win the wars? Aren't our progeny better served by at least trying to honestly understand all perspectives, as Mary wished to do?

Only twenty feet away at that moment stood an old Cherokee warrior, watching that exchange at the Dead Angle on June 27, 1914. He had fought near there, of course, but he had a much deeper perspective, a longer-term perspective. He knew men had fought over that red-clay of Georgia long before the War Between the States. His ancestors, the ancient Cherokee, had fought both the Creeks and the early settlers to keep this land, long before the men in blue and grey fought at the Dead Angle. Like the old Confederates present that day, the Cherokee had also lost.

Still that old Cherokee warrior alone on that mountain suspected more was to come. He had thought on the matter deeply as the Cherokee always do, and even then he believed that the red earth of Georgia would once again see men fighting over the land. As he watched men whom he'd fought, and men he'd fought beside at the Dead Angle, he understood that the questions that caused that war were still not addressed.

While slavery was a settled issue, a question settled by history in the United States in 1865, there were other questions. The future of the Cherokee, while not an issue in the War Between the States, had never been settled prior to the war. It is indeed, not settled to this day. Nor are questions on the rights of the states compared to the responsibilities of the national government in Washington City. Who is, in fact, subordinate to whom? How do state and federal powers align to maximize freedom for all? Those questions are still very real and pertinent even as this book is written some 150 years after the fight at the Dead Angle.

Maybe that dynamic, that tension, is the fundamental American condition. Maybe real freedom in our nation depends somehow on that tension, and the checks and balances in our states and in our nation.

Perhaps my great-grandfather, that Cherokee who fought near the Dead Angle—the same warrior who sat watching events at the Dead Angle in 1914, was correct in his suspicions. He had shared those thoughts with his children and they have been shared within our family through the years. Perhaps that dynamic tension between governments represents our joint future, and if that is the case, then Tom Jefferson was indeed correct so very long ago, when he said, "The tree of liberty must be refreshed from time to time with the blood of patriots and tyrants." Perhaps men will, one day, fight again over this land.

It is most ironic that the wisest words on that dynamic American tension were not uttered by Jefferson, or Jeff Davis, or Major Turnbull, or Joe Johnston; not by Crazy Billy, or even by the greatest orator of his day, President Lincoln himself. Rather the wisest summation may have been the words of an unnamed black man those many years ago along a creek bank in northern Georgia. "Dis be de price of Freedom. Dis be de price of de Jubilee!"

## The End

# Other historical novels by Jimmy C. Waters

"These stories are our stories; every generation faces challenges and we can both celebrate those brave men and women on whose shoulders we stand while taking comfort in knowing that they survived and thrived under conditions much worse than we will ever know inspiring us to persevere in meeting our challenges."

*– Tom Campbell, Star New, Wilmington, NC*

"Waters' book reads like a good novel and it even has a title appropriate for a good suspense story. This title was not contrived but refers to an actual Cherokee custom, *The Blood Oath*, which is very important in the history of the Cherokee, as the book abundantly demonstrates."

*– Forrest W. Schultz for: The Historical News*

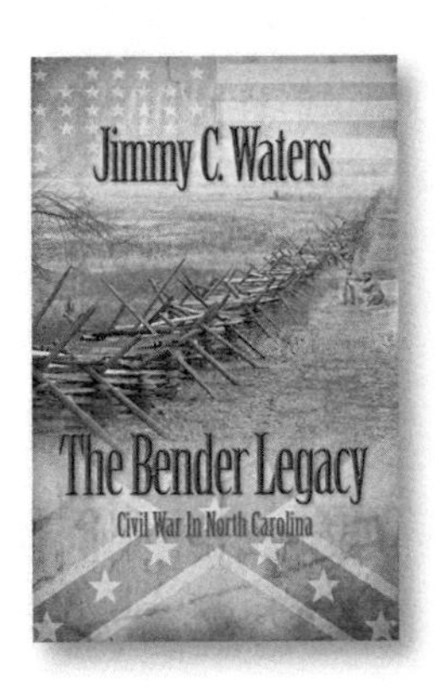


"Great book (*The Bender Legacy*) about the history of New Bern and the surrounding areas during the Civil War. I would highly recommend this book."

*– Comments by a reader, Ms. Sally Edittoe*